PRAISE FOR ROBERT DUGONI

FOR *THE EIGHTH SISTER*

"*The Eighth Sister* is a great mix of spycraft and classic adventure, with a map of Moscow in hand."

—Martin Cruz Smith, international bestselling author

"Is there anything that Robert Dugoni can't write? With *The Eighth Sister*, he boldly steps into the espionage arena with an expertly crafted tale of a long-retired CIA agent sent to modern Russia to hunt an assassin killing US spies. Told at a whipsaw pace in clear, muscular prose and filled with nuanced characters, nothing is as it seems or can be predicted in this tale. Indeed, everything about *The Eighth Sister* feels so fresh and authentic we could see the story breaking in the headlines tomorrow."

—Mark Sullivan, bestselling author of *Beneath a Scarlet Sky*

"Exhilarating . . . A tightly written, flawlessly executed espionage novel that takes the reader on a refreshingly unique, white-knuckle journey through the byzantine world of modern intelligence. Dugoni weaves a complicated web of deception and doubt around his unlikely hero, building tension and keeping the reader hooked until the end."

—Steven Konkoly, *USA Today* bestselling author

FOR THE TRACY CROSSWHITE SERIES

"One of the best crime writers in the business."

—Associated Press

"Dugoni is a superb storyteller."

—*Boston Globe*

"[A] swift, engrossing story."

—*Seattle Times*

"[Dugoni's] characters are richly detailed and true to life."

—*Kirkus Reviews*

"Dugoni does a masterful job . . . If you are not already reading his books, you should be!"

—Bookreporter

"Dugoni continues to deliver emotional and gut-wrenching, character-driven suspense stories that will resonate with any fan of the thriller genre."

—*Library Journal* (starred review)

THE EIGHTH SISTER

ALSO BY ROBERT DUGONI

The Extraordinary Life of Sam Hell

The 7th Canon

Damage Control

The Tracy Crosswhite Series

My Sister's Grave

Her Final Breath

In the Clearing

The Trapped Girl

Close to Home

A Steep Price

The Academy (a short story)

Third Watch (a short story)

The David Sloane Series

The Jury Master

Wrongful Death

Bodily Harm

Murder One

The Conviction

Nonfiction with Joseph Hilldorfer

The Cyanide Canary

THE EIGHTH SISTER

ROBERT DUGONI

This is a work of fiction. Names, characters, organizations, places, events, and incidents are either products of the author's imagination or are used fictitiously. Any resemblance to actual persons, living or dead, or actual events is purely coincidental.

Published by Thomas & Mercer, Seattle

www.apub.com

ISBN-13: 9781503903036 (hardcover)
ISBN-10: 1503903036 (hardcover)
ISBN-13: 9781503903319 (paperback)
ISBN-10: 1503903311 (paperback)

Cover design by Kaitlin Kall

Printed in the United States of America

First edition

To my daughter, Catherine, who has always made me laugh and smile.

College is just your next adventure.

Time to fly. Time to crow.

Then you will know the truth, and the truth shall set you free.

John 8:32

The truth will set you free, but first it will piss you off.

Origin Debated

Prologue

Moscow, Russia

Zarina Kazakova stepped to the glass doors of Belyy Dom, the Russian White House, and peered out at the leaden sky threatening to suffocate Moscow. It was not *if* the sky would unleash the first flurry of snow, but *when.* Meteorologists had forecast evening temperatures below zero, and as much as six to eight inches. Zarina sighed at the thought of another difficult winter as she forced her fingers into the soft fur of her mittens. Bogdan, one of the guards, stood near a metal detector with his body angled to peer out at the cloud layer darkening by the minute. *"Pokhozhe, chto eto budet dolgaya zima, Zarina."*

"When is it not a long winter?" Zarina replied in Russian. She intended her question to be rhetorical, and Bogdan, a true Muscovite, did not bother to answer it. They both knew "long" did not accurately describe Russian winters; "oppressive" more readily came to mind.

"Do you have plans this evening?" Bogdan asked. He wore his somber green-gray military uniform beneath his equally somber wool coat. His peaked cap sat square on his head.

"I always have plans," Zarina said, being purposefully vague and hoping to discourage Bogdan before he got started. In her early sixties, she had her mother's genes—just a sprinkle of gray in her auburn hair and skin as smooth as a woman half her age. Her mother had emphasized good living to be the key to a Russian woman keeping her looks, the one thing she truly possessed and thus needed to carefully guard. Zarina dressed impeccably, and she had never undertaken two of Russia's national pastimes—smoking and drinking excessively, especially vodka. She'd also been single since her divorce, and it seemed every man in Belyy Dom knew of it.

Bogdan smiled. "You're dressed as if to go out."

Indeed. Her heavy winter coat and rabbit-skin collar matched the fur of her *ushanka*, which she pulled snug on her head, the earflaps lowered to protect against the anticipated wind and cold.

"Can I only dress this way for a date?" Zarina asked. "Hmm?" She pulled the muffler over her mouth, not interested in Bogdan's response, and moved toward the door. *"Dobroy nochi."*

"Spokoynoy nochi," Bogdan replied, wishing her a peaceful night as he pushed open the door for her. Zarina stepped into a gusting wind hurtling up the Moskva River with the fury of an approaching freight train. Tonight's storm would be fierce.

She navigated the concrete steps and hurried across the courtyard, head down. After passing through the ornate gate, she stepped onto Krasnopresnenskaya Nab, marching along the bank of the river to her bus stop at the corner of Glubokiy Pereulok. The deafening roar of buses and the blare of horns in Moscow's twenty-first century "Putinstan" echoed above the wind, commuters scurrying to get home before the first flurry of snow. At the bend in the Moskva River, the Hotel Ukraina, a hulking mass of Stalinesque excess, dominated Zarina's view. Stalin had commissioned seven such buildings following the Second World War to glorify the Soviet state and to impress the West, which was busy building skyscrapers. The persistent rumor was the dictator had also similarly designed each of the seven to confuse American bombers, if they were ever to fly into Moscow. Given the paranoid propensity of Russian leaders, Zarina believed the rumor.

Preposterously Russian, each building was grossly overbuilt, with a stout base rising to a spire adorned with a red star, and infused with Greek, French, Chinese, and Italian architectural influences. Zarina wondered what Stalin's reaction would have been to learn that the Hotel Ukraina had become the Radisson Royal Hotel, a symbol of western capitalism.

Hissing air brakes and the smell of petrol refocused Zarina's attention, and she shoved and squeezed her way through the folding doors of her bus; chivalry had long since given way in Russia to self-preservation. Remarkably, she found an empty seat at the back of the bus and removed her gloves and hat so she didn't overheat. The humid, stale air had condensed on the windows and held the pungent smell of body odor, poorly masked by strong perfumes and colognes.

The bus wound its way along the Moskva River, already filling with chunks of floating ice, another harbinger of the wicked winter to come. Thirty minutes after Zarina boarded, the bus reached her stop in front of the supermarket on Filevsky Bulvar. She crossed the bleak park, listening to the spindling tree limbs click and clack with each wind gust. Soviet-era apartment buildings stood like sentries around the park, grotesque concrete blocks with tiny windows and tagged with graffiti. Zarina pushed open the brown metal door to a Spartan lobby. The light fixtures had long ago been stolen—along with the marble floor and brass stair railing. Russians had interpreted capitalism to mean: "Steal what you can sell." Attempts to replenish the buildings had only led to more thefts.

Zarina rode the elevator to the twelfth floor and stepped into a hallway as drab and bare as the lobby. She undid the four locks to what had once been her parents' apartment, wiped the soles of her boots on the mat so as not to mark the oak floor, inlaid with an intricate geometric design, and hung her coat and hat on the rack before she stepped into the living area.

"We were beginning to wonder if you were coming home, Ms. Kazakova."

The man's voice startled her, and Zarina screamed. He did not react. He sat on her couch, his legs crossed. A quick assessment of his uncreased gray slacks, black turtleneck, and long leather jacket, and Zarina concluded he was police, possibly FSB—the Russian counter-intelligence agency and successor organization to the KGB. A second man, hidden in her kitchen, emerged into the hall behind her, preventing retreat—not that she contemplated it. He was as square and thick as a refrigerator.

"Please, sit," the man on the couch said. On the coffee table beside his ushanka and fur-lined leather gloves was a bottle of Zarina's best vodka, which she saved for guests, and the two crystal glasses she'd inherited from her mother. "I hope you don't mind," he said, noticing her eyes shift to the table, "but Stolichnaya is almost impossible to afford on a government salary. I'm wondering how it is that a secretary in the ministry of defense can afford such a luxury?"

"It was a gift," Zarina said, trying not to sound nervous. "Take it with you and leave. I do not drink."

"Don't be so hasty. Please. Come. Sit. Allow me to make introductions."

Zarina remained standing, uncertain what to do. She'd long contemplated the possibility of this day, and had hoped it would never come.

"No? Well then, I am Federov, Viktor Nikolayevich." He gestured to the refrigerator. "And this is Volkov, Arkady Otochestovich."

Federov's formal introductions did not bode well, nor did the fact that he did not bother to show Zarina his FSB credentials. Zarina felt weak in the knees but mustered defiance. "I have many friends in the ministry of defense." She checked her watch. "One will be here at any moment, a guard."

"Had," Federov said.

"Excuse me?"

"You said 'have.' I think you meant the past tense, which is 'had.' And no one is coming, Ms. Kazakova. We have watched your apartment for several weeks, and no one has yet to come. Why is that? You are single and very good-looking." Federov reached for and poured himself a shot of vodka. He looked up at her with hardened, dark eyes. "May I?"

"What is it you want?" she asked.

He sat back, glass in hand. "Right to the business. Good. I like that. No wasting of time. Very well." He raised the glass. *"Za tvoyo zdarovye!"* He drank, then set the glass down on the table. "Tell me, what do you know of the seven sisters?"

The question perplexed her. "Are you mad?"

Federov smiled. "Let us assume I am not. What do you know of them?"

"I am not a tour guide, and I am not here to amuse you. Buy a book if you want to know. I'm sure there are many."

"Oh," Federov said, uncrossing his legs. "You think I am referring to Stalin's seven buildings. A reasonable mistake. No. I do not wish to know of buildings. I wish to know of the seven sisters, of which you are one, who have spied for the Americans for almost four decades."

Zarina felt a trickle of sweat roll down her back. The room had become as warm and as humid as the bus. She had never heard the term "the seven sisters" for anything but the buildings. Were there six others like her?

"Is it hot in here?" Federov asked Volkov. "I was a bit cold, though the vodka does help." He redirected his attention to her. After a long moment, he said, "You see, Ms. Kazakova, the other two women also claimed they, too, did not know of the seven sisters, and do you want to know something?"

A pause. Was he expecting Zarina to answer? No words came to her. Six others like her. My God.

"I believe them." Federov sat back. "Arkady can be very convincing. I would also like to believe that you, too, do not know the identities of the others, but I cannot leave here without similar assurances. We all have bosses to answer to, don't we?"

"I have no idea what you're talking about," Zarina said. "You've made a mistake. I am a secretary in the ministry of defense and have been for almost forty years. My credentials have been checked and approved dozens of times. You can confirm this."

"You deny the existence of the seven sisters?" Federov asked.

"As you have defined them, I certainly do."

Federov picked up his gloves and hat from the table and stood. He looked grave. "To me, it is a sad song I do not wish to hear. To Arkady, your denial is music to his ears."

PART I

1

Camano Island, Washington

Charles Jenkins dropped to a knee and picked at the leaves and twigs cluttering the two graves. It had become his routine along his five-mile morning run to visit Lou and Arnold, his two Rhodesian ridgebacks that he'd buried along the creek bed. The wooden crosses had long since been swept away when the creek had overflowed its banks. He hadn't considered that possibility when he'd hastily buried his two boys.

Max, his mottled female pit bull, scurried from the brush as Jenkins stood from his crouch. "Still got you though, don't I, girl? You're the last of the Mohicans." Max, too, was getting long in the tooth, her coat now more gray than brown. Jenkins couldn't be sure of her age, having rescued her from a man who had abused her. He guessed she was at least eleven, two years older than his son, CJ. "Come on, girl. Let's get home and see CJ off to school."

He picked up his pace down the gravel road, Max doing her best to keep up. He wanted to get another dog. CJ was old enough to learn responsibility by caring for an animal, but Alex was dead set against the idea with a second baby on the way, and Jenkins was smart enough not to argue with a pregnant woman.

He walked the final ten yards, his hands clasped on his head as he sucked in the cool November air. Sweat dripped from beneath his knit cap and heavy blue sweatshirt. He ran three mornings a week—his knees wouldn't take another day—and lifted weights in his basement. At sixty-four, he could no longer stay in shape just watching his diet. It required blood, sweat, and yes, a few tears, but after a year of intensive and consistent exercise, he was six foot five and once again 235 pounds, just ten pounds heavier than his peak weight when he'd worked as a CIA case officer in Mexico City nearly forty years ago.

The Range Rover idled in the gravel drive of their two-story home, the engine warming while Alex conducted the daily fire drill to get CJ out of bed and out the door in time for school. This morning, a Thursday, Alex tutored students who needed help in math, which added to the stress. Jenkins made CJ's daily lunch and ensured his backpack was organized and near the front door so he could run without feeling completely guilty.

"CJ, come on! We're going to be late." Alex stood in the doorway, yelling into the house, her tone already one of exasperation.

Jenkins heard CJ's reply from somewhere inside. "I can't find my soccer cleats."

"That's because you left them in the car," Jenkins said under his breath.

"They're in the car where you left them," Alex shouted.

"Do you have my lunch?" Jenkins said softly.

"I can't find my lunch," CJ said. "Do you have it?"

"Yes," Alex said, clutching the brown paper bag.

"Where's your jacket?" Jenkins whispered. "I don't need one. Yes, you do. It's thirty-eight degrees. Grab the jacket off the hook."

"Where's your jacket?" Alex asked when CJ ran out the door. The boy wore shorts and a T-shirt.

"I don't need one."

"It's freezing out. Grab your down jacket off the hook."

CJ ran back inside and returned with his jacket. The boy was all arms and legs, tallest in his class—which was to be expected with a father Jenkins's height and a mother half an inch over five foot ten. He looked like a mixture of Alex's Hispanic heritage and Charlie's African American roots. He even had his father's green eyes—likely from a recessive gene passed down from Jenkins's distant Louisiana ancestors.

CJ ran past Jenkins. "Hi Dad. Bye Dad."

"Kiss your father," Jenkins said.

CJ returned and allowed Jenkins to kiss him atop the head. "Have a good day at school." CJ turned for the car. Jenkins followed. The boy climbed into the back seat. "Any more trouble with that boy?" Jenkins asked.

"No, it's fine."

"If there's a problem, you call. You remember the code?"

"Yes," CJ said, sounding impatient as he buckled in.

"What is it?" Old habits die hard. Jenkins had a family code, just as he'd had a code when he'd worked in Mexico City, in case the shit ever hit the fan and they needed one another's help.

"Dad . . ."

"We're wasting time."

"How's Lou?" CJ sighed.

"He's sleeping at the moment."

"Could you wake him?"

"If it's important."

"It is."

Jenkins tousled CJ's hair. "Good boy." He shut the door.

Alex rolled her eyes. "He'd forget his feet if they weren't attached to his legs. And the doctor wonders why I have high blood pressure."

"You're going in for a checkup today?"

"At two."

Alex was twenty-three weeks pregnant, and her last doctor's visit revealed that she had high blood pressure, which the doctor said explained her headaches and upper abdominal pain. He'd diagnosed preeclampsia and told her to slow down and take it easy. The only cure for preeclampsia was to deliver the baby, and Alex was nowhere near term. Jenkins had taken over all the bookkeeping and administration of CJ Security from Alex, in addition to performing the fieldwork. They'd named the family business after their son.

Jenkins kissed her. "Promise me you won't overdo it, Alex."

"I won't. They have a desk and chair in the classroom for the pregnant lady." She got behind the wheel and buckled in. "Have you spoken with Randy?"

"Alex . . ."

"I'll have less stress if you tell me you have."

"I have a call in to him."

"How much do they owe us?"

"Let me handle it. I'm sure we'll get paid by the end of the month."

"I think you should tell them you're pulling everybody out until they're current. That would get their attention."

"I'm sure it would. Don't stress about it. The doctor said stress isn't good for the pregnant lady."

CJ shouted from the back seat. "I'm going to be late, Mom."

She rolled her eyes. "*Now* he's worried." She kissed Jenkins and shut her car door. "Call Randy," she said, lowering her window and speaking as she drove away. "Give him until the end of the week. Tell him he's stressing out a pregnant lady and if I go postal, he's first on my list."

Jenkins smiled and called after her. "I'll let him know."

The Range Rover spit gravel as Alex navigated the center turn around the large sequoia and drove toward the asphalt road.

CJ Security provided services for the Seattle-based investment company LSR&C. The company's CFO, Randy Traeger, was a fellow soccer parent who had approached Jenkins after learning that Jenkins had security experience working for Seattle attorney David Sloane and his clients. Traeger explained that LSR&C was expanding quickly, with satellite offices in San Francisco, Los Angeles, and New York, and that it intended to expand overseas. Jenkins could coordinate much of the security work—protecting employees as well as wealthy clients who visited the office—by phone, thereby avoiding commuting an hour and a half in ever-worsening Seattle traffic.

The Range Rover turned left at the end of the road and disappeared behind trees and shrubbery. Jenkins looked to Max. "The security contractors won't wait until the end of the month to get paid," he said.

The dog gave him a fretful look.

"Yeah. That's how I feel."

—

Jenkins disconnected after leaving Randy Traeger another message. If Traeger didn't call him back today, Jenkins would drive into Seattle and make a personal appearance at LSR&C's office in the Columbia Center. He clicked through the documents open on his computer. Forming CJ Security had required a hefty business loan and much of their savings, but the work had initially been strong. With the recent change in the market, LSR&C had slowed in paying CJ Security's bills and was now more than fifty thousand in arrears. Jenkins could not draw again on his business loan to make the midmonth payroll to his security contractors and vendors, and he did not have the money to float LSR&C. He tried to present a calm front for Alex's sake; additional stress would only exacerbate her preeclampsia, putting both her life and the baby's at risk. He kept reminding himself that LSR&C had been late paying its bills before, but it had always eventually come through.

Jenkins shoved his cell phone into his pocket, grabbed a cup of coffee from the pot on the kitchen counter, and stepped outside to get some fresh air. Max trotted along at his side. He walked down to his vegetable garden, which looked like it had been hit with an atomic blast, nothing but withered stalks, wooden stakes, and shriveled leaves. He hadn't had time to button it up for the winter while running the business by himself.

Jenkins thought he heard tires crunching gravel—Max's bark confirmed it—and he looked to the south. A car navigated the dirt-and-gravel path across his neighbor's property. Many years ago, an easement had allowed the cars to continue along the path onto Jenkins's land, but when that easement expired, the adjacent neighbor put in a gate and planted blackberry bushes to prevent cars from driving all the way to Jenkins's home. Charlie built his driveway and an alternative road at the back of his ten-acre lot.

The car stopped when it reached the overgrown blackberry bushes and locked gate. At least the engine shut off. A car door slammed.

Jenkins walked to the front of his house. By the time he got there, a man stood as if admiring the property.

"Can I help you?" Jenkins said.

The man turned—a ghost from Jenkins's past. Still tall and lean, he had the bronze skin of someone regularly in the sun, but with hair now a shock of white. Carl Emerson peered at him with familiar, piercing blue eyes.

"Been a long time," Emerson said.

2

Jenkins entered the living room and handed Emerson a mug of coffee.

"So, this is where you've spent your time?" Emerson stood at the picture window, looking across the horse pasture to what had once been a dairy farm but now stood fallow.

"This is it," Jenkins said.

Emerson sipped his coffee to cover an awkward silence. "Private security?" he said. He'd done his research or had someone do it for him. The question was why.

Jenkins nodded.

Carl Emerson had been Jenkins's CIA station chief when Jenkins served as a case officer, but Jenkins had not had contact with Emerson, or anyone else from the agency, since abruptly leaving that post some forty years ago.

"You enjoy it?" Emerson asked.

"For the most part," Jenkins said. "It has its ups and downs, but it's mine."

"The buck stops with you." Emerson took another sip of coffee, smiled, and walked from the window to the river-rock fireplace. He considered framed family pictures on the mantel, one of Alex on their wedding day. "You married another case officer. Her father consulted for us in Mexico City, didn't he?"

Jenkins ignored the question. "And you, what are you doing these days?"

"Keeping busy as a desk jockey in an office in Langley," Emerson said. "Though I should have retired by now."

"And yet, here you are," Jenkins said.

"Here I am." Emerson set his mug on the mantel. "Mr. Putin has brought Russia back to the forefront of American intelligence, making people like you and me, who worked through the Cold War, a hot commodity. *Vy yeshcho govorite po-russki?*"

"Not in a long time," Jenkins said.

During his training at Langley, Jenkins learned he had an affinity for foreign languages. He spent a year in foreign-language school learning Russian and Spanish before being sent to Mexico City to counter what had become a haven for KGB officers at one of the largest Soviet embassies in the world. "Why are you here, Carl?"

"The seven sisters."

Jenkins shook his head, unfamiliar with the term.

"Seven Russian women, chosen from dissident parents, trained almost from birth to infiltrate various institutions of the former Soviet Union and provide the United States with intelligence. It's one of the few times the agency exercised patience," Emerson said.

It distinguished the CIA from the KGB, at least when Russia had been the Soviet Union. Soviet intelligence had always moved with great deliberation and patience, and it was accepted in the intelligence community that Russia had agents in the United States who had been inserted as children.

"The seven sisters were to be totally clandestine," Emerson continued. "Only a select few in the agency ever knew of the operation, and fewer knew the sisters' names. I am not among those select few."

"They still exist?" Jenkins asked.

"Some," Emerson said.

"We didn't deactivate them when Gorbachev instituted *glasnost* and *perestroika* in the 1980s?" Jenkins said.

"No," Emerson said. "And now things have changed both inside Russia and in our relationship to it. Putin is not Gorbachev."

Putin had been a KGB foreign intelligence officer who rose to the rank of lieutenant colonel, and he was generally considered untrustworthy and immoral by the intelligence community.

Emerson spoke as he walked to one of two red leather chairs. He sat and crossed his legs. "Putin is on record as saying that the breakup of the Soviet Union 'was the greatest geopolitical catastrophe of the twentieth century.' It's a particularly telling statement when one considers the twentieth century produced two world wars and the Holocaust."

Jenkins lowered himself onto the leather couch across from Emerson, the coffee table between them. "Why are you here, Carl?" he asked again.

"Three of the sisters have been killed within the last two years."

"Killed as in—"

"As in they've quit reporting and disappeared."

"Maybe they don't want to be involved any longer."

"Unlikely. The more Russia reverts back to a dictatorship, with a constitution that is largely perfunctory, the more it goes against everything the seven sisters were trained to oppose."

Jenkins sat back. "You think someone inside Russia has determined their identities and executed them? Why wouldn't they execute the other four at the same time? If they had three, they would have the names of the others—Russian interrogation techniques are ruthless."

"The sisters do not know one another, nor do they know the name of the operation. They don't even know they're part of an operation. Each believes she is acting autonomously."

"They can't give each other up."

"No. They cannot."

Jenkins gave that some thought, then said, "So I ask again. Why are you here?"

"The millennials have come of age, Charlie, and they've moved into the intelligence community. They are very good with computers and electronic intelligence. Human intelligence, however, boots on the ground, has become a lost art. You speak the language or could reasonably do so again quickly. Your employment provides you with a legitimate cover; LSR&C has an office in Moscow, does it not? It would make your presence within the country easy to backstop. You would not need training."

"You want to reactivate me?" Jenkins asked, disbelieving.

"We do," Emerson said.

"For what purpose?"

"We assume that if three of the sisters have been identified and killed, it is just a matter of time before the others are also terminated."

Jenkins should have said "No," but instead he asked, "How much do we know?"

"Not enough. What we know is Putin first learned of the seven sisters' possible existence while he worked as a KGB agent, and that he tried unsuccessfully to verify their existence and to identify them."

"And he never gave up looking?"

"*He never forgot* might be a better way to put it. The FSB is not the KGB. It is a more refined version, with better technology. We have reason to believe Putin verified the operation and activated a counteragent, what he refers to as an eighth sister."

"How very James Bond of him," Jenkins said.

"Subtlety has never been his hallmark. You've seen the pictures of him with his shirt off? Perhaps while riding bareback?"

"Russian virility," Jenkins said, recalling how the Russian officers thrived on thinking they were stronger than their CIA counterparts.

"The eighth sister is in reference to an eighth building Stalin commissioned but never saw built. We need someone to identify who that person is before any more sisters are killed."

Jenkins shook his head. "Russian intelligence would pick me up the moment the Border Guard scanned my passport, and they will have a dossier on me from my time working in Mexico City."

"I'm counting on it." Emerson smiled. "A disgruntled former CIA agent now working in Moscow. The FSB will be wary, but also very interested," he said. "You would start slowly, provide information to interest them but which does not compromise active operations. When you establish their trust, you will indicate that you can provide the names of the remaining four sisters. When you do, we have reason to believe the eighth sister will present herself."

"And then what?"

"Your role would end upon identification."

"I'd be a shoehorn agent."

"Yes."

Jenkins shook his head. "And my successor would kill the eighth sister?"

"As you said, Charlie, Russian interrogation techniques can be brutal. The remaining four sisters have risked their and their family's personal safety to provide sensitive and important information."

"So, tell the director to get them out. Russia is no longer a closed country. Have the remaining four sisters travel to Europe or have them travel here."

"Unfortunately, pulling them out might expose them, and recent events in Britain have proven that pulling them would not protect them from Putin's wrath. We'd also lose a link to vital information at a time when we cannot afford to do so. Putin has never hidden his nostalgia for the Soviet Union. He restored lyrics chosen by Stalin to the Russian national anthem, marshaled Soviet-style military parades in Moscow, and restarted a national fitness program Stalin first began in 1931."

"Maybe he thinks he's Jack LaLanne."

Emerson smiled, but it waned. "With his intervention in Ukraine and his annexation of Crimea, not to mention Russia's role in Syria, in the 2016 election, and the nerve agent attack in Britain, the days of the Soviet Union seem to once again be upon us."

Jenkins stood and paced. "I walked away decades ago and did so for a reason."

"Which is what makes you an asset now. What happened in the past was a mistake, Charlie."

Jenkins could still see the Mexican village, men and women lying dead on the ground, and the attack based on reports he had filed. "A mistake? That's an interesting way to describe it."

"The attack was based in part on your intelligence."

He grew angry. "And I've had to live with that. That's been my punishment." Jenkins checked his emotions. He'd buried the past. He'd never forgotten it. "I don't have any desire to get involved again. I have a wife and a child, and a second on the way. Find someone else."

"There is no one who has your unique skill set who could be quickly activated and believed."

"I could go into Russia a dozen times and come up empty, Carl. What makes you think I would have any more success finding this eighth sister than anyone else?"

"The moment you discussed the seven sisters, you wouldn't have to find the eighth sister. She would find you."

Jenkins had loved that life in Mexico City. The job had given him a sense of purpose, a team intent on doing something important. He'd loved the games he'd played with the KGB officers, and he'd been good at it, better than good. His career had been fast-tracked, before the slaughter in the Oaxacan village changed his perspective.

"I'm not that guy anymore, Carl."

Emerson stood, reached into his suit coat, and pulled out a small business card. "My number, in case you change your mind."

Jenkins didn't reach for it. "I won't."

Emerson placed the card on the mantel and walked from the room.

Jenkins did not follow.

After Emerson had left, Jenkins crossed to the mantel and picked up the card, considering the number. He carried the card with him to the plate glass window, and stared out at what had once been a productive dairy, but which had been left to go fallow, despite its potential.

3

It had been a week since Jenkins's deadline to LSR&C, and despite Randy Traeger's assurances the company would come current on CJ Security's outstanding bills, LSR&C had made a payment of just $10,000. It had not been enough to make full payroll. Jenkins had security contractors threatening to quit, and vendors and creditors discussing legal actions. Worse, because of a personal guarantee Jenkins had to sign to obtain his business loan, his own assets were also at risk. He stood to lose everything, including the family farm, if the bank called in the loan.

He'd told Alex that LSR&C had made a payment and had promised another, but she knew the severity of their situation.

Jenkins paced his home office. He'd been unable to reach Traeger for two days, and he was quickly running out of options. Even if he sued and won, payment would take months, maybe years, if there was anything to recover. By then he would have lost everything. He'd be bankrupt and homeless with a wife and two children. For the third time that morning, Jenkins opened his desk drawer and took out the card Carl Emerson had left on his mantel, flipping it between his fingers. There was no business identified, no name or title, no address, just a ten-digit number.

—

At noon, Jenkins walked the cobblestone street of the Pike Place Market, hearing fish hawkers call out and hungry seagulls caw. Many of the restaurants and shops had already been decorated for Christmas, though Thanksgiving was still a few days away.

Radiator Whiskey, a restaurant inside the two-story building at the mouth of the market, had an open floor plan. Ductwork, exhaust fans, and light fixtures hung between wood beams. Pots and pans dangled from a center rack over a noisy kitchen, and bottles of whiskey and aged wooden barrels lined a back wall. The space was flooded with natural light, streaming in through the multipane arched windows, which looked out at the iconic, red Public Market Center neon sign and clock.

Carl Emerson sat at a table near the window. A chalkboard displaying a handwritten daily menu hung on the wall.

"How'd you find this place?" Jenkins removed his black leather coat and draped it over the back of a chair.

"A friend recommended it," Emerson said. "She said it had a retro feel and good food." A waitress approached the table. "Can I get you a drink?" Emerson asked.

Emerson had a glass of Scotch over ice. His choice in alcohol hadn't changed.

"Just water," Jenkins said.

The waitress departed. "I'm told the pork shank is excellent," Emerson said, handing Jenkins the menu.

Jenkins set the menu down without considering it. "How would I find this eighth sister?"

Emerson picked up his glass, sipping at the Scotch. Then he replied, "As I said, once you mention you have information on the remaining four sisters, we believe she will find you. Russians are curious and paranoid by nature. It comes from looking over their shoulders during eighty years of communist rule."

"And how do I establish credibility?"

"As you said, the Russians will vet you the moment they scan your passport. When you make contact, you let it be known that you're a CIA case officer—"

"Former case officer."

"A former case officer wouldn't have much in the way of valuable information, not unless you worked at Lockheed or some such place. No, you lead them to an understanding that while it appeared you left the agency, you're very much still in play, and have information you believe would interest them. Given your hermit-like existence on your farm these past decades, they won't have a way to verify or disprove what you tell them. As I said, it is the perfect cover."

Jenkins had spent years living off of an inheritance supplemented with cash from selling honey, jams, and Arabian horses. "Hiding in plain sight," he said.

"Exactly."

"And the information I have is the identities of the other four sisters?"

"You say that and you'll likely find yourself in a Russian cell at Lubyanka," Emerson said, referencing the building that had housed the KGB and now housed the FSB. "Initially you will tell them you have information you wish to sell. Remember, the Russians are sloth-like in this process. They will wait you out, make it look as though they are uninterested, and likely test you before they trust you."

"And why am I doing this?" Jenkins asked. "If I'm still active, why am I betraying my country?"

"The best cover is always one—"

". . . closest to the truth," Jenkins said.

"You have a business that is seriously low on operating funds."

"How do you know that?"

"An old operative's intuition—you wouldn't be here if you were thriving, would you?"

"How do I establish trust?"

"I will provide you with names of Russian agents, long since exposed, who worked for the CIA, but who were never acknowledged by the Kremlin or by the agency."

"If they were never acknowledged, then how would I have access to such information?"

"Because they were KGB officers we turned in Mexico City. If the FSB checks, and they will check, they'll determine you are telling the truth. That should be enough to stir their paranoia pot and pique their curiosity. Once you have established trust, you will tell them you may have access to the names of the remaining four sisters, for an increased price. The number doesn't really matter, but do recall that the Russians are miserly."

Emerson slid a manila file across the table.

Jenkins opened the back flap and peered inside. He saw a Polaroid picture clipped to a worksheet of a man who looked to be midforties.

"Colonel Viktor Nikolayevich Federov," Emerson said.

"The eighth sister works for him?"

"Unlikely. We believe her identity is known only at the very highest levels within the FSB. Federov, however, is known to be ambitious. The moment you mention the seven sisters, he will understand the significance, and he will report the information up his chain of command. When the eighth sister presents herself, you will get out with a promise to provide the names of the remaining four sisters. You will provide the eighth sister's identity to me. We'll take it from there."

"And what if the Russians decide not to play by the rules? What if they decide they'd prefer that I stay as a guest in their country?"

Emerson never blinked. "If anything goes wrong the agency will disavow the operation. Your work can never be publicly mentioned or acknowledged. To do so would put the remaining four sisters at greater risk."

"What about my wife and my son?"

"Your wife can know nothing about what you are doing."

"I understand that. What assurances do I have that if anything were to happen to me they would be taken care of?"

"None," Emerson said.

Jenkins sat back. "At least you're honest."

"Would you have believed me if I had said anything different?"

"I want two hundred and fifty thousand dollars, fifty thousand up front, the other two hundred paid upon my providing you with the name of the eighth sister."

"That's a lot of money," Emerson said.

"It's a lot of risk, and I have debt I need to resolve. Think of the first fifty thousand as an advance. I'll ask the FSB for a similar amount to divulge the first name. When I receive that money, I'll give it to you."

Emerson smiled. "You haven't changed. Still sticking it to the KGB."

"I've changed a lot," Jenkins said.

"I can't get you a payment in advance," Emerson said. "When we are certain the FSB is interested, I will authorize payment of fifty thousand. When we have the name of the eighth sister, I will seek another hundred thousand."

One hundred and fifty thousand would get CJ Security out of debt and provide a cushion for Jenkins if LSR&C continued to falter.

The waitress returned with Emerson's plate. She asked Jenkins if he wished to order, but he waved her away, not hungry. Emerson looked down at his pork shank, topped with red peppers and a green aioli sauce. "Do we have a deal?"

"Yeah," Jenkins said. "We have a deal."

"Brush up on your Russian."

—

Jenkins looked over the top of the book, expecting CJ to be asleep or close to it, but his son remained awake. Alex had not allowed CJ to read the Harry Potter novels when he'd been younger. She said the stories contained adult themes frightening for a child. On his ninth birthday, CJ asked again to read the books. Jenkins had sided with CJ. Big mistake. Alex relented, but only if Charlie read CJ the first two novels.

"Next time, just tell me to keep my mouth shut," Jenkins had said to her.

Ordinarily, Jenkins loved this time with his son, but tonight he'd been distracted. LSR&C had made another $10,000 payment, but that didn't compensate for the additional debt. Jenkins was performing a juggling act, trying to appease the security contractors, the vendors, and the bank.

"Dad," CJ said. "Are you all right?"

Jenkins realized he'd stopped reading. "Yeah. Yeah, I'm fine." He looked at the glowing red numbers of the clock on the dresser—9:00 p.m. "We better stop for the night."

"Finish the chapter."

"It's the end of a section and the next section looks pretty long." Jenkins closed the book and put it on CJ's nightstand. He moved his chair back to the corner beside CJ's soccer cleats, shin guards, and uniform. "How was soccer this afternoon?"

"It was okay," CJ said, sliding beneath the covers.

"Just okay?"

"Coach wants me to play defense. Stopper."

"That's great. That's one of the most important positions."

"You don't score goals from stopper."

"Yes, but if the other team doesn't score, your team has a better chance to win, doesn't it?"

"I guess so," CJ said.

"Sometimes the most glamorous positions aren't the most important," Jenkins said. "Sometimes the most important positions are the ones that aren't as flashy."

He bent and kissed CJ atop his head. "You know I love you, right?"

"I know," CJ said, and he rolled onto his side.

Downstairs, Alex had a fire burning in the stone fireplace and sat on one of the burgundy leather sofas with a blanket draped over her legs, reading another book on parenting. Just thirty-nine, Alex was far too young for him, but also far more mature. He figured the latter was because she was the only child of two highly educated professors. Her father had worked as a consultant to the CIA during Jenkins's time in Mexico City. Jenkins met Alex thirty years later when she came to his farm on Camano. She delivered a package from Joe Branick, Jenkins's partner in the Mexico City field office. Branick had told Alex that if anything happened to him, Alex should get the package to Jenkins.

Alex looked up from her book as he approached. "Did he put up a fight?"

"Not too bad," Jenkins said.

"I'm thinking of getting him the audiobooks. The counselor said having CJ listen to a narrator while he follows along will improve his vocabulary."

Jenkins enjoyed his time reading to CJ. "Let's not rush it," he said.

"You were quiet at dinner, Charlie," Alex said.

"Was I? I guess I just have a lot on my mind."

"Come sit by the fire for a bit."

Jenkins walked around the couch, and she pulled back the blanket. He slid beneath it, the two of them watching the flames flickering an array of colors behind the glass cover of the fireplace insert.

"What did Randy say?"

"The investments are strong, but they've had some expenses opening additional foreign offices, so cash flow is tight. He says he'll work to get us and our vendors caught up. Things will work out." He paused, considering the flames. Then he said, "LSR&C has asked me to fly to London to help them open their office and assess potential security risks. Randy will be there. It will be a good chance for me to speak to him in person about getting current."

"When do you leave?" she asked.

"When things get set up. Could be just after Thanksgiving."

"How long will you be gone?"

Jenkins couldn't be certain, but he recalled an agent once telling him that counterespionage was like dating. You didn't want to make yourself too available too soon. The initial date was simply to spark interest. "Probably a week."

"I like it better when you're home," Alex said, nuzzling close to him.

"Freddie's in the closet," Jenkins said. It was the nickname they'd given the sawed-off shotgun Jenkins kept in a gun locker in the bedroom closet. Before Alex and CJ, he'd slept with the shotgun at the side of his bed.

Alex ran her hand below the blanket. "Freddie is not what I had in mind."

"What did the doctor say about sex?"

She kissed him. "She said it was fine as long as I didn't exert myself. Looks like you're on top."

4

A week after Thanksgiving, at 10:30 p.m., Jenkins boarded Aeroflot flight 2579 from Heathrow Airport to Sheremetyevo Airport, roughly twenty miles from the Moscow city center. Two days before, Jenkins had called LSR&C's office in Moscow to advise that he would be flying in to evaluate their security measures.

Though the flight was roughly four hours from Heathrow, the entire trip was seventeen hours from Seattle. With the layover and multiple time changes, he'd arrive in Moscow at five in the morning. To maintain his cover, Jenkins used the company credit card to arrange both the flight and his accommodations at the Metropol Hotel in downtown Moscow. He didn't worry about Alex finding the charges; she rarely checked the company card since her preeclampsia diagnosis.

Unable to sleep on the plane, Jenkins put on earphones and practiced his Russian and the Cyrillic alphabet. Though it had been decades since he'd last studied the language, he was still able to pull that knowledge from some recess in his mind. By the time the airplane's wheels touched down, he was far from fluent, but he could understand and speak enough to get by. Jenkins looked out the plane window at a dark sky along the horizon and hoped it indicated snow in Moscow and was not a harbinger of things to come.

Inside the terminal, the immigration official closely considered Jenkins's passport, then turned to his computer terminal and typed.

After a moment he shook his head and handed the passport back to Jenkins. *"Nyet."*

"Chto sluchilos'?" Jenkins asked. *What's the matter?*

The man looked surprised Jenkins spoke to him in Russian. *"Nyet,"* he said again and attempted to wave Jenkins out of line.

"Ya prozhdal chas," Jenkins said. *"I u menya yest' delo, po kotoromu mne nuzhno popast' v Moskvu." I've waited an hour, and I have business I need to get to in Moscow.*

At Jenkins's pronouncement, the man stepped from his booth and called to someone, though Jenkins couldn't pick up what he'd said. A second man, this one in a drab suit, came quickly. The two men kept their voices low, speaking for a few minutes. Then the man in the suit took Jenkins's passport and said to him in English, "Come with me, please."

Figuring that arguing was not going to speed up the process, and knowing that when things go bad in Russia they can quickly go very bad, Jenkins followed the man through the airport to a general detention room, certain he was about to be processed and put on a plane back to the United States. The man in the suit left him in the room alone. Jenkins set down his backpack and his roller bag. He tried the door. Locked.

"Nice," he said. "I can't even get *into* the country."

After thirty minutes, Jenkins tired of the game. About to bang on the door, he heard men's voices just before the door burst inward and a man with a shaved head and broad shoulders entered and approached Jenkins as though he'd found a long-lost cousin. The man in the drab suit entered the room looking pale and worried.

"Mr. Jenkins," the first man said in accented English. "Please, apologize for the inconvenience. I have been waiting at baggage claim for your arrival. I am Uri, your driver and your head of security here in Moscow."

Jenkins had not asked for or expected a driver. "What's going on, Uri? Why have I been detained?"

"A misunderstanding." Uri shot the man in the suit a sharp, withering look. Given their disparity in size, the man looked like a chastised schoolboy. Uri shouted in Russian: "This is an important businessman. Where is his passport?"

The official quickly surrendered Jenkins's passport. "You see? A misunderstanding." Uri smiled and picked up Jenkins's luggage. "Come. Do you have more baggage?"

"No," Jenkins said, following Uri out of the room.

"You are smart to travel light," Uri said over his shoulder. "It can take another hour to get your bag from the plane. I think it eats them." He smiled again. "Come."

"Uri," Jenkins said, catching up as they hurried down a hallway. "I didn't ask the office to provide a driver."

Another smile. "In Moscow, is understood. Construction now is everywhere, tearing down and building up, and more people and more traffic every day." Uri turned left, proceeding down a long, bland terminal. "Without driver you would not get very far or very fast."

It was all very plausible, and Uri a convincing actor. His presence at the airport could have been to pick up his boss—but Jenkins also knew that his passport had triggered an alarm. His detention had provided the immigration official an opportunity to alert the FSB, and gave them time to get people in place to shadow Jenkins's movement while in the country. One of those people could very well be Uri. It was not uncommon for the Russians to put KGB, and now FSB officers inside American companies.

Jenkins might now be a United States businessman, but years earlier he had been CIA, and Russian memories, like their winters, were very long.

Once in Moscow, Uri looped around the Kremlin on Marx Prospekt, giving Jenkins the chance to see the onion-shaped, colorful domes of St. Basil's Cathedral. A few people milled about the square, braving the cold in warm winter clothing.

Uri drove to the front entrance of the Metropol Hotel, and Jenkins stepped from the back of the car into a biting cold that stung his cheeks and hands and made it hurt to breathe. He'd packed a knit hat and gloves in the outer compartment of his bag, but instead of removing them, he took the moment to play tourist. He looked across the heavily trafficked road as if to admire the Kremlin's clock tower, but focused his attention on the two men in the black Mercedes Geländewagen. He'd first noticed the car in the side mirror on the drive into the city.

"You will be at office at two o'clock today. I will come for you at one thirty, yes?" Uri said, placing Jenkins's bag on the ground. "You will sleep but not too deeply."

Jenkins thanked him, picked up his bag, and climbed the steps. A valet opened the door to a marbled hotel interior. Ornate, beaded chandeliers hung from a boxed ceiling above gold statues and marble pillars. Expensive watches glistened in lobby display cases, and a harpist plucked the strings of her instrument. The clerk at reception spoke perfect English, and within minutes Jenkins entered his fifth-floor room. He had to fight the urge to lie down on the king-sized bed, knowing that if he slept, it would be "too deeply" as Uri had warned. Jenkins had work to do.

He walked into the bathroom, shut the door, and turned on the shower. Then he reached behind the toilet and felt the duct tape. Peeling free the tape, he pulled out a manila envelope. He sat on top of the toilet lid, opened the envelope, and removed several sheets of paper, reading the name of the inactive operation and the identity of the Russian double agent he would use to get the FSB's attention.

Jenkins had the bait. Now he had to cast his line and hope for a strike.

—

After committing the materials provided by Carl Emerson to memory, Jenkins creased each page into an accordion fold, placed the first page onto the rim of the toilet, and ran the flame of a lighter across the top of the page. The folds caused the paper to burn without smoke or smell, and thus did not set off the smoke alarms. When the page had burned down, he pushed the stray ashes into the bowl and continued with the remaining pages, except for a small piece of paper he tore off and set aside.

Emerson had provided the telephone number to the FSB headquarters in Lubyanka Square. Jenkins opened his suitcase, pulled out a burner phone, and keyed in the number. He trusted his memory, but he was no longer a midtwenties kid without a care in the world. He hoped nerves, and not something worse, explained why his right hand had started to shake. The tremor was slight, but not one he'd ever had.

He shoved the burner phone into his coat pocket and grabbed his thick wool cap and fur-lined leather gloves from his suitcase. Then he committed to memory the position of every object in the room, which would be searched.

He walked to the door and dropped to a knee, as if to tie his shoe, and placed the piece of paper he'd torn from the dossier beneath his sole so the breeze when the door opened would not disturb it. Standing, he pulled open the door and stepped out, carefully shutting the door.

In the hotel lobby, the valet asked Jenkins if he desired a cab. Jenkins declined. "Just going for a walk," he said, practicing his Russian. "I don't suspect I'll get very far in this cold."

He zipped his jacket and pulled the knit hat down over his ears as he stepped outside. A gust of Russian winter smacked him in the face like a fist. He stopped just outside the door to slip on his gloves, which provided a moment to confirm the continued presence of the black Mercedes parked across Teatral'nyy Prospekt.

He walked north, each breath marking the air as he approached the burnt-orange building in Lubyanka Square. The rectangular edifice had once been one of the most feared in the world, home to the KGB and its infamous prison.

Emerson said the KGB had been Keystone Cops compared to the FSB, and that when Putin seized power, he made strengthening his position and the state top priorities. He created his own oligarchy, bringing friends and colleagues with him from Leningrad, then planted them inside the FSB to keep him apprised and to ruthlessly stop anyone who challenged him.

Across the square from the Lubyanka Building stood Jenkins's destination, the massive, multistory building once called Detsky Mir, home to more than one hundred children's stores. Jenkins trudged to a glass door entrance decorated for Christmas with three large neon figures—a young girl, a bear, and Pinocchio. He wondered if they had political significance—the young girl, new Russia; the bear, old Russia; and Pinocchio, a character caught in between. What Jenkins cared about, other than the building's location, was that mothers and their children would pack the stores, particularly this close to Christmas. He wanted a public place for his first meeting, if a meeting was to take place at all.

Inside the mall, Jenkins removed his gloves and hat and shoved them inside his coat pockets. His face tingled as if he'd spent the morning at the dentist and the Novocain had begun to wear off. He found a Starbucks coffee shop on the ground floor, ordered a grande cappuccino, and carried it to an open table beneath an ornate and colorful glass atrium roof. Shoppers' voices—a low hum—nearly drowned out Christmas music. Jenkins busied himself on his cell phone to give his two Russian handlers time to catch up. The two men entered the mall and stood near an ornate lamppost, one of the men with his head buried in a folded newspaper.

Jenkins took a deep breath and placed the call. It rang several times and he thought it would go to voice mail. Then a male voice answered. "Federov."

"Dobroy dien," Jenkins said, greeting him in Russian, then speaking English. "I'm an American businessman in Moscow, and I have information I think would be of interest to the Russian government. I would like to meet with somebody to discuss a proposal that may be of value to you."

Federov paused, likely scrambling to record the conversation. *"Kakaya informatsiya?"* he said, using Russian, though he no doubt spoke English. Language was a means to control a contact, and you never wanted to divulge how much you understood.

"Information that must be discussed confidentially," Jenkins said, again speaking English.

Federov paused. Then in English he said, "We don't handle anything like that. If you've lost your passport or are in need of directions, why don't you go to the American embassy?"

"I don't believe they would be as interested in the information as the FSB. But if you're not interested, then I'm sorry to have wasted your time."

"Podozhdite," Federov said quickly.

"Yes," Jenkins said. "I'm still here."

Another pause. Federov asked, "Where did you learn to speak Russian?"

Jenkins smiled. The game had changed little in the intervening decades. This was an opportunity to impress. "Mexico City in the 1970s. But I'm finding that it is like riding a bike."

"Riding a bike?"

"An American expression. Once you learn, you never forget."

"You wish to come to Lubyanka?"

"No. If you or someone else is interested in speaking to me, you can call me back at this number. I'm close by. I'll tell him where to meet." Jenkins did not wait before rattling off the burner phone's number. He could hear Federov searching for a pen and paper.

"I won't be here for more than fifteen minutes," Jenkins said. "Once I finish my coffee, I will leave. You might want to tell the two men following me that mothers tend to get uncomfortable when they see men in a children's store unaccompanied by a child. *Proshchay.*"

Jenkins disconnected and sat back, watching his two Russian minders in his peripheral vision. Within a minute, the one closest to him turned his head ever so slightly to try to hide the wire snaking up from the collar of his jacket to his ear. He was receiving a call.

Fifteen minutes passed. No one returned Jenkins's call. Like the KGB, the FSB would be patient. It preferred to do things on its terms.

Jenkins picked up his drink, sipped the final contents, and discarded the cup in a garbage can as he left the building. He walked past his minders and just couldn't resist the chance to tweak them and in the process communicate he was an experienced field officer.

"Vy mozhete byt' arestovany za besporyadok v detskom magazine," he said. *You could be arrested for loitering in a children's store.*

—

Jenkins spent the afternoon going over security measures with Uri for LSR&C's offices in Moscow. When they'd concluded their meeting, the investment team suggested dinner at a Chinese restaurant. Jenkins, who hadn't eaten since a snack on the plane, readily accepted. He kept vigilant that evening but did not see anyone who appeared to be shadowing him, or watching him while at dinner.

Toward the end of the evening, Jenkins excused himself to use the bathroom. Standing at a urinal, he heard the door swing open and another man enter. Though there were several open urinals, the man stood at the one adjacent to Jenkins. Jenkins flashed back to his training and realized his mistake. He'd been taught to never use a urinal, leaving his back to the door and his hands occupied.

"Mr. Jenkins." The man spoke without turning his head or shifting his eyes from the white tile above the urinal. "I am Federov, Viktor Nikolayevich. We spoke this morning by phone. We would be interested in speaking with you. Come to the lobby of the Lubyanka tomorrow morning at ten a.m. Do you know it?"

"Too well," Jenkins said. "So, you'll excuse me if I decline your invitation. Old prejudices die hard. I prefer someplace neutral."

It was a matter of keeping a fish on the line but not making it too easy.

Jenkins heard Federov inhale and exhale sharply. "You are familiar with Zaryadye Park?"

"Is that where the Hotel Rossiya once stood?" Jenkins said, sensing another opportunity to impress Federov as an American intelligence officer, though Federov had likely found that out already. The Hotel Rossiya, once the largest hotel in the world, had housed all foreign visitors during Soviet times. After the fall of communism, a new owner had sought to remodel the hotel but was forced to tear it down when his contractor found the walls to be filled with cameras, listening devices, and pipes to distribute gas. Putin, it was said, convinced the owner to walk away from the building so as to prevent a national embarrassment. He built the park instead, and called it a gift to the Moscow people.

"It is," Federov said.

"I believe they built the hotel on the foundations of a skyscraper never built, the Zaryadye Administrative Building, did they not?" Federov did not answer. "The building would have been the eighth of what are now referred to as Moscow's 'Seven Sisters,' would it not?" Federov turned his head. Jenkins had his attention, and in the process he got a good look at the man.

"You can walk from your hotel," Federov said. "There is an eleven a.m. showing in the media center, a documentary on the 1812 fire of Moscow. Sit in the second-to-last row."

5

Jenkins positioned his body to block the breeze when he opened his hotel room door and glanced at the carpet. The scrap of paper had moved. He did not let his gaze linger for long. Technology now made it possible to put a camera on the head of a pin, and he would be watched.

He dropped his winter clothing on the bed and checked his watch. Moscow was eleven hours ahead of Seattle. That meant Alex would be in the middle of getting CJ to school and wouldn't have a lot of time to talk, or to ask questions.

Using his cell phone, he called her at home. Alex answered on the second ring.

"Hey," she said, sounding rushed.

"Just thought I'd call to let you know I arrived safely and to find out how you're doing."

"I'm trying to get CJ out the door." She yelled, "CJ, let's go. You're going to be late again, and if you're tardy I'm not going to bail you out this time." Then she said, "Sorry. How are things going?"

"Everything is fine. Listen, remember your blood pressure. Yelling isn't going to help. If he's late he can face the consequences. It's the only way he's going to learn."

"Yelling reduces my blood pressure," she said.

"Just don't overexert yourself."

"I have your lunch and your jacket," he heard her say to CJ. "I'm starting the car."

"Sounds like you have your hands full. Give CJ a kiss for me."

"Will do," she said.

"I love you, Alex." It wasn't his nature to tell her he loved her each time he called. He hadn't been raised that way, and so it never became second nature.

She paused. "I love you too," she said. "I'm looking forward to you coming home."

"See you soon."

Jenkins disconnected, felt suddenly sick, and hurried into the bathroom. He shut the door and turned on the shower. Then he threw up in the sink. After a few minutes he straightened. His reflection in the mirror looked pale, and he felt light-headed and dizzy, and a cold sweat chilled him. He gripped the sink counter to steady himself and took several deep breaths, holding each before exhaling. When he no longer felt light-headed, he quickly undressed and stepped into the shower, allowing the needles of hot water to prick his skin.

He'd accomplished what he'd intended. He'd cast the bait, and Federov had seemingly taken it, but Jenkins knew Federov would be patient. He would be cautious. He would try to manipulate each situation so he'd be in charge. Federov could do so. Jenkins was on Federov's home turf, and they both knew he could make Jenkins disappear—in an instant.

Forty years ago, in Mexico City, Jenkins had teased the KGB agents. He took pride in being a pain in their side, and he had enjoyed every minute of it. But it had been different back then. He'd had nothing to lose. It was not unlike the feeling he'd experienced in Vietnam, where he'd discovered young men, soldiers, who had stopped caring whether they lived or died, believing death in the jungle to be inevitable. Jenkins swore he would not become like them. He swore he would make it out of that hellhole alive, that he would not forget all the reasons he had to live.

And then he had.

He, too, came to accept death as inevitable, and he, too, had stopped caring.

He'd carried that same attitude with him to Mexico City, and it had allowed him to be fearless in whatever he'd been asked to do.

But this was not that time, and he was no longer that person.

Jenkins lifted his right hand. The shake evidenced how much he cared, and how much he had to lose—a woman he loved and who loved him, a son he adored, and another child on the way. No, he was not dodging bullets in the jungle, but he knew this game he was playing could be every bit as deadly.

6

Jenkins rose the following morning after a fitful night, dressed warmly, and headed out into the Moscow cold. He wanted to collect his thoughts before meeting Federov—if Federov showed. Russian KGB officers had frequently set up meetings and drops with no intention of showing, as a way to exert power over the individual and to control the situation. Jenkins sensed the FSB operated similarly.

He exited the hotel and walked toward the Lubyanka Building. This time, however, he turned right beneath a "50 percent off" sales sign written in English, and proceeded down a cobblestone pedestrian path dusted with a light snow and lined with restaurants and high-end stores such as Giorgio Armani, Saint Laurent, and Bottega Veneta, all decorated for Christmas.

This was definitely not your grandfather's Moscow.

He paused, as if to look in the store windows, and allowed his eyes to scan the reflections of the people on the street, to determine if his minders were following. He didn't see them. He continued to Red Square, the Kazan Cathedral on his right, and the GUM department store, decorated with thousands of sparkling Christmas lights, to his left. Across the square, a line of tourists waited in the cold to enter Lenin's Mausoleum. Jenkins continued past St. Basil's Cathedral and exited Red Square across from Zaryadye Park on the banks of the Moskva River. The park looked to be a mix of freshly planted trees and lawns along with gleaming glass buildings. Jenkins crossed a busy intersection to a glass-domed building, paid the entrance fee, and obtained a map and brochure in English that touted Zaryadye to be the first public park built in Moscow since 1958, and applauded Putin for this gift to the Moscow people. The brochure omitted any mention of the scandal-ridden saga of the adjacent Zaryadye Hotel. Construction of the hotel had necessitated demolition of a valuable art nouveau building owned by billionaire businessman Dmitry Shumkov. Shumkov resisted the demolition of his building and was subsequently found hanging in his Moscow apartment. Investigators described his death as a "noncriminal" suicide.

Following the brochure map, Jenkins crossed the floating bridge and walked past curvaceous structures seemingly carved into the sloping grass lawns until he came to the Media Center. He paid an admittance fee and searched for the room showing the fire of Moscow in 1812.

Jenkins suspected that Federov's choice in films had a purpose. He'd studied Russian history as part of his training and knew that the 1812 fire had been deliberately set by retreating Russian forces, leaving Napoleon's invading French army without food, shelter, or people to rule. Napoleon had ridden into Moscow victorious but had no choice but to flee the city or starve and freeze to death.

Russia would not be dominated.

As instructed, Jenkins took a seat one row from the rear among a sparse crowd.

At eleven fifteen, with no sign of Federov, Jenkins concluded this had been another FSB test. He gathered his coat and belongings, about to leave, when he noted two men entering the darkened theater and moving purposely toward him, the first being Federov. The FSB agent sat in the seat beside Jenkins. A second man, this one built like a block of cement, took the seat directly behind them, which made Jenkins think of Peter Clemenza from the *Godfather* movies, specifically the scene when Clemenza sat in the back seat of a car so he could strangle Talia Shire's husband in the front passenger seat.

"You wish to speak?" Federov said in English.

Jenkins nodded. "I do."

"All right, but if you want us to cooperate, you'll have to come to Lubyanka," Federov said, trying to sound disinterested. "You're the person making the proposal. We're willing to listen, but if you want to talk to us, you must come over."

"Ya dumayu, chto ya dostatochno blizko. Krome togo, korotkaya progulka po russkomu kholodu khorosha diya zdorovya, net?" Jenkins said, deliberately speaking Russian. Ordinarily he never would have divulged how much Russian he knew or understood, but he wanted Federov to believe he controlled this meeting. *I think I am close enough. Besides, a short walk in the Russian cold is good for the health, no?*

Federov glanced at him, and the two men held one another's gaze. Saving face—projected strength—meant everything to Russian men. Jenkins purposefully broke eye contact first.

"Besides, the noise in here makes it next to impossible that anyone could hear us or record our conversation," Jenkins said in English. "I think that is best to suit our purposes this morning. I assume you do also, which is why we're here."

Federov stared at the screen. "Perhaps we should start with your purpose?" he said.

"Fair enough. As I said on the phone, I'm an American businessman with information I think the Russian government would appreciate."

"What kind of business?"

"Security."

A grin inched across Federov's lips. "In Russia, some would say we have enough security, maybe too much."

"And in the United States, some would say we don't have enough to protect us from those who seek to harm us." He sighed. "My job is a convenience for my presence in your country."

"Why don't you tell me why you are here."

"Have you ever visited Mexico City?" Jenkins asked.

Federov's eyebrows inched closer together. "No. I have not."

"You're too young." Jenkins estimated Federov to be midforties. "In my day, you couldn't throw a rock without hitting a Russian KGB officer in Mexico City."

"And what was your business in Mexico City?"

Jenkins smiled. "Throwing rocks at Russian KGB officers."

Federov glanced at Jenkins for a moment, then laughed.

"Yo era un turista estadounidense en México," Jenkins said in Spanish. *I was an American tourist in Mexico.*

"I see. So tell me, what then is the nature of your information?"

"The names of Russian KGB officers I hit with those rocks."

"I do not understand."

"Stones that found their mark."

"Russian KGB officers who defected?"

"No. Those who stayed."

"I see." Federov was clearly intrigued but would not show it. He shrugged. "This was many years ago. The Soviet Union is no more. What makes you think we would still be interested?"

"Yes, I've read all about glasnost and perestroika. So perhaps I am wrong in my assumption that someone like me would have anything of value to offer this new Russia."

"Perhaps not," Federov said, but then added, "one can only try."

Jenkins nodded. It was time to boat the fish. "Alexei Sukurov. I believe he was a former colonel in your KGB, and for forty years he provided the United States with valuable information regarding Soviet weapons technology. The operation went by the code name Graystone."

"I have not heard of this man."

Jenkins smiled. "Because he would be an embarrassment to your country. Look him up, Mr. Federov. If he interests you, let me know."

"How long will you be in Moscow, Mr. Jenkins?"

"One never knows," Jenkins said, noting that Federov had not asked where he was staying.

"And if this man is of interest, what is it that you would want in return?"

"What every American wants," Jenkins said. "What every Russian wants, at least from what I saw on my brief walk this morning. We're all capitalists now, aren't we?"

7

The call to Jenkins's burner phone came the following afternoon, as Jenkins hurried up the carpeted runner into the Metropol Hotel's marbled lobby after another round of largely unnecessary meetings with LSR&C's Moscow office. He'd scheduled the meetings only because he wanted to give Federov time to do his due diligence on Alexei Sukurov. According to Emerson, Sukurov, a high-ranking KGB officer, had for years provided the United States with detailed information on Soviet technology before his death. His name itself was, therefore, inconsequential. The hope was Federov would be curious about whether Jenkins had access to more relevant but equally sensitive information.

The call confirmed Federov was curious.

The FSB officer again requested that Jenkins come to the Lubyanka Building. Again, Jenkins declined. He suggested instead that they meet in a restaurant. In an effort to soothe Federov's ego, Jenkins further suggested that Federov pick him up at the hotel, then drive until satisfied Jenkins was not being followed by any CIA case officers—a procedure which, in Jenkins's day, had been called "dry cleaning."

An hour later, Jenkins walked down the steps outside the back of the hotel. While he waited, heavy snowflakes drifted on a light breeze before settling on the paved courtyard like fall leaves, tempering sound and giving Moscow a tranquil feeling.

A black Mercedes pulled into the courtyard and stopped at the base of the stairs. Federov sat in the passenger seat, staring out the windshield. Jenkins heard the click of the door locks disengage, and the valet pulled open the rear door. Jenkins slid into the back seat behind Federov. The block of cement drove. They did not exchange pleasantries.

The driver merged onto surface streets. Jenkins noticed both men checking mirrors for a tail.

The driver made a sudden and sharp right turn, forcing Jenkins to grab the ceiling handle and fight against the centrifugal force threatening to throw him across the back seat. The bottom of the car scraped concrete. The wheels bounced. When they stopped, the headlights illuminated a narrow brick alley, barely the width of the car. The driver shut off the ignition and killed the lights. Then he and Federov quickly exited the car. Federov opened the back door.

"Step out, please."

Jenkins stepped out, hoping this was not their final stop. The alley reeked of the sour scent of garbage.

The driver patted down Jenkins from his head to his feet. When he'd finished, he nodded to Federov, who gave a hand signal down the alley. Headlights from a second car, parked in an arched tunnel, illuminated the alley. The car inched forward from its hiding place. Three men, one as tall as Jenkins, emerged from a red Audi and walked quickly and silently to the black Mercedes. The tallest sat in the back. The new driver drove down the alley, turning right on the intersecting street.

Jenkins followed Federov and his driver to the Audi and climbed into the back seat. They exited the alley in the direction they had entered. The block of cement resumed making unexpected turns and slowing and accelerating to time traffic signal lights. When satisfied no one followed, the driver pulled to a stop on Tverskoy Boulevard in front of a Baroque-style building with a gold plaque bearing the name Café Pushkin.

Jenkins followed Federov and the driver into the restaurant, passing through a modest crowd seated in the bar. They climbed a narrow staircase to the second floor, where the maître d' waited, as if expecting them. He led them through what looked to be an elaborate personal library, with dining tables tucked behind ornately carved bookshelves displaying the gold spines of antique books. Tiny lamps with shades hung from the ends of bookcases. With dark mahogany wood, arched windows, and hunter-green tablecloths, the room had the look and the feel of one described in the Harry Potter novels Jenkins read each night to CJ.

On a snowy weeknight, the room was sparsely populated, though Jenkins heard soft voices speaking Russian and the clink and ping of silverware and glasses. The smells emanating from the kitchen made his mouth water, and he realized that he hadn't eaten since breakfast. The maître d' maneuvered his way around another bookshelf and gestured to a table positioned in the corner. Two drinks—vodka from the look of it—had been placed on the table. A waiter in a white shirt, red vest, and an apron that extended below his knees offered menus. Federov declined, ordering on the spot. Jenkins struggled to understand what was being ordered but deciphered sparkling water, champagne, caviar, and veal cutlets with fried onions.

Either the Kremlin had really liked Jenkins's information, or Federov, like many American government employees, saw an opportunity to expense a meal and decided to do it right.

"Your agency must pay you well. Far better than in the United States," Jenkins said, looking about the room after the waiter had departed.

Federov said, "I'm sorry for the theatrics, Mr. Jenkins, but one cannot be too certain when first meeting."

"I take that to mean that you verified Alexei Sukurov?"

"Mr. Sukurov is deceased," Federov said.

"Natural causes?" Jenkins asked.

Federov picked up his drink. The second drink sat on the table before Jenkins. He poked his thumb in the direction of the block of cement. "He's not drinking?"

"Arkady Volkov," Federov said. "And no, he is not drinking. He's driving. It would be irresponsible." Federov raised his cocktail glass. *"Za fstrye-tchoo." To our meeting.*

Jenkins returned the toast and put the vodka to his lips but did not drink.

Federov set down his glass. He kept his voice low. "You worked in Mexico City in 1978 with a man named Joe Branick, deceased. A suicide, I believe, no? An interesting explanation." Jenkins did not respond. "You left Mexico City and returned to the United States. That is where your history seemingly ends, Mr. Jenkins."

And so it did, in a sense. Disillusioned and guilt-ridden, Jenkins left the CIA and sought isolation on his Camano farm, living alone until that fateful morning when Alex arrived.

Jenkins unfolded his napkin and placed it in his lap. "I wasn't particularly happy with my employer."

"Yes. It seems you were sent into the mountains of Oaxaca to report on a growing communist threat by a fabled Mexican leader known as El Profeta. Not long thereafter, the inhabitants of that village were massacred. The massacre was said to be the work of a right-wing Mexican militia. Another interesting explanation, no? How is my information so far?"

Jenkins nodded but did not answer, due to the waiter's timely return. The man set a plate of appetizers on the table, speaking while gesturing. "Rye-bread bruschetta with eggplant spread. Marinated mushrooms, and pickled vegetables. *Naslazhdat'sya.*"

Federov picked up a piece of the bruschetta and spread the eggplant with a butter knife. "Please," he said, gesturing to Jenkins. "You will enjoy."

Jenkins chose the bruschetta and spread, mimicking whatever Federov ate. The driver sat resolutely.

"He doesn't eat either?" Jenkins said. "Where do you replace his oil and batteries?"

The driver slowly turned his head and stared at Jenkins. After a moment, he gave Jenkins the tiniest hint of a smile. This guy would be a riot at a comedy club.

"To be clear, Mr. Jenkins." Federov popped a mushroom in his mouth. "We are not interested in the names of dead former KGB officers."

"And yet, here we are," Jenkins said.

"Yes. Well, I assume that your purpose in advising me of Alexei Sukurov was to allow me to verify that at one time you had access to classified information. Yes?"

"Yes."

"And you say that you have other information more currently relevant?"

"I have access to information I believe would be very relevant."

"And how is it that an unhappy former case officer of the Central Intelligence Agency has such access after so many years, Mr. Jenkins?"

"He wouldn't," Jenkins said.

Federov paused, just a beat. Then he picked around the edges of the appetizers and Jenkins's statement. "So, you are wasting our time?"

Jenkins set down what remained of his bruschetta and wiped the corners of his mouth with his napkin. "On November 16 of this year, a secretary in the Russian Ministry of Defense, Zarina Kazakova, left the Russian White House, what you refer to as Belyy Dom, shortly after five p.m. to return to her apartment in the Filyovsky Park District." He recited information Carl Emerson had provided. "Ms. Kazakova worked in the ministry of defense for nearly forty years. She received favorable reviews and had been recognized as a member of the party in good standing before glasnost. Her standing did not change thereafter.

And yet, she would not return to work the next day or the day after. Her whereabouts, and the circumstances of her disappearance, are unknown." He paused to take a bite of his bruschetta. "An interesting development, wouldn't you say?"

Federov's Adam's apple bobbed. He attempted to hide this with a sip of his vodka, but whether it was the news or the alcohol, he began to cough into his green napkin, suffering through an ill-timed hacking fit. The driver flinched but otherwise did not move. If Federov *had* been choking, he certainly would have died. The coughing slowed and finally ceased.

"Excuse me," Federov said, voice harsh. He sipped water. "I believe your saying is 'the wrong pipe,' yes?"

"Yes," Jenkins said.

Federov placed his elbows on the table and made a steeple with his hands. "Your information is interesting," he said. "Of course, it would need to be verified for its accuracy."

"Of course," Jenkins said, though the coughing spasm had already done that.

"Is there more?" Federov asked.

Jenkins said, "Two other women, Irena Lavrova and Olga Artamonova, both similar in age to Ms. Kazakova, have also disappeared during the past eighteen months. They, too, left their employ with the Russian government and never returned. Would you like to hear about them?"

Federov nodded. This time he sipped his water, not his vodka. He was interested. He was very interested.

For the next ten minutes, Jenkins told Federov of the other two of the seven sisters, and the circumstances of each woman's disappearance. He told Federov that in each instance, the Moscow police professed to have very little in the way of leads, or any hope they would find the three women, despite the pleas of family and friends.

When he had finished sharing the information, Jenkins said, "You see, Viktor, sometimes the best disguise is no disguise at all. One can simply disappear in plain sight, and everyone speculates as to why he has done so, until they lose interest in him altogether. It is then that the person is most valuable . . . and the most dangerous. Wouldn't you agree?"

"And what then would motivate such a person?"

"My motive is not complicated, nor is it altruistic or patriotic. It is strictly financial," Jenkins said. "My business is failing and I am financially tapped out. I can't meet my payroll expenses and I'm about to lose everything I have worked so hard to achieve. I've signed personal guarantees on business loans, which puts my home and everything else I own at risk."

"You have a family?"

"That is not relevant," Jenkins said. He sat back. "Besides, you checked with your superiors and you confirmed my identity. Leave it at that. Now check with your superiors regarding the three women, whom I believe your agency refers to as three of 'the seven sisters.'"

Federov paused. "And you can provide the names of the other four sisters?"

This was where things got dicey. If Jenkins said yes, there was very little preventing Federov from taking him immediately and seeking to extract the information, perhaps in one of the remodeled cells inside Lubyanka.

"No. Not at present."

"But you have access to this information?"

Jenkins shrugged. It should have been obvious that he did.

"What is it you are proposing, Mr. Jenkins?"

"I want fifty thousand dollars as a sign of good faith."

Federov smirked. "For information we already possessed? I don't think so."

"Consider it a down payment. Any further information will cost an additional fifty thousand. Prior to my delivery of the seventh and final name, you will pay me a bonus of two hundred and fifty thousand dollars."

"Five hundred thousand dollars," Federov said, doing the math.

"Consider it a deal." Jenkins removed a sheet of paper with a bank account number on it and handed it to Federov. The number, again, had been provided by Carl Emerson. "The down payment will be wired to this bank before I leave tomorrow morning to catch my flight home. If it is not, I will assume your superiors are not interested. If it is, you can call the number you called earlier and simply say 'The down payment has been completed.'"

The waiter returned, carrying trays of food and set them on the table. When he'd finished, Federov dismissed him. "I believe that my superiors will pay your initial expenses, Mr. Jenkins, but I see no basis—"

"My terms are nonnegotiable," Jenkins said, eating one of the mushrooms and issuing Federov his first challenge.

"Then I will be discussing your terms with my superiors," Federov said, offering no commitment. He took a piece of the veal and buried it under onions. As he cut his meat he said, "And I wish to provide you with information."

Jenkins nodded but he had not expected this.

"Chekovsky, Nikolay Mikhail," Federov said.

"Who is Nikolay Chekovsky?" Jenkins asked, certain this was a test, though not yet certain of the purpose.

"A name for you to remember. But do not disclose this name . . . to anyone." Federov smiled but kept his eyes focused on his plate as he cut into his veal. "You are seeking a lot of money, Mr. Jenkins. My superiors wish to be sure you are not, how shall we say . . . playing us." He took another bite, set down his utensils, and raised his cocktail glass. *"Za tvoyo zdarovye,"* he said. *To our health.*

Jenkins raised his glass in his left hand. Beneath the table, he felt his right hand quiver.

8

Christmas morning, less than a month after his trip to Russia, Jenkins sat in his leather chair, sipping coffee and considering the array of empty boxes and wrapping paper strewn across the family room floor. CJ sat on the floor assembling an app-enabled droid that looked like something from a *Star Wars* movie—a rolling black ball. In the fireplace insert, pine and maple burned a bright red-orange, and the fan pushed out warm air. He could smell Alex's cinnamon rolls baking in the kitchen and hear Max gnawing on a massive bone—her annual Christmas present—beneath the dining room table.

Jenkins had awoken at just after 4:30 a.m., which had become his routine since his return from Russia. Initially, he'd related his inability to sleep to jet lag, but his insomnia had persisted. He'd awake with his mind churning over the minutiae of the security work, and of Russia and the operation.

Unlike in his younger days, he could not compartmentalize his job, could not separate his work from his personal life. Though he was home on Camano, Russia remained on his mind, as did the ramifications of everything that could go wrong. He used his left hand to steady the mug and sipped his coffee. His restlessness would escalate until he got up to run, or to do enough push-ups, pull-ups, and sit-ups that his muscles ached and he was gasping for air. When he had finally exhausted his body and cleared his mind, he'd grab a book and a blanket and lie on the couch in the family room. Most mornings sleep still didn't come, despite his growing fatigue.

He couldn't hide this from Alex. When she asked, he told her he was worried about the business, got up because he didn't want to disrupt her sleep, and said he'd get through it. Alex didn't buy it. A psychiatrist diagnosed Jenkins with panic attacks and generalized anxiety, and related both to what Jenkins had told her—worry about his business failing, and the uncertainty of becoming a parent, again, at sixty-four years of age. The psychiatrist said the attacks could get better when the issues resolved. In the interim, she prescribed mirtazapine, which Jenkins took at night to help him sleep, and propranolol for attacks during the day.

"All right you two, breakfast is served." Alex carried a platter of cinnamon rolls topped with melting frosting to the dining room table. CJ dropped the droid and nearly beat her there.

"They're hot. Don't burn your mouth." She placed one of the rolls on a plate and handed it to him, along with a napkin. CJ began to peel the bun, which released wafts of steam. She served Charlie a roll, but he set it aside.

Alex sat in the adjacent leather chair and looked down at Max. "She loves that bone, doesn't she?"

Jenkins nodded to CJ. "Almost as much as he loves your cinnamon rolls. Next year I think we should forget the presents and just make him a week's supply."

"Do you think we overdid it?"

Jenkins had no idea of the final tally. "Probably, but this is his last Christmas as an only child. You feeling okay?" Jenkins asked. "You look tired."

"I am tired." She'd been complaining of fatigue since his return. She was twenty-eight weeks pregnant now, and the doctor wanted her to go as long as possible before he would schedule her for a C-section.

"That was a nice Christmas gift from Randy," she said. "That should help, shouldn't it?"

"Definitely made my contractors and our vendors happy," Jenkins said. He had told Alex the $50,000 payment had come from LSR&C. It had actually come from Carl Emerson. Jenkins had paid his security contractors and many of the company's vendor invoices. It didn't bring CJ Security current, but they were closer than they had been.

"Randy said he'll do his best to bring us current by the end of the year," Jenkins said. "Personally, I'm worried LSR&C is growing too fast. I told Randy I didn't really see the point of the office in Moscow, or in Dubai for that matter. Randy didn't say it, but I think he agrees with me. He said the offices were Mitch's idea, that he wants to take advantage of emerging markets." Jenkins referred to Mitchell Goldstone, LSR&C's chief operating officer. "What time do we need to be at David's?"

Since neither Jenkins nor Alex had immediate family, they spent most holidays with David Sloane, who had lost his wife, Tina, to a murder.

"David said anytime," Alex said. "It'll be nice to see Jake again. I'm happy he's back. Nobody should have to wake up alone on Christmas morning."

Jake, Tina's son, had been living in California with his biological father, but he had moved back to Seattle to attend law school and once again lived with Sloane at Three Tree Point on the shores of Puget Sound.

Jenkins stood. "I'm going to get the paper and another cup of coffee. You want anything?"

"I'm good," she said.

Jenkins filled his coffee cup in the kitchen, then walked out the back door. The temperature felt cold enough for it to snow, if they got any precipitation. The meteorologist had indicated that was not likely. Jenkins picked up the paper and slid it from the plastic sheath. The front page included a picture of a homeless shelter beneath the headline *Happy Holidays*. Articles below the fold included the president's Christmas dinner at the White House, and another on the continuing battle to increase national park fees.

Jenkins took the paper into the kitchen and stood at the counter, flipping through the pages and glancing at articles. On an inside page, in a section reporting on world news, a small headline caught his attention.

Russian Laser Pioneer Found Dead

Beneath the fold was a picture of a dark-haired man wearing glasses. Nikolay Chekovsky.

Jenkins felt the familiar rush of anxiety as he read the article. Chekovsky had been found hanging in his Moscow apartment, and his wife was pushing the police to investigate the death as a homicide.

Chekovsky, considered one of the leading laser scientists in the world, had been an outspoken critic of the use of lasers in military applications, which placed him at odds with members of the Kremlin.

Jenkins felt heat spreading throughout his limbs, and the now familiar ache in his joints. His right hand shook enough to rattle the newspaper. He set it down and rushed through the kitchen into his den, found the bottle of propranolol in the bottom drawer of his desk, and dry swallowed one of the green tablets.

9

Early evening, the day after Christmas, Jenkins walked Waterfront Park in downtown Seattle. The weather remained cold and blustery, with wind gust warnings for those traveling home from the holidays. Emerson stood at the railing at the end of the pier looking west, across Elliott Bay's blackened waters. He wore a long tweed coat and black gloves. His hair fluttered in the wind, but otherwise he seemed impervious to the stiff breeze blowing whitecaps across the bay. To Jenkins's left, the Seattle Great Wheel, festively lit in Seahawks blue and green, rotated high above the water. Farther south, the roof of the football stadium glowed purple. Faint notes, Christmas music, carried on the gusting wind, which also brought the briny smell of Puget Sound.

Jenkins pulled up the collar on his black leather car coat against the cold and thrust his hands deep into its pockets as he approached Emerson. Though he wore a black knit ski cap, he could feel the cold on his earlobes.

"Who was Nikolay Chekovsky?" he said.

Emerson never acknowledged the question, or seemingly even heard it. He stared blankly at a decorated ferryboat churning toward the pier.

"Was he one of ours?" Jenkins asked above the howl of the wind.

"You read the paper." Emerson spoke so softly Jenkins almost didn't hear him. "He was a scientist and Russian dissident who spoke out against the Putin regime. In Russia that can be enough to get one killed."

"Was he one of ours?" Jenkins asked again, this time more forcefully.

Emerson shot him a glance, then, as if thinking better of whatever he was going to say, disengaged and returned his attention to the crossing ferry. "Whether he was one of ours or he wasn't is irrelevant."

Jenkins stared at the side of Emerson's face. "To you maybe, but not to me. I want to know. I have a right to know."

"No, you don't." Emerson turned and looked Jenkins in the eyes, holding his gaze. "You have no right to know."

"If I am back in this—"

Emerson raised his voice and his tone. "This is the way the FSB works. You know this. It's the way the KGB worked. If you are interrogated, anything you know they will also know. So, I say again, you have no right to know."

"I'm done with this. I'm done with this whole thing." Jenkins turned to walk away.

"You can't walk away this time, Charlie."

"The hell I can't."

"If you walk away and this assignment fails, four women who have served this country for nearly forty years will die, and for that you will never forgive yourself."

The words stopped Jenkins in midstep. He shut his eyes, fighting against the ache in his muscles and the burning in the pit of his stomach. Guilt, he knew, was a horrible reason to do anything, but it was also a powerful motivator. He turned back. "You could have got him out. I told you his name. You could have come up with some excuse, some reason for him to leave the country."

"You know why the Russians told you his name," Emerson said. "This was how the KGB operated in Mexico City. They told you Chekovsky's name because they had already decided to kill him. Using him to test whether you would give his name to the agency was just a convenience. You know if I had moved to get him out, whatever the reason, they would have known you were not trustworthy, that you had given up the name and the information to someone at the agency. What then? What of your mission?"

"This isn't about—"

"The next time you tried to enter the country they would have detained you and sent you home or, worse, allowed you to enter and made arrangements for you to permanently disappear. If pushed, they would have painted you as a traitor to your country who, when confronted, committed suicide, thereby ruining not just your good name, but that of your entire family. I told you, Charlie, the FSB is a more refined version of the KGB."

A seagull, fighting the breeze, spread its wings to land on one of the piers, a relatively simple task, but the wind blew the bird backward, and it gave up without really trying.

Emerson changed his tone. "You have nothing to feel guilty about. You were given a name, and you provided me with that name. I made the decision that it go no further. If anyone is responsible for Chekovsky's death it is me, not you."

Jenkins hadn't thought of how the news might impact Emerson. He'd been too busy being angry and feeling sorry for himself. Emerson was right. Jenkins had done all he could by disclosing the name. He had not made the decision to abandon Chekovsky. That decision had been made by people well above his pay grade. But it did little to assuage the angst he felt since he'd read the news of Chekovsky's death.

"Federov will call," Emerson said. "He will feel emboldened by these events, and he will try to make you feel responsible for not having disclosed Chekovsky's name."

This, too, had been a common tactic of the KGB to gain leverage over an informant. They used the information to blackmail the person so he could not back out.

"To Federov," Emerson continued, "you will have put yourself in a no-win situation that requires you to do exactly what he wants when you next meet."

"And what do I give Federov when we meet?" Jenkins said.

Emerson opened his coat, reached inside, and handed Jenkins an envelope. Jenkins snatched it before the stiff breeze blew it down the pier.

"The fourth sister," Emerson said.

Jenkins eyes narrowed. "How did you get her name—"

"I didn't."

"I don't understand."

Emerson nodded to the envelope. "Uliana Artemyeva died two years ago of cancer at sixty-three years of age. She worked in the Russian nuclear industry sector as a top-level analyst. For the past decade she provided the CIA with classified information exposing Russia's energy officials engaging in bribes, kickbacks, and money laundering designed to grow Vladimir Putin's atomic energy business worldwide. Of course, the FSB does not have any knowledge of this individual's betrayal." He nodded to the envelope. "That will prove it, and it will again prove that you are capable of providing them with highly classified information."

"Federov told me his superiors are not interested in information on dead Russian double agents."

"But he also expressed interest in identifying the remaining sisters, did he not?"

"Artemyeva was one of the sisters?"

"I highly doubt it," Emerson said, "given that her involvement with the agency only began ten years ago. But the Russians don't know when her involvement began, she is the same age as the other three sisters they've already identified, and the information she provided is similar in nature to the information provided by the other three."

"They'll assume she was one of the seven," Jenkins said.

"They may doubt you, but they will have no means to prove or disprove what you tell them. This information will get you one step closer to meeting and identifying the eighth sister."

"Will you attempt to get the other four sisters out of Russia?"

"That decision is above me. Remember, though, that the other sisters do not believe they are in any danger because they do not know the three women killed were three of seven."

Jenkins shook his head.

"Something else bothering you?" Emerson asked.

Jenkins couldn't precisely pinpoint the nature of his concern. "Where did the eighth sister get her information on the other three?"

"I suspect you will know soon enough. You will have provided Federov with too much information for him to ignore. He'll make contact. When he does, tell him you are returning to Russia."

"Did he at least pay the fifty thousand dollars I demanded?"

Emerson smiled. "Of course not. He's Russian. After eighty years of communist rule, Russians never pay for anything they can steal or get through blackmail. But he will pay when you disclose that information." He nodded to the envelope. "He can't afford not to."

10

The telephone call from Federov came just after the new year. The conversation was brief. Federov invited Jenkins to return to Russia. Jenkins asked if Federov's superiors had agreed to his financial demands—mainly just to tweak him. Federov assured, "All matters discussed are being handled."

Until that was actually the case, Emerson was reimbursing Jenkins cash for his expenses.

The second week of January, Jenkins left the rain on Camano Island for Russia's snow and bitter cold. He told Alex he had to return to London to check on the progress of his security team at LSR&C's new office in advance of a visit from two English billionaires. That part of the story was true. He also said he would travel to Paris, a possible expansion site for LSR&C, to scout potential office locations. That part was not true.

He didn't like lying to her, but his purpose in doing so was twofold. The less a spouse knew of the case officer's work, the less she could ever divulge in an interrogation—by either side. More practically, he didn't want to worry her, knowing that worry could be harmful to her and to the baby.

This time, when his flight from Heathrow to Sheremetyevo International Airport landed, Jenkins had no problem with customs officials. He met Uri at baggage claim. Jenkins had called the office to ask for a ride—to not do so would have looked suspicious—and Uri had been more than happy to oblige him. Uri dressed in a black turtleneck and black leather jacket. He looked like a Russian mobster. For all Jenkins knew, he might be.

"Good that you are back, Boss." He grabbed Jenkins's bag and bulldozed a path through people scrambling to find luggage.

When they arrived at the Metropol, Jenkins presented himself at the registration desk, and the smiling clerk greeted him by name. Jenkins doubted the man's memory was that good, even if six-foot-five black men were not the norm in Moscow. The clerk also provided Jenkins with a room key card without asking for a credit card. The room would be free, but it also meant there would be no record of Jenkins having stayed at the hotel on this occasion. Federov had spoken to the hotel, it seemed. Jenkins was uncertain what to make of this.

Jenkins made his way to room 613, tossed his bag onto the bed, and considered an expensive bottle of champagne wrapped in a towel and plunged into a bucket of ice. On the counter was a three-by-five white envelope and in it, a card with a message welcoming Jenkins back to the Metropol and confirming that his car service would pick him up in the courtyard at the rear of the hotel at eight fifteen that evening.

That gave Jenkins twelve hours to catch up on sleep, though not in this room. He picked up the phone and called the front desk.

"Yes, Mr. Jenkins?"

"Mne ne nravitsysa moya komnata. Ya by predpochel druguyu." I don't like my room. I'd prefer another.

"Did you receive the bottle of champagne?" the flustered clerk asked.

"I did, thank you," Jenkins said. "But it didn't improve the room."

"Is there something specific then, Mr. Jenkins?"

"I'd prefer the opposite side of the hotel," Jenkins said. He wanted to be able to see the front entrance. At present he was looking at the wall of an adjacent building.

"I meant is there something specific about your room?"

"Not unless you can move it to the opposite side of the hotel," Jenkins said.

"I'm sorry," the clerk said. "I'm afraid those rooms have all been reserved for the evening. We're full."

"A higher floor, perhaps."

"I'm sorry," the clerk said again, clicking computer keys before responding. "We don't have any open rooms."

"Then I'll be checking out," Jenkins said. "Thank you for your hospitality."

"Wait," the clerk said.

Jenkins did not respond.

"We've had a cancellation, Mr. Jenkins. I'll send the bellboy to your room in one hour."

"I'd like to be asleep in one hour," Jenkins said, knowing the delay was to bug the alternate room. This clerk had been in contact with Federov. "Send the bellboy now."

He hung up the phone before the clerk could respond, grabbed the champagne and the note, and picked up his bag. Within minutes the bellboy knocked on his door and escorted Jenkins to a room on the opposite side of the hotel and two floors higher.

"*Spasibo.*" Jenkins handed the young man the bottle of champagne and a twenty-dollar bill. Then he said, "I'd like to know if anyone comes to the front desk asking about me."

The bellboy nodded. "No problem."

That evening, prior to departing his hotel room, Jenkins again placed a scrap of paper on the carpet near the door. He'd also opened the closet door several inches, unscrewed his mechanical pencil, removed a filament of lead, and slid that filament onto the door hinge. If someone did search his room, they'd be savvy enough to leave the closet door similarly ajar, but they'd have no way of putting the lead filament back together once it snapped when they opened the closet, in the unlikely event they even saw it.

Jenkins stepped out the back door of the hotel at 8:15 p.m. Federov was not prompt. Jenkins suspected the FSB officer and his partner, Arkady Volkov, were sitting in a parked car with the heater blasting, taking great pleasure knowing Jenkins stood in the cold, freezing his nuts off.

The Moscow temperature had plunged with nightfall; meteorologists said a cold wave rippling across the country would drop the temperature to minus thirty degrees Celsius. Jenkins stood beneath a decorative lamppost—the light like a candle flame in an oxygen-deprived room. Soon the cold seeped into his joints, despite his heavy coat and the hat with earflaps he'd purchased in Seattle. Jenkins moved his arms and his legs, trying not to freeze. After fifteen minutes he'd had enough. He walked back through the lobby doors into the warm hotel interior.

As he made his way across the marbled lobby, the bellboy he'd generously tipped appeared with an envelope. "Excuse me, Mr. Jenkins, a message came for you." The bellboy paused and looked about. "There's a taxi waiting out front."

"Spasibo," Jenkins said.

Jenkins considered the lobby but did not see anyone overly interested in him. He opened the envelope.

Change of plans. Take taxi out front.

Jenkins swore, stuffed the envelope into his coat pocket, and slid on his gloves as he walked across the marbled foyer, down the steps, and out the front door. A man stood outside a waiting cab, his shoulders hunched against the cold. Smoke from a cigarette filtered from his nostrils. When Jenkins made eye contact, the man tossed the cigarette butt into the snow and quickly moved behind the wheel.

Jenkins slid into the back seat. The driver didn't ask where Jenkins wanted to go or flip the lever on the cab meter. He appeared to be driving without a destination, though certainly with a purpose—to determine if Jenkins was being followed. Jenkins used the Kremlin, lit up in the hazy night sky, as a landmark, and confirmed they were driving in circles. After fifteen minutes, a cell phone rang. The driver answered it, listened, then set down the phone and pulled a U-turn in the middle of the street. They crossed the Moskva River. Jenkins again kept note of the street signs. The taxi made another right, this time on Krymsky Val. Minutes later he pulled to the curb and stopped.

The driver pointed down a pedestrian walkway in what looked to be a park. "Carousel."

When Jenkins stepped from the cab, the cold again engulfed him. He pulled up the collar of his jacket and pressed the flaps of his hat tight against his ears as he walked a path illuminated by old-fashioned streetlamps struggling to provide a sallow light. The path led to a children's playground with several colorful carousels, but neither Federov nor the black Mercedes. More waiting. So Russian.

Several more minutes passed before the Mercedes slowly approached, driving toward Jenkins on the deserted pedestrian walking path.

Jenkins raised his hand to deflect the glare of the car's lights and watched Federov exit and approach, smoking a cigarette. The streetlamp cast a tempered glow across the car's windshield, illuminating Volkov's presence in the driver's seat, and the red glow of his cigarette. "This is a pedestrian walkway," Jenkins said to Federov. "You could get a ticket if a police officer comes by."

"I'll take my chances," Federov said. Despite the cold, he wore only a leather car coat, no hat or gloves—no doubt another display of Russian men's physical and mental virility. Jenkins really didn't care. He wasn't out to impress Federov with feats of strength—physical or mental. He shoved his gloved hands into his coat pockets, preferring not to get frostbite.

"Where are we?" Jenkins asked, looking about.

Federov feigned surprise. "Do you not read, Mr. Jenkins? I took you to be a man of the arts."

And that place where Jenkins had stored information from the past, including the street name, revealed itself. "Gorky Park," he said.

Federov smiled, nodding. "Very good. Your Martin Cruz Smith, I believe."

"You've read it," Jenkins said.

"I read everything about Russia."

"I didn't take you to be much of a reader."

"You've misjudged me," Federov said. "Though I prefer Russian writers. Dostoyevsky and Tolstoy."

"*Crime and Punishment*?"

"A masterpiece," Federov said. He removed a crumpled pack of cigarettes from a coat pocket, tapped the pack against his palm and withdrew a cigarette with his lips, then offered the pack to Jenkins, who declined.

"You Americans." Federov shook his head. "You don't smoke. You don't drink. You work out every day. Something must kill you; it might as well be enjoyable." He flicked his lighter and touched the blue flame to the tip of the cigarette. The tobacco burned red as Federov inhaled, seeming to savor the taste. When he exhaled, the tendril of smoke lingered, as if trapped by the oppressively thick air. "I wished for you to be comfortable for our meeting. Someplace in Moscow perhaps you are familiar with, no?"

"I read it many years ago," Jenkins said, feeling the cold seeping through every seam in his clothes. *Comfortable my ass.* "I'm afraid I don't remember all of the details."

"No? Inspector Arkady Renko?" Federov pointed to a spot to his right. "Three bodies shot and mutilated and left buried in the snow. A—how do you say . . . murder mystery? No? They didn't find the bodies until the melt in April."

"Gruesome," Jenkins said, wondering if Federov's point had been to intimidate. "Did you know it almost wasn't published?"

"*Gorky Park*? No?" Federov said.

"The publisher didn't think a book involving a Russian detective would sell, that Americans wouldn't be interested."

"Look around you—Russia is a very interesting country," Federov said. "I believe the killer was an American, though, yes?"

"Spoiler alert."

"Izvinite?"

"It means you gave away the ending of the book. You spoiled it."

"You Americans are odd." Federov took another drag on his cigarette, speaking as the smoke filtered out his nose and mouth. "You said you have additional information?"

"I also said I had financial demands."

"My superiors were not impressed with the information provided. Perhaps this will be more impressive."

"I'm not sure we'll find out."

"No?"

"No."

"You read of Nikolay Chekovsky?" Federov asked, right on cue.

"Yes," Jenkins said. "I did."

"A shame a man so talented must die."

"As you said, something must kill you."

"Yes, something." Federov dropped the butt of the cigarette and ground it out with the toe of his shoe. "You could have saved him."

"I doubt it."

"No?"

"I assume you had him under surveillance long before you told me his name. So, even if I had been inclined to tell the agency his name, which I wasn't, what really could have been done?"

"No daring American rescue like your adventure novels?"

Jenkins gave a thin smile. "Not likely."

"But the fact remains that you did know his name, and yet you did nothing to warn your superiors. How do you believe they will respond if they were to learn of this?"

"Who would tell them?"

Federov smiled.

"I want fifty thousand dollars deposited by the end of the week or I get on a plane and I don't return."

Federov gravely shook his head. "That is a lot of money, Mr. Jenkins. Perhaps you have not been following the news. Oil prices are falling each day. Russia's economy is in recession."

"I'm sure your bosses can scrape up the money. Perhaps one of the Russian oligarchs is a patriot." He smiled again. "That was the deal."

"Yes," Federov said. "In principle, certainly. But my superiors would be more inclined to pay once they have this additional information."

Jenkins paused, though only for effect. He wanted Federov to think he had Jenkins over a barrel and that Jenkins knew this. Jenkins said, "You are searching for four of the remaining seven sisters."

"We have had this discussion."

"Number four," Jenkins said.

"You know the identity—"

"Uliana Artemyeva," Jenkins said. He watched Federov's eyes shift to Volkov as he provided the details of Artemyeva's betrayal and the CIA's use of that information to undermine Putin's nuclear industry sector. Jenkins was being recorded, likely filmed.

Jenkins reached into the interior pocket of his jacket and produced the manila envelope Carl Emerson had given him. He handed it to Federov. Then he said, "Fifty thousand in the account I gave you. Otherwise, our conversations, much as I have enjoyed them, will come to an end." Jenkins turned and started up the path.

"You will freeze to death walking in this cold," Federov said.

Jenkins turned back and smiled. "Something must kill us."

11

The walk back to the Metropol Hotel might have killed Jenkins. Ironically, he was saved by an ambulance that stopped as he reached the other side of the Crimean Bridge. He would have considered this a good deed, or perhaps a practical solution by two men who figured if they didn't help him they'd be by later to pick up his corpse, but when the driver opened the door he asked for "forty American dollars." Jenkins had read that Moscow vehicles of all types—even hearses and garbage trucks—were picking up pedestrians. In a city where so many struggled to make ends meet, every ruble helped.

He gladly paid the not-so-altruistic ambulance driver.

When he returned to his hotel room, the scrap of paper remained on the floor where he'd placed it, and the pencil lead balanced on the closet-door hinge. He bolted and chained the door and collapsed onto the bed.

His ringing cell phone awoke him. Caller ID indicated Alex. Jenkins checked the time: eleven a.m. He'd slept almost twelve hours, which was six more than he normally slept on a good night. He looked about the room, considering whether it was possible he'd been drugged. If he had been, he felt no side effects. Everything looked to be in place.

"You sound like you're still sleeping," she said.

"I had a bit of a late night last night," he said. "The Brits enjoy their pubs. I hope to be home in a day or two. How are you?"

"Tired. CJ negotiated an additional chapter of Harry Potter tonight. I think that kid is going to be a lawyer."

She sounded down. "Everything okay?" he asked.

"I don't want to alarm you."

Jenkins sat up. "What is it?"

"I had some spotting today," she said. "The doctor said it could be nothing, but he wants me to put my feet up for a couple of days."

"I'll come home," Jenkins said. He'd never forgive himself if anything happened to Alex or to the baby.

"No, don't," she said. "I spoke to Claire Russo and she's agreed to pick up CJ in the mornings and take him to school and to soccer practices. All I have to do is get him out of bed and out the door on time."

"I'll call CJ today and tell him we need his help."

"Don't," she said. "I've already spoken to him and he's trying. He made dinner tonight."

"I'll bet that was special," Jenkins said.

"Turkey sandwiches. And they were pretty good. I'm going to bed. I'm tired. I just wanted to hear your voice. I love you."

"I love you too," Jenkins said.

He disconnected and stared at the phone. What the hell was he doing? What the hell would he do if Alex lost this child because he was in Russia, working again for the CIA? He didn't belong here. He was too old to be out at night in the bitter cold talking to FSB officers about classified material. He should be at home, taking CJ to school and caring for his wife. He thought again of why he'd started CJ Security. Was it to provide his family with financial security? Or was it his ego, his never-satisfied quest to try something new, something different, something challenging? That might have been okay when he was young and could afford to make mistakes, but he was sixty-four years old, with a nine-year-old son and a pregnant wife. He wouldn't be much good to them dead, and he wasn't so naïve that he hadn't considered that a distinct possibility. The Russians did not like to be fooled. If Jenkins was successful, and he determined the identity of this eighth sister, he could be looking over his shoulder for the rest of his life. The CIA would not protect him or his family. Emerson had made it abundantly clear that if things went sideways, they'd disown the mission faster than a busted teenager disowned a bag of pot. Jenkins needed to move. He needed to find the eighth sister and get the hell out of Russia.

Jenkins returned to the Metropol Hotel at just after six in the evening following another meeting at the LSR&C Moscow office. The clerk at reception greeted him with a wave and handed Jenkins an envelope.

Jenkins thanked him. Stepping inside his hotel room, he noticed the scrap of paper on the carpet where he had placed it. He took off his coat, hat, and gloves, set them on the bed, and opened the envelope. Inside was a folded sheet of paper. When he unfolded it, a ticket fluttered to the carpet. Jenkins bent and picked it up. The ticket was to the Vakhtangov Theatre for the 7:30 p.m. performance that evening of the play *Masquerade*.

Federov wanted to meet. He also apparently seemed intent on convincing Jenkins he was not just a brute, but a man of the arts.

Jenkins wasn't buying it.

Jenkins exited his cab and walked the Arbat, a cobblestone street rich with history. At present, the Arbat looked to have become gentrified, which was to be expected given its proximity to the center of Moscow.

Tonight, the pedestrian foot traffic was light due to the blistering cold. A crowd stood outside the Vakhtangov Theatre, sucking on last-minute cigarettes, their breaths trailing them like smoke from steam engines.

At one of several entrances, a woman scanned his ticket and Jenkins shuffled inside. He quickly shed his coat, hat, and gloves, but decided not to check them in case of the unexpected. He handed his ticket to an usher. Rather than lead Jenkins down the aisle, she directed him to a staircase and said something about following the stairs to the third level.

Jenkins did so, and eventually made his way to a private booth with six red velvet seats. Predictably, Federov and Volkov were not there. Jenkins took the seat closest to the railing. The curtain remained drawn across the stage, and a cacophony of voices, atop instruments being tuned in the orchestra pit, echoed up, along with the audience's strong odors of perfume and cologne.

Jenkins sat, once again waiting. At least this time he wasn't outside, freezing.

With the theater seats nearly full, the house lights dimmed. As if on cue, a part of the rehearsed play, Federov entered the booth. He'd dressed in a dark suit and striped tie. Volkov followed, dressed in jeans, a polo shirt, and winter coat. He also carried a briefcase, which seemed odd given the setting.

Federov looked at Jenkins and said, "Would you mind switching seats?"

Jenkins stood, wondering about the possible reason for the request, but he took the outside seat in the first row. Volkov sat behind him, which again made him think of *The Godfather* and Peter Clemenza.

"Have you ever seen this play, Mr. Jenkins?" Federov asked, keeping his voice low.

"I don't believe so," Jenkins said. "Thank you for the ticket." The orchestra made a few final noises, then fell silent. Jenkins could see the conductor's raised arms, poised to begin. "I would wait before you are thanking me," Federov said. He handed Jenkins a program. "The play was written in 1835 by Mikhail Lermontov. I am told that it is often compared to Shakespeare's *Othello*." The orchestra burst into music, the conductor's arms frantically waving. Federov leaned closer so Jenkins could hear him. "The hero, Arbenin, is a wealthy middle-aged man with a rebellious spirit. Born into high society, he ends up murdering his wife."

"So, another uplifting Russian comedy," Jenkins said.

"Life is not always uplifting or comedic." Federov sounded resigned. His breath smelled of garlic and beer.

"Nor is it always depressing and humorless," Jenkins said.

"You should live through the winters here in Russia before you decide. You may have another opinion."

"I'm sure I would." A beat passed and Jenkins said, "I didn't take you as a man of the arts."

Federov chuckled. "Do you have children, Mr. Jenkins?"

Jenkins did not answer, making it clear that any questions about his family were off the table.

"I have two daughters," Federov said, picking lint from his slacks. "My oldest, Renata, is in the play tonight—an inconsequential role, one of the servants."

Jenkins turned his head to see if Federov was being serious. The Russian shrugged. "My ex-wife has seen her now three times. I am the bad parent. I am the parent who is always working late and cannot be here. I have promised my daughter that I would attend on three occasions, and each time I have had to disappoint her. Trust me when I say there is nothing worse than a disappointed daughter and a vindicated ex-wife."

Jenkins smiled. It was the first bit of humor Federov had displayed. Perhaps the information Jenkins had provided the prior evening was causing Federov to warm to him. "That's why you wanted the seat by the railing."

"That is why," Federov said. "Remaining in character is not Renata's acting strength. She will invariably look up here to see if I came."

"And so here we sit," Jenkins said.

"And so here we sit." Federov pointed at actors coming on stage. "There. You see the dark-haired woman in the white dress. That is my daughter."

"She's beautiful," Jenkins said. "You must be proud of her."

Federov shrugged. "The beauty and theater come from my side of the family. My mother sang in the Russian opera."

"Theater is in your blood."

"For the amount I have spent on Renata's training, I could be watching a doctor operate, but I'm told that young people now are not concerned with things like money and living decently. They want to be happy. Everyone wants to be happy. I'm supposed to accept that, while paying the bills, of course."

"Of course. Still, she's in a major production in Moscow. That's something."

"She stinks, Mr. Jenkins. That she gets from my ex-wife's side of the family. When my wife sang at home, the neighbors feared she'd sucked the cat into our vacuum cleaner. My daughter's singing is not much better."

Jenkins smiled. "How then did she get the part?"

Federov rolled his head toward Jenkins and raised his eyebrows. "She benefits from having a father who knows people who know people, though neither she nor her mother know of this."

Jenkins chuckled. "And for the briefest of moments, you were starting to sound almost human, Federov."

Federov shrugged. "We are not so different, Mr. Jenkins. We want our wives and our children to be happy, no? I failed at my marriage. I am trying not to fail with my children." Moments later, when Federov's daughter left the stage, the FSB agent stood. "Come," he said.

"We're leaving?" Jenkins asked.

"She does not return until the third act. She will not know we have left. Think of it as a reprieve." Jenkins paused, still uncertain if Federov was joking. "The play is typical of Russian theater," Federov said. "Far too long and far too depressing. Spoiler alert—the wife dies. Come."

Jenkins followed Federov from the booth, Volkov trailing them with his briefcase. Jenkins wondered if it contained money. Rather than turn right toward the hall leading to the theater entrance, Federov turned left. They continued down the hall to a back staircase that would, presumably, lead outside. Jenkins followed the Russian FSB officer down a narrow staircase to the bottom floor, but Federov walked past the green exit sign that was over a door.

"Where are we going?" Jenkins asked.

"Someplace to speak in private," Federov said.

Somewhere behind him, Jenkins heard the orchestra and singers building to a faint crescendo. Federov stopped and pushed open a door. Jenkins took a step forward before realizing he had stepped into total darkness. Behind him the door slammed shut. He heard Federov, or Volkov, flip a switch. A bright light emanated from a bare bulb hanging from a wire, revealing the room to be a windowless, concrete square. In the center of the room, just beneath the light, someone had placed a lone metal chair.

When younger, and better on his game, Jenkins would have assessed all of this in an instant, and just as quickly disabled both men, but his reactions were no longer what they once had been, and by the time it all registered, he was too late.

He felt a dull blow to the back of his head.

12

The sharp smell of ammonia caused Jenkins to sit up. Blurred images danced and shimmered. When his vision cleared, he saw Federov seated beside Volkov in folding chairs, both sucking on cigarettes. From the haze of smoke above their heads and the collection of crushed butts littering the floor, Jenkins could tell he had been out for a while. He had a throbbing ache at the back of his head where he'd been hit.

"I told Arkady he hit you too hard," Federov said, voice calm. "He doesn't seem to understand the word 'soft.'" Volkov stood and walked to a folding table at the edge of the light. On it, he'd set his briefcase. He clicked it open.

Jenkins felt plastic strips binding his wrists to the bars at the back of the chair. His ankles were likewise bound to each chair leg. His jacket and his shirt had been removed, draped on a hanger hooked to a nail hammered into the wall. The nail appeared to have caused a spiderweb of cracks.

"I removed your jacket and shirt so as not to damage them unnecessarily," Federov said, following Jenkins's gaze.

"What the hell is this, Federov?" Jenkins asked, trying to sound more tired than scared. This was an unexpected development—unlike anything he'd experienced in Mexico City. He needed to buy time to determine its purpose. Was it simply to scare and intimidate him, or had he pissed off somebody in Lubyanka?

Volkov unfolded the briefcase on the table. In it, Jenkins saw duct tape, pliers, knives, and a blowtorch.

"I am on a schedule," Federov said, checking his watch. "If I am not back in the box before the start of the third act, my daughter will know that I left and then . . ." He shrugged. "For me and for you it is not so good."

"So your daughter is actually in the play?" Jenkins asked, stalling for time.

"Of course," Federov said. "And I would not want to disappoint her again. You asked, I believe, 'What is this?' No?"

"Yeah. What the hell is this?"

Federov took a final pull on his cigarette, dropped the butt to the floor, and stood, crushing the embers beneath the sole of his shoe. Smoke escaped his nostrils and mouth as he spoke. "This is a room several stories beneath the stage. Its history is somewhat uncertain and, I think, embellished. So, hard to say. Some say Catholics used to come here, under the guise of attending the theater, but really to attend mass during communist times. Others say that is a myth, that the room was used only for storage. Still, others say it is one of the hundreds of rooms used by Stalin to interrogate dissidents. They say the blood of those men stains the walls and cannot be covered with paint. Do you see the red tint? It is not so easy in this light."

"Sounds like the plot of another Russian play," Jenkins said.

"One doesn't really know the truth, which, ironically, is also why you are here, Mr. Jenkins."

Jenkins fought to remain calm. At least with his right hand cuffed to the chair it was not trembling. He kept his voice even and, hopefully, unconcerned. "This is all very theatrical, Federov. You want to try again, this time without the histrionics?"

Federov paced. "You are here, Mr. Jenkins, because I told you once my superiors are not interested in, and will not pay for, the names of dead women. Of which you have provided me."

"What is that supposed to mean?"

Federov stepped in front of him. "It means that Uliana Artemyeva died several years ago from natural causes."

"So?"

"So, you can see my dilemma, no?"

"No, I can't. How does that diminish the information?"

"Because we have no way to confirm or to disaffirm that Ms. Artemyeva was one of the seven sisters."

"I told you she was one."

"Yes, but someone who would betray his country for money is not exactly a bastion of integrity and honesty. Is he?"

At the table, Volkov twisted the nozzle onto the torch, turned the valve, and struck a match. It made a scraping sound on the table. The burner ignited in a blue-and-yellow flame, and Volkov adjusted the nozzle until the flame became a crisp blue triangle.

"Why would I provide you the information if it was inaccurate?"

Federov diverted his attention when he heard the pop of the blue flame, then reconsidered Jenkins. "With which of the fifty thousand reasons would you like for me to start?"

"How about one of the fifty thousand you haven't paid me? I provided that information in good faith, Federov, with the understanding that I would be compensated. Don't treat me like some amateur. I'm getting tired of it. You want the information. I'm providing it. I can't be held responsible if one of the seven sisters had already died of natural causes."

"It is convenient for you though, no?"

"Does this look convenient to you?"

Volkov removed a knife from its sheath and sliced a ribbon of paper that fluttered to the ground.

Jenkins looked back to Federov. He needed to outsmart him. "Tell me, Federov, how is it that you confirmed the other three women were three of the seven sisters? Did they tell you when you tortured them?

Or did they tell you they did not know what you were talking about, that they did not even know the term 'the seven sisters'?"

"They might have been trained well to resist, Mr. Jenkins."

Jenkins laughed, but inside his stomach churned. "If that's the case, then you boys have fallen well off your game since I was sparring with the KGB. I understood the FSB was a more refined version of the KGB. Maybe I heard wrong, if you could not get three sixty-year-old women to admit anything to you."

"We are going to find out if we have fallen off our game," Federov said. He considered his watch. "I will go back to the booth," he said, speaking Russian to Volkov. "You will excuse me, Mr. Jenkins. Our superiors have orders, but this is ugly business in which I do not wish to participate."

"You're not thinking this through, Federov."

"You wish to enlighten me?" Federov sat again in the chair across from Jenkins. He folded his legs. "Enlighten. Please. But be conscious of the time. The second act is long, but not that long."

"Why would I provide information on a Russian double agent that your people could easily verify wasn't true? The information I provided to you would be, if divulged to my agency, enough to put me in a penitentiary for the remainder of my life. So why would I risk providing you with false information now? What purpose would it serve?"

Federov bent forward, inches from Jenkins's face. "I am thinking it is because you want to make me look like the fool to my superiors, Mr. Jenkins. And I will not be made to look like the fool."

"What I want is my money, as we agreed. I don't give a good Goddamn about your image with your superiors, and based on what you're telling me, I'm not sure I have much respect for them either. At least tell me your superiors performed their due diligence and determined the information is accurate." Jenkins waited for an answer. When it didn't immediately come he chuckled. "Seriously? How else did the FBI and the CIA know that the Russian nuclear industry officials were engaged in a conspiracy of bribery and extortion, unless they were receiving classified information from someone in a position of knowledge?"

"Artemyeva is dead, which means—"

"It means you can't verify the information simply by torturing her. It means you have to get a bit more creative, like searching through documents and engaging in human intelligence. How were the FBI and the CIA able to thwart so many companies doing business with Russian energy companies, unless they had knowledge of the kickbacks and the extortion and threatened to make that information public? The illegal activities were made known to the CIA by a 'confidential witness' with intimate knowledge of the Russian atomic energy commission. That confidential witness was Uliana Artemyeva."

At the table, Volkov removed a large snipping tool and held the cutting edges to the flame of the torch until the tool glowed red.

"Maybe she was and maybe she wasn't this confidential witness," Federov said, again picking at imaginary lint from his suit leg.

It was a tell. Almost everyone had a tell, even some of the best agents Jenkins had gone up against. Picking imaginary lint was Federov's tell. He was not as confident as he was projecting. His daughter was not the only actor in the family who stunk.

"It does not mean she was one of the remaining seven sisters," Federov said.

"No?" Jenkins said, becoming more confident. "She was sixty-three years old when she died. How old were Zarina Kazakova, Irena Lavrova, and Olga Artamonova?"

"Which would be the reason that you chose to disclose this name as opposed to another."

"As opposed to some other woman working in the Russian atomic energy industry who just so happens to be the same age as the other three and who, through a little bit of work on your part, you would know was providing the US with confidential information? You disappoint me, Federov. I was a fool to deal with you. I should have asked for someone above you—someone with some intelligence." He smirked. "You go ahead and throw away the only potential source of information you'll ever have that might be able to provide you with the names of the other sisters because you think I could be a double agent feeding you a bunch of bullshit."

Federov sat in silence, but his body language spoke volumes. Jenkins had gotten to him. He'd gotten to Federov's ego, in front of Volkov, who had put down his play toys and now also looked uncertain and, maybe, concerned.

"I guess we're at a crossroads," Jenkins said. "And not unlike the crossroads you face with your daughter?"

Federov looked up. "How so?"

"You can either swallow your pride and accept your daughter's chosen profession so you can have a relationship with her, or you can let your pride get in the way and lose any hope of ever having any relationship." Jenkins waited a beat. Then he said, "So what's it going to be, Federov? Are we going to have a relationship? Or are you going to let your pride get in the way and lose the best opportunity you'll ever have in your career to make a name for yourself?"

13

The clerk at the Metropol Hotel reception desk gave Jenkins a quizzical stare, as if seeing a ghost. He walked out from behind the counter.

"Are you not well, Mr. Jenkins?" he asked over the sound of the harp strings being played in the lobby.

Truth was, Jenkins felt sick and probably did not look well. He'd talked his way out of Volkov using his body as an ashtray, or maybe snipping off a couple fingers, but he didn't feel clever or vindicated, as he had in Mexico City when he'd outfoxed a KGB agent. "I think I might have overdone it at dinner," Jenkins said.

"Is there anything I can get you? Some aspirin perhaps?"

"No. Thank you. I'll just head up to my room and lie down."

He entered the elevator feeling drained and exhausted. As the doors closed, a hand knifed between them. Jenkins jumped back and instinctively raised his hands. The doors opened and the bellboy, the one Jenkins had given the champagne and the twenty-dollar tip, stepped into the car. He nodded before he hit the "Close" button multiple times. When the doors closed he turned to Jenkins.

"A woman came to the desk asking for you. She said she was a friend of yours. The desk clerk would not provide her with your room number, but this is Russia, Mr. Jenkins, and everything can be bought for a price."

"What did she look like?" Jenkins asked.

"I would guess mid-to-late forties, but it was hard to tell. She wore large glasses and had much hair."

"What was the color of her hair?"

"Dark. Almost black. The glasses were big, oval shaped."

"What about her clothes? Do you remember anything?"

"She wore a long winter coat with a fur collar and a scarf."

The coat and the scarf, along with the glasses, could be easily and quickly discarded, giving the woman a completely different appearance, if necessary. The more perplexing question was why the woman had gone to the clerk asking for Jenkins. The clerk certainly would have told Federov that Jenkins had switched rooms when he checked in, and Federov would have told the woman, if she was the eighth sister. Only two scenarios came to mind. Either Federov did not know the eighth sister, or the woman was not the eighth sister. If not, then who was she? If Federov had not sent the woman, Jenkins had to assume the desk clerk would have alerted him by now that someone had come to the hotel asking about him—though Federov had gone back to the play to watch his daughter in the third act and may not yet have received that message.

"Did she say anything else?" he asked.

"No. When the clerk told her he could not confirm a guest's presence at the hotel or provide a room number, she left. But as I said, Mr. Jenkins, in Russia, everything has a price."

"Spasibo." Jenkins reached into his pocket for additional cash.

"No." The young man raised a hand. "Now we are . . . even. Yes?" He pushed the button for the next floor. When the elevator stopped, he stepped off. "Good luck to you, Mr. Jenkins . . . whatever it is that you are doing."

Jenkins rode the elevator to the eighth floor. Trays with empty plates, glasses, and discarded napkins and cutlery littered the carpet. Jenkins checked the trays as he walked to his room, looking for anything he might use as a weapon if, as the bellboy had implied, the woman had been able to bribe someone and get a key to his room. He spotted a steak knife and picked it up, along with the napkin. He cleaned the blade and fit the handle of the knife up the sleeve of his shirt.

At the door to his room he removed the "Do Not Disturb" sign he'd hung on the handle, and swiped his card key, hearing the mechanism engage and unlock. He dropped to a knee, not wanting to take a bullet to the forehead if the woman was inside, pulled down on the handle, and gently shoved open the door three to four inches. The scrap of paper remained on the carpet where he had placed it.

He let out a sigh, stood and entered his room. Inside, he removed his coat, and tossed it, along with his hat and the steak knife, on the bed. The events of the evening hit him hard. He felt a panic attack continuing to gain traction. In the bathroom, he shook out one of the green pills and washed it down with water, then took deep, slow breaths to calm himself. In the mirror he looked as gray as the Moscow winter night. He turned on the cold water, lowered his head, and splashed water on his face. His wrists burned where the cuffs had bit into his skin, leaving red abrasions.

In minutes his breathing slowed and his anxiety eased. Whatever the reason for Federov's test tonight, Jenkins had seemingly passed—though one never knew with the KGB and, he assumed, the FSB. He hoped the bellboy's news of a woman seeking his room number was further proof of his conclusion.

As he calmed, Jenkins felt pangs of hunger and considered his watch. Room service would be his best option. He dried his hands, exited the bathroom, and walked to the antique desk. Out the windows he saw the fountain in Teatralnaya Square and, across it, the columned entrance to the Bolshoi Theatre with the statue of Apollo crowning the peaked façade. To his right, down the street, the squat Lubyanka Building was ablaze with lights, a subtle reminder that the FSB never slept.

Jenkins picked up the amenities binder from the desk and flipped to the tab for in-room dining, then punched in the three-digit code on the desk phone. His gaze drifted to his left, to the gap in the open closet door, which remained as he had positioned it. His focus then shifted to the gold hinge.

A man answered the line. "Yes, Mr. Jenkins, how may I be of service?"

The lead filament did not rest on the hinge.

"Hello? Mr. Jenkins?"

He looked to the carpet, where the filament had fallen, snapped in half.

14

Jenkins turned his back to the closet, as if admiring the view out the window, but kept his attention on the mirror on the adjacent wall, assuming someone, the woman perhaps, was inside the closet.

"I'd like to order some food," he said.

"My pleasure, Mr. Jenkins. What can I get for you?"

Jenkins flipped the pages in the binder but kept his gaze on the mirror. "I'd like the cheeseburger," he said, "with fries. And a beer. Whatever you recommend."

"How would you like your cheeseburger cooked?"

"Medium," Jenkins said.

"Very good, Mr. Jenkins. Is twenty minutes acceptable?"

"That would be fine."

The man hung up, but Jenkins continued talking. "I have a free day tomorrow. Do you recommend any place in particular that I might visit here in Moscow? Something close, given this cold spell?" He picked up the phone cradle, gripping the cord snaking behind the desk, turned his back to the closet, and yanked the telephone cord from the wall.

Then he paced.

"That sounds like it could be interesting. I think I would enjoy that very much."

He continued talking as he paced, keeping an eye on the mirror. He noticed a slight change in light inside the closet, someone moving.

He paced the opposite direction, so the phone was in his right hand. "What about theater performances? Are there any that you would recommend?"

He waited, keeping up the imaginary conversation, looking for an opportunity. A cylindrical tube protruded from the closet door opening. He was out of time.

Jenkins threw the phone but didn't wait to find out if his aim had been true. The phone crashed with a loud clang. He followed it, hurling his 235 pounds into the closet door and the person inside the closet. They hit the back wall with a thud. He found the hand holding the gun and shoved the barrel at the ceiling just before hearing a pop. Jenkins felt a knee come up fast and hard and quickly shifted. The strike missed his groin, and struck him in the right thigh. He bent the wrist holding the gun and heard the gun pop a second time, before it dropped to the carpeted floor. A hand clawed at his face, fingernails raking skin. He'd had enough. He delivered a short, powerful blow, and felt the person go limp, then sag to the floor.

Jenkins dragged the body from the closet. A woman. He dropped her onto the floor and retrieved the gun, shoving the barrel into the waistband of his pants at the small of his back. He turned the woman over. She wore no glasses. A black wig sat askew on her head. Her clothes were dark—black jeans, a black turtleneck, black boots. He pulled off the wig, revealing light-brown hair tied in a bun. She had angular, Slavic features. He quickly pulled the cord from the phone and used it to tie her hands behind her back. For the next several minutes he went through the pockets of her coat and other clothes looking for any form of identification, finding none.

Someone knocked on the hotel room door. Jenkins moved back to the closet and picked up the woman's coat, searching it. In the pocket he found the scarf the bellboy had described.

A second knock, three short raps.

"Just a minute," Jenkins called. He fit the scarf between the woman's teeth and tied it around the back of her head. Then he dragged her into the closet and shut it. Moving toward the hotel room door, he caught a glimpse of himself in the mirror. His shirt was torn. Claw marks lined his chest and had drawn blood down the right side of his face. He couldn't open the door looking like this.

Another knock.

At the door, Jenkins stood to the side of the doorframe and leaned out to peer through the peephole. A man in a white jacket stood in the hall beside a rolling cart with a silver tray.

Jenkins moved away from the door in case the man also had a gun. "I'm just stepping from the shower," he said. "Leave the tray on the cart, please?"

"With pleasure," the man said. "Would you like me to leave the bill as well?"

The man was worried about his tip. "Yes, please. I'll take care of it."

Jenkins waited a beat, then looked out the peephole. The young man had departed. Jenkins opened the door and rolled the cart into the room. Then he hurried back to the closet. The woman had opened her eyes, dazed but coming to. He grabbed her and dumped her into the desk chair, then took a moment to examine the gun—a Ruger 22 with a suppressor. Efficient. An assassin's weapon. The bullet would have been enough to kill him, but not so large as to splatter his brain and blood all over the room.

It raised additional questions, foremost being: If this was the eighth sister, why had the woman come to kill him? If she was the eighth sister, why hadn't she come to find out what Jenkins knew of the remaining four sisters? Why hadn't she known his room number without asking the clerk?

The woman sat, staring at him.

"If I remove the gag, are you going to be quiet?" he asked in Russian.

She nodded.

"If you scream, if you make a sound, I will shoot you and put your body under the sheet on that cart. Then I'll leave you in the stairwell. Do you understand me?"

The woman gave another nod.

Jenkins spun the chair and untied the gag. He stepped back, out of range, in case she flung herself at him or attempted another kick to the groin. The woman squinted several times and opened and closed her mouth. He hadn't broken her jaw or her nose. His aim in the dark had been off, but she would have a black left eye in a matter of hours.

"Let's start with you telling me your name. Who are you?" Jenkins said, this time in English.

The woman responded with a blank stare.

"Nothing?" Jenkins said. "All right then. Why did you try to kill me?"

Again, she did not respond.

"Kto ty?" he said. *Who are you?*

"I speak English, Mr. Jenkins." Her English was heavily accented.

"I could call the police," he said. "And tell them that you tried to kill me."

This time her lips slowly spread into a knowing grin. "And I would tell them that you tried to rape me and I fought back, bravely. The gun, I would say, is not mine. It is yours. Do you really want the Moscow police to be looking into your presence here?"

Did she know the reason for his presence? What he needed to determine was whether she worked for the FSB. He was beginning to think she did not. "I could call the FSB," he said. "I'm sure they could extract information from you."

Again, it drew no verbal response. He went to his coat on the bed and pulled out the burner phone. "No?" He shrugged. "Very well." He punched in a number.

"Wait," she said.

Interesting. "Something you want to say? Are you FSB?"

"If I were FSB, why would I want to kill a man willing to betray his country and the lives of seven women who may have done more harm to Russia than any others in its history?"

Rather than clarify, her answer complicated his situation. If she was not FSB, not the eighth sister, then how did she know of the seven sisters? He moved to the window and looked down at the hotel's front entrance, but he did not see a Mercedes. "I don't know. Why would you?"

"I wouldn't," she said.

"If you're not FSB, then what are you?"

"Tell me first, Mr. Jenkins, why you are betraying these women? Why are you betraying your country?"

"I need the money," he said, sticking to his story. "My business is failing."

"You would so easily trade these lives for money?"

He shrugged. "I don't bleed red, white, and blue."

"And yet you did not kill me just now, though you had the chance. You still have the chance. I'd say the odds favor you. So why don't you kill me, Mr. Jenkins? Why don't you call the FSB and tell them to come and dispose of my body?" Before Jenkins could answer, she said, "No. You did not do so because you are having doubts. You asked me my name. What purpose would my name serve in making you money to save your business?"

"I'm curious."

Her eyes bore into him. "I think I have misjudged you, Mr. Jenkins. I think that you wish to know my name because you are not here to tell Viktor Federov or Arkady Volkov the names of the remaining four sisters. That is why you provided them with the name of a dead woman. No. You did not come here for that purpose."

Intrigued where this conversation was going, and why, but conscious of the minutes passing, Jenkins said, "So why don't you tell me why I came here?"

"You came here to find the eighth sister."

"Are you the eighth sister?" he said, now doubting that to be the case.

"Tell me if I am correct, Mr. Jenkins. What do you have to lose? I am bound and you are holding my weapon. You can kill me at any time. It doesn't change your circumstances."

"Why do you want to know?"

"Because, Mr. Jenkins, I am smelling a rat. And I think it has bitten us both."

"What rat would that be?"

"The rat who sent you to Moscow to learn my name. The rat who told you that I work for the FSB and that I am killing the seven sisters. The same rat who is divulging the names of the seven sisters to Federov, and being paid much to do so."

"*You're* divulging the names to Federov."

She laughed. "If I were, why would I try to kill the man who says he can provide the remaining four names? Why would the clerk not give me your room number if I worked for Federov?"

And those were two of the questions that continued to bother Jenkins. Logically, she was right, and Jenkins, too, was starting to smell a rat. He went again to the window and peered down at the entrance.

"Who do you work for?" he said.

"I suspect the same agency that you work for."

Jenkins turned from the window, considering her.

She shrugged.

"Tell me why I should believe you."

"Common sense."

He stepped from the window and leaned against the desk. "Okay, explain it to me so it makes sense."

"First, let's discuss what you were told. You were told that I am the eighth sister and that my purpose is to determine the names of the other seven sisters. Correct?"

"Keep going."

"But the circumstances of our encounter do not support what you were told."

"Let's say I'm questioning what I was told."

"My purpose is not to determine the names of the remaining seven sisters for the FSB. My purpose is to determine the name of the person disclosing the names of the seven sisters to the FSB. Is that you, Mr. Jenkins? No." She shook her head slowly. "I do not think you are the rat. I think, Mr. Jenkins, that the rat sent you to find me so the rat can kill me before I find him."

Jenkins again looked down at the street. A black Mercedes had pulled to the front of the building. The reception desk had reached Federov. The FSB officer emerged from the passenger's door. Volkov stepped from the driver's side and came around the back of the car.

"They are coming, aren't they, Mr. Jenkins?" the woman said. "They are coming to—how do you Americans say it—kill two birds with one stone."

Jenkins was far from convinced of anything, but he also couldn't dispute that things were not as they'd been presented to him by Carl Emerson. Was Emerson the rat? He didn't know. But he wasn't about to wait here to find out the answer. He needed to get out of the hotel. He needed time to seek answers. And his best option at the moment was to keep the woman alive to find out what else she knew. He assumed she had the same goal. It made for what case officers referred to as an uncertain but necessary alliance.

He grabbed the steak knife, moved behind the woman, cut the cord binding her hands, and discarded the knife. "We need to go."

"Yes," she said. "We do."

He grabbed his backpack with his passport and what cash he had, then stepped into the bathroom and shoved his shaving kit with his medicines in as well. He picked up his coat, hat, and gloves, and stepped to the door. "How well do you know Moscow?"

"I was born here," she said. "This is my city."

"Then I suggest you get us out of here or we're both going to die."

"My wig." She moved quickly to the closet and flipped the black wig on her head, adjusting it in the mirror as she moved toward the door. She slid on the large, round glasses, picked up her coat and the scarf, seemed to rethink the decision, and dropped them on the floor. "Better for us if they think we have left the hotel."

"We *are* leaving."

"Yes, but we must make them believe they are too late, that we have left in a hurry. It is the only way."

Reluctantly, Jenkins dropped his winter coat, hat, and gloves back onto the bed.

She pulled open the door to the room and looked in both directions before stepping into the hall. Jenkins moved toward an exit sign above the stairwell.

"They will guard the stairwells and the elevator," she said. She moved down the hall, stopping to pick up a wineglass from a dinner tray and knocked on the hotel room door. She directed Jenkins down the hall so he was out of the view through the peephole.

Jenkins turned and looked to the elevator. The woman knocked again. *"Vpusti menya,"* she said in a drunken voice. *Let me in.* She began to sway. She rapped three more times. *"Vpusti menya."*

Jenkins turned again to the elevator.

A man spoke from behind the door. *"U vas nepravil'naya komnata." You have the wrong room.*

"Otkroy dver'. Ya zabyl svoy klyuch." The woman slurred. *Open the door. I've forgotten my key.*

The elevator bell pinged the car's arrival. At the same time, the man unlocked and pulled open the door. *"U vas nepravil'naya—"* he began. The woman bull-rushed forward. Jenkins followed, shutting the door behind them.

The man started to protest, but swallowed his words when Jenkins raised the gun and pointed it at the man's forehead. He clasped his other hand over the man's mouth. The man's eyes widened with fear. He stood naked but for white cotton briefs, his hairy stomach protruding over the waistband.

"Listen to me," the woman said, speaking Russian in a hushed tone. "If you scream or make any noise, he will kill you. If you stay quiet, we will leave in due course. Sit down on the bed." The man hesitated, eyes fixated on the gun. "I said, sit down on the bed."

The man retreated two steps until the backs of his legs hit the mattress, and he collapsed onto the bed, shaking.

Jenkins moved to the door and looked out the peephole. Federov and Volkov, along with two others, hurried down the hall from the elevator. He felt the vibration of the floor as they approached and continued past. If the woman was FSB, now was the time for her to scream. She remained silent.

Federov held a room card and motioned to the others to stand on either side of the door to Jenkins's room. Each man held a gun, muzzle pointed at the floor. Federov swiped the key and pulled down on the door handle. The men barged inside.

The woman whispered to the man on the bed. "There are men coming to kill us. These are not police. These are not good men."

"Mafiya?" the man said.

"Da, mafiya," the woman said. "If they find us in your room they will kill us and then they will kill you. They will leave no witnesses. Do you understand?"

The man nodded.

Jenkins watched the men exit his room. Federov motioned for them to move to the doors at each end of the hall. They did so, but not to stand guard. They entered the stairwells. Volkov stepped from the room holding the woman's long coat and scarf as well as Jenkins's winter clothing. Her plan had worked. They thought Jenkins had already left.

Jenkins heard muffled conversation between Federov and Volkov, but he could not understand what they were saying. Federov looked displeased. He hurried down the hall in the direction of the elevator, Volkov jogging to catch up.

"It's almost over," the woman whispered to the man. "We will soon leave. But let me warn you. If you tell anyone we were here, those men will find you and they will kill you. Do you understand?"

"Da," the man said softly.

"You were sleeping. You had too much to drink. You did not see or hear anything."

"Da," the man said again.

"Go back to sleep," she said. "You are having a nightmare."

15

Jenkins peered through the peephole before opening the door. Clear. He stepped into the hall, wishing he could have taken his winter clothing so he wouldn't freeze to death.

"How did you get here?" he asked the woman.

"A car, parked at the back of the building." She moved to the door beneath the red exit sign at the end of the hall, opened it, and looked up and down the stairwell. Jenkins listened for footfalls, hearing none. She gestured for him to follow. They descended the stairwell, stopping every so often to listen. Hearing no other footsteps, they continued to the bottom floor. Again, the woman peered out a crack in the door before she stepped into the hall and turned to her right, winding her way through abandoned hallways, Jenkins following.

They emerged in a darkened dining area and hurried across the room, exiting to another hallway. They continued until they heard voices and music.

"The hotel bar," she said, pulling Jenkins to her as she backed up against one of the marbled pillars. They resembled lovers, perhaps discussing whose room they would use to continue their evening.

She whispered to him as she ran her hands over his shoulders. "The back entrance to the hotel is just down the marble steps. I will go first. Wait five minutes before you walk outside."

"I don't think so," he whispered back. "We haven't exactly developed that kind of trust."

"Then I suggest you develop it," she said. "At the moment they don't know what I look like, only my disguise. If I walk out that door I am a woman who was drinking in the bar. If you walk out that door with me and they are watching, you blow my cover."

Jenkins knew the woman's anonymity would allow her to walk out the door. He also knew it was a possibility she would get in her car and not look back, leaving him to fend for himself. He also knew he didn't have much choice.

"Two minutes," he said.

"Five minutes," she said, more forcefully.

"Why five?"

"Because the Bolshoi gets out in five minutes. In five minutes you walk out the back door and cross the street to the fountain. If anyone is following, lose them in the crowd exiting the Bolshoi."

"And then what? Where am I going?"

"To the ballet. Everyone will be coming out. You will be going in."

"How—"

She spoke over him. "Listen. We don't have time for questions. If anyone stops you, tell them you left your jacket and gloves at the coat check. Inside, there will be another crowd. Follow the signs to the coat check. Just past it you will find a door. Go through it. The hallway leads backstage to where performers change. There is a back exit the performers use to avoid the crowds at the front of the building."

"How do you know this?"

"Listen carefully," she said, more urgently. "Go out the back door. You will be in an alley. Cross it to the building behind the Bolshoi. There is a restaurant on the second floor where many in the Bolshoi go after the performance, and so the door in the alley will be unlocked. Climb the stairs to the second floor. You will be arriving through the back entrance, but do not go into the restaurant. You will see a metal cage blocking a staircase to your right. The metal cage is broken. Open it and descend one flight. You will have to cross a darkened hall leading to an exit into a second alley. I will flash the car's headlights once. Can you remember this?"

"Yes."

"Give me the gun," she said.

"I don't think so."

"If I am accosted and have to kill someone, I must do so quickly and quietly."

"So must I."

"Yes, but without a car, neither of us is getting very far, very fast, and not likely alive."

Again, Jenkins couldn't fault her logic, but logic and trust weren't the same thing, and giving up his only weapon to someone who hadn't yet earned his trust—far from it. But, as she said, what choice did he have? They couldn't walk out of the hotel together, and they wouldn't get far without a car.

"What do I do while I'm waiting?"

"Use the bathroom." She looked to her left. Jenkins saw the men's room door just behind the marbled pillar.

Reluctantly, he lifted his shirt. She grabbed the Ruger, slipping it in the waistband of her jeans and covering it with her sweater.

"Pozhelay mne udachi," she said. *Wish me luck.*

—

Paulina Ponomayova tilted her head and let the bangs of the black wig flow across the left side of her face, hoping the hair and the glasses would cover much of her left eye, which was already swelling shut. She stepped past a security guard standing beside the first set of glass doors.

"Mogu li ya pomoch'?" he said. *May I be of assistance?*

Ponomayova kept her eyes down. *"Nyet, spasibo."*

The second set of doors separated with a whoosh, and the Moscow cold cut through her sweater and stung her uncovered face and hands. She moved purposefully past Mercedes and BMW sedans parked in stalls beneath poles displaying the flags of numerous countries. The valet sat inside a green wooden kiosk. A black-and-white wooden arm extended across the parking lot exit. The valet had the door to the shack closed against the cold. As Ponomayova neared, he slid the door open a crack. Ponomayova felt a blast of warm air from an electric heater beneath the man's sitting stool.

He put his hand through the opening, and she handed him the valet tag. He matched the tag to a set of keys among several sets hanging on hooks along the back wall of the shack.

"It will just be a minute," he said, getting up from the stool.

"Nyet," she said, holding out five rubles. "No reason for us both to be cold."

He smiled and took the money. "*Spasibo.* I don't remember a January this bad in quite some time." He stepped from the shack and pointed to the back of the lot. "There, you see it?"

"Da," she said.

"Are you all right?" he asked, staring at the side of her face.

"Da," she said. "Just a small accident."

Ponomayova crossed the lot to her car, an unassuming gray Hyundai Solaris. Across the street, the well-lit walls of the Kremlin illuminated the filtered winter haze that continued to suffocate the city. She clicked the button and unlocked her car door. As she did, she heard a man speaking in a rushed tone.

"Excuse me. Excuse me."

Ponomayova froze. *"Da,"* she said, without turning.

"We are looking for someone," the man said. "Can you look at this picture?"

Ponomayova turned but kept her head tilted to the left and allowed the hair to obscure that side of her face. The man, whom she did not recognize, held a photograph in an outstretched arm. Charles Jenkins.

"Nyet," she said. "I have not seen him."

"And what is your business at the hotel tonight?"

She smiled. "What business is my business of yours?"

"Tell me . . . what happened to your eye?"

"Piss off."

The man held up identification. FSB. "Tell me."

"I walked into a door. Too much vodka."

The man put away his credentials. "Identification, please."

Paulina recalled a time when no Russian would refuse to produce identification, but that had been the old Russia. "I don't carry identification with me when I'm out drinking. It is too easy to lose."

"Identification," the man said, more forcefully.

"Okay. Okay. It's in the car is all I meant. Give me a second."

Ponomayova reached for the door handle with her left hand and grabbed the butt of the gun with her right. In one quick motion, she turned, raised the nozzle, and fired. The gun made a *pfft* sound, the noise partially masked by Moscow's traffic. The man dropped like a sack between the two parked cars. Blood trickled from the nickel-size hole in his forehead. Ponomayova pulled open her car door and quickly slid behind the wheel. She turned the key. The engine groaned but did not kick over.

"Shit," she said and tried again. The engine struggled, then kicked to life.

She backed from the stall slowly, not wanting to draw attention to herself or the body on the ground. She drove around the lot to the valet shack and raised a hand as if to wave but actually to block the valet's view of her face. The wooden arm raised and she departed, breathing a heavy sigh of relief.

Charles Jenkins checked his watch as he stepped into the men's room. Elevator music played from ceiling speakers, a Russian version of an American song. His intent was to go into one of the stalls but that changed instantly. A solitary man stood in a black leather coat at one of several urinals mounted on the wall. Arkady Volkov.

Before Jenkins could retreat, Volkov turned, in the process of zipping his fly. He froze. A fraction of a second passed before the recognition registered, but that was all Jenkins needed. Volkov's eyes widened and his right arm swept across his body, but Jenkins, without a weapon, had rushed forward. He hit Volkov, and the two men crashed through a stall door, stumbled around the toilet, and fell against the tiled wall. Jenkins had one hand on Volkov's face, fingers gouging at his eyes. His other hand gripped the hand holding the butt of Volkov's weapon, which the Russian was struggling to pull from its holster. Volkov's other hand was under Jenkins's chin, forcing his head back at an unnatural angle. The two men stumbled for leverage inside the stall, twisting and turning. Volkov was as strong as he looked—his short arms as powerful as pistons. Despite Jenkins's efforts, he felt Volkov's hand pulling the gun from its holster, and he knew he would lose this battle of strength. He had to use Volkov's strength against him.

Jenkins relaxed his right hand. Volkov's head shot forward. When it did, Jenkins issued a short, sharp blow with the palm of his hand, driving the back of Volkov's head against the tiled wall. The tile cracked and shattered. He slammed Volkov's head a second time and a third, but the gun continued to progress, the nozzle turning, now just inches from Jenkins's stomach.

Jenkins grabbed Volkov by his collar and spun him, shoving him out the stall door and across the bathroom. They hit the far wall together. Jenkins pirouetted, and used centrifugal force to spin Volkov a second time, this time slamming his back hard against one of the urinals. The porcelain cracked and a portion of the urinal crashed to the floor, water spraying from the broken pipe. Volkov groaned in pain. Jenkins spun him again, this time across the room, slamming Volkov's back into the sink counter, then spun him yet again, hoping to disorient him, back toward the urinals. Volkov's feet slipped on the wet floor, and the two men stumbled and fell. Jenkins lost his grip on Volkov's hand holding the gun, and it jerked from his grasp.

Jenkins rolled and picked up the broken urinal. A bullet pinged off the porcelain just before he slammed it down on Volkov's arm, which the Russian had moved to cover his face. Jenkins heard a sickening crack, this time not the porcelain. The Russian's limbs twitched, then stopped moving.

Breathing heavily, Jenkins grabbed the weapon and struggled to his feet, about to stumble to the door. He caught a glimpse of himself in the mirror, his shirt torn and wet, and his face scratched. He turned back to Volkov and quickly moved the urinal. He yanked off Volkov's leather coat and slid it on. The coat was tight across the back, and the sleeves ended above his wrists. It would have to do. He shoved Volkov's gun in the waistband of his pants and held the coat over it. Then he took a deep breath and pulled the door open. Stepping out, he nearly collided with a man, stumbling drunk, about to enter.

"Ya by vospol'zovalsya vannoy na vtorom etazhe-skazal on," he said. *"Kto-to ostavil ogromnuyu kuchu der'ma na polu." I would use the bathroom down the hall. Someone left a huge pile of shit on the floor of this one.*

—

Viktor Federov stood in the hotel lobby, listening to the desk clerk provide a description of the woman. Federov snapped his fingers and another FSB officer brought him a coat and a scarf. "Is this the coat and scarf?"

"Yes. Definitely."

Federov tossed the coat back to the second officer. "You said she wore glasses? Describe them."

"Big. Round. The frames were clear."

"What color were her eyes?"

"They were a light color . . . blue, I believe. Maybe hazel or green."

Federov spoke to the man holding the jacket and scarf. "Not likely if her hair was that dark. Probably contact lenses or a wig, maybe both."

"Do you want a sketch artist?" the second officer asked.

"No point," Federov said. "It is doubtful the woman still looks anything like the woman this man is describing. Check every trash bin for a wig and glasses."

As the officer departed, Federov returned his attention to the clerk. "Tell me what this woman said when she approached you. Exactly, please?"

"She said she had an appointment with Mr. Jenkins and asked for his room number."

"Anything else?"

The man massaged his temples. "No."

"Think," Federov said. "You are sure? Nothing else?"

"No. Just that she wanted his room number."

"And you gave it to her."

"Not initially," the man said. "There were others around. I followed her outside and gave her the room number."

Federov nodded. "How much did she pay you?"

Beads of sweat marked the man's forehead and upper lip. "I didn't—"

"How much?"

"Ten thousand rubles."

Federov held out his hand. "I must confiscate the bribe. It is now evidence."

The clerk removed the rubles from his pocket and handed them to Federov, who shoved the bills into his pants pocket.

Federov checked his watch. He'd sent Volkov to the bar twenty minutes earlier to ask those present if they had seen the woman or

Jenkins. "Stay here. I may have more questions." Federov started down the hall and flagged the second FSB officer. "See that the desk clerk does not leave."

Federov's shoes slapped the marbled floor as he strode past the elevators and down a set of stairs to the hotel bar, which remained in full swing, men and woman seated at tables and bar stools. He looked for but did not see Volkov. He called Volkov's cell phone but he did not answer, which was unlike him. Federov stepped to the bar and made eye contact with the bartender.

"I'm looking for a man who was here asking questions about guests of the hotel. Short but very stocky."

"Yeah. He was just here."

"Do you know where he went?"

"I saw him go down the steps to the bathroom."

Federov pulled out the picture of Jenkins. "Have you seen this man?"

The bartender shook his head. *"Nyet."*

Federov descended the steps, pushed open the bathroom door, and stepped in. Water splashed beneath his shoes. Volkov lay on the floor in the corner, without his jacket, a broken urinal nearby.

Federov hurried to him. He grabbed Volkov's wrist. His pulse was weak but he remained alive. He looked for Volkov's gun but did not see it. From the looks of the bathroom, there had been one hell of a fight. The only logical conclusion was Volkov had stumbled onto Jenkins and Jenkins was now likely armed. Federov stood and exited the bathroom, fishing in his pocket for the picture of Jenkins as he approached the hotel guard standing just inside sliding glass doors.

Federov held up the picture and his FSB credentials. "Did this man leave the hotel?"

"Yes, just a few minutes ago."

"You recall him?"

"Definitely. He was wearing a black leather coat, but no hat or gloves. He said he left them in his car and was going out to retrieve them. He looked as if he'd been in a fight."

"Was he with a woman?"

"No. He was alone."

Federov removed his cell phone from his pocket, punched in numbers, and spoke as he rushed out a second set of sliding doors into the hotel parking lot. His head swiveled left and right, his eyes searching for possible exits, and for the officer he had assigned to watch the back entrance and the parking lot. "I need you to perform a cleanup in the hotel bathroom near the bar," he said into his phone. "Call an ambulance but be discreet. I do not want any other police agencies involved. Then close the bar and clear it."

He disconnected. When he did not see the officer, he ran toward a valet seated inside a wooden shack. A couple stood outside the shack waiting to retrieve their car. Federov stepped to the front of the line and banged on the door. The young man quickly slid it open. Federov held up the picture of Jenkins and his FSB credentials. "Did you see this man leave?"

"I don't think so."

"Then think more clearly. Did you see him?"

"I didn't see him," the valet said. "But I've been running to and from cars, with the Bolshoi just getting out."

"What about a woman?"

The young man frowned. "There have been a lot of women. What did she look like?"

Federov turned toward the sound of a woman's scream. He hurried across the lot to where a woman stood beside a man, both bundled in winter clothing, both staring at a body on the ground.

"I nearly stepped on him when I got out of the car," the man said to Federov. "I thought maybe he was homeless and had frozen to death."

Federov shoved the man aside and looked down at the FSB officer. He'd been shot in the forehead, a kill shot, the hole no larger than a nickel and the amount of blood minimal given the cold evening temperature.

"Go inside and speak to the front desk," he said to the man and woman. "Tell the man in the dark suit there's a dead man in the parking lot. Go! Go!"

The couple hurried across the lot to the back entrance of the hotel.

Federov ran to the sidewalk and looked up and down the street, then across it to the plaza and the fountain. Behind it, people streamed out the doors of the Bolshoi. Jenkins could not have gone far. And he would seek a crowd to get lost in. Federov looked again to the Bolshoi's exiting patrons.

—

Charles Jenkins jogged across the street to the fountain. His confrontation with Volkov had left him several minutes behind schedule. Would the woman wait for him? Had she ever intended to wait for him?

Couples bundled in winter clothing took selfies beside a fountain, but they quickly moved when he approached, no doubt deducing from his tattered and bloody appearance, and his lack of winter clothes, that he had to be insane. So much for blending in. Getting lost in a crowd would not be easy, nor would getting inside the Bolshoi.

He hurried to the front entrance, holding the coat closed to hide his torn shirt. Most of the men exiting wore long wool coats over tuxedos or expensive suits. Jenkins looked like a homeless vagrant. He dodged and weaved his way through the crowd to one of the doors. A middle-aged man in a black vest and matching bow tie stood just inside the doorway, thanking patrons for coming and wishing them a good night.

"Izvinite," Jenkins said. *"Ya ostavil svoi veshchi s proverkoy pal'to." Excuse me. I left my belongings with coat check.*

The man considered Jenkins from head to foot and quickly dismissed him. *"Nyet,"* he said.

"I left my hat and gloves at the coat check," Jenkins said again in Russian. "I need to retrieve them."

The man looked repulsed. "Where is your ticket for your belongings?" he said.

"I've misplaced it," Jenkins said.

"Then show me your ticket for tonight's performance."

"Please. It will only take a moment."

The man shook his head. "Very convenient, but no."

"Then let me describe my belongings and you can get them for me." He needed to get the man away from the door.

"I am not your valet. Go away or I will summon the police."

Jenkins stepped back, hoping to find another door either unattended or with a less diligent doorman. If he had to, he'd go around the building and see if he could find the alley. He glanced at the crowd in the plaza, the Bolshoi patrons streaming away from the front of the building—everyone except one man, who was charging forward.

Federov.

Federov looked above the heads in the crowd. At six foot five, Charles Jenkins was seven inches taller than the average Russian male. As he surveyed the crowd, Federov heard people shouting and turned toward the noise. A commotion appeared to have broken out at one of the doors to the building. He rushed toward it. Several people lay on the ground. He pushed and shoved and stepped over the bodies, drawing protests and some resistance.

"Police business!" Federov shouted. He held up his credentials to get people to back away. "Police business!"

He helped a man in a black vest and tie to his feet. The man looked flustered but unharmed. "He ran into the building," the man said. "He said he left his hat and gloves. A vagrant."

"What did he look like?" Federov rushed, fumbling in his pocket for the photograph.

"Black," the man said. "He was black and very big."

Federov didn't bother with the picture. "Which way?" he said.

"That way." The man pointed. "He said he was going to the coat check."

Federov entered the building and hurried down the hall, avoiding those people he could, knocking others to the side. Farther down the hall, he saw people being similarly knocked aside, like bowling pins in an alley. Then he saw a head above the others. Charles Jenkins turned and looked over his shoulder. The two men made eye contact. Jenkins took off.

Federov stepped over and around the people Jenkins had strewn on the floor, following signs for the coat check. A crowd had gathered around the desk, clerks taking tickets and retrieving coats, fur hats, and gloves. Federov leapt up and down, like a man on a pogo stick, trying to see above the crowd. To the far left he saw a door open and shut.

"Excuse me," he said. "Step aside. Police business. Police business. Move."

With effort, he reached the door but paused before pushing it open, uncertain whether Jenkins waited to ambush him on the other side or to shoot him with Volkov's gun. He pushed the handle and slowly opened the door. No shots rang out. Instead he heard the piercing wail of an alarm and saw the metal door at the far end swing shut. He ran toward it, reached for the metal bar, and slammed into the door. It did not budge.

He stepped back and barreled his shoulder into the door. It moved, but only an inch. He stepped back again, raised his shoe, and kicked at the handle near the latch. The door shook but did not open. Jenkins had blocked it, somehow, from the other side.

Bolshoi security ran into the hallway, shouting at him.

"Help me!" Federov held up his credentials. "Help me to get the door open."

The three men pressed their shoulders against the door, grunting and groaning. The door opened another inch. They stepped back, counted to three, and rushed forward. The door opened a foot. Federov looked out the opening. On the other side, a large blue garbage bin had been shoved against the door. "Again," he said.

They pushed again. The door opened enough for Federov to squeeze through, and he stepped into an alley. He looked left. A dead end. He rushed to his right, to a street, and looked in both directions. People leaving the Bolshoi hurried to get out of the cold. He did not see Jenkins. He pulled out his phone as he jogged back down the alley, issuing orders and instructions. As he spoke, he heard voices filtering down from above, and he looked up at a strand of lights crisscrossing a restaurant. He reached for a door in the alley. It opened. He took the steps two at a time, coming to a landing at the back of a café. Inside, neatly dressed people from the Bolshoi ate pastries and drank coffee, with no indication of a commotion or disturbance having recently passed through. Jenkins had not come this way.

Federov turned, about to climb the stairs to the next landing, when he noticed a gate blocking a descending staircase. He pushed on the gate. It, too, swung open. Going up would make no sense. Jenkins would be trapped.

Federov removed his gun from its holster and slid down the stairs with his back pressed to the wall. He swung his body around the landing, taking aim. No one. He continued down the final set of stairs to ground level, crossed a darkened hall, pushed on the handle of another door, and stepped out into a second alley. He heard a car engine, turned, but saw no lights. The car emerged from darkness. Federov leapt to his right. The car clipped his leg and spun him. He hit the ground hard, rolled, and sat up, firing several shots as the car reached the end of the alley and turned left. Federov got to his feet and stumbled to the street, gun raised, but the car had turned again, and was gone.

16

As they drove out of Moscow, Charles Jenkins again asked the woman her name. Again, she declined to tell him, but not for the reason he thought. "It would not be good for either of us if you were to know my name," she said. "In fact, I would suggest that you close your eyes and not pay attention to any of the details of where we are going."

Jenkins believed her, though he was far from convinced he could trust her. Still, she had been true to her word. She could have left the hotel and not looked back, left Jenkins to fend for himself, but she had not. Regardless of whether he could fully trust her or not, at present he had two goals: to keep moving forward and to determine what she knew.

The woman tossed her glasses out the window. Ten minutes later, she pulled to a stop and discarded the wig in a drainage ditch. Without her wig and glasses, she looked to Jenkins to be mid-to-late forties, though heavy smoking might have prematurely aged her. She had crow's feet around her eyes and her lips, and she'd lit up a cigarette the moment they'd left Moscow's city limits. The interior of her car smelled like an ashtray. He cracked the window to get fresh air.

"It's a bad habit," she said. "Especially when stressed."

After a thirty-minute drive and three cigarettes, she exited the expressway and weaved along suburban streets, eventually parking outside a multistory apartment building, one of several in a cluster. "We must be quiet when we go in," she said. "Communist doctrine remains prevalent in the elderly, and it was not so long ago that neighbors spied on neighbors to gain favor with the state. People here do not mind their own business."

They stepped from the car into the cold. The moon peeked out from behind the haze, painting the tableau a charcoal gray. The trees, stripped of leaves, stood silent in the planters. As Jenkins approached the woman's apartment building he heard a dog bark, a mournful, far-off wail. They stepped inside the lobby undetected and moved to the elevator. It arrived empty. They rode it to the fourth floor. The woman stepped off first. Jenkins followed. At her apartment door she used a key to open several locks and hurried inside, Jenkins behind her. He set his backpack on the floor as the woman closed the door, reapplied the locks and slid a chain into the slot. Only then did Jenkins let out a sigh of relief and allow himself a moment to relax.

"Vodka?" the woman said.

"Yes," Jenkins said.

The apartment was typical of what Jenkins had read about Soviet-era housing, when personal space was considered to be antirevolutionary. It consisted of the small entry with a coat stand and a narrow closet. The kitchen was to the left; a sitting room to the right doubled as a bedroom, partitioned with a four-panel divider. The kitchen was just large enough for one person to stand between a two-burner stove on one side and a sink beneath two cabinets on the other. As with the car, the apartment smelled of cigarette smoke, despite a cold breeze from the kitchen window opened a fraction of an inch.

The woman turned on a radio and lowered the volume. She opened a freezer and removed a bag of vegetables, pressing it to her eye, before she retrieved a bottle of Stolichnaya.

"Sorry about that," Jenkins said, keeping his voice soft.

"I would have done the same." She retrieved two glasses from the cabinet and poured two shots. She lifted her glass. Jenkins reciprocated.

"Here's to luck," she said.

The vodka burned the back of his throat but tasted good just the same.

"Do you wish for some tea?" she asked.

"Sure," he said.

"I have pastries." She opened the refrigerator. "They are not fresh but—"

"No, thank you," he said, continuing to evaluate her.

She kept the kitchen light off, but ambient light from the moon seeped through the sheer curtains covering the windows, painting the kitchen in black-and-white. She grabbed the kettle with her free hand and set it on the counter. The lid pinged when she removed it, and she filled the kettle from the faucet. Jenkins pushed aside the curtains and looked down on an interior courtyard crisscrossed by clotheslines, some bearing articles of clothing.

He removed the weapon he'd taken from Volkov and placed it on a half-round table beneath that window. The woman turned at the sound of the gun hitting the table.

"Where did you get that?" She set the kettle on the front burner.

"I ran into one of the FSB agents who knew me in the hotel bathroom."

"Did you kill him?" she asked.

"I don't know. Possibly."

She struck a match and turned a knob. The burner emitted the faint odor of gas before igniting in flaming blue fingers. She adjusted the knob and dropped the spent match into the sink. Still holding the bag of frozen vegetables to her face, she moved toward the table.

"It is a PSS," she said.

"What is a PSS?"

"*Pistolet Spetsialnyj Samozaryadniy.* Semiautomatic. Accurate up to twenty-five meters. The sealing cartridge neck prevents the escape of a flash or smoke and virtually no noise."

"No suppressor needed?"

"No. It makes the weapon easier to conceal and is favored by FSB special forces." She pulled out the chair across from him, the legs scraping against the linoleum, and sat, looking as emotionally and physically spent as Jenkins felt. He'd been running, literally, on adrenaline.

"We can expect that Federov will have much at his disposal to find you," she said.

"Can he track you somehow? What about your car?"

She gave this some thought. "The disguise will make that unlikely, and the car has plates for another since destroyed. Still, we should not stay long. Tell me why you are here."

In for a penny, in for a pound, Jenkins decided. Talking might also be the only way to learn the woman's involvement. "The first visit, I was to provide discreet knowledge of a Russian double agent, information the FSB presumably already possessed, but that would make me look as though I was capable of obtaining highly classified information. On the second visit I was to provide Federov information on a woman who worked in the Russian nuclear energy department."

"Uliana Artemyeva," she said.

"You know of her?" Jenkins asked.

"I know she was suspected to have been the confidential source providing the information. However, that was never confirmed. Russia does not like to broadcast each time it has its nose rubbed in the mud."

"How did she die?"

She shrugged. "Natural causes, but many in Russia suspected of betrayal die of natural causes . . . or suicide."

The kettle on the stove whistled. She left the frozen vegetable bag on the table and moved to retrieve the kettle. "You told your FSB contacts that Uliana Artemyeva was one of the seven sisters, yes?" She pulled two mugs and two saucers from a sparsely furnished cabinet, and a box of tea from a drawer below it. She set the box on the table and filled the two mugs with hot water.

"Since she was dead," Jenkins said, "the information could not be confirmed nor denied."

"It was information meant to impress your contact." She set Jenkins's mug on the table. "Cream or sugar?"

"No," Jenkins said. "And in answer to your question, yes, the information was intended to impress that I could obtain classified information." He pulled a packet of tea from the box, opened it, and dunked the tea bag in his mug.

"Who sent you here?"

"I can't tell you that."

"What did this person tell you?"

Jenkins sipped at his tea and felt the water burn his upper lip. He blew on the liquid and set the cup down. "He said Vladimir Putin knew of the seven sisters during his time working for the KGB."

"This is true," she said.

"He said Putin commissioned an eighth sister to hunt down the other seven and that she had already identified and assassinated three of the seven."

"This I do not know," she said, "though I would doubt its accuracy."

"My job was to determine the name of the eighth sister."

"And what?"

"Then I was done."

"Zarina Kazakova and Irena Lavrova," the woman said. "Who is the third sister?"

"Olga Artamonova."

She sat back, seeming to ponder this.

"Who do you work for at the CIA?" Jenkins asked.

"If you are a case officer then you know I cannot tell you that," she said. "If you are not, then, Mr. Jenkins, it is better for all concerned if I do not tell you about myself or my handler. But let me ask, how well do you know this contact of yours?"

Jenkins blew on the surface of his tea before sipping again. "I worked for him years ago when I was a new agent. But I haven't worked as a case officer for many years."

She looked to be considering this, then asked, "Why then did he choose you?"

Jenkins gave her question some thought. "I speak Russian. And I had a built-in cover for coming to Russia. My business provides security for an investment company with a branch office in Moscow. And I've had experience with the KGB. I was tactically trained and could start immediately."

"If you have not been a case officer for many years, why did you agree to do this?"

Soft music, the strings of a violin, came from the radio on the counter. Jenkins thought of Alex and CJ and his unborn child and explained his situation. "Ordinarily I'm not a man motivated by money. Never have been. But things have changed."

"You had a pressing need."

"Yes," he said. "I do."

She looked to a clock on the wall. "If we are going to do anything, we need to move now. By this time tomorrow I suspect your face and name will be all over Moscow television and newspapers. And you are not exactly hard to miss."

Jenkins shook his head. "Federov won't do that. He won't want to be embarrassed that I've gotten away. He was very concerned that I was trying to make him look like a fool to his superiors. I suspect the FSB will keep this quiet and try to find me some other way."

"Even so, the FSB oversees border security, so you can expect that your picture will be sent to all border guards and customs officials by morning, if not already. Getting you out of Russia will not be easy."

Another thought chilled him. If he had been set up, and that now seemed likely, whoever was responsible would learn he had gotten away and possibly go after the people Jenkins loved the most. "My wife and son," he said, standing.

She stood. "Wherever they are, it would be best if they left quickly."

17

Viktor Federov was in no mood for half answers or ambiguities. His best suit was torn in the knees and soiled from the snow and dirty water in the alley. His left knee had swollen and was painful to the touch where the car had clipped him. He had an assortment of other aches and bruises—the largest was to his ego. Charles Jenkins was gone, very likely with the help of the woman who had come to his hotel room. The pressing question at the moment was, Who was she? Federov's contact in the United States said Jenkins had been sent to Russia not to disclose names, but to determine the name of the woman hunting for the leak that was providing the FSB with the identities of the seven sisters. Had that been the woman who came to Jenkins's hotel? But if so, why would the woman have helped Jenkins to escape? Wouldn't she have believed Jenkins was the leak? Wouldn't she have killed him?

Something had not gone according to script, and Federov's contact within the CIA was more than upset it had not. Federov was told, quite adamantly, that neither Jenkins nor the woman was to leave Russia, otherwise Federov's contact would "disappear" without providing the names of the remaining four sisters, leaving Federov to explain to his superiors how that had happened. As much as Federov's reputation had risen in the past two years, his fall would be significantly farther.

Federov limped back to the hotel parking lot. Two of his colleagues stood in the cold, speaking to the valet, their words punctuated by white puffs of breath. The younger officer, Simon Alekseyov, broke away from the conversation as Federov approached. "Colonel, are you all right?"

Federov dismissed the question. "I'm fine. What have you learned?"

"We have the hotel security staff pulling video for the past two hours," Alekseyov said.

"Did you find the woman's glasses and the black wig anywhere in the hotel?"

"Not yet. No."

"Unless you do, the security video will be of no more use in identifying the woman than the interview I already conducted of the reception desk clerk. The woman disguised her appearance."

"Colonel?" The second officer stepped toward them. "I think you should hear what the valet has to say."

"I've already spoken to him."

"Yes, well, he remembered something. I think it could be important."

Federov motioned for the officer to lead the way. The valet stood outside the wooden shack, smoking a cigarette and otherwise looking cold and nervous.

"You remembered something?" Federov said, dispensing with formalities.

"Yes."

"Well? Do you intend for us to stand here in the cold guessing? What is it?"

"It's about the woman. I remembered that she had dark hair and round glasses."

"We know this already." Federov turned to the second officer, not trying to hide his displeasure. "We know this already. Why are you wasting my time?"

"She had a black eye," the valet said.

Federov returned his attention to the valet. "What did you say?"

"The woman had a black eye, or at least the start of one. She had her hair down to conceal the side of her face, but I could see the area around the eye was already red and swollen. I asked her if she was all right."

"What did she say?"

"She said it was just an accident. Too much alcohol, but it didn't look like an accident. It looked like someone had punched her or slapped her."

"Did she say anything else?"

The valet sucked his cigarette to the butt and flicked it across the pavement. He shook his head, releasing white tendrils as he answered. "No. I offered to get her car, but she said there was no reason for both of us to be cold."

"Which eye?"

The valet shoved his hands in the pockets of his gray coat and thought for a moment. Then he said, "Left. It was her left eye."

The blow would have most likely come from a right hand. So maybe Jenkins and this woman had not started out as friends after all. "Where was her car parked?" Federov asked.

"Over there." He pointed to where the body of the dead FSB officer lay.

The shooter had struck the man in the center of the forehead, a kill shot, a shot made quickly and accurately by someone likely to have been tactically trained. Federov had assumed it had been Jenkins, but not any longer.

"Did you hear the shot?"

"No," he said. "But I was inside with the electric heater making a racket."

Federov turned to Alekseyov. "Find out if anyone heard a shot," he said. "Ask the man at the door into the building."

If no one had heard the shot, it was likely the woman had used a suppressor, further indicating she had tactical training.

"What type of car was she driving?" Federov asked.

"A Hyundai Solaris. Gray."

"What year?"

"I don't know the year."

"Was it new? Old?"

"It was new. I would say within the last few years."

"Did you park it?"

"Yes."

"Did you notice anything more about the car or the woman you have not told us?"

The valet looked to Alekseyov. "I told him that she smoked Karelia Slims. There was a pack on the passenger seat."

Federov raised a hand. "I'm going to have this officer put together a statement. If you think of anything else, do not hesitate to tell him, or to call me." He handed the valet a card. "Anything at all." Federov hobbled inside the hotel, speaking to Alekseyov. "I want you to put out a bulletin to every government office. We are looking for a woman with a bruised left eye. Ask for the names of every woman who does not report to work tomorrow, for any reason." Federov stopped, a thought coming to him.

"Colonel, that would require—"

Federov raised a hand, silencing Alekseyov. He paced in a small circle in the hotel lobby. "Start with the FSB," he said.

"Colonel?"

"I want the names of every woman who works for the FSB, in any capacity, who fails to report to work tomorrow. Crosscheck those names with vehicle registration for anyone who drives a Hyundai Solaris. And make sure that the hotel provides any tape they have of the parking lot. Go."

18

Jenkins didn't want to use the burner phone he'd used with Federov, or his actual cell phone, which was likely being monitored. He had to assume his home phone, and possibly Alex's cell phone, were also being monitored. If he used the woman's cell phone, he was taking a different risk. If the call could be triangulated, as in the United States, it could be another clue to the woman's identity, putting her in still greater danger.

With little practical choice, and not a lot of time, he decided it best to use his own phone and keep the call short. The woman excused herself and stepped into the other room to give him privacy.

Jenkins dialed Alex's number, paced the small kitchen, and prayed she answered. While he waited, he realized that he'd agreed to be reactivated to help his family, and now he was calling because he had put them in danger.

"Hey. I was just lying here thinking of you," Alex said, answering.

He felt overwhelming relief. "I was thinking of you too. You're in bed?"

"Just as the doctor ordered. What are you up to? When are you coming home?"

"I've hit a few complications that could delay things," he said.

"What kind of complications?" she said.

"How's Lou?"

Alex paused, but just a beat. "He's sleeping at the moment."

"When he wakes up, have CJ take him for a walk, would you? You know how much he loves to get out of the house."

"He does," she said. "I'll get him out now."

"Great. And take Freddie with you."

"Okay. Listen, CJ just walked in. I'll call you later," she said.

"I love you, Alex," he said, but she had already hung up.

19

Jenkins drove the woman's car south on the M4 highway through farmlands covered beneath snow while she continued to press the bag of vegetables to her eye. A wind had picked up, gusts blowing snow across the road and making the car rattle and shake. Jenkins struggled to see, and to keep the car from being pushed off the road. If the wind did not let up, the road would soon become impassable.

"You are worried . . . about your wife and your son?"

Jenkins nodded. "And about this weather."

"You're lucky," the woman said. "To have someone to love so much."

Jenkins hadn't thought of it that way. He corrected the steering wheel when the car shuddered from another blast of wind. "Let's hope the wind dies down," he said. "I'm not sure we can drive much farther if it doesn't."

"We have no choice. If we stop, we will freeze to death. I didn't come this far to freeze to death in my car, and I suspect you did not as well."

"How far are we going?"

She looked at him from the passenger seat and shrugged.

"Another need-to-know basis?" Jenkins said. "Really? If we get caught now, they'll catch us both."

"The Black Sea." She flipped down the visor and checked her eye in the illuminated mirror. Her skin had started to discolor, yellow and dark purple around the edges, but the swelling had been curtailed by the bag of frozen vegetables. "There is small town where friends keep a safe house in times of need." She flipped up the visor.

"Are these American friends?"

"They are friends to anyone who opposes this regime. Once we are there I can make arrangements to have you taken out of country."

"What do you mean, me? You're not coming?"

"Russia is my home, Mr. Jenkins. I have lived here all my life. I have no intention of leaving now."

"If they figure out who you are, they'll torture you for information about me and the seven sisters."

"You don't know anything more about the seven sisters than they already know," she said. "Neither do I."

"They'll torture and kill those you love."

"I love few, Mr. Jenkins. My parents are dead. My only brother is dead. My marriage ended many years ago."

"Do you have children?"

"No."

Jenkins had not seen any photographs in the woman's apartment. "Why did you do this? Why are you working for the CIA?"

"It is long story, Mr. Jenkins."

"And we have a long drive," he said.

After a silence she said, "My brother is the reason I do what I do."

"Did someone kill him?"

"The state killed him. They killed what he loved, what he lived for. My brother took his own life."

"I'm sorry."

"It was many years ago."

He let a moment pass. Then he asked, "What was his love?"

"The ballet," she said softly. "The Bolshoi."

"That's how you knew the building so well. He danced for the Bolshoi."

"No. He never did. That was his dream. That was his love. You see, Mr. Jenkins, for many years, after my parents divorced, my mother would take my brother and me to the Bolshoi on nights that she performed. She was not one of the stars, but she worked regularly in the cast. She did not make enough money to have someone watch us. I used to explore backstage, to imagine that I was living other places, other countries. I had to use my imagination, because Ivan would watch almost every performance. I used to get mad at him. I would say, 'Ivan, it is the same show tonight as last night and the night before and the night before. Come. Let us play.' But Ivan loved the Bolshoi more than anything in the world, and he wanted only to someday perform as my mother did. He worked very hard for that opportunity. When he surpassed what my mother could teach him, she saved every ruble and begged and pleaded to get him into the prestigious Bolshoi Ballet Academy in Moscow. The academy is almost as old as your country, and it has produced some of the finest dancers the world has ever known." She paused. Jenkins heard the wind howling outside the car. Then in a whisper she said, "My brother would have been one of those dancers. He had the drive, the ambition, and he had the talent."

"What happened?" Jenkins asked.

"My brother fell in love," she said. "He fell deeply and hopelessly in love with one of his instructors, a married man many years his senior, and this man led Ivan to believe that he also loved him. He told Ivan he could be instrumental in Ivan's career, that he could get Ivan leading roles in some of the most prestigious shows in all of Russia."

Jenkins sensed what was coming.

"But he was using him," the woman said, "along with several other students. When he'd had his fill, he discarded Ivan as if he was trash. In his anger, Ivan made the mistake of threatening to expose this man as a homosexual. You see, Mr. Jenkins, Russia is not so accepting as in your country, not even today. Back then, it was worse. The man went to Ivan's instructors and told them Ivan did not have what it takes to dance for the Bolshoi. He said he had told Ivan this, and that Ivan had threatened him and made spurious allegations that this man was a homosexual. Ivan was expelled from the academy."

"What about the other boys? What about the others this man was abusing?"

She smiled but it had a sad quality to it. "They saw the handwriting on the wall, as you say in your country. They saw what happened to Ivan. They weren't about to make the same mistake. Ivan was alone with his allegations and with his failure. He was alone with the knowledge that he would never dance for the Bolshoi, or any other company. Devastated, he climbed to the roof of the Bolshoi and jumped to his death."

The woman paused and Jenkins could tell she had become emotional. After a minute she again found her voice. "I had taken him there many times. It had been a place to look at the lights of Moscow and to dream of what life had to offer each of us."

"I'm sorry," Jenkins said.

"Yes, for many years I, too, was sorry," she said, now sounding more adamant, more determined. "I was sorry my brother could not see his way out of his misery. I was sorry my mother and I had to live with his decision. Then I realized that what happened to my brother was not his fault. It was not even the fault of this man who had abused him. What happened to my brother was the fault of the institutions that made this man go into hiding in the first place, that punished my brother simply because he had loved another man. I swore I would get my revenge, and I would not stop until Russia was a real democracy, and all the people had real options and real opportunities. I thought that day had come when Gorbachev took power, but it was a fleeting and false hope. Each year, Russia falls farther and farther away from a true democracy." She looked at him. "So you see, Mr. Jenkins, I will not stop now. Not even if it means that I must die."

If it was all an elaborate story, it was a good one, one she told with honesty and emotion. "How were you recruited?" Jenkins asked.

"I have a proficiency for computers and for math. I studied at Moscow University. One day I made a call to the US embassy. A week later I was at home and there was a knock on my door. The courtship took several months. I was asked to perform many mundane tasks."

Jenkins knew from his own experience that an agent motivated by money could not be trusted. Instead, the agency recruited or responded to those who had an ideological or a more personal reason for wanting to betray their country. "They were testing you," he said.

"Yes, whether I could be trusted." She shrugged.

They drove in silence for several miles. Then Jenkins said, "What did you dream of on the roof of the Bolshoi?"

"It does not matter any longer."

"You said you had dreams. What were they?"

She smiled. "I dreamed that I would become the Bill Gates of Russia. I would start my own business and develop my own software that would someday be used in every computer in the world."

"You said that you used to dream of other countries, of America. Now you can go. You can still have your dream."

She pointed out the windshield. "Tollbooth."

Jenkins slowed as they approached flashing lights reflecting in the blinding snow. The tollbooth looked like a gas station, with multiple lanes beneath a solid-blue awning. Everything was automated, which gave Jenkins a second thought.

"Do they have cameras?" Jenkins asked.

"I would suspect so, but Federov will have no reason to suspect me, and I told you the plates are for a different car."

Jenkins didn't think the woman was giving Federov enough credit. He knew there were too many possible ways to identify her—and the car. "Maybe not. But I'd prefer we ditch this car and find another."

"What is 'ditch'?"

"Hide," he said, "and take another car."

"Look around you. There is no one. And if we steal a car, then they will look for that car."

She made a point. Jenkins slowed and powered down his window, struggling to insert a bill into the machine. When he'd succeeded, the red-and-white arm across the road lifted. He drove from the tollbooth back into snowy conditions. "How many more hours do we have?"

"Many," she said. "Stay on M4. I think that I will sleep. Try not to kill us."

"Listen, if we're going to be driving together for that many hours, at least tell me what I should call you if you don't want to tell me your name."

"You can call me Anna," she said. "I always wanted the name Anna since I first read *Anna Karenina*."

"All right, Anna. Will you ever tell me your real name?"

"Perhaps," she said, tilting back her seat and turning her head toward the window. "Perhaps when I know that you are again to be free. Then I will tell you."

20

Viktor Federov stood in his office watching his computer screen and drinking another cup of black coffee, despite his stomach's protests. He hadn't eaten dinner or breakfast, and the coffee felt as though it was burning a hole in the lining of his stomach. Federov wore the same suit as the prior evening, the pants ripped in the knees and wrinkled where they had gotten wet. He hadn't bothered to go home to change. There was much to do, and little time to do it. Jenkins and the woman, whoever she was, would be working to quickly get out of the country, and with Russia's vast borders, and its often disinterested border guards, that was not an insurmountable challenge. Federov had ordered that Jenkins's picture be provided to every border-crossing guard, and that an alert be put on his passport, but those measures would only work if Jenkins used his passport and the border guard paid attention to the alert. Neither was a given.

Federov set down his coffee cup and pressed a button on his computer to fast-forward through another hotel security tape. He'd started with footage of the parking lot. They'd located the Hyundai Solaris, but the camera was of poor quality and so, too, was the image. They had enhanced it enough to read the license plate, but the plate number turned out to be for a Lada Granta, which further research revealed had been totaled in an accident. It would be of no help identifying the owner, only the car. He moved next to hotel footage of the reception counter and watched the woman in the dark wig and glasses approach. Her long coat nearly touched the floor. The scarf and large eyeglasses covered everything but small portions of her face, which eliminated any chance of obtaining a screen shot to perhaps identify her. Everyone who worked in a government office was fingerprinted and photographed. With facial recognition software, they might have been able to get a match. The woman appeared to know this—further proof, perhaps, of her employment at the FSB. A mole. In addition to the scarf, she kept her body turned to the left, as if she knew the location of the hotel cameras in the ceiling.

Federov switched to different footage, this film from a camera on the eighth floor. He watched the woman step from the elevator and walk down the hall toward Jenkins's room. Again, she kept her head down, likely to prevent the camera from obtaining a meaningful shot of her face. She used a key card—one she had purchased with the rubles—to gain access to Jenkins's room, and slipped inside.

Sometime later, Jenkins exited the elevator. Before reaching his room, he stopped and retrieved something from a food tray. Federov backed up the tape and watched again in slow motion, zooming in on the plate. A knife. Jenkins had picked up a knife and slid it up the sleeve of his coat.

"Interesting," Federov said.

When he reached his room, Jenkins did not immediately enter. Rather, he dropped to the ground—as if anticipating a gunshot—reached up from his knees, and pushed the door open. Only then did he step inside and allow the door to close behind him.

"He suspected she was in his room," Federov said. "How?" He made a note to talk again to the clerk. Someone had alerted Jenkins to the woman's presence at the hotel.

The only reasonable deduction from Jenkins's actions was that he also knew, or at least strongly suspected, the woman could be in his room. And his retrieval of the knife strongly indicated he did not consider the woman a friend, at least not initially, though something had apparently changed his perspective.

Roughly fifteen minutes after Federov had been informed by his hotel contact that the woman had come to the desk and asked for Charles Jenkins—after the third act of his daughter's play but before the cast party Federov had promised to attend but did not—Federov and Volkov arrived at the hotel. Federov watched the tape of the eighth floor to determine how they had missed Jenkins and the woman. He sat forward as Jenkins exited his room. He had a black backpack slung over his shoulder. The woman followed. Jenkins initially moved toward the staircase at the end of the hall but stopped and turned back. The woman had said something to him, most likely that the staircase would be covered. It had been.

Whatever had happened inside the hotel room, Jenkins and the woman were now acting as a team.

Without the long coat and the scarf, which Volkov had found in Jenkins's hotel room—a ruse to make Federov believe Jenkins and the woman had quickly fled—Federov got a better look at the woman. He estimated her to be five foot seven or eight, based on a comparison with Charles Jenkins. She also looked to be in good physical condition, with developed shoulders and a thin waist. The woman walked across the hall, stopping to pick up a champagne flute from a room-service tray. She knocked on the hotel room door. Federov felt sick to his stomach and it had nothing to do with the coffee. He knew what was to happen next. The tape only confirmed it.

Federov noted the hotel room into which Jenkins and the woman had fled. He would send someone to speak to the guest and find out what, if anything, Jenkins or the woman had said to him.

Simon Alekseyov knocked on Federov's door as he entered the office. "I have the list of female employees who did not report for work this morning. There are six."

"Did you cross-reference them with their car registration?"

Alekseyov nodded. "Two drive a Hyundai. One is blue. The other is gray."

Federov motioned for Alekseyov to hand him the sheets of paper. He stared at a picture of Paulina Ponomayova. Forty-eight years of age, she was attractive, with light-brown hair, brown eyes, and a strong jawline. She was also five feet eight inches and weighed 130 pounds, which comported to what Federov had just seen on the tape.

"What do we know of her?"

Alekseyov read from a sheet of paper. "She was hired by the FSB fresh out of Moscow University, where she earned degrees in computer science and systems hardware, and mathematics. At the FSB she has had an exemplary work history, with promotions to positions requiring higher and tighter security clearance."

Based on the ages of the three sisters already detected, Ponomayova was not one of the seven. Federov looked through her personal life, which was equally unremarkable. She'd been married in her early twenties but divorced. She had no children. Her parents were deceased, as was her only sibling, a younger brother, Ivan.

"She has very little to live for," Federov said.

"She works as a computer systems analyst for the Directorate of Records and Archives," Alekseyov said, which meant that Ponomayova would have computer access to all reports filed by all personnel, including reports by and about Russian assets and targets, such as the reports Federov had written about Charles Jenkins.

"You have an address?" Federov said, already moving around his desk to his coat stand.

"Yes."

Federov grabbed his heavy winter coat and hat from the hook and started from the office, then stopped. "What do you know of Volkov's condition?"

"He is in the hospital but he is alert," Alekseyov said.

Federov would stop by to see him when he got the chance. At present, he had a man to catch. "Come. You will drive. I wish to review the file."

—

Federov stepped from Paulina Ponomayova's apartment into the drab hall. Inside, FSB technicians would continue processing the apartment, but it appeared to have been cleaned. The shelves and walls contained no framed photographs of family members or friends. They found no photo albums on the shelves and no personal mail, not even junk mail, in any of the drawers. They did not find a computer. The kitchen was spotless and smelled of a lemon-ammonia product, though they had found a spent match in the sink. The rest of the furnishings were equally Spartan. Even the trash bag had been removed from the wastebasket in the kitchen. Federov had a junior officer checking the garbage bins in the parking lot, though he thought it highly unlikely Ponomayova would have dumped anything compromising in so accessible a location.

In fact, the room was so clean, Federov initially wondered if it was a false address, an address Ponomayova had provided on her employment files, but not a place where she actually lived. Her neighbors, however, confirmed that she did live in the apartment, and the match in the sink indicated she had been there recently. The neighbors described her as quiet, said she did not socialize, and revealed very little about herself. No one could recall seeing anyone else at the apartment, and no one had heard her come home the prior evening.

Federov continued to scour an FSB dossier on Ponomayova, which he'd read front to back on the drive to her apartment. It confirmed what the tenants were telling him, and it all pointed to someone working diligently to remain anonymous, and to have largely succeeded. Fingerprint technicians would dust her apartment, but the lemon-ammonia smell made it equally unlikely they would find Jenkins's prints.

As Federov read the dossier, looking for something he might have missed, Alekseyov hurried down the hall toward him, grinning like a young boy on Christmas morning.

"We have the car," he said.

Federov felt his adrenaline spike. "Where?"

"A tollbooth camera on M4 recorded the license plate. Subsequent tollbooths confirm the car continued south throughout the night."

"They're heading to the Black Sea," Federov said. He checked his watch. "They should almost be there. Find us a plane or a helicopter. Alert the local police in the towns along that route of the car's potential presence. Tell them if they locate the car they are to keep an eye on it, but they are not to approach. Am I clear? They are not to approach the car or any house or apartment where the car is parked. Go. I will be right behind you."

21

After hanging up the phone with Charlie, Alex grabbed Freddie from the gun safe, a go bag she kept with a change of clothes for her and for CJ, basic toiletries, medications, and $5,000 in small denominations. Old habits died hard, for her and for Charlie.

She drove to CJ's school and pulled him from class, then drove directly to David Sloane's law office in the SoDo district. Sloane had bought a warehouse and converted the building in an up-and-coming area south of Seattle's downtown. Charlie would know to call Sloane's office to reach her. They had established this plan if ever needed. Alex had never thought it would be.

As she pulled into the parking lot, a commercial train crossed at the intersection behind the building, bells clanging and the train's horn blaring. Max sat up in the back of the Range Rover and barked.

"Stop it, Max," CJ said, pouting. He wasn't happy to be missing soccer practice. He'd talked to his coach, just as Charlie had prepped him, and the coach told him he would play striker in their next game. Alex didn't have the heart to tell her son that wasn't going to happen, at least not until she determined what was going on.

What have you gotten yourself into, Charlie?

Alex, CJ, and Max took the elevator to the third floor of the pet-friendly, converted warehouse.

Within minutes of checking in at reception, Carolyn, Sloane's secretary, walked into the lobby. Close to six feet, Carolyn protected Sloane's calendar like a hawk. "Alex," she said. "And CJ." She looked to Tara, the receptionist. "You didn't tell me it was family." She bent to pet Max. "What brings the three of you here?"

"I need to speak to David," Alex said.

"He's in a deposition, but he should be finishing soon. Why don't you wait in his office? I'll let him know you're here." She looked at Alex's stomach. "You look like you're getting ready to bust."

"Not too soon, I hope," Alex said. "I have several more weeks to term."

"Tara, can you call Jake and tell him Alex and CJ are here?"

"I know where his office is," CJ said, and he took off running down one of the halls, Max in pursuit, setting off dog barks in the offices as they went.

Carolyn led Alex to Sloane's office in the front corner of the building, told her to make herself comfortable, and departed. The office was large, with a desk in one corner, a couch in the other, and a round table with two chairs. Alex sat at the table and took out the laptop they used for CJ Security business. Her mind churned. They had never used the protocol before, and she had no idea why Charlie had used it now, or what danger she and CJ could be in. She felt better now that they were in Sloane's office and she could set her mind to determining what had happened.

She logged onto the Internet and studied Charlie's search history, scanning what he'd been doing, looking for his travel itineraries. She found his most recent itinerary and noted his flight to Heathrow, but what followed sent a chill down her spine. After a two-hour layover, he'd taken a connecting flight to Sheremetyevo Airport, Russia.

Alex broke out in a cold sweat. She researched further and found a second flight coinciding with his current trip. It, too, included a stopover in London before a connecting flight to Sheremetyevo.

She opened a second tab and quickly accessed CJ Security's business accounts, scanning the recorded charges on the company credit card. She found charges for multiple nights at the Metropol Hotel in downtown Moscow. The dates of the charges coincided with the dates Charlie first flew to Sheremetyevo Airport. She did not find hotel charges coinciding with his current trip, at the Metropol Hotel or any other hotel in Russia.

She found the Metropol Hotel's website and called the number. The phone in Moscow rang several times before a man answered, speaking accented English, the clerk probably alerted by the international number.

"I'm trying to reach Charles Jenkins. He's a guest at your hotel."

"One moment, please."

The clerk put her on hold and she suffered to hotel music for several minutes. Anxious, she stood from the desk and looked out the windows to the beat-up RVs and trailers in the lot across the street.

The desk clerk returned. "I'm sorry, but we don't have a guest by that name registered at the hotel."

"Did he check out?"

"I'm afraid you've misunderstood. We have no record of anyone by that name having stayed at the hotel."

Alex provided the clerk with the reservation dates for the trip in December, along with the confirmation number.

"Yes, a Mr. Jenkins was here on those dates," the clerk said.

"But nothing more recently?" she asked.

"I'm afraid there is no other record," the desk clerk said, rushing her now. "Can I be of any further service?"

"No, thank you." Alex hung up just as Sloane walked into his office.

"Hey," Sloane said. He set down a notepad and stack of documents on the round table and greeted her with a hug. "Is everything okay?"

Alex grimaced from a cramp.

"Are you all right?" Sloane asked.

"Give me a second." When the pain passed, she said, "I'm worried about Charlie. He's in some kind of trouble."

"How do you know he's in trouble?"

"He called me and, in short, he told me to get out of the house, pick up CJ from school, and come here. He also told me to arm myself. It's a protocol we have if something goes wrong."

"He didn't say why?"

"No, which means he's worried our calls could be monitored. He also isn't in London, as he told me."

"Where is he?"

"Moscow."

"Russia?" Sloane said, sounding surprised. "Why?"

"I don't know why, but he has airline reservations, a hotel reservation, and credit card expenses in Moscow for December, and a second airline reservation to Moscow just a couple days ago. I called the hotel; they said they had a record of him staying there in December, but nothing more recent."

"Another hotel?"

"Maybe, but I didn't see any other credit card charges coinciding with this second trip."

"You're certain he took the second flight?"

"I'm not certain of anything yet, but we have a code in case any one of us is ever in trouble. He was definitely telling me to get out of the house. Charlie's also a creature of habit. He would have stayed at the same hotel."

"But the hotel has no record?"

"That's what they told me. I also know that without a record, it's easier to say the person was never there." She grimaced when she felt another pain.

"Take it easy, Alex. We'll get this figured out. You have no idea where he is now?"

She shook her head. "Not at the moment, and I can't call his cell until I find out what is going on. I don't know for certain, but this smells very much like a CIA operation."

Sloane blanched. "Charlie would never do that. He walked away years ago."

"I know," she said. "And I know he'd never do it for himself, but he might for me and CJ."

"What do you mean?"

Alex explained CJ Security's financial situation. Then she said, "I'm worried, David. If he's somehow involved again and he's in trouble . . ."

"We don't know that," Sloane said.

They didn't, but Alex also knew Charlie had spent his time in the CIA running operations in Mexico City against the KGB, and that the Russians had long memories and were very patient when it came to getting what they wanted.

22

After nearly twenty hours of continuous driving, Jenkins drove the Hyundai into the town of Vishnevka on the Black Sea coast. They'd stopped only to pay tolls, to change drivers, fill the car with gas, and use the restroom. By midmorning, the snow and wind had given way to rain and fog, but at least they were no longer being pushed all over the road or driving blind. The better weather had allowed them to make up time. Anna explained they would not stay in Vishnevka, but only stop for food, water, and other supplies.

Vishnevka sat on a slope above the Black Sea and, from first appearances, looked to Jenkins to be a beach town largely deserted in the winter. Anna said the population in the beach towns tripled during the busy summer months.

The diminished population was a problem. Jenkins still wanted to ditch the car for another, but with fewer people, there were fewer cars, and a stolen car would be quickly noted. He looked at the gas gauge, which was below a quarter of a tank, and said, "We should get gas while we're here, just in case. How much farther do we have to go?"

"Not far."

"When we get there we should look for someplace to hide the car."

He pulled into a Lukoil station and they both got out—Jenkins to fill the car, Anna to walk across the street to a small market to buy food and supplies.

After fitting the nozzle into the gas tank, Jenkins walked into the attached convenience store, ordered a coffee, black, and asked the attendant if he could use the bathroom at the rear of the store.

After relieving himself, Jenkins washed his hands at the sink while considering his image in the dull mirror. He had not slept in thirty-six hours, maybe longer. His eyes were bloodshot and puffy, and dark bags had formed beneath them. He could run three times a week and watch his diet, but there was no reversing the aging process. Days like this, he felt his years. He hoped that, wherever they were going, he could crash for at least a few hours.

He stepped from the bathroom into the store, scanning the shelves for something decent to eat but finding mostly junk food—chips, donuts, candy, and products he could neither identify nor pronounce. The glass freezers contained soft drinks and alcohol. He hoped Anna had better luck in the store across the street. He looked out the windows as a beat-up compact car with a blue stripe along the side and a light bar across the top pulled into the petrol station. Police. The car continued past the pumps and parked. A young police officer got out, but he did not walk to the store. He went around the back of the Hyundai, pulled a slip of paper from his breast pocket and looked to be comparing what was written on the paper with the car's license plate.

They'd been found.

The officer peered through the driver's-side window, then tried the door handle, which Jenkins had locked. He looked to the convenience store and started toward the front entrance. Jenkins moved back into the restroom but kept the door partially open so he could hear what was being said.

"Dobroye Utro," the officer said to the attendant. *"Vy znayete, ch'ya mashina nakhoditsya snaruzhi?" Do you know whose car that is outside?*

The store clerk nodded to the bathroom. *"Chelovek prosto voshel. On v vannoy." The man just came in. He's in the bathroom.*

The officer turned and pointed. "He's in there now?" he asked.

"Da."

The officer walked toward the bathroom. Jenkins let the door close and retreated to the stall. He shut the door but did not latch it, sat on the toilet seat, and braced the door with one hand. He heard the outer bathroom door open and swing shut. Beneath the stall door two black shoes came to a stop. The officer rapped on the door, a metallic ping—a key perhaps. Then he stepped back.

"On ispol'zuyetsya," Jenkins said. *It's in use.*

"U vas yest' avtomobil' snaruzhi, Hyundai?" Do you own the car outside, the Hyundai?

"Da. Chto iz etogo?" Yes, what of it?

"I need you to come out now," the officer said, continuing to speak Russian.

"Who the hell are you?" Jenkins said, also speaking Russian.

"Politsiya."

"Is it illegal to take a shit?"

"Come out," the officer said.

"Well, you're going to have to wait until I'm finished."

"Come out now," the officer said more forcefully.

"Okay, okay," Jenkins said, not wanting the officer to get any more suspicious and call for backup, if he hadn't already done so. "Can a man not take a shit in peace?"

Another rap on the door. "Now. Come out now. And keep your hands where I can see them."

"Can I at least use my hands to pull up my pants?"

"Pull up your pants. Then come out."

"What is this about?" Jenkins asked, hoping the officer would step closer to the door.

"Come out."

Jenkins stood but paused, as if to pull up and belt his pants.

When the officer stepped toward the door, Jenkins lifted and unfurled his leg, striking the door with his heel. The door sprang open, both surprising and striking the young officer. He stumbled backward, off balance. Jenkins advanced quickly and delivered two blows to the face, knocking him out.

He flexed the fingers of his hand and felt a sharp pain. "Really have to stop getting into fights in bathrooms," he said.

He didn't have a lot of time. If the officer had called for backup, they were in serious trouble. He hoped, in a small town, off-season, that backup was not readily available. He half carried, half dragged the man into the stall and propped him on the toilet. Then he removed the officer's handcuffs and quickly cuffed the man's hands above his head to a pipe extending down the wall. He took the officer's keys and tossed them outside of the stall, then removed the officer's shoes and his socks. He shoved one sock in the officer's mouth, slipped the second sock between the man's teeth, and tied the ends around the back of his head. That was the best he could do. He shut the stall door and deposited the shoes and the keys in the trash bin before walking back into the store.

The attendant sat at the counter. Jenkins thumbed through rubles and paid for his coffee and gas.

"*Spasibo,*" the man said, speaking Russian. "What happened to the police officer?"

Jenkins looked to the door at the back of the room. "I don't know. I guess he has to go."

"He asked who owned the Hyundai." The attendant pointed to the pump.

"*Da.* His wife wants to buy one, but he is against it. He asked me how I liked mine."

The man made a face as if he understood. "How do you like it?"

Jenkins frowned. "I'd like a Mercedes, but that's not in the budget." He smiled, as if sharing a joke. "The Hyundai doesn't have much power, but it gets good gas mileage, and today that is more important."

"Da," the man said, making another face. "They say the price is going to go up another eight to ten percent because of the sanctions by the Americans."

"Good for you. Not so good for me." Jenkins pointed over his shoulder with his thumb. "Too bad they can't bottle what he's putting out in there. They could run a city on his natural gas."

The attendant laughed.

"I would let it air out before you go in there. You're liable to suffocate," Jenkins said, moving to the front door.

"Da. Thanks for the warning."

Jenkins departed the store, walking casually to the car, resisting the urge to look back to see if the attendant had moved to the bathroom. His right hand ached from punching the young officer, and he wondered if he had broken a knuckle. He removed the nozzle from the car's gas tank and returned it into the pump, using the opportunity to look inside the convenience store. The attendant remained seated, watching the television mounted above the counter. Jenkins got behind the wheel and drove across the street to the market with the red tile roof, arriving as Anna walked out the door. She carried plastic bags in each hand. Jenkins pushed open her car door.

"Hurry," he said. "We have a problem."

23

Alex sat at the round table in Sloane's office going through Charlie's laptop. Jake sat beside her, working on his own laptop, searching the Internet. Sloane moved back and forth from his desk, going over documents Alex printed out for him. They'd left CJ and Max in the lunchroom with pizza they'd ordered for dinner, a soft drink, and cable television. The boy was in heaven.

Outside the office windows, night had fallen. Streetlamps illuminated rain tapping on the warehouse roof. A loud whistle signaled the approach of another train. Alex pored through CJ Security's credit card records and their personal credit card records, as well as Charlie's e-mails and text messages. She'd made a list of the charges Charlie incurred while in Russia, places where he had dined, and plotted those locations on a map of Moscow she'd printed out. The charges confirmed Charlie's second trip, but not his second stay at the Metropol Hotel.

She'd called LSR&C's Moscow office. Uri, the head of security in that office, confirmed Charlie had visited the office twice in the past month, and that he had stayed at the Metropol on both occasions—at least that was where Uri had dropped him off and picked him up.

Someone was lying.

"How far behind in payments was LSR&C?" Sloane asked, setting down another document on his desk.

"In November it approached fifty thousand dollars."

"Why didn't Charlie tell me? I could have written the company a letter."

"The CFO kept telling Charlie he'd bring us current, and he did eventually make two ten-thousand-dollar payments, but the bills and vendor invoices kept mounting." Alex stood and walked to where Sloane sat, showing him a timeline she'd created. "Look at this. Just before Christmas, after Charlie made his first trip to Russia, we received a check for fifty thousand dollars, enough to pay our security contractors and bring our vendors current. I'm having trouble finding that check, though the increased balance appears in CJ Security's checking account."

Sloane studied the timeline for a moment, then asked, "And you can't think of any business reason for Charlie to be in Russia?"

"That office has been set up for some time. It wasn't like he was going over to get it up and running. Uri said Charlie came to discuss security measures. I think that was just an excuse."

"Excuse for what?"

"If Charlie has been reactivated, he'd need a cover to get into the country, a legitimate reason for being there."

"Okay, but I'm assuming that, cover or not, the Russians would have a means to detect a former CIA operative's entrance into their country," Sloane said.

"No doubt," she said. "The company gave him a reason to be there, and he got in, but it didn't mean the Russians would trust him, or accept his presence as legitimate."

Jake lifted his head from the computer. "Locke, Spellman, Rosellini and Cooper," he said. "That's what LSR&C stands for?"

Alex nodded.

Jake lowered his head and continued to type, studying his computer screen.

"If Charlie's in trouble do you have any other way to get in touch with him?" Sloane asked.

"No. And I wouldn't. Our agreed-upon procedure was he would call you or this office. I ditched my cell phone because that would be the first thing someone would trace, if they were trying to track my location."

"I thought so," Jake said, sitting back. He turned his computer screen toward them. "Locke, Spellman, and Rosellini are the names of former Washington State governors."

"Are you sure?" Sloane stepped closer to the screen. Neither he nor Alex had been raised in Seattle or knew much about its history. Jake had been raised in Seattle, at least until high school.

"Gary Locke was governor from 1997 to 2005."

"That I remember," Sloane said.

"John Spellman was governor from 1981 to 1985. He passed away in January of 2018. Albert Rosellini served as governor from 1957 to 1965. He died in 2011."

"So it's not very likely they were investors or officers of the company," Sloane said, reading Jake's laptop. He turned to Alex. "Could they be relatives?"

"I don't know," Alex said. "I've never met anyone except Randy Traeger, the CFO."

"One name is possible," Jake said. "Two is an unlikely coincidence. Three is deliberate. Isn't it?"

"If it's an investment and wealth management company, those names would give the company prestige," Sloane said. "If the company is trying to entice people to invest, those are names that could go a long way toward convincing people to do so."

Jake turned his laptop around and his fingers danced across the keyboard. After a moment he said, "The company was incorporated in Delaware in 2015."

"Delaware?" Alex said. "The home office is in Seattle."

"A lot of companies incorporate in Delaware," Sloane said. "The business laws are more favorable, and there is no state corporate income tax so long as the company does not transact business within Delaware." He turned to Jake. "Where does LSR&C have offices?"

Jake pecked at the keyboard as Alex spoke.

"Seattle and New York, Los Angeles, London, and Moscow."

"New Delhi, Taiwan, and Paris," Jake added. "According to the company website anyway."

"I've never heard of an office in New Delhi or Taiwan. And I understood Paris was only under consideration," Alex said.

Sloane picked up his desk phone. "Do you have Randy Traeger's number?"

"His cell number was in the phone I got rid of."

"I got the office number," Jake said. He rattled off the number to Sloane, who punched it in, leaving the call on speakerphone. They got an after-hours recording.

Sloane checked his watch, hung up the phone, and spoke to Jake. "I want you to do some digging. Find out who is really running the business, and anything else you can about the company. Something doesn't smell right."

24

As they fled the gas station and convenience store, Jenkins told Anna the details of what had happened with the police officer.

"If they found the car, we have to assume that means they found you. We're out of time. We need to hide the car and do whatever it is we're going to do," Jenkins said.

Anna directed him along a narrow dirt-and-gravel road with significant potholes that caused the car to pitch and bounce. The road followed the contour of the land, the Black Sea to their right, though shrubbery obscured most of their view. Jenkins drove past piles of scrap wood, and gravel and cinder blocks for the construction of new homes on vacant lots. He looked through the windshield at the overcast sky. "If Federov knows we're here, he'll have satellite cameras pinpoint this area to search for the car. The marine fog will keep him from seeing much of anything while it lasts, but we can't take the chance of the fog lifting. We need to get rid of the car, someplace undercover, to make him think we've moved on."

To his right, Jenkins saw a yellow flame burning atop a rusted metal tower—the flare stack to a natural-gas refinery. Red tanker ships anchored offshore. The road turned to the left, away from the coast. He drove inland, finding fewer homes and more vacant lots.

"Here." Anna pointed to a two-story concrete-block home behind a fence that looked to be made from pieces of scavenged metal. Across the street, and to their immediate right, were barren lots with spindly trees and unkempt shrubs.

Jenkins stopped at the wrought-iron gate. Anna got out of the car and unlocked a link of chain. It rattled as she pulled the links through the metal bars, and the gate emitted a squeal of protest when she pushed it open. Jenkins drove the car forward. Anna came around to the driver's side as Jenkins stepped from the car. "Take the supplies to the back of the house and wait for me there," she said.

"Where are you going?"

"To ditch the car," she said, making the word sound like "deetch." "A neighbor down the street has a shed. They will not be here for months. If I can fit the car inside, I'll hide it there. If not, I shall do my best. Shut the gate behind me and replace the lock. There is an easement behind the houses I will use to return."

Anna backed out of the driveway and Jenkins shut the gate with another squeal and relocked the chain. He carried the bags around to the back of the two-story cinder-block house. White paint peeled from the blocks, revealing that the home had once been a bright pink. At the back of the house, Jenkins encountered an overgrown yard. Two rusted poles protruded from the ground, with line strung between them. Stacked rocks and chunks of concrete overgrown by vines and shrubbery delineated a backyard. Behind the crumbling wall was more open land. They wouldn't have to worry about nosy neighbors.

A strong breeze blew in from the water, bringing a stinging cold and a briny smell. Jenkins set down the bags on a step and shoved his hands into the pockets of Volkov's jacket, moving around the corner so the house blocked the wind while he waited.

Ten minutes after Anna had departed, he saw her coming down an easement behind the houses. She hopped the fence and approached. "Any problems?" Jenkins asked.

"No," she said. "It was tight, but it will work."

"The question is for how long. Federov will go house to house if he thinks we're here, and he'll check every hiding place for your car. From what I can see, there aren't a lot of either."

"Then we will not be here long."

She moved past him and lifted a rock in a patch of overgrown weeds, revealing a key, stepped up three wooden steps, and unlocked the back door. The glass pane rattled when she pushed the door open.

They entered what looked to be a mudroom off the kitchen, which had lime-green countertops and dark-brown cabinets. The house smelled musty and the air stale. "Keep the lights off," Anna said. "And the drapes and blinds closed. I'll open a back window to get some fresh air."

Jenkins put the plastic bags on the counter and opened the refrigerator. The light did not go on. He heard Anna go upstairs, footsteps on the floor. He shut the door and flipped the switch on the wall quickly to test for power.

"The power is turned off," he said when Anna returned.

"Good," she said, taking two plastic bottles of water and tossing one to Jenkins. She led him from the kitchen to a sitting room with a couch and two recliner chairs. When Jenkins sat, the chair emitted a puff of dust. Anna collapsed on the couch.

"When's the last time anyone was here?" Jenkins asked.

"I don't know," she said.

"If the power is off, I'm assuming there is also no heat."

"I'm sure everything was shut off for the winter, including the water."

Jenkins was worried about possible connections that could lead Federov to the house. "Who owns the property? Does the person have any connection to you? Any ties of any kind?"

"No," she said. "None."

"We can't drive out of here. Not unless we can find another car."

"We must also assume Federov will have boats at his command, since the Russian Coast Guard patrols the Black Sea," she said. "That will complicate things."

"Your contact will come by boat?"

"Yes," she said. "The second-story window faces the sea. I put a red card in the window. At night, I flash a beam of light and look for a beam in return. One flash and we go. Two and we wait another day."

"How does he get to us?"

"He does not," she said. "It is too risky to come to shore, especially if the coast guard is patrolling the coast line. We must go to him."

"You have a boat?" Jenkins asked.

Anna stood from the couch. "Come."

Jenkins followed her into a room at the back of the kitchen and saw two large storage boxes. Anna bent and opened one of the boxes, revealing diving equipment.

25

The helicopter touched down in a red circle in the center of a high school's green Astroturf soccer field. Federov and Simon Alekseyov ducked as they departed the bird, the wind from the spinning blades causing Federov's suit jacket and coat to flap as they crossed the turf to an awaiting police officer. Students stood outside the school buildings, watching with their hands raised against the wind, observing this unusual break in their routine.

"Colonel Federov?" The police officer shouted over the thumping blades and extended his free hand. His other hand held the police hat on top of his head.

Federov gave the hand a perfunctory shake. He'd received a call that Paulina Ponomayova's car had been located at a gas station in the town of Vishnevka, and he told Alekseyov to make arrangements to get them there as quickly as possible.

"I'm Chief of Police Timur Matveyev. Please," Matveyev said, still shouting and gesturing to a waiting police car.

Matveyev removed his hat and put it on the car's dash as he slid behind the wheel. Federov climbed into the passenger seat. Alekseyov sat in the back.

"I understand you've located the car," Federov said as soon as he'd shut the door and muffled the thumping blades.

"Yes," Matveyev said. "We believe so."

"Where is it?" Federov asked.

"That's the problem," Matveyev said. He recounted what had happened to his young officer.

"My instructions were very simple and clear," Federov said, seething. "The car was to be identified but not approached."

"The officer is young and inexperienced," Matveyev said. "It is a mistake."

"It's more than a mistake," Federov said. "It could result in a breach of national security. You do not have the car?"

"No," Matveyev said. "But it can't be far."

"You do not know its current location?"

"Not at this time," Matveyev said, then rushed to add, "but we know that it was here, at the gas station, very recently."

Federov suppressed his anger, knowing that it would do no good. He reached into his pocket and unfolded the map he'd brought with him. The M27 motorway ran along the coast from Novorossiysk to Russia's border with Abkhazia, the region that Russia took from Georgia. A handful of roads intersected M27, leading into Russia's interior, but Federov dismissed those, convinced Jenkins and the woman were attempting to flee the country, either southeast to Georgia, northwest to the Ukraine, or across the Black Sea. Federov did the math in his head, calculating the approximate distance to each border and the likely speed of the car. He spoke out loud. "If the car was in Vishnevka at approximately 8:30 this morning, then they've had little more than an hour to drive north or south. Given the terrain, the winding road, and this fog, that's roughly forty to fifty kilometers in either direction," he said to Alekseyov, who leaned forward, between the seats. "Get an alert issued to police departments in the towns along M27. I want to know if that car is spotted. Tell them to check traffic film as far back as an hour ago. And alert the border service that Jenkins may try to cross." He turned to Matveyev. "Do you have traffic cameras?"

"Some," Matveyev said. "In town."

"Take us to your office."

Matveyev's office was a double-wide trailer situated on a vacant lot at the edge of town. The police chief had obtained the videotape from the convenience store at Federov's order, and the three men sat around an antiquated desk watching the tape on the computer monitor.

The footage quality was poor, grainy, and in black and white.

"Fast-forward," Federov said to Matveyev. Matveyev did so. "Stop."

They watched Jenkins exit the store and get back into the Hyundai. He drove away from the pump, made a U-turn, and drove across the street, stopping a second time. A woman walked out of the store carrying plastic bags and got into the car. Federov assumed it was Ponomayova, though he could not see details at that distance.

"I want any video footage from inside that store and I want to know what she purchased."

Matveyev shouted at the young officer who had endured the humiliation of having been handcuffed to the bathroom toilet. The man had a split lip and a black eye and looked to be in considerable pain.

"Go!" Matveyev said. "Find out."

"Play," Federov said to Matveyev. The tape resumed.

With Ponomayova in the car, Jenkins again made a U-turn, but he did not drive toward M27. He drove east, toward the water. Federov checked his map. "There is a road here, along the water?" he asked.

"No," Matveyev said, looking over his shoulder and running his finger along the map. "Those are train tracks. They follow the water's edge to the gas-refining plant. This, here, is a walking path for pedestrians to access the beach."

"How do the people who live in these homes access them?"

"There is a road." Matveyev turned the map, studied it. "Your map does not show it, but the road follows the beach to this point, then turns left, providing access to these homes and eventually intersecting with M27, here. You see?"

Federov sat back, thinking. Jenkins did not know the area. He would have been following directions, likely provided by Ponomayova. If their intent had been to gain access to M27 and beat a hasty retreat, Jenkins could have driven north after picking up Ponomayova from the store. He hadn't done that. In fact, he'd made a deliberate move not to do that. He'd made a U-turn and drove toward the beach. Federov put himself in Jenkins's position. Jenkins had clearly deduced the police officer had identified the car. He would have also known, therefore, that it would be dangerous to continue driving. That meant he had either hidden the car and found another, or he and Ponomayova had no intention of leaving Vishnevka, at least not immediately, and remained in hiding somewhere close by, perhaps waiting for transportation. Jenkins, as a trained CIA officer, would also know Federov had access to satellites that could focus on this area and identify the car, though not with this current weather. Still, Jenkins would not take the risk of the car being again spotted. Fog or no fog, Jenkins would have hidden the car under cover.

"Find out if anyone has reported a stolen car within the last few hours," Federov said to Matveyev. "I want to know of any such report immediately."

Matveyev stepped to a nearby desk. Federov accessed the Internet and pulled up Google Earth. A few more strikes of the keyboard and he was looking at a picture of the Russian coast along the Black Sea. He pinpointed Vishnevka and zoomed in to better see the access road Matveyev had showed him, but which was not on his map. He saw how it turned to the left, away from the water, and continued past no more than twenty homes before intersecting the M27.

"These homes," he said, speaking over his shoulder. "Is it safe for me to assume they are used primarily in the summer months?"

"Yes," Matveyev said. "Though not every home."

"I need to borrow your car," he said.

26

Jenkins stared at the scuba equipment and immediately felt his anxiety level rise. He stepped away from the locker, suddenly short of breath. Fearing the onset of a full-blown panic attack, he hurried into the living room and grabbed his medications from his backpack, dry swallowing a propranolol.

"Are you all right?" Anna asked, entering the room.

Jenkins closed his eyes. Though it was cold in the house, he felt himself perspiring.

"Mr. Jenkins?"

"I just need a minute."

She stepped closer. "You are not all right."

"I'm fine. It's a panic attack," he said. "Anxiety."

"About the scuba dive?"

He nodded. "I'm also a bit claustrophobic. Is there any other way to reach this ship?"

She shook her head. "He will already be violating international treaties by being in Russian waters. He cannot come to shore, and we have no boat to meet him. It is the only way. We cannot delay. As you said, the FSB will eventually find us."

"What kind of cover does he have, to be out on the water? What will he tell the coast guard if they find him?"

"He is a commercial fisherman in Turkey. If he is stopped, he will tell them he must have drifted, that his GPS has been on the blinking . . . is not working."

"How far out do we need to swim to meet him?"

"I will have to check the coordinates, but a minimum of three hundred meters."

"And you've done this before?" Jenkins asked.

"No." She slowly shook her head. "I have had no reason to go before this."

"Please tell me you have, at least, scuba dived before."

"Yes. I am trained. But I must tell you that a three-hundred-meter swim is about the capacity of the tanks."

"No, you didn't have to tell me that." He sat down, feeling his anxiety calm but not his concern. He tried to gather his thoughts. "How do we find the boat if we're underwater?"

"I will have the coordinates of the ship and we will follow a compass."

"A compass? What about currents? What if we drift, or the boat drifts?"

"The ship will not drift. He is experienced. We will follow our compass and, once in place, I will inflate a buoy with a beacon to alert him to our presence."

"And if we're off, then we've swum three hundred meters and what?"

"We will not be off."

"But if we are?"

"If we are off, then we will be up the shit creek, I believe is how you say it."

"Terrific." Jenkins blew out a breath of air. "How long does the tank of air last?"

"That depends on how much you are breathing. You are big man and your anxiety will not help, but if you remain calm and follow me, then the tank will last approximately thirty to forty-five minutes, but perhaps longer since we will not be diving deep. No more than three meters. Remain calm and you will be fine."

"What about sharks?" Jenkins asked.

"Only the kind like in your movie *Jaws*. Nothing to worry about." Anna paused. Then she smiled. "It is joke. No sharks." She checked her watch. "It is dark at 4:20. I will look for his response. One light and we go half an hour after sunset. That gives us a few hours to check the equipment and make you more comfortable."

"If you want me more comfortable, I'd suggest you find a way to put a cruise ship in that equipment box."

27

Using Matveyev's personal car, Federov drove the gravel road, the car pitching and bouncing with each pothole. To his right, in between bushes and paralleling the beach, he saw the train tracks and power poles leading to the natural-gas refinery. He drove slowly up an incline, the road just wide enough to accommodate Matveyev's car. Shrubs on each side threatened to engulf the road. Federov looked for shrubs that had been knocked down or otherwise disturbed—a possible place to hide a car.

At the top of the slope he came to a series of expensive, and more recently built, homes. He slowed and looked through fences, but he did not see any cars or any place to hide one.

As he continued along the road, now driving inland, the quality of the homes decreased significantly. Piles of construction materials overflowed the lots to the edge of the road—rusted pipes, blocks of cement, and other materials. Men stood in the road loading materials into the back of a lime-green flatbed truck. Federov stopped and exited the car. He approached the men with a picture of the Hyundai and a picture of Charles Jenkins. The photographs fluttered and flapped in the breeze off the sea.

"Izvinite za bespokoystvo. Ya ishchu etu mashinu. Vy videli eto?" I'm sorry to bother you. I'm looking for this car. Have you seen it?

The first man considered the picture, then shook his head. The two other men walked toward Federov, studied the picture, and also shook their heads.

"Nyet," they said.

"What about this man? Have you seen him?"

Again, they shook their heads.

Federov believed them honest, but Russians had once again become distrusting of their government and those who worked for it. "How long have you been working on this street?" he asked.

"A couple of hours," one of the men said. "We are just finishing."

"Spasibo," Federov said. He got back into the car and continued along the road, looking left and right and asking himself, *What would Jenkins and the woman want more than anything?*

"Privacy," he said.

He stopped outside a house with a vacant lot on its left and across the street. A six-foot wrought-iron gate attached to a fence made from aluminum siding protected the home. Federov parked the car and stepped out, peering over the top of the fence. He did not see the car or a place to hide it. He walked to the gate and pulled on a chain, rattling the padlock, which appeared to be rusted shut. He looked again to the house, but he did not see any lights. No smoke came from the chimney.

He returned to the car and continued down the street, noting houses in various stages of construction and of various quality. He considered cars in driveways, and when he could not see over walls, he got out to look. At a fork in the road he noted a one-story home with a sloped red roof and, to its right, a shed made from sheets of corrugated metal. Federov parked on the gravel, got out, and walked to the shed. The doors did not have exterior handles, though they were hinged. A stone on the ground kept the doors shut. Federov heard wind whistling through cracks in the metal siding. He removed the stone and pulled on the bottom of the door, which remained stubborn, scraping dirt as it opened. The lack of any marks in the dirt almost caused him not to bother, but he persisted and managed to create a gap wide enough to slip his hand inside and grip the door's edge. With a better hold, he lifted as he pulled. When he'd opened the door enough to step inside, he held up his phone and turned on the light, illuminating a gray Hyundai.

His heart hammered in his chest.

The shed was too narrow for him to walk to the back of the car, but this did not stop him from climbing over the hood and the roof. He used his phone to illuminate the license plate, which he'd committed to memory. The plate matched.

The car had been parked facing out, with easy access to M27 if the need arose to quickly get away—if Jenkins and Ponomayova even remained close by. The possibility existed that Jenkins and Ponomayova had switched vehicles, maybe with a car that had been inside the shed.

Federov exited the shed and watched the house for any sign of people inside. Seeing no such indication, he returned to the shed, closed the doors, and put the rock back in place. Then he did his best to obscure the line in the dirt made by the door, as well as his footprints.

Back inside Matveyev's car, he drove to the fork in the road and parked behind shrubs. He called Alekseyov on his cell phone, who told him that there had been no sighting yet of the Hyundai on the M27 or in any of the towns along it. "Border security has been alerted as well as the coast guard."

Federov told Alekseyov he wanted as many men as Matveyev had available to guard each end of the road, from the sea to the intersection with M27. "Tell them no one drives in, and no one drives out without the car being thoroughly inspected. Do you understand?"

"Da."

Federov provided Alekseyov with the house number associated with the shed. "Determine the owner. Send people to wherever they are currently and find out when they were last here, and also any cars they own and keep here."

"Where are you?"

"I have found the car in a shed at the end of the road. I am going to the house now to determine if Jenkins is inside."

"Do you want more men?"

Federov did not want others. He did not want anyone who might give away his position. Jenkins was a smart and formidable foe. Federov knew from his research that Jenkins had served in Vietnam and therefore that he could have experience with trip wires or other such things to alert him to someone's approach. Ponomayova, too, was capable, given her shot of the FSB agent in the hotel parking lot. And both, he assumed, were armed. Beyond all of that, Federov did not want to answer to anyone. Not now and not later.

"*Nyet.* Position the men at each end of the road. If Mr. Jenkins is here, they are trapped. And this time he will not get away."

28

Jenkins heard Anna reenter the house through the back door, one of several trips she'd made to map their path to the beach. The boat had made contact. One light. They were good to go. Earlier she had reported that the wind had died down and the seas had calmed, a good thing. This time, however, when she returned, she looked grave.

"There are men out front." She said the words without emotion, the way one might say: "There are rocks on the beach." But Jenkins knew what it meant. He knew the ramifications. Getting to the beach might be harder than the swim to the boat.

"We can't stop now," he said. "We move forward."

They laid out the scuba gear on the brown shag carpet. Jenkins's suit was more than a little tight, but he could squeeze into it—he didn't have much choice.

"Can we get around the men?" he asked as they worked.

Anna shook her head. "No. Two men are sitting in a car at the end of the road where the path leads down to the sea."

"Is there another path?"

"No. It is too steep and would be very difficult to climb down even without equipment. With tanks, is not possible. More men are also positioned at the other end of the road, near where I parked the car."

"The gas station likely had a camera, maybe the store too," Jenkins said. "Federov would have seen me make a U-turn and drive toward the sea. He assumes we stayed."

"It is a logical deduction," she agreed.

"If they found the car, they'll start searching houses. We're going to have to find a different path down to the water, or a way to get the two men to leave."

"There is no other path. And the men will not leave unless they think they are pursuing us. You will have to go alone."

Jenkins wasn't sure exactly what she meant, but he deduced it meant that Anna would be the distraction to get the two men away from the path. "No. I'm not going without you. We'll find another way."

"There is no other way," she said in that soft, resigned voice.

"There is always another way," he said. "Don't quit on me, Anna."

She smiled, but it had a sad quality to it, the smile of a woman just before the state executed her. "I'm not quitting, Mr. Jenkins. I'm doing my job."

"It's Charlie, damn it. My name is Charlie."

Another smile. "I'm not quitting, Charlie. You have to understand that if you survive, if you get back, then I have done my job. You must get back and stop whoever is leaking the information on the seven sisters, before others die."

"They'll kill you, Anna."

"Paulina," she said. "My name is Paulina Ponomayova."

"No," he said. "Do not tell me your damned name now. This is not the end."

"They will come door-to-door, Charlie. They will find us both. You yourself said so."

"Then we'll fight."

"If we stay, we both lose our only chance. The boat will not wait, and it will not return. How long can we fight? How many?"

Jenkins paced.

"Please," she said. "Let me do this for my brother."

"For your brother—"

"What I have done, all these years, I did to avenge his death. But I have spent my entire life living in the shadows, Charlie. I have never loved after my divorce—because I could not take the pain of losing another person. You are married. You love your wife. You have a son and another child on the way. You have love in your life, Charlie. I was never so fortunate. I want this chance to step from the shadows, and to look the people in the eye who killed Ivan. I want to tell them that everything I have done, I have done because I love him."

Jenkins sat on the sofa across from her. "It won't be that simple, Paulina. They'll torture you to find out what you know about me, and where I have gone."

Again, she smiled. "They will never have the chance, Charlie."

Jenkins knew she meant that she would take her own life when the time came.

"I will tell them that for decades my brother did them more harm than they could ever have imagined doing to him, or to me. And they will have to live with the knowledge that revenge has eluded them, once again."

Jenkins sighed, fighting back his emotions.

"Do not be sad for me, Charlie. This is a day I have anticipated, and for which I have long prepared. I am at peace with my God, and I am anxious to see my brother dance the ballet in the greatest ballroom in all eternity. Give me this gift. Give me this opportunity to know that I have harmed them one last time."

"What will you do?"

"I will get to the car, and I will lead them away from here. When I do, you must go quickly. There is a gap in the fence at the back of the property. The lot behind us is vacant but filled with trees and shrubbery to provide cover. Make your way to the access. It will lead you to the water's edge. Have everything prepared so that when you reach the water you can submerge."

"The compass," he said. "I don't know how to use it."

She removed the compass from her wrist and fastened it to his. "You keep this arm straight. The arm with the compass you bend at a ninety-degree angle, gripping the other wrist, like this." She showed him. "You follow a compass heading of 210 degrees."

"How do I—"

"We will set the compass bezel until the north arrow is aligned, like this." She moved the bezel counterclockwise. "This red line is the lubber line. This we will adjust to 210 degrees. In the water, this button is the light to illuminate the watch, but the compass will glow continuously, and you will be able to see the direction you are heading. Keep your arm and the compass as level as I showed you, and keep the lubber line on 210 degrees as you kick."

"What about the current?"

"The Black Sea does not have any appreciable tide. Just follow the lubber line and kick hard. It is not an inconsequential distance, and keeping the course will be difficult, but it can be done. How well do you swim?"

"It's been a while."

"You look to be in good shape. Your legs are strong, yes?"

"Yes," he said.

"You must be in the water no later than five forty-five. Thirty minutes is a decent time to swim three hundred meters. Stay under the water no more than three meters to conserve your air. The boat will come between six fifteen and seven o'clock. It will not appear one minute before, and it will not stay one minute longer."

"How will I see it?"

"He will drop a light into the water. You must look for the light. When you see it, release your beacon but keep the string wrapped around your wrist. He will have the coordinates. He will come to you. Surface only when he comes."

"What if I run out of air before he gets there?"

"You are going to have to relax. Breathe calmly. You can do this, Charlie. Do this for me and do this for Ivan. Do this for your wife and your son and your unborn child." She paused, staring at him as if there was something else to tell him.

"What?"

"Your wife will have a daughter," she said softly.

Jenkins took a moment, considering her. She seemed so certain. "How could you know that? I don't even know that."

She shrugged. "I do not know, but about this I feel strongly."

Jenkins nodded. "If we do have a daughter, I'll name her Paulina, and when she is old enough, I'll tell her about the sacrifice you have made."

Ponomayova looked to be fighting emotions. She stood and checked her watch. "We must go now." She moved to where she had placed her black coat and black knit hat.

"Paulina?"

She turned and smiled, but she spoke no words. No words came to Jenkins either. He watched her walk to the back of the house. A second later, he heard the back door open and click closed.

29

Alekseyov called Federov with news regarding the house with the shed. FSB agents found the owner at his apartment in the Yasenevo District just northeast of downtown Moscow. He told the officers that he and his wife inherited the beach property from her parents and used it during the summer months. He stored his truck and his tools in the shed. He had no other car. The shed should have been empty.

Like the house.

"They are not in the house," Federov told Alekseyov after he'd gone room to room. "Tell the men to go door-to-door starting with the first house at the end of the block. I want every room in every house checked. If no one is home, break down the doors."

Federov disconnected and slid the gun back into his shoulder holster. He walked to the back of the house and stepped into the yard, still fuming at the police officer's stupidity for engaging Jenkins at the gas station, thereby alerting him that Federov had discovered the car. Had the officer not done so, this matter would have likely already concluded and Federov would have had Mr. Jenkins. Or his body.

Soon enough, he thought. *Soon enough.*

30

Paulina slid out the back door into the yard. The clotheslines swayed in a breeze and the poles creaked as if with displeasure. She slid through an opening in the stone wall, moving down the easement toward the house and the shed where she had ditched the car. The marine layer tempered sounds, and the quiet reminded her of those final days in Moscow, when a thick blanket of snow had fallen over the city. She would not see Moscow again, or the Bolshoi, where she and Ivan had once roamed the hallways and the secret rooms, and climbed to the roof to gaze out at their city. Those were good memories she had of her brother, those and the memories of him dancing. He'd looked like an angel trying out his first pair of wings.

She would cling to those memories now, but she could not dwell on them.

She proceeded down the easement, gun in hand, eyes and ears attuned to every movement and sound. A dog barked, but it was a distant echo, the wail of a dog pleading to be let inside, not the barking of a dog disturbed. She continued on.

When she reached the stone fence at the back of the home closest to M27, she paused to study it. The house looked as it had, dilapidated and deserted. As she started to go over the stone fence, movement caught her attention. She retreated and ducked behind the wall. A man, dressed in a long coat, exited the back of the house.

She watched him remove a pack of cigarettes from his inner coat pocket and flick the blue flame of his lighter. The flame briefly illuminated a hardened face she recognized. Federov. The red ember glowed as Federov sucked in the tobacco, then blew smoke into the night air.

She could think of only one reason for Federov to have been inside the house. He had discovered the Hyundai parked in the shed, and he had suspected she and Jenkins were in the house. Now that Federov knew they were not, the FSB and local police would go door-to-door, as Jenkins had said. She did not have much time.

She rested the handle of the pistol on the top stone. The shot was no more than five to seven meters. She would not miss. More importantly, the reverberation would echo and draw attention away from Charlie. She might even have time to get into the Hyundai and get away, if they had not disabled it. She would drive as far as she could, hopefully far enough. She took aim just as Federov tossed his cigarette butt into the yard and moved down the side of the house, in the direction of the front yard.

Time for her to move.

She climbed the wall and dropped into the yard. She crossed to the shed, keeping watch for others. At the back of the shed she paused again and peered around the side of the building. She saw another glowing ember; someone watching the garage. This was a problem.

She retreated, took just a moment to catch her breath, and moved to the opposite side of the shed, sliding to the corner. She picked her steps carefully so as not to disrupt a misplaced sheet of aluminum siding or inadvertently kick a can. She peered around the front of the building. The guard paced as he sucked on his cigarette. She estimated he was no more than three meters from her, an easy shot. She looked down the road—to where others had likely established a roadblock of some kind, trying to keep her and Jenkins from escaping on M27.

She'd deal with that if she got the car out of the shed.

She had run out of time. So, too, had Mr. Charles Jenkins.

She removed the silencer, which was no longer needed, raised the barrel, and peered around the edge. When the man turned toward her, she took aim.

"For you, Ivan," she whispered.

Jenkins jumped up and down and pulled and tugged on the stubborn dry suit, eventually getting it over his shoulders. When he had done so, he reached for the long strap of fabric attached to the zipper key. Finding it, he sucked in his stomach, thankful he'd lost weight, and raised his arm, tugging on the strap. The zipper slowly pinched the suit together, moving up his back. When the zipper cleared his shoulder blades, it slid easily up his neck.

The suit was tight. So be it.

He sat to pull on his booties and his gloves. Then he took the ziplock bag with his medications, his passport, and his rubles and dollars, and slid it into a pocket of the buoyancy vest, what Paulina had called a BC. He zipped the pocket closed. He'd also take the gun he'd removed from Arkady Volkov. If he reached the beach, he'd discard it in the water. A gun would be of no help to him once he dove.

He crouched down and slid the straps of the vest onto his shoulders, then straightened and lifted the tank from the kitchen table, feeling its weight. He fastened the clips and straps so the vest rested on his hips and was otherwise snug, as Paulina had instructed. Moving with the tank on his back would be easier than trying to carry it, along with his fins and his mask, and it would allow him to keep a hand free in case he needed the gun. He was also mindful of Paulina's last instruction. When he got to the water, he needed to be ready to submerge.

He picked up his fins and his mask by their straps, moved to the front of the house, and pulled down a blade of the blind. It crinkled and pinged. Peering out the gap, he saw the car still parked in the street, and he hoped that whatever Paulina did, it would be enough to get the two men to move away, and quickly.

He was about to let the blind snap shut when he noticed movement inside the car. The two men got out simultaneously. Something was up.

The driver talked on his cell phone, looking up and down the street as he did. Then he lowered the phone, slid it into his coat pocket, and said something to the passenger, who had come around the back of the car. Together they walked toward the house. They'd probably been instructed to search door-to-door.

"Shit," Jenkins said.

He watched them tug on the gate. It shook and rattled. Not about to give up that easily, the first man moved to the aluminum siding used for fencing, gripped a gatepost, climbed atop the fence, and jumped into the yard. The second man mimicked his moves. When he'd landed, the two approached the front of the house.

Jenkins moved to the door at the back of the house, gun in hand.

One of the men knocked on the front door. After a pause, he knocked again, this time with more force, more insistent, and called out, asking if anyone was home. About to open the back door and move toward the easement, Jenkins caught sight of a shadow on the blinds covering a window along the side of the house. The second man had started to work his way to the back of the house. Was the man at the front of the house a decoy, someone to draw Jenkins's attention?

He retreated from the door into the shadows of the room, bent to a knee, difficult with the weight of the tank on his back, and pressed against the wall. His hand holding the gun shook. He wouldn't hit much if he couldn't calm his nerves. He took deep breaths to steady his aim.

He heard feet outside and followed the sound to the back door. The man climbed the steps. Jenkins could see his shadow on the thin piece of cloth covering the window. The door handle turned. Locked. A sharp ping followed, and a large piece of the glass fell inward, shattering on the floor. The man reached his hand through the hole, unlocked the door, and reached for the doorknob.

Jenkins raised the gun, gripping his right wrist with his left to steady it. He couldn't wait for whatever it was Paulina planned to do.

He'd have to shoot and take his chances.

Paulina pulled the trigger. The agent's left shoulder looked as though someone had yanked a string attached to his back. His feet came out from under him and he hit the ground hard. The crack and thump of the shot echoed in the still night air. Most would mistake the sound for a car backfiring, but those who knew guns, like Federov, would not.

Paulina moved quickly and deliberately to the agent on the ground, removed his gun from its holster, and tossed it into the bushes. *"Vy budete zhit,"* she said. *You'll live.*

Hurrying to the front of the garage, she picked up the rock holding the doors shut, flung it into the yard, and yanked open the doors. She squeezed along the driver's side of the car and managed to open the door enough to press inside.

She inserted the key, said a silent prayer, and turned the ignition. The engine came to life. "Time to run, Ivan."

She dropped the car into drive, saw headlights approaching from the intersection at the end of the road, and, not wanting to get pinned inside the shed, gunned the engine. The car leapt forward, the back end fishtailed on the dirt and gravel before the tires gripped and the Hyundai straightened. She aimed directly at the oncoming car.

She glimpsed two men in the front seats just before the driver yanked the wheel and their car swerved and plowed through shrubbery, striking the trunk of a tree with a loud thud, followed by the persistent blast of a car horn.

Charles Jenkins had his distraction. She hoped it worked.

Paulina accelerated toward the intersection. Without headlights, she saw gray shadows in the road, two cars serving as a roadblock. She aimed for the gap between the front bumpers, powered down the driver's-side window, and shot at the police officers getting out of their vehicles. They ducked and sought cover. Just before impact, she brought her arm in, dropped the gun into her lap, gripped the steering wheel with both hands, and braced herself.

The Hyundai crashed between the two cars and forced its way through the narrow opening. She felt her body jolt forward, the safety strap digging into her shoulder and across her lap then being pulled back hard against the seat. She hit the brakes, yanked the steering wheel to the right to correct the back end, and punched the gas. The car sputtered up the M27 incline. Behind her she heard more shots.

She wouldn't get far, but hopefully she'd get far enough to give Charles Jenkins time to run.

—

Jenkins released pressure on the trigger when he heard the echo of a gunshot fired from somewhere down the street. Paulina. The man at the back door heard it also. He paused, then removed his hand and stepped away. The man at the front of the house shouted something, and the man at the back took off running.

Jenkins stood, struggling for balance, and moved to the door. He stepped outside and heard the sound of tires spitting gravel. No time to waste, he moved as quickly as he could across the backyard, stopping to slip through the gap in the stone fence. The bottom of his tank clanged against a rock. Stepping through, he hurried across the adjacent empty lot, toward the path leading to the Black Sea. Down the street, the opposite direction, he saw the taillights of the car that had been parked in front of the house.

He came to another stone fence, this one just a couple feet high, but it slowed him as he struggled to get over it. Wearing booties, he felt every rock and branch he stepped on. He crossed another yard and came to a house under construction. This was the house at the turn in the road. The path to the beach was across the street and about fifteen yards west. Jenkins moved along the side of the house to the front yard. He paused, looked left and right, saw no one. As he was about to move forward, the bushes rustled. Jenkins took aim. A dog came out of the brush, startling him. It briefly considered him, then curled its tail between its legs and scurried down the road.

Jenkins moved forward, sweat dripping down his face and burning his eyes, blurring his vision. With his hands occupied, he had no ability to wipe the sweat away.

He crossed the road. Now he was exposed. He picked up his pace, feeling the tank bouncing against his back, the weight belt digging into his hips. He cleared the bend in the road and slipped down the path. Another ten yards and he was on the rocky beach. Again, the bottom of his feet felt every stone as he picked a path to the water's edge. Reaching it, he dropped his fins, mask, and gun, and pulled the hood of the dry suit over his head. It snapped tightly into place. He felt along the edges, tucking in stray strands of hair.

He picked up the rest of his equipment and walked knee-deep into the blackened water. The calm night air had stilled the surface and the waves were minimal, helping his balance. He had no use for the gun now and tossed it, hearing it splash somewhere in the darkness. He lifted his left leg, struggling to balance on the rocks, and slipped on the long fin, then repeated the process and pulled on the second fin. He tried to spit in his mask but his mouth had gone dry.

He spotted the headlights of a car on the road that looked to be accelerating toward the path to the beach.

Again, Jenkins tried to spit, this time producing minimal saliva. He rubbed it against the glass until it squeaked, rinsed it, pulled his mask over his face, and adjusted the snorkel. The approaching car came to a stop. Men got out quickly.

Jenkins stuck the regulator in his mouth and fell backward into the frigid water.

—

Federov walked down the road to meet with Alekseyov and the other FSB agents but came to a sudden stop when he heard the gunshot. The shot came from the end of the block—from the house he'd just inspected. He'd left an officer at the shed.

He turned and ran, at first a jog, his knee painful, but he swallowed that pain and lengthened each stride until he was sprinting. He heard a car engine and watched as the Hyundai burst from the shed. It fishtailed, corrected, and accelerated. One of the police cars, the officers no doubt alerted by the sound of the gunshot, sped toward it, a high-stakes game of chicken. The police car flinched and veered suddenly to its right, barely missing the Hyundai, and plowed through bushes and hit a tree.

Federov didn't stop or raise his weapon to shoot, knowing it more important that he get to the roadblock as quickly as possible. He watched the Hyundai take aim at the two cars parked across M27 and heard a rapid succession of gunshots. The car did not decrease its speed. If Matveyev's men had returned fire, they'd missed their mark.

The Hyundai smashed between the gap in the two cars, causing a horrific crunching of metal and shattering of glass. Federov thought for a brief moment that the crash would disable the car, but the force of the impact separated the two cars enough for the Hyundai to push through. The back end again fishtailed, but the driver corrected and collected speed, driving south.

Federov was losing them, again.

When he reached the two police vehicles, now damaged, Federov raised his weapon and unloaded his clip. The Hyundai never slowed.

Federov considered the police cars, their front ends smashed so badly he knew they could not be driven. Down the road, however, headlights approached. Federov stood in the middle of the road waving his arms. Alekseyov skidded to a stop. Federov hurried around the hood to the driver's side.

"Get out! Get out!" He yanked Alekseyov from the car.

The young officer stumbled from behind the steering wheel, fell to his knee, and scrambled out of the way. Federov got behind the wheel and accelerated before the officer who'd escaped from the passenger seat had time to close the door. The velocity caused it to snap shut.

He maneuvered around the two damaged police cars, punched the accelerator, and increased speed as he ascended the slope in the road. He figured he was a mile or two behind the Hyundai, but the Hyundai had hit two cars at a high rate of speed. The damage to its front end had to be significant. He could only hope the engine would give out sooner rather than later.

Three-foot stone walls and heavy brush bordered the narrow two-lane highway, which made it difficult to pass, and dangerous to do so where M27 intersected cross streets. Having studied the map, Federov knew those cross streets led to housing tracts, but they provided no discernible way out of Russia and were therefore dead ends as far as Jenkins and Ponomayova would be concerned. Federov was more convinced than ever that the two were desperate and making a futile run for the border.

He quickly came up on the bumper of a white commercial van, swerved into the adjacent lane to pass, and just as quickly retreated when headlights appeared around a bend in the road. When the oncoming car passed, Federov swerved again. Seeing an opening, he pressed down on the accelerator and passed the van just as the road veered to the left. He braked and pulled the steering wheel hard into the turn, though not hard enough to keep the right side of the car from scraping against the metal guardrail that had replaced the stone wall. Sparks flew, and the side mirror violently snapped off.

Federov accelerated and braked into the next turn. When the road straightened he picked up speed, honking the horn and flashing his lights as he passed another vehicle. This continued for several miles, until Federov began to wonder if Jenkins and Ponomayova had evaded him, perhaps hiding out on a cross street. Just as he had that thought, however, he came around another bend and saw red taillights. Federov quickly closed the distance. The Hyundai drove well below the speed limit, smoke spewing from beneath its hood.

Finally, he'd caught a break.

Federov hit the accelerator and slammed into the back bumper. The Hyundai swerved, but the driver corrected. Federov steered to his right and tapped the rear bumper, a move favored by police. The Hyundai spun. This time the driver could not correct. The car slid across the center white line and the adjacent lane before it slammed into the trunk of a tree, coming to a violent and certain stop.

Federov hit his brakes and spun a U-turn. He parked ten meters back from the car, considering the windows for any movement. Seeing none, he removed his gun and got out, using the door as a shield. He took aim at the back window.

"Vyydite iz mashiny, podnyav ruki na golovu!" Get out of the car with your hands on top of your head.

There was no response. Smoke rose from the shattered engine.

Federov repeated the order.

Again, he got no response.

He raised up from behind the door and shuffle-stepped forward, finger on the trigger. He moved deliberately to the driver's side and used his left hand to yank on the door handle. It opened with a metallic crunching noise. The woman, Ponomayova, lay draped over the steering wheel. Federov looked across the seat, then to the back of the car. He did not see Jenkins. Infuriated, Federov grabbed Ponomayova by the neck and yanked her backward. Blood streamed down her face from a cut on her forehead.

"Gde on?" he shouted. *"Gde on?" Where is he?*

Ponomayova's eyes cleared momentarily and she smiled, her teeth red from the blood. *"Ty opozdal. On davno ushel,"* she said, voice a whisper. *You're too late. He is long gone.*

Federov stuck the barrel of the gun to her temple. "Tell me where he is. Where did he go?"

She laughed and spit up more blood. "So very Russian of you to threaten to kill a dying woman," she said, speaking through clenched teeth.

"Where is he?"

She smiled again, this one purposeful, and this time Federov saw the white capsule wedged between her teeth.

"For Ivan," she said. "May those of you who killed him rot in hell."

31

Jenkins swam into darkness, the blue glow of his compass his only spark of light. Tucked tightly in his dry suit, the mask pressed to his face, he fought against his claustrophobia and anxiety, and focused on that light and his struggle to keep the degree heading aligned with the lubber line. Whenever he lost focus, or found himself starting to panic, he thought of Paulina, knowing she had given her life for him to have this opportunity, one he would not waste.

Let me do this, for Paulina, for Alex and CJ and my unborn child.

He told himself to relax and to kick in long, languid strokes, not to exert himself or breathe too deeply. Paulina said the swim would take roughly thirty minutes. He checked the dive watch frequently. He'd been swimming for nearly half that time. When he wasn't watching the compass, he looked up to search for a light in the water, not seeing one. Miss that light, and he knew he would not have enough air to get back to shore and, even if he did make it back, somehow, he would have nowhere to go.

He checked his depth gauge. In the darkness, it was difficult to read, but he saw enough to know that he remained three meters below the surface, just deep enough that he could see the distinction in the color of the water. He propelled himself forward. Though Paulina had told him the Black Sea did not have any appreciable current, he felt a pull, and he had to fight against it to maintain his course.

Another ten minutes of kicking and he sensed he was getting close, but to what? He did not see a light. He checked his submersible pressure gauge, thankful that the equipment was American made and he could at least understand what he was reading. The SPG had started at four hundred pounds per square inch. It was now down to 100 psi. When the gauge reached 50 psi, his remaining compressed air would be in the red, the tank close to empty.

He swam another three minutes and checked the compass. He was in position. He looked for a light, didn't see one. He checked his watch: 6:35 p.m.

He was on time. He was in position.

The boat, however, wasn't there.

—

Federov pulled out his cell phone as he rushed back to his car and called Alekseyov. Ponomayova and Jenkins had split up. Her sacrifice had clearly been to lead Federov and his team away from Jenkins. With M4 being watched, he doubted Jenkins would try to get to the border. That left the water.

"Jenkins is heading to the water," he said when Alekseyov answered. "Get a car and get to the water. Look for a boat and any vessel anchored offshore. And call the coast guard. Tell them to intercept any ship in Russia's territorial waters."

He disconnected, considering Paulina Ponomayova and what she had said to him. He had studied her dossier. He knew "Ivan" had been Ponomayova's brother, and that he had committed suicide by jumping from the roof of the Bolshoi Theatre. Ponomayova's comment indicated she held the Russian state responsible for her brother's death. Her anger had likely been the reason for her treason and also the likely reason she had done what she had done, directing their attention away from

Jenkins so that he might slip away. Whatever the extent of her betrayal, she must have seen this moment as a fitting ending.

Federov would never stomach anyone who betrayed her country, but he had begrudging respect for someone who would give her life to a cause, no matter how misguided.

He slowed when he came to the damaged police vehicles. The roadblock was no longer needed, nor had it been of any use. Matveyev had no clue about what he was doing.

Federov powered down his window, waving at the two cars to separate further so he could pass. He accelerated between them and continued down the dirt-and-gravel road leading to the Black Sea. When he reached the far end, just before the turn, he parked, pushed out of the vehicle, and hobbled on his aching knee down the access path, careful not to roll his ankle on a rock or step into a hole.

Alekseyov stood at the water's edge, looking through binoculars. He turned at the sound of Federov's approach. Federov took the glasses without a word and focused on the horizon, scanning left to right, searching for a boat or a light, not seeing one. The marine fog layer remained thick enough to hide a boat, especially if the boat was running without lights.

"Have you seen anything?" he asked Alekseyov.

"No, Colonel, I have not."

"You've contacted the coast guard?" he asked, eyes still pressed to the binoculars, fingers adjusting the knob between the lenses.

"They have dispatched a Rubin-class patrol boat to search this area."

"One?" Federov lowered the binoculars. "They have one vessel?"

Alekseyov shrugged. "I stressed to them the urgency of this matter, Colonel—"

Federov swore, raised the binoculars to his eyes, and continued searching. *"Ya naydu tebya, Mr. Dzhenkins, I kogda ya eto sdelayu, ty rasskazhesh', mne vse. V etom vy mozhete byt' uvereny." I will find you,*

Mr. Jenkins, and when I do, you will tell me everything. Of this you can be assured.

—

Jenkins checked his SPG. It was now becoming a habit, like a person in a car running low on gas repeatedly glancing at the descending gas gauge. The needle on his SPG had dropped another 10 psi, down to 60. Another 10 and he'd officially be in the red. It didn't mean he was out of air, just getting dangerously close. He knew it would be prudent not to allow the gauge to dip farther, but Jenkins didn't have much choice, or options, other than to surface, something Paulina had said not to do.

He checked his compass. The lubber line pointed straight and true to 210 degrees. The question now was whether he had swum far enough, or whether the current, what little existed, had been just enough to slow his pace, in which case the boat remained farther out. He was beginning to think the plan had been doomed from the start—the ship trying to find a drop of water in an ocean. Then he remembered the search-and-rescue transponder, and Paulina's instruction. He disconnected the conical device from his belt, opened the plastic casing, and turned the switch to the black dot just as Paulina had instructed. A light began to flash. He wrapped the string around his wrist, and let the rest of the string unfurl. The transponder floated to the surface and gently tugged on his arm.

Nothing left to do now but to hope and wait.

He swam in circles to keep warm, one eye focused on the compass, the other searching for a light. Not seeing one.

Could the compass be off? He tapped the face. Could Paulina have somehow set it wrong, sending Jenkins swimming in the wrong direction, making the transponder out of range of the boat, and making Jenkins hopelessly lost? He fought to remain calm and to control his breathing. If he panicked, he'd suck what remained of the compressed air from the tank, and then he'd be both lost and without air. He looked again to the SPG—50 psi. He was in the red. The gauge seemed to be dropping faster. He was breathing too quickly, or too deeply. He again contemplated surfacing, but Paulina had warned against doing so prematurely. He could inflate his vest and float on the surface. At least then he wouldn't be sucking what remained of his air.

He was about to surface when he heard a dull, distant thrumming sound. He stopped moving and held his breath, listening more intently. The noise increased in volume. A boat engine. He couldn't pinpoint the sound, magnified under the water. The noise sounded as if it was all around him. He turned in circles, searching the surface.

There!

A wake cut through the surface, the hull of a boat approaching at a slow speed. Trailing behind the boat's stern, perhaps three feet below the hull's lowest point, was a blue LED light.

It glowed like a small lighthouse. Charles Jenkins's salvation.

Jenkins kicked his fins, moving toward the light, closing the distance from forty feet to twenty feet and finally to ten feet. About to inflate his BC, he heard another thrumming, this one even louder than the first, a much larger engine to a much larger boat, and one that sounded as if it was traveling at a much higher rate of speed. The water above him churned. The hull of the boat was deeper than the first boat, deep enough to crush Jenkins. And it was quickly closing on him.

The LED light extinguished.

Jenkins stopped swimming, frantically using his hands to help him sink. The hull of the boat passed over him, but close enough to spin him in the rush of the moving water. When he'd stopped spinning he checked his SPG. The exertion of the swim toward the boat had caused him to suck in more compressed air. The gauge now read just 30 psi. It was firmly in the red, and quickly fading to the black.

32

Demir Kaplan had been a fishing boat captain for almost twenty-five years, and, at sixty-three, he knew the waters of the Black Sea, Bosphorus strait, and Marmara Sea as well as any man. Prior to owning his boat, he'd spent fifteen years in Turkey's navy, the last ten in an amphibious marine brigade, after five years in special forces detachments. He'd retired, largely out of boredom, and set to work on his father's fifty-foot fishing boat. When his father died from too many cigarettes and too much booze, Kaplan became the fishing boat's captain. For years, fishing had provided his family a good living. The fish he caught—anchovies and shad—filled the fish sandwiches sold by the vendors beneath Istanbul's Galata Bridge. Turkish fishing, however, had been in sharp decline for years, a victim of commercial overfishing, illegal netting, and lax regulations. Where once Kaplan could fill his nets with thirty different species of fish, he was now lucky to catch just five or six, and none in great quantities. In a bid to replenish the stock, the government had banned fishing in the summer months to allow the fish to reproduce, but these regulations impacted only Turkish fishermen. The Russians did not abide by any such laws, did not honor territorial waters, and they stripped the Black Sea through gill netting, then grossly underreported their catch counts. After spending eighty years learning how to cheat the government, cheating had become ingrained in the Russian way of life.

Kaplan had made a decent living, enough that he could build family homes on the cliffs of the strait for himself and for his two sons and their families, but as he aged, and retirement beckoned, he grew concerned that his sons could not make a living fishing, so much so that he had become reacquainted with valuable contacts from his days in the navy. For the past several years he'd supplemented his dwindling fishing income with money earned from transporting refugees out of Iraq and Syria, and smuggling—weapons and people—American, British, and Israeli special agents. In this regard, he'd become like the Russians. As long as he was paid, he didn't care about the outcome. Besides, he hated the Russians, a trait he had inherited from his father. He considered smuggling agents who opposed the Russian regime to be a way to even the playing field. And he was paid handsomely to do so, receiving more money for one smuggling run than he could make in a fishing season—but only if he safely delivered his target. Tonight, with each passing minute, that prospect seemed more and more unlikely.

Kaplan circled the coordinates he had been given for his pickup and scanned the ship's radar—a gift from the Turkish government to improve his fishing. He used the radar to search for transmissions between 9.2 and 9.5 gigahertz, the frequency of the transponder; which was below the frequencies used by the Russian Coast Guard. If he found the transponder signal, he would instruct his sons to lower an LED light beneath the hull of his boat to visually alert his pickup.

He'd been circling in the dense fog for nearly seven minutes without any sign of the transponder on his radar. He told his sons, well-trained in these missions, and the only men he fully trusted, to drop the LED light into the water anyway, hoping to lure the diver to the boat.

The dense fog was both a blessing and a curse. It would make finding a diver more difficult, but it would also make it more difficult for the Russian Coast Guard to find them. If the coast guard did find Kaplan, his excuse was well rehearsed. He would circle as if to drag in his nets, unaware that he had inadvertently drifted into Russian territorial waters. If the Russians did not buy Kaplan's excuse, the penalty could be the sinking of his ship.

Kaplan again looked at his watch. He would not linger. He would wait exactly thirty minutes, as agreed, not a minute more or less. He would depart at seven o'clock, passenger or no passenger. He had twenty-three more minutes, but he could have twenty-three days. He would not find his package, not without a signal. Without a signal, he was blind, unable to see more than ten or fifteen feet in any direction in this cursed fog, making the chances of visually spotting a diver impossible.

He slowed his boat, stepped from the pilothouse, and turned on the spotlight, moving the beam over the water's surface. The marine fog continued to plague them, and the light only made it more difficult to see, like turning on a car's high beams on a foggy road. He kept the beam low to the water to try to cut the glare.

"Do you see anything?" Emir, the older of his two sons, asked.

"No," Kaplan said.

"And nothing yet on the radar?" Emir asked, keeping his voice low.

"Nothing."

"How much longer?" Yusuf said. The two boys looked and sounded apprehensive, knowing the potential consequences of being this far into Russian waters, which they had never done before.

Kaplan checked his watch. "Twenty-one minutes," he said. He walked back into the pilothouse and noticed a blinking green light on his radar screen, initially thinking it the transponder, then quickly realizing the light was closing on his location at a high and unexpected speed.

"Bok!" He rushed to the door. "A boat," he yelled to his sons. "Closing fast. The Russian Coast Guard. Quickly, drop your nets."

Kaplan cut his engines and the boys moved with practiced precision, this process well rehearsed. A spotlight appeared over their bow and, from the thickening fog, the outline of a boat materialized like a ghostly apparition. The spotlight blinded Kaplan. He raised an arm to shield his eyes. As the boat moved from his starboard to port side, Kaplan recognized the blue hull with the vertical red, blue, and white stripes on the bow.

The Rubin-class Russian Coast Guard boat fell under the control of the FSB. This must be a high-value target Kaplan sought.

A voice came over a loudspeaker, talking in Russian. Kaplan ignored it.

The voice barked additional orders as the boat slowed, using thrusters to turn the bow and the stern to position it alongside Kaplan's vessel. Kaplan could understand Russian, when he chose to. Tonight, he did not choose to understand. He'd play his part as the distressed Turkish fisherman with a tangled mess of netting.

He stepped from the pilothouse onto the deck and stood beside his two sons. The voice spoke yet again, telling Kaplan to prepare to be boarded. He looked at his sons, then to the netting. As the Russian skiff lowered and approached, Kaplan lowered fenders over the side of his boat. Moments later, he caught the Russians' mooring line tossed up to him. His son, Yusuf, caught the second line and they secured the ropes to the cleats on deck. Kaplan lowered an aluminum ladder over the side of his boat and two of the three men climbed aboard—the second man armed with a Kalashnikov rifle slung over his shoulder. This was not normal procedure.

The officer wore a pristine, double-breasted peacoat with the collar turned up to protect his neck against the cold. On deck, he fit his black cap on his head. His face looked prepubescent, far younger than either of Kaplan's sons. His hands were soft and pink, and without calluses—an officer from the academy, not a man who had lived and worked on a boat. Kaplan knew his type. Officious, he would not deviate from regulations, and he would seek to enforce his authority. Kaplan hoped the man's inexperience would act against his rigidness.

"Papers," he said in Russian, trying to sound authoritarian. Kaplan stared at him, shaking his head as if not understanding.

"Kàğitlar," the officer said in Turkish.

Kaplan nodded his understanding and said his papers were in the pilothouse.

"Get them, please."

Kaplan moved to retrieve them. The officer and his guard followed. Inside the pilothouse, Kaplan pulled open a cabinet and retrieved his and his sons' papers. As he did, he heard twelve short beeps coming from the radar, but he resisted the urge to look.

The transponder.

His pickup had arrived.

"What is taking so long?" The officer sounded agitated.

Kaplan tossed the papers onto the radar screen to conceal the blip, though he could do nothing about the beeping. He fished through the papers as if searching for something, then handed them over. The officer showed no emotion. *Such a sullen people unless inebriated,* Kaplan thought. He took the moment to consider the brass name tag on the man's right breast pocket. Popov.

"Why are you fishing in Russian waters?" Popov asked as he flipped through the pages.

Kaplan shrugged. "I must have drifted in this damned fog. We are having problems bringing in our nets. They have tangled and I am concerned they will get caught in the prop. To cut them would be prohibitively expensive."

Popov walked from the pilothouse back outside and crossed to the netting hanging over the side of the boat. He could not have helped but notice the knotted tangles. Kaplan looked past them, to the water, but did not see a blinking light in the fog.

"So you see," Kaplan said, smiling. "We are far from fishing anywhere."

"Do you have your fishing papers?" the officer asked.

"Yes, for me and for both my sons. Would you like for me to get them for you as well?"

"No. We wish to search your vessel."

"For what purpose?" Kaplan asked.

"Because you are in Russian waters and we have the right to do so," Popov said.

Kaplan shrugged. He was well past arguing with a snot-nosed shit. "Please," he said, gesturing for them to proceed. "May I inquire as to what you seek?"

"No. You may not," Popov said.

Popov nodded for the man with the rifle to follow him. They proceeded to the pilothouse. Kaplan looked to his sons but he did not speak or make any gestures, knowing that others on the patrol boat likely watched.

"You, Captain," the second man shouted from the pilothouse door. "Come here."

Kaplan nodded to his sons and walked to the pilothouse.

Popov stood near the radar. "What is this?" he asked.

"That is my radar," Kaplan said. "The Turkish government provided it to improve fishing."

"I know it is your radar. Why is it beeping?"

Kaplan stepped forward and pointed out the window. "Your ship," he said. "I turned on the radar because of this damned fog. I don't want to inadvertently drift into something that might cause damage. You see? The beep is stationary. It is your ship."

The officer looked again to the radar. The blip on the screen was not his ship. It was far too small, but Kaplan hoped the ruse would work.

Popov departed the pilothouse back onto the deck, and Kaplan exhaled a sigh of relief. The officer and mate descended a ladder into the ship's hold. On these missions, Kaplan kept a pile of rotted anchovies in the hold, in case anyone decided to search. The smell would persuade them to be quick. Popov came back on deck with a foul look.

"Your fish are rotting," Popov said.

"Bait," Kaplan said. "Anchovies. The stronger the smell the better the attraction."

Popov walked to the back of the boat. "What is this?"

"It is an inflatable, in case the ship was to sustain damage."

"You are to leave Russian territorial waters at once."

"I am sorry," Kaplan said. "We are doing our best to get untangled and to move on."

Popov displayed no sympathy. "Yank the netting out of the water and proceed back to Turkish waters. You can untangle your nets there. If not, I will cut them."

"As you wish," Kaplan said.

The officer nodded to his mate, and the two climbed over the side of the boat and back down to the skiff, which transported them to their patrol boat.

"Bring in the netting," Kaplan said in a loud voice. He checked his watch: 6:57 p.m. He softened his voice. "We have lost this one."

33

Jenkins kept watch from beneath the hulls of the two ships. He had one hand extended, having yanked down the transponder so it rested just below the water's surface. He did not know for certain, but he assumed the larger vessel to be a Russian ship, navy or coast guard, most likely. He hoped the smaller vessel was his rescue ship, lured to his location by the transponder, though at the moment it was of little use to him.

Minutes before, a rubber raft had cut between the two ships and was now tied to the fishing boat.

He checked his SPG. The psi had dropped below 15, seemingly decreasing more slowly as he hovered, barely moving. Still, in minutes, he would be sucking on an empty tank and he would have no choice but to surface or suffocate. He tried to remain calm, tried to expend as little energy as possible. Despite the dry suit, now that he was no longer moving, his limbs had begun to ache in the frigid water. His fingers and toes had gone numb.

Minutes passed. Jenkins checked his gauge: 8 psi. He checked his watch: 6:55. Paulina said the rescue boat would leave at 7:00 p.m., though she had probably not anticipated the vessel being boarded. Would it stay? Could it? Would the Russian Coast Guard impound the boat for being in Russian waters?

He heard an engine and looked up. The small inflatable churned away from the fishing vessel, returning to the larger boat. Jenkins checked his gauge: 5 psi. Another minute and he heard the sound of engines starting, first the engines of the Russian vessel, then the engine of the fishing boat.

Both boats were leaving. His heart pounded: 4 psi.

The Russian vessel pulled away, the sound of the engine increasing in volume and intensity as it sped off, churning the water and leaving a wake of white foam. Jenkins unfurled the string wrapped around his wrist, let the transponder rise, and kicked hard for the surface. The water bubbled and churned. When he breached the surface, he saw the fishing boat slowly moving away. Two men stood at the railing, pulling in something. He spit out the regulator.

"Hey," he yelled. "Hey!"

He lowered his head and swam, kicking hard, but the boat continued to pull away. It was too far to reach, but he sensed something in the water, something dragging behind it, kicking up turbulence. Jenkins kicked harder and reached. Netting. He missed it, kicked again, reached.

The netting pulled farther from his grasp. The ship increased speed, departing.

He'd missed his ride out of Russia. His SPG was on empty, and he was adrift, far from shore, his limbs freezing and quickly going numb, without hope of rescue.

34

Demir Kaplan watched the Russians hook the inflatable to the winch, and the skiff lifted from the water. Popov and his two men stepped back on board the coast guard vessel and disappeared inside the bridge. Moments later, the engines churned and the boat departed, picking up speed and disappearing into the fog until even its lights were swallowed by the gray mist.

Kaplan throttled back the power, not wanting to accidentally get their netting caught in the engine prop. Then they'd really have a problem. His radar continued to emit twelve short beeps from a location on his boat's starboard side, but that was also the location that the Russian patrol boat had departed. He could not risk going back to look for his pickup. He could not risk the lives of his two sons, both married and raising families. He shook his head. He knew he was likely leaving his pickup to die, either in the Black Sea or, if the person made it back to shore, at the hands of the Russians. It made him sick. He could only hope the person would have another opportunity to escape.

He reached for the throttle, about to turn the wheel and head for home, when he heard one of his sons shouting.

"Bok!" Kaplan feared they had sucked the netting into the engine prop. His son stuck his head into the pilothouse, gripping the doorjamb, a wild look in his eyes.

"Tekneyi durdur! Tekneyi durdur!"

Kaplan stopped the engine.

"Emir thinks he saw something in the water!"

Kaplan hurried onto the deck, knowing he was taking a risk stopping to search the water. The Russian patrol boat could return at any moment. He turned on the searchlight anyway. *"Nerede?"* he asked. *Where?*

His son pointed. Kaplan directed the light beam in the direction of his son's outstretched arm and finger. The fog lit up, looking like a spider's web enclosing its trapped prey. Kaplan lowered the angle of the light to cut the glare, then slowly rotated the light to the right and to the left, sweeping the water's surface.

"There is nothing," he said.

"I saw something in the water," his son said again.

Kaplan swept the light back to the right. He could hear the ping of water against the side of his boat. "Nothing," he said again.

Jenkins listened to the fading sound of the engine and watched the fog engulf the fishing boat. His heavy breathing marked the chilled air with white puffs. He felt himself tiring, felt the heat being sucked from his body. He knew he had to keep moving, to keep swimming. The cold would kill him. It might kill him anyway. But now he was tired. So damn tired.

And which direction should he swim? In the gray shroud, he could not see the shoreline. If he swam in the wrong direction, he could end up swimming farther out to sea, a certain death.

Think.

He needed to calm his mind. He needed to think logically. Ironically, at this moment of high stress and desperation, he felt no anxiety. Maybe what he'd needed all along was a hopeless situation and a certainty of death. He smiled at the absurdity of it, not that he was resigned to his fate, not when he still had a chance. He would not quit, not on Paulina or her brother, not on himself, and, more importantly, not on his family. He wanted CJ to have lasting memories of his father. He wanted to impart whatever wisdom he could share to make his son's life better than his own. He wanted his unborn child to know him, and he was determined to see that child's face.

His compass.

He looked at the compass on his wrist. He had been following a course out to sea set on 210 degrees. If he reset the arrow on north and set the lubber line to that same reading, then he could determine the reading exactly 180 degrees in the opposite direction, which, theoretically, should be the heading to take him back to shore. Yes, there were likely problems when he reached shore, but as Paul Newman had said to Robert Redford in *Butch Cassidy and the Sundance Kid* when Redford refused to jump from a cliff into a river because he couldn't swim, "Hell, the fall will probably kill you!"

No sense worrying about the shore until he got there. If he got there.

Another problem was his stamina. Could he make it? He was in good shape from running and dieting, but swimming used a different set of muscles. First thing he needed to do was to lighten his load.

He disconnected his weight belt and let it sink to the bottom of the sea, already feeling more buoyant. Next, he needed to release his tank. He'd never done this before and imagined it would be more complicated than the belt. He didn't want to remove his buoyancy vest, which still had air in it and would keep him afloat. He recalled how he and Paulina had secured the tank to the vest with a strap just beneath the valve on top of the tank. Another strap pinched the tank tight to his back.

He reached behind him, feeling for the bottom strap, and followed it as far as his arm allowed. He gripped the unsecured end of the strap and pulled it loose. Then he reached over his head and found the valve to the tank. Just below it, he felt the fabric and inched along it until he found the clip, pinched it, and felt it snap free. The tank slid down his back and dropped like a stone into the depths.

He found the inflator hose attached to the buoyancy vest and blew air through it, inflating the vest and increasing his buoyancy. Then he slid on his mask and put the snorkel's mouthpiece between his teeth. He lowered his head and put his right arm in front of him as Paulina had instructed, found his bearing, and began kicking, he hoped, toward shore.

Within seconds, he felt himself laboring, the cold kicking in, his muscles thick and his movements slow. He imagined his blood like oil in an engine in subzero temperatures. But he couldn't fixate on those thoughts, or on the cold, or even on his labored breathing. *Just keep moving.* That's all he needed to do. *Keep moving.* He had at least thirty minutes of kicking in front of him. He'd take one minute at a time. He'd resist the urge to lift his head, to take his mouth off the snorkel mouthpiece, to fall prey to his body's desire to stop and rest, if only for a minute.

To stop was to die.

He kept repeating their names in his head. *Alex and CJ and . . . baby-to-be.* They hadn't decided on a name. Didn't know the sex. Paulina said it would be a girl—How? Jenkins didn't know, but in that moment he, too, saw a baby girl. *Alex and CJ and baby-to-be. Alex and CJ and . . . Alex and CJ . . . Alex and . . . Alex. Alex.*

He heard underwater thrumming, thinking at first it was just his imagination, his desire. It persisted. He stopped and looked up, but he was having difficulty connecting the sound to anything in particular. *A boat? Yes. No . . . An engine. A boat engine.* The thrumming grew louder. The boat getting closer. He looked into the gray shroud. Was it his imagination? Was it the desperate hope of a condemned man?

Was it the Russians, returning?

A spotlight pierced the darkness, illuminating the gray.

Not his imagination. The fishing boat.

The light swept left and right. Then it stopped. He thought he heard voices. Men shouting.

The light swept right again, blinding him. With difficulty, he raised his arm and flung it back and forth over his head.

"Nerede?" he heard.

Then, *"Orada! Orada!"*

Not Russian.

The boat inched closer, materializing out of the fog. On deck, two men stood at the railing, one pointing down at him. The second threw something overboard. It spun in the air before hitting the water. A life preserver.

Jenkins kicked to it, looped an arm through the opening, and held on as the men pulled in the line, dragging him to the ship.

It took what little strength he had remaining, and two men pulling and tugging and finally grabbing the straps of his vest, to yank Jenkins onto the boat. He fell over the railing and flopped onto the deck like a fish gasping for air. Three men stood over him, speaking to him in short, quick bursts of English, an urgent tone. He could not catch his breath long enough to respond.

One of the men gripped Jenkins beneath his shoulders and dragged him across the deck to the pilothouse. The oldest looking of the three hurried to the steering station, taking the wheel and throttling forward on the engine. Jenkins rocked backward as the engine kicked in and the boat gained speed.

He could not feel his hands or his feet, and he'd begun to shiver violently. One of the men held out a mug. Steam drifted up from the surface of the liquid inside. When Jenkins reached for it, his hands shook so violently he could not hold the mug.

The man knelt in front of Jenkins and pulled off his gloves. Each movement sent thousands of needles shooting through his hands and his fingers, and Jenkins groaned in agony. After the man had removed the gloves, he stuck Jenkins's hands beneath his armpits.

"How are your feet?" he asked in accented English.

"I can't feel them," Jenkins said, his teeth chattering.

The second man—they were brothers perhaps, based on their similar appearance—returned from the back of the pilothouse with thick wool blankets, draping them over Jenkins's shoulders. He helped his brother remove Jenkins's rubber booties. Like his hands, Jenkins's feet ached.

"I am Emir," the man said, rubbing life back into Jenkins's feet. "This is my brother, Yusuf. The captain is our father, Demir."

"I thought I lost you," Jenkins said, still shivering. "I saw your boat leave."

Yusuf vigorously rubbed Jenkins's hands and he winced at the intense pain. "I am sorry," Yusuf said, "but we must get the blood to circulate again."

"The Russians must want you very badly," Demir said from the wheel of the boat. "For them to alert the coast guard is a serious matter."

"Who do you work for?" Jenkins asked. He began to feel his hands and his feet, but with that return of feeling came more of the stabbing needle pain.

"For myself," Demir said.

"You're not with Turkish intelligence?"

"I am a fisherman who works when called upon. My reasons for doing so are my reasons. I was told to find you and to bring you back to Turkey, to Istanbul. I do not care to know the details."

"I'm grateful you came back," Jenkins said. He pulled his hands from the brother's grasp and flexed his fingers. They felt thick and swollen, but he slowly regained dexterity. Emir handed him the mug. He cradled the warmth in his hands, sipping at the hot and very thick

Turkish coffee while Yusuf used sharp scissors to cut him out of the dry suit.

“Emir will take you to change into dry clothes, though that will be a challenge given your size—and to get you something to eat,” Demir Kaplan said. “He can also show you to a bunk to lie down and sleep. You must be very tired.”

Jenkins stood, his legs weak, and followed Emir to a narrow interior doorway. He stopped and looked back. “Thank you,” he said.

“Do not thank me yet,” Demir said. “It is a long way to Istanbul and I suspect the Russians will not give you up so easily.”

35

Viktor Federov stepped into the run-down beach house; the interior cold, the air musty and carrying a strong odor of mildew. His men had been going door-to-door, finding most of the beach homes empty and no sign anyone had been there. This one, too, was empty, but it had not been for long. Bags of groceries remained unpacked on the kitchen counter, a box of crackers open. Inside the bags Federov also found juice and bottled water, cheese, and chocolate bars. He grabbed the box of crackers from the counter and took it with him into the living room, eating them. The crackers tasted better than he anticipated, or maybe he was just that hungry. He could not even recall his last meal.

He considered the articles of men's clothing strewn across the furniture. On the floor lay scuba equipment, though just one set—a buoyancy vest and a tank, full from the weight of it, a mask, fins, and a dry suit—a woman's.

His men had rifled through the clothing but did not find any identification. Federov did not need any. He knew whom the clothes belonged to and who had intended to use the equipment.

Paulina Ponomayova had clearly given her life so that Jenkins could get away, and that raised further questions regarding the importance of this man and his mission. Federov wiped his fingers on his pants, handed the box of crackers to one of the other men, and spoke to Simon Alekseyov.

"A man scuba diving without propulsion can get approximately forty minutes of air from a full tank. Jenkins is a big man, so perhaps less, say thirty minutes—unless he is well trained, which we must now assume to be so. Calculate roughly three hundred to three hundred and fifty meters on a calm night such as this. Call the coast guard. Tell them we are looking for a diver. Give them the coordinates. Have them call me without delay if they encounter any boats in the area."

Alekseyov pulled out his cell phone to make the call. Federov walked outside and crossed the yard. He could not see the beach, but he could see the blackened waters engulfed in fog. Minutes later, he turned to find Alekseyov hurrying across the yard with a look of purpose.

"The coast guard stopped a Turkish fishing boat roughly three hundred meters offshore. The captain of the vessel said he had been fishing when his nets became tangled, and his crew was working to free them. Colonel?"

Federov had looked back to the blackened horizon, thinking. There was no way a man could meet a ship in that fog, in the dark—even with coordinates. He would need a way to transmit his location to the boat, something small—like the kind used on buoys to alert captains to rock croppings, or other underwater perils. "Get the person you spoke with immediately on the phone. Tell him I want to speak to the officer of the coast guard vessel who boarded the fishing boat."

Alekseyov dialed the number as Federov moved toward the water. Within a minute, Alekseyov handed Federov the phone.

"Yes. What is your name?" Federov asked.

On the other end of the call, the man said, "I am Captain Popov."

"I understand you came upon a Turkish fishing vessel a short time ago?" Federov said.

"Yes, maybe an hour ago."

"What was the ship doing here?"

"He said he had been fishing when his nets became tangled. He was working to free them. In the process he drifted into Russian waters."

"This far?" Federov asked. "Did you search his ship?"

"Personally. His papers were in order."

Federov didn't give a damn about the boat's papers. "How many men?"

"Three. A father and two sons."

"You did not find anyone else?"

"No."

Federov had his doubts as to how thoroughly Popov had searched the ship. Smuggling vessels were known to contain hiding places in which to conceal illicit drugs, weapons, and people.

"How did you locate this boat in this fog?"

"It appeared on radar."

"Did anything else appear on your radar?"

"No," Popov said.

"Nothing?"

"No," he said again. Then, after a pause, "I don't think this is important, but when we boarded the Turkish ship *its* radar did pick up a signal."

"What kind of signal?"

"A stationary green light. I inquired about it and the captain said it was the ship's radar detecting our presence."

Federov felt his knees weaken. "Could it have been a transponder, Captain?"

"I . . ." Popov began to answer, then caught himself.

It was a sufficient enough answer for Federov. The captain had not considered the possibility.

"Where are you now?"

"Still on patrol, in roughly the same area."

"I want you to scan the entire range of your radar frequencies. Call me back and advise whether you get any other hits. Then return to Anapa and meet me there."

Federov hung up the phone. "Get the helicopter ready. We're going to Anapa."

Alekseyov shook his head. "It is not possible, Colonel. The fog is too thick to fly."

Federov cursed. "How long is the drive from here?"

"I do not know exactly, but at least several hours under good conditions. Tonight, it could be much longer."

Several hours would put the Turkish fishing vessel close to Turkish waters, perhaps too late to intercept. Federov could not take that chance. He redialed the previous number. "Captain Popov, this is Colonel Federov. You said you remain close to Vishnevka?"

"Relatively, yes."

"And you have an inflatable you used to board the fishing trawler, no?"

"Yes, of course."

"Return to Vishnevka and send your inflatable to shore. Look for flashing lights. I'm coming aboard."

—

With a change into dry clothes nearly large enough to accommodate him—he didn't button the top two buttons of the shirt or his pants, which also stopped a couple inches above a pair of work boots—Jenkins was once again warm. After changing, Jenkins followed Yusuf to the ship's galley. The Turkish coffee, so dark and thick a spoon almost stood upright, made his limbs buzz and placed him on full alert, despite not having slept much the past seventy-two hours. Food had helped to temper the effect of the coffee, and it had never tasted so good. They served him lamb with rice, scrambled eggs with onions and pepper, and bread. After they finished eating, Yusuf and Emir went to rest. They, too, had endured a stressful evening.

Jenkins walked back into the darkened pilothouse where Demir Kaplan stood watch. The lights of the console reflected under his bearded chin, casting his face in a blue-gray light. Demir looked like his sons, though he had the weathered skin of a man who'd spent his life at sea, or had seen too many tragedies. Deep depressions migrated like rivulets from the corners of his eyes. He stood with his shoulders hunched from too many years standing at the helm, and his chest and arms were thick from manual labor. He turned his head as Jenkins ducked through the interior doorway and stepped into the pilothouse. A space heater beneath the console warmed the room to a comfortable temperature.

"You should be sleeping," Demir said. "Too much worry?"

"Too much coffee," Jenkins said.

Demir grunted and said, "We Turks like our coffee as we like our women."

"Black?" Jenkins said, smiling.

Demir glanced at him, his lips inching into a grin. "Thick and full of energy."

Jenkins laughed. Then he stuck out his hand and said, "Thank you for coming back. You saved my life."

"Do not make this personal, Mr. Jenkins. You are nothing more than cargo that I am transmitting to Turkey."

"I understand. I just wanted to say it."

Demir shook the hand. "You're welcome."

They traveled in silence, listening to the hum of the boat's engine and feeling the bow rise and fall with each wave. After several minutes, Demir's curiosity got the better of him. "Whoever you are, you must be very valuable to your country and very dangerous to the Russians."

"I'm not so sure anymore," Jenkins said. "Things have become much more complicated than I anticipated."

"As they always do," Demir said.

"The other two—they are your sons?"

"Yes, although both are better looking than me. They have their mother in them. Me, I have the sea in me."

"They're good men," Jenkins said.

"Money can buy much, but it can't buy blood. Not Kaplan blood. Do you have children, Mr. Jenkins?"

"A nine-year-old son," Jenkins said. "And another baby on the way."

Demir considered him while rubbing his beard. He nodded. "Good for you."

"I got started late in life."

"Because of your career?"

"For some time, yeah, that was the reason. Then I just never really had the chance."

Demir glanced at him. "And now you have much to lose."

"Too much."

"Then why do you do it?"

"I had to support my family, and I thought I was serving my country. I'm no longer sure that is the case."

Demir sighed. "When I was a young man I had a naval career before coming to work for my father. The fishing was abundant. It was a good life. Now the fishing is not so good. I have seven grandchildren, an eighth on the way. We do what we must for our families."

Jenkins nodded. "How long before we get to where we are going?"

"We will be in Turkish waters in an hour. We will be in port an hour after that."

"If you don't mind the company, I'd like to stay here, keep watch with you."

"I do not mind," Demir said.

—

Federov and Alekseyov boarded the Russian patrol boat from the inflatable. Popov greeted them on deck and wasted little time leading them up a staircase and inside the pilothouse.

"We have picked up something on the radar," he said, moving to one of the console's instruments.

"A ship?" Federov asked.

"No, much smaller. A buoy of some type, but not in a location one expects to find a buoy, nor at the frequency we would expect. This appears to be drifting."

"How close is it from where you boarded the Turkish fishing boat?"

"Maybe half a mile, but given the direction it is drifting, it would have been very close to the fishing boat an hour ago. Do you wish to track it down or try to find the boat?"

"Track down what is transmitting. We will better know whether the boat is culpable or its presence was simply a coincidence. I do not wish to embark on another wild goose chase. If the boat captain proves culpable you can find him?"

"We can find him," Popov said. "And we will run him down."

"Good," Federov said. "Because I would hate to tell your superiors that you allowed him to get away."

Popov visibly blanched. His cheeks colored a splotchy red. "Yes, Colonel." He gave the order to lock on to and locate the buoy.

Twenty minutes later, Popov, Federov, and Alekseyov stood on the ship's deck along with half a dozen seamen. Beams of light crisscrossed the surface of the fog-shrouded water.

"There," one of the men said, pointing. "There."

Federov, Popov, and Alekseyov stepped closer to the deck railing. The seaman dropped a grappling hook over the side, snagged a cylindrical red tube with a flashing light, and slowly dragged it out of the water and onto the deck.

"It is a transponder," Popov said. "It's used—"

"I know what it is used for," Federov said. "And what it was used for in this instance. You said you could find the fishing trawler?"

"Yes."

"Do so."

—

In the pilothouse of the fishing boat, Jenkins handed Demir Kaplan a cup of coffee. "Six sugars?" Jenkins asked.

"I do not drink it for the taste," Demir said. He sipped at the rim and set the cup in a rack to prevent it from tipping over.

"I noticed the boat is named *Esma*. What does that mean?"

"Esma is my wife, and she has been my wife for forty years. She used to say that I loved the sea more than I loved her, so when I inherited the boat . . ." Kaplan shrugged. "Now I say, 'I am with you, Esma, even when I am at sea.' With Allah's grace we will have many more years together, many more grandchildren." He looked at his instrument panel. "Not far now from Turkish waters. Twenty minutes."

"You're almost home," Jenkins said.

Demir looked at him and sighed. "But you are a long way from being home, I fear. The FSB has many assets in Turkey, and there are many people who will give you up for very little lira. You are an easy man to remember. You will need to be careful."

Jenkins heard a beeping noise from the console. Demir turned to the ship's radar, his eyes studying the glowing green light. "Call my sons," he said.

"What is it?"

"I do not know. But it is tracking our same coordinates."

"How close is it?"

"Not far. And moving fast. Too fast for us to make the strait." Demir pushed down on the throttle and Jenkins felt the boat lurch forward with the increased speed.

"Can you outrun it to Turkish waters?"

"If it is a Russian patrol boat, Turkish waters will not save you. The Russians do not respect territorial waters when they want something, and it appears they want you very much."

"How would they know?"

"I do not know. Perhaps they found your transponder. We had no choice but to leave it, and now they know why we were there in the first place. Go. Call my sons. If we are smart, we can deceive them. Tonight the fog is a blessing from Allah."

—

With Federov's urging, the Russian patrol boat made good time and had been tracking the Turkish fishing vessel, the *Esma*, for almost half an hour. The fishing vessel moved at a strong clip and was not changing course. The *Esma* was taking the shortest and most direct route back to Turkey.

"It has increased speed," Popov said to Federov. "They know we are coming. The captain is trying to make the Bosphorus strait."

"That cannot happen," Federov said.

"He cannot outrun us. We will intercept him in minutes." Popov paused. Then he said, "We will be in Turkish waters, Colonel."

Federov ignored the statement. "I want that boat stopped and searched. If it comes down to it, we will say it invaded Russian territorial waters and is smuggling cargo."

"And if the boat will not heed our warnings?" Popov asked.

"Then you will sink it," Federov said, "and take on board anyone who lives."

The patrol boat quickly closed the distance. The radar image, despite the thick fog complicating satellite communications, projected clearly what was most certainly the Turkish fishing trawler.

"I am picking up other ships, closer to the Turkish shore," Popov said.

"Turkey is filled with too many fishing boats," Federov said. "Ignore them. Stay on the trawler."

"I am going to try to hail him," Popov said.

"No," Federov said. "You will not."

"The *Esma* has radar," Popov said. "We are not a surprise to them."

"Then there is no point hailing them," Federov said.

"The boat is two hundred yards off our starboard side," a technician said.

"Slow your speed," Popov said, "but stay on course."

Another minute and the fishing trawler appeared, shrouded in the gray mist, still running hard.

"I must hail it," Popov said. "To not do so is to risk a collision."

"Issue a warning shot across its bow," Federov said without hesitation. He wanted the captain to understand the ramifications of his continued actions, that he was putting himself, his men, and his boat and livelihood at risk. Federov suspected the trawler captain to be nothing more than a well-paid courier who would feel no kinship to Jenkins. He had somehow fooled Popov, but he was not about to fool Federov.

Popov nodded to his men. The order given, a large echo exploded from a gun on the deck of the ship. Seconds later, Popov said, "It has slowed."

Federov nodded. "Now that the captain knows you are serious, you may hail him and advise him to stop his engines immediately. Tell him we wish to board his vessel."

Popov did as Federov instructed, and the fishing boat stopped. Federov pulled open the door and walked onto the deck. The temperature had warmed, though not much. He shoved his hands into his coat pockets as he descended the stairs and waited for the men to lower the Zodiac inflatable. When they had, he climbed down a ladder, along with Popov and two armed guards. Within seconds the skiff had crossed between the two vessels, and Federov was assisted onto the deck of the *Esma* by the captain and his son.

"You are the captain?" Federov spoke Russian to a stout man with a salt-and-pepper beard.

The captain looked at him as if confused, then looked to Popov, who repeated the question in Turkish.

"As I was several hours ago when you boarded my ship," the captain said. "Did you think things would change?"

"Search the ship, thoroughly," Federov said to the armed guards. Then he said, "For your sake, Captain, I hope things have not changed. I am Colonel Viktor Federov of the Russian Federal Security Service. Tell me, what were you doing in Russian waters?" Federov asked.

Again, Popov translated.

"I told the captain that our nets became tangled and we were working to untangle them."

"And you drifted all that way? Nearly to the Russian shoreline? On a calm night such as this? I find that difficult to comprehend," Federov said. Popov began to translate. "Enough," Federov said, eyeing the captain. "This man has played you for a fool. He understands every word I am saying. He could not have fished the Black Sea for so long and not have learned Russian. He chooses not to acknowledge you."

Federov turned to one of the guards. The man handed him the transponder. "What is even more perplexing is that this transponder was found and calculated to have been in the exact area that your vessel was initially boarded."

"It is not mine," the captain said, still speaking Turkish. "Though I thank you for retrieving it and being so determined to return it."

Popov translated.

"You were following this transponder's signal because it was leading you to your pickup."

"I was not following anything," the captain said, "and I do not pick up things out of the water unless they are fish."

"Where is your other son?" Popov asked.

"What?" the captain said.

"Where is your other son? There were three on board. Where is he?"

Kaplan did not answer.

"Find the other man," Federov said to the guards, then redirected his attention to the captain. "Do not play games with me, old man. My patience is waning and I am in no mood for your games."

After almost ten minutes the two guards returned from searching the ship. Both shook their heads. "There is no one else on board."

Federov continued to stare down the captain. "You will tell me where your son and Mr. Jenkins have gone, Captain, or I will order the patrol boat to sink your ship."

Kaplan spoke Turkish. "I do not think that would be wise."

"No?" Federov said, smiling at the man's hubris.

"No. We are in Turkish waters and tensions between our two countries have been high since the war in Syria, when your Mr. Putin called us Turks terrorists."

Federov looked to Popov, who translated. "Good point," Federov said. "So, maybe we will not fire upon you, Captain. Maybe we will simply ram your boat and blame this damn fog. A tragic accident."

"The inflatable is gone," one of Popov's men announced.

Federov said, "Tell me where your son and Mr. Jenkins have gone, and I will not sink your ship, Captain. Refuse and we will do so, and I will still get the information from you. What is it going to be?"

"And I told you, Colonel Federov, that would not be wise," the captain responded in Turkish. "I have alerted the Turkish coast guard to your presence in Turkish waters. They are old friends of mine. Check your radar. They are fast on their way. The way I see it, you have very little time to get back to your patrol boat and get back in Russian waters."

Federov appreciated the man's courage. "Perhaps your son can tell us where they have gone."

Emir shook his head. "I do not know."

"No?"

Federov removed his pistol and stepped to Emir, pressing the barrel to his forehead. "As you said, Captain, we don't have much time. I'm going to ask you again, just this once, and I want you to think very carefully before you answer me, in Russian. Yes? Now, where are your son and Mr. Jenkins going?"

36

The inflatable skimmed across the water's surface, the rigid hull slapping at the waves as the rubber bow bounced. Yusuf had the twenty-five-horsepower engine open full throttle, the boat going as fast as possible. Jenkins knelt on the rigid fiberglass floor in the middle of the boat to provide ballast. He wore a life jacket over a red survival suit. His hands gripped the rope holds on each side of the inflatable, and he felt each bounce reverberate in his back and his knees. Several times the waves were so jarring he thought the inflatable might flip. Those hours of warmth on the *Esma* now proved to be a curse, contrasting sharply with the cold air and the spray of frigid water.

Yusuf used a compass to keep the bearing he and his father had agreed upon. If he stayed on course, with the *Esma* running parallel to the inflatable, it would shield them from the Russian Coast Guard's radar, and he might just make it to the Bosphorus strait. The technique was called radar shadowing. Demir had learned it in the navy. If done correctly, it would allow Demir to defeat the Russian radar, which would see just the larger boat, the *Esma*, on its monitor. By the time the Russian patrol boat stopped the *Esma*, took the time to board it, and the additional time to notice Yusuf's absence, the inflatable boat would be half an hour closer to shore—if it didn't capsize first. At least that was the plan.

Jenkins's hands hurt from gripping the handholds, and the muscles throughout his arms and his core ached as he fought against inertia threatening to throw him overboard. The wind and the noise of the engine prevented the two men from speaking. The only thing Jenkins could do was look into the fog and hope he spotted an oncoming ship or floating debris before it killed them.

Thirty minutes after launching, Yusuf reduced speed, and the boat's shimmying and bouncing decreased enough that Jenkins dared to remove his hands from the holds. He balled his fingers into fists, then cupped his hands and blew hot air into them. As he did, the fog suddenly dissipated and Jenkins stared up at a blanket of stars sparkling in the blackened sky. The stars seemed to descend all the way to the water's surface, but a closer inspection revealed lights from hotels and houses littering hillsides rising on both sides of the tiny boat.

"The Bosphorus strait," Yusuf said. "I think, Mr. Jenkins, we might just make it."

Under other circumstances the setting would have warranted stopping the boat and taking time to appreciate the beauty. This was not that time. They passed beneath an enormous suspension bridge spanning between the two land masses. Lights atop the towers flashed a warning to approaching planes.

Jenkins kicked out his legs from beneath him and stretched his limbs. The waters had calmed considerably inside the strait. Yusuf slowed still further and fit the end of a metal rod with a blinking blue light into a hole. Jenkins quickly saw why. As they made their way through the strait, they passed large tankers, anchored in place, and cargo ships getting an early start to their day. Hit one of them and it would be like a gnat colliding with the windshield of a car.

Yusuf further reduced his speed as they approached a marina, and he deftly maneuvered around a rock outcropping providing protection for the boats moored there. That proved to be the easy part. A myriad of boats of different shapes, sizes, and colors crammed the marina, all seemingly moored without consideration to boat slips. Yusuf guided the inflatable around trawlers as large as the *Esma* and fishing boats no larger than their craft. There seemed to be no organization to the moorage—the boats stacked three and four deep, in the same slip, as if a tsunami had swept through, lifted the boats, and dropped them in a haphazard manner.

Yusuf maneuvered the inflatable boat to the far end of the marina and cut the engine, letting the rubber hull bump against a wooden boat docked in the last slip. He tied a mooring line to a cleat on the wooden boat and gripped the railing to pull the inflatable close. "Climb up," he said to Jenkins.

Jenkins stood slowly and uneasily, feeling like he was skating on ice. He grabbed the railing and lifted himself onto the boat's deck. Yusuf did the same, though with much greater ease.

"Come," Yusuf whispered.

The night air was perfectly still and quiet, without the sound of moving cars or voices. Somewhere in the distance, a foghorn bellowed. It sounded almost alive. Yusuf led Jenkins to the other side of the boat and jumped a three-foot gap to a concrete pier. Jenkins followed him past wooden benches to the street, where a small town awaited dawn—two- and three-story buildings, colorfully painted, with retail stores on the ground level and apartments above them. Cars lined the street, parked with as little attention to parking spots as the moored ships to their slips, and seemingly making the street too narrow for even a single car to pass.

Yusuf led Jenkins down the sidewalk to a commercial van. He moved to the front and reached under the bumper, snatching a key and unlocking the side door, sliding it open. Jenkins climbed inside. The interior smelled of vegetables and was packed with empty cardboard boxes and wooden crates.

"Stay down," Yusuf said. "The fewer who see you here the better."

Jenkins did as instructed.

Yusuf slammed shut the door. A moment later he opened the driver's door. The dome light remained dark. Yusuf slid behind the wheel, started the engine, and drove from the curb. "You can sit up now," he said. "But stay in the back, away from the windows."

Jenkins sat up, removed his survival suit, and rested against the crates to see out the windshield. The road ascended from the marina, cutting through foliage. Between the trees and shrubs, Jenkins got occasional glimpses of the strait and the lights of the anchored tankers.

"Where are we going?" Jenkins asked.

"If the patrol boat followed us, the Russians know we have you. If they stop my father he will stall for time, but he will not risk his son or his boat to save you."

"I understand."

"The Russians have many assets in Turkey, especially in Istanbul. Many of your spy novels have been written about Istanbul, and with good reason. Those assets will be searching for you, and for me. They will find me eventually, and I will have to tell them where I have taken you."

"Where are you taking me?"

"The only safe travel for you now is by bus. It will not be convenient, but you can buy a ticket without showing identification, and you can get off of one bus and onto another. Remember, good information is disinformation. So this you will need to do often. Leave false trails."

"Where am I going?"

"I will drive you to Taksim. There you will catch a bus to Izmir and from Izmir to Çeşme. Once in Çeşme, secure passage across the Aegean Sea to Chios."

"Greece," Jenkins said.

"You can practically skip a stone and hit Chios from Çeşme. From Chios you are on your own."

"How much time do I have?"

"The bus ride to Izmir will take seven to eight hours depending on how often you get on and off. To Çeşme is another hour. I will stay away for as long as possible, but no longer than midday. I cannot risk staying away longer. I worry for my family. When confronted, I will tell the Russians that I dropped you at a bus station in Istanbul, but that you refused to tell me where you were going."

"Don't lie for me," Jenkins said.

"I will not. I will stay away as long as I can, and I will do my best to stall them, but if they threaten my family, I will tell them that you are bound for Çeşme. Hopefully it will be enough time for you to get there and get out of the country."

Thirty minutes later, the landscape changed dramatically. The highway continued past hillsides covered with apartment buildings. Another fifteen minutes and Yusuf exited the highway, driving the surface streets of a city awakening. He drove into a large, open square and pulled the van to the curb.

"Across the street. You see the white awning? You can buy a bus ticket from the kiosk when it opens. Look for Istanbul Çevre Yolu. Remember to get on and off the bus frequently. Disinformation. Be very careful."

"I have no lira," Jenkins said. "Only rubles."

"You can exchange your rubles. There is a bank, just down the street."

"Thank you for your help, Yusuf. I will never forget you, your father, or your brother."

"I'm afraid that would be a mistake, Mr. Jenkins . . . for all of us."

37

Jenkins made himself disappear in Gezi Park, across the street from where Yusuf had dropped him, while he waited for the businesses to open. He sat with his back against a tree and his knees pulled to his chest. Convenience stores and fruit vendors were the first to open, at four thirty in the morning. Cars soon appeared, along with a smattering of people. He stood and massaged the pain in his knees before he crossed the street. He did not go to the bus kiosk. He walked down the street, past retail stores on the bottom floor of five-story apartment buildings, to the business Yusuf had pointed out, Alo Döviz. He didn't know what it meant, but there were two ATMs and behind them a glass-enclosed counter with the universal sign for money—the dollar sign. As he approached, Jenkins saw the flags of the United Kingdom, the United States, and Russia. He handed the man behind the counter 10,000 rubles. He would need more, but too much would make him too easily remembered.

The man counted the rubles, pressed the buttons on a calculator, turned the machine, and showed Jenkins the conversion: 850 Turkish lira. Jenkins nodded. *"Spasibo,"* he said. Jenkins held up his hand, as if holding a cell phone to his ear, and asked where he could purchase a phone, speaking Russian.

The man pointed down the street and indicated Jenkins should veer to his right at the corner. *"Yuva iletisim,"* he said.

Jenkins took his money, thanked the man, and proceeded down the street, finding the store. Inside, he explained to a young man, again using Russian and again with some difficulty, that he wanted to purchase two burner cell phones with international calling plans that would allow him to call other countries. After further discussion, the man directed him to something called a Mobal World Talk & Text Phone for 112 lira, which was roughly nineteen dollars. Jenkins declined the young man's attempts to upsell him, said the phones were simply for business calls, and departed the store with two of the Mobal World cells.

With the phones in the pocket of his coat, Jenkins hurried back to the bus station. Again, he didn't immediately approach. He watched the people near the station, looking for anyone standing about, trying to look busy. Seeing no one suspicious, he approached the counter and repeated what Yusuf told him to say. The teller took his lira and issued him a ticket, then stood up, speaking Turkish and gesturing emphatically to a bus at the curb. Jenkins deduced from the man's gesticulations that he had to hurry, and he took the ticket and ran across the street. He reached the bus just as it was about to leave. The driver opened the door, Jenkins stepped up, showed the man his ticket, and took a seat toward the rear of the bus.

He wasn't sure what he had been expecting, but the bus was surprisingly modern—the interior temperature and the seats comfortable. Jenkins sat back, feeling fatigue settling into his joints. He put his head against the window and closed his eyes, hoping for even a few hours of precious sleep, though conscious of Yusuf's instructions that he get on and off the bus frequently. Disinformation.

—

Yusuf stayed away from his home for as long as he dared—enough time, he hoped, for Charles Jenkins to be well on his way out of Istanbul. He returned to Rumeli Kavaği at just after noon, and wound his way along the road above the marina to one of the homes his father had built on the cliffs above the Bosphorus strait. His brother and his father lived in houses down the street. He parked the van, descended the stairs to the gated courtyard, and crossed to his front door. The gate slapped closed and clicked shut behind him.

Yusuf opened the front door but stopped advancing when he saw his wife seated in the living room, the plate-glass window behind her offering a spectacular view of the strait, though that was not the focus of his attention. His father and his brother also stood in the room, along with three men. Yusuf's three children were, thankfully, at school.

"Ah," one of the men said. "So good of you to join us, Yusuf. We've been awaiting your arrival."

"Who are you?" Yusuf said. "And what do you want?"

The man smiled. "You know who we are."

"I know you're Russian."

"Yes," the man said. "We are the Russians who stopped your father's ship in search of Mr. Jenkins. Mr. Jenkins has committed serious crimes in Russia, including the murder of Russian FSB officers."

"I know nothing of his crimes," Yusuf said.

"No?"

"No."

"But you know where he is?"

Yusuf shook his head. "At the moment I do not."

The man smiled but it had a tired quality to it. He pulled his gun from his holster and held it to Yusuf's wife's head. She cried. "Do you really want to do this?" the man asked.

"No," Yusuf said. "I do not. But how can I tell you what I do not know?"

"Where did you take Mr. Jenkins?"

"That is a different question. I took him to the bus terminal in Taksim. He told me that is where he wished to go so I took him there."

"And where is he going?"

Yusuf looked from Federov to his father and his brother. His father nodded.

"He said he intended to leave the country through Greece."

"More specific, please."

"I can only assume he is headed to the Turkish coast and will seek to get across the Aegean Sea. I do not know where he intends to go once he is there."

"And did you help Mr. Jenkins obtain any travel papers to assist him in his efforts?"

"No. I swear. I just drove him to the bus station. That is the last I saw of him."

The man nodded to the others and they made their way to the door. He lingered near a shelf and picked up a picture of Emir and his family, Yusuf and his family, and his father and his mother. Then he turned to Demir. "You have a beautiful family, Captain. In the future I believe it would be prudent if you were to spend more time with them."

Jenkins's head bumped against the bus window, awakening him. He quickly sat up, momentarily disoriented and confused. He looked around the bus, but others also appeared to be sleeping or not paying him any attention. He had no idea how long he had slept or how far they had driven. When the bus slowed and exited the road, Jenkins pulled out a map he'd picked up at the bus terminal from the inside pocket of his jacket and checked his watch to determine how long they had traveled. He ran a finger along the bus route, and concluded they were entering the city of Bursa. Signs soon confirmed his deduction.

The bus pulled into a terminal and stopped with the hiss of air brakes. The driver shouted in Turkish and the passengers made their way to the exits at the front and rear of the bus.

Jenkins stepped off with his eyes scanning the terminal. It appeared to be in the middle of a dirt lot. He made his way to where several taxi drivers stood outside beat-up cabs and approached the first driver in line. "Bursa?" he said.

The man responded in Turkish. Jenkins tried Russian but the man shook his head. Thinking for a moment, he spoke English, unfolded the map, and pointed to Bursa. The taxi driver smiled and nodded. Jenkins jumped into the back seat.

They drove for approximately fifteen minutes, into what Jenkins surmised from the congestion to be downtown Bursa. The man spoke from the front seat, undoubtedly asking Jenkins where he wanted to go. Jenkins saw signs atop buildings for several hotels and pointed to one of the hotels situated on a busy intersection congested with cars, buses, and retail stores. The driver stopped at the entrance. Jenkins checked the fare on the meter and paid the man a generous tip, one he would remember. Then Jenkins stepped out, dodged pedestrians, and went inside the Central Hotel.

Speaking English, he asked for a room for two nights. The desk clerk asked Jenkins for a credit card. Jenkins shook his head. He took out his money and said he would pay in cash. The man smiled and nodded his approval.

"Sorun Değil," he said.

Jenkins smiled in reply.

Key in hand, Jenkins made his way to the elevators and ascended to the third floor. His room was second from the end on the left. The interior was Spartan but clean. Jenkins removed a burner phone from his coat pocket and tossed his jacket onto his bed. He called David Sloane, uncertain of the time difference between Seattle and Turkey. Sloane sounded groggy when he answered the phone.

"David."

He heard the sound of someone getting up. "Charlie?"

"Is Alex at your house?"

"Yeah, she's here with CJ."

"How are they doing?"

"They're worried about you. We all are. Are you all right?"

"I don't have a lot of time."

"I'll get her."

Jenkins heard more commotion, then a voice that made his heart soar. "Charlie?" Alex said.

"Hey. You're okay? CJ's okay?"

"We're fine. Where are you? How are you?"

"I'm on my way home, but I'm going to need some help. Do you remember Uncle Frank from Mexico City?"

"Who?"

"Do you remember me telling you about my Uncle Frank in Mexico City, the man with an artistic flair for documents? You and I visited him on one of our trips back to Mexico City, maybe eight or nine years ago."

There was a pause. Then Alex said, "Yeah. Yeah. I remember. The forger."

"He'd be in his seventies now. He owned that antique store in Mexico City. *Antigüedades y tesoros.*"

"Antiquities and Treasures."

"Yes—165 República del Salvador."

"Hang on. Hang on. I have to get a pen. Okay, repeat that."

Jenkins did. "I'm going to need at least one passport," he said. "Canadian. And I'm going to need someone to bring it to me."

"Where are you?"

"Turkey. I'll provide more explicit instructions when I get to Greece."

"Charlie, I can't fly. I'm on bed rest."

"I know. David is going to have to do it," he said.

"David can't do it, Charlie. If they see you we have to assume I am being watched and they know I am here. They'll follow David."

Jenkins sat on the edge of the bed, rubbing his forehead, trying to think despite his exhaustion. Then he heard another voice through the phone.

"I'll do it."

38

Federov smoked a cigarette as he watched the buses arrive and depart the Bursa bus terminal, spitting black petrol smoke out their exhaust pipes. Taxi drivers shouted "Taksi" outside their worn and tired-looking cars and vans. Simon Alekseyov moved from one driver to the next, showing each Charles Jenkins's photograph. Dressed in a suit and tie, Alekseyov stood out like the proverbial sore thumb. Most men wore jeans or slacks, untucked long-sleeve shirts, and leather coats. They looked as if they hadn't shaved in days. The women, too, wore casual dress, though a few wore hijabs and even fewer the burka with the headdress.

Federov took a drag on his cigarette and blew smoke out the open car window. The weather had warmed to a comfortable fifteen degrees Celsius, but it had also produced a brown haze that hovered over the bus terminal.

Alekseyov pulled open thc passenger door of the rental car. It gave a metallic snap. He got in, shaking his head. *"Nichego,"* he said. *Nothing.* He put the picture of Jenkins on the dash of the car, and he and Federov continued their wait for the arrival of the next round of buses and taxi drivers.

Federov knew Jenkins had taken at least one bus. The ticket agent at the bus terminal in Taksim recalled Jenkins and remembered that he had purchased a ticket first thing that morning when the booth opened.

Jenkins had paid lira, and the man said he looked to have a significant amount. He also said Jenkins had to run to catch the first bus out of Istanbul.

On a whim, Federov had found a currency exchange office down the street from the bus terminal and showed the teller Jenkins's picture. The man recalled Jenkins exchanging 10,000 Russian rubles that morning and said he had assumed Jenkins to be Russian both because of the rubles and because he spoke Russian. The man also said Jenkins asked for directions to a store to purchase a cell phone, and he had directed Jenkins down the street to a store in one of the alleys.

The store clerk also identified Jenkins from his picture, and said Jenkins purchased two burner phones, each loaded with roughly thirty minutes of call time. He said Jenkins expressed interest in making calls out of the country. Federov left the store and called his contact in the United States. Federov's contact told him that Jenkins might be attempting to reach his wife and tell her of his plans for getting out of Turkey.

Federov then tracked down and spoke to the driver of the first bus to have left Istanbul that morning. The man specifically recalled Jenkins getting onto the bus because Jenkins had nearly missed it, and he recalled Jenkins because of his size. He said Jenkins did not request any unplanned stops, and that his bus had emptied when he reached the station in Bursa. In case Jenkins had gotten back onto the bus, or a different bus, Federov had agents in Çeşme asking the bus drivers arriving in that city if they recalled seeing him. If Jenkins hadn't gotten back on the bus, then he'd likely taken a cab at the bus terminal, maybe to lay low in Bursa for a day or two, though with roughly 850 lira, he also could have had the cab take him all the way to Çeşme.

"There's another one." Alekseyov pointed to another taxi pulling into the bus terminal and parking at the back of the line. He picked up the picture from the dashboard and crossed the parking lot to the taxi stand. Moments after showing the driver Jenkins's photo, Alekseyov turned his head and waved his arm for Federov to come quickly. Federov stepped from the car, took a final drag on his cigarette, and flicked the butt across the lot as he walked toward them.

Alekseyov stepped to Federov as he approached. "He recalls him."

Federov felt a jolt of nervous energy. "Does he speak Russian?"

"Little," Alekseyov said.

Federov took the photograph and showed it to the driver, speaking Russian. *"Vy pomnite etogo cheloveka?" You recall this man?*

"Evet," the man said, nodding. *"Ono bu sabah Bursa şehir merkezindeki biro tele götürdüm." I drove him to a hotel in downtown Bursa this morning.*

Federov looked to Alekseyov for help. "He said something about driving him to a hotel in Bursa." Alekseyov looked to the driver. *"Kogda?"* he asked, then caught himself, struggling with the translation. *"Ne zaman?" When?*

"Bu sabah," the man said.

"This morning," Alekseyov said to Federov.

"Ask him where he took him," Federov said. "To what hotel?"

"Otel neydi?"

The driver looked at Alekseyov, then at Federov, and held out his hand, rubbing his thumb and index finger together, a universal sign. Federov nodded. Alekseyov pulled out forty lira from his pocket and handed it to the man.

"Central Hotel," the man said.

Federov turned without another word and walked back to their rental car. As Alekseyov caught up, Federov pulled open the driver's door and spoke across the roof. "Get me the directions," he said, "but first let everyone in the area know to keep an eye out for him. Tell them not to go near the hotel until I arrive."

Twenty minutes later, Federov drove past the Central Hotel on a busy street in downtown Bursa. The street fed into a roundabout littered with honking city buses, vans, scooters, and other vehicles seemingly paying no attention to lanes. On the sidewalk, vendors hawked their wares, adding to the cacophony of sounds. Federov took the roundabout, then backtracked until he found parking one hundred yards past the hotel, in front of a bank ATM.

"Tell the others we will meet them here," Federov said. He lowered his window and shook free another cigarette. Before he could light it, a bank employee came out of the front door of the bank, gesturing and telling Federov to move his car. The employee pointed to a sign Federov could not read and did not care to. Federov nodded to Alekseyov, who got out of the car and intercepted the man, speaking to him in animated Turkish before handing him a few lira. The man considered the notes, shrugged his shoulders, and left without further complaint.

Eventually, four other agents met Federov and Alekseyov. Federov sent one of the men to scout the exterior of the hotel for exits Jenkins might use to escape. He returned ten minutes later.

"On the far side of the hotel there is a glass door leading to an alley with restaurants and outdoor tables and shops. It is crowded at the moment. The near side abuts a hardware store. There are no exits. There is a third exit at the rear of the hotel, but it also leads to the same alley."

Federov instructed two men to position themselves at a table where they could see the door at the back of the hotel, and the other two to sit somewhere with a view of the door on the far side of the hotel. He and Alekseyov would enter the hotel through the front door. When the men were in place, Federov and Alekseyov approached the reception desk. The hotel looked to be a traveler's rest stop, clean but nothing fancy, a place to sleep for the night for a modest price. Brochures stuffed in a rack just to the right of the counter advertised local activities, from the zoo to sightseeing bus tours. The tours perhaps explained the innumerable small white buses cluttering the street outside the hotel. The interior smelled of Turkish cigarettes, and Turkish music played from ceiling speakers.

At the counter, a man in an open-collared white dress shirt looked up and greeted them. Alekseyov slid Jenkins's photograph across the counter and said, "We are looking for this man and understand he rented a room here this morning."

The man removed a brochure from one of several slots on the counter and placed it over the photograph. Then his eyes shifted to his right, and Federov saw a camera bolted to the ceiling, the lens directed at the front desk. The clerk looked at Alekseyov and Federov in much the same manner as the taxi driver. He recognized Jenkins, but to breach hotel policy would come at a price.

Alekseyov picked up the brochure as if contemplating it, turned his back to the camera, and subtly placed twenty lira and the photograph inside the fold. He set it back on the counter. The man opened the brochure but his look conveyed he was not impressed. He did not pick up the lira. "I do not know," he said. "We get many guests. He may be familiar."

Federov nodded and Alekseyov pulled back the brochure and repeated the process. This time, the man did not hesitate. He picked up the brochure and casually slid the lira into his pants pocket while considering the photograph inside the brochure. "Yes," he said looking up at them and keeping his voice low. "He came in this morning, spoke English, and rented a room for two nights. He paid cash."

Federov's heart pounded. "Did you see him leave the hotel?"

"I did not. He looked exhausted. I assume he is sleeping."

"What room?" Federov said.

The man looked again to Alekseyov and placed the brochure on the counter. Federov placed his hand over the brochure before Alekseyov could pick it up, and glared at the clerk. The man got the message. He turned to his computer and quickly typed. Then he picked up a pen and wrote "312" on the back of Jenkins's photograph.

"I have lost the key to my room and will need another," Federov said.

The man slid a room key into a machine to activate it, then handed the key, and the photograph inside the brochure, to Federov.

Federov walked to the elevator bank just behind the counter and deposited the brochure in a garbage can. They stepped on board the elevator. When it stopped on the third floor, he nodded for Alekseyov to step off, then he switched off the elevator before he also stepped into the hall. He removed his gun and pressed it against his thigh. Alekseyov mimicked him. The two walked down the hall, considering room numbers on doors. Room 312 was on the left side of the hall, which meant the windows faced the street. Federov hoped Jenkins had not seen them entering, but if he had, and if he had attempted to flee, the other men would know it. He and Alekseyov took up positions on each side of the door, guns now raised.

Federov removed the key from his pocket and slid it through the lock mechanism. The light flashed green. He pressed down on the handle, pushed the door open, and entered quickly, gun in front of him.

39

David Sloane paced the hardwood floor behind his family room couch and shook his head. He repeated himself, one arm raised as if to say, *Speak to the hand.* "No. No way."

Music filtered through the room from speakers in the ceiling—loud enough to drown out their voices, in case anyone was listening, but not so loud as to wake CJ, who was sleeping upstairs. Sloane had also lowered the blinds.

He talked to Jake, who stood on the throw rug between the two white leather couches, imploring Sloane to listen to reason.

"Alex can't go, Dad." Alex sat on a couch. She looked tired and forlorn. "She's on bed rest."

"I'll go," Sloane said. "I can go."

"You can't go, especially not now," Jake said. "If Alex was followed here, or to the office, they already know who you are. It would take someone about ten seconds to look up who owns this house, if they haven't already. Besides, you're not exactly anonymous, given your career, and Charlie worked for you. If you go, they'll follow you. They wouldn't even have to follow you. They'd just look for your name and determine where you were flying and on what airline and what flight."

"You can't go, Jake. No. No."

"I'm twenty-three years old. I'm not a kid. I can handle myself, and I can handle this."

Sloane continued to shake his head. "Not this you can't. These people are professionals."

Alex spoke. "Your father is right, Jake. It's too dangerous."

Jake shook his head. "It's dangerous for anyone, but it's the least dangerous for me. They aren't going to expect me." He turned to Sloane. "I have a different last name than you, and they won't know it. You can buy a ticket to some other place, South America or Japan—be a decoy—and I'll get a ticket under the name Jacob Carter."

Alex turned to Sloane. "He actually makes sense."

"I don't care. He's not going."

"We can't just leave Charlie," Jake said. "We have to do something. I'm the only one—"

"I don't intend to just leave him," Sloane said. "And I'm not losing you the way that I lost . . ." Sloane caught himself and took a breath. After several seconds he continued. "If I can't go, we'll hire someone to go."

"Then you put that person at risk. And you heard Charlie—his contact in Mexico City isn't going to trust just anyone. We can't even call to confirm he's still there. Charlie said he doesn't own a phone, and he would never acknowledge himself to someone over the phone. It has to be in person. If we send just anyone, and this guy, Uncle Frank, says no, the guy will leave. He has no stake in this beyond what you pay him."

"Why would the guy in Mexico City, if he's even still alive, trust you?" Sloane said.

"Because Charlie's my godfather, and I'm young and naïve and desperate, and I'm not going to take no for an answer."

Sloane stopped pacing, pulled out a chair, and sat at the kitchen table. He had his hands folded, as if in prayer. After a moment he looked to Alex. "What about someone else who Charlie knows?"

"What are you going to tell them, Dad? That you need them to pick up a package and 'Oh, by the way, someone might be trying to kill you'?" Jake said. "I'll be careful. I'll take a taxi from the airport and I'll double back to make sure I'm not being followed before I go into the store."

"And if you are being followed?"

"If I am then I will abort, and we'll think of something else."

"How do we stay in touch?"

"In the morning I'll buy burner phones for you, me, and Alex. Alex can call Charlie and tell him our plan."

Sloane took a deep breath.

"They aren't going to try and kill me, even if they could somehow follow me. They want Charlie, not me. The smart play would be to allow me to get the papers, then follow me to wherever Charlie wants me to drop them."

Sloane looked from Jake to Alex. "He's right, isn't he?"

Alex nodded. "I don't want him to do it either, David, but, yeah, he's right. They don't know him and even if they figured it out, they don't want him. They want Charlie."

"There's a chance it will work," Jake said. "If you go, there's no chance. Our best bet is to use you to draw them away and increase my odds. They'll follow you to South America. You can lead them on a wild goose chase, then get on the plane and come back."

Sloane nodded. It did make the most sense. "You sure you want to do this?"

"Yeah," Jake said. "I do."

"There's another reason why this makes sense," Alex said. "I don't know what's going on, but if Charlie makes it back home, he said he could need a lawyer, and if you help him to do this, to break the law, you'd definitely be disqualified from representing him, and very likely disbarred."

Sloane nodded. He hadn't thought of that either. He turned to Jake. "Can you get computer access at Seattle U?"

"Absolutely."

"Go to the library, to a terminal unconnected to you, and look up flights to Mexico City leaving tomorrow. Purchase a ticket using your own credit card and go to the airport straight from school. Take Uber or Lyft. Don't drive. Make sure you're not followed. If at any time you suspect you're being watched or followed, you promise me you'll abort."

"I promise," Jake said.

He looked at his watch, then at Alex. "I'm assuming you have instructions for him, things to do and to look out for?"

Alex nodded and looked at her watch. "I'll teach him everything I can in the time that we have."

Sloane moved toward the kitchen. "I'll make coffee."

40

Viktor Federov swung the barrel of the gun left, then right. The hotel room was empty, the bed made. There was no closet door, just an area with a clothing bar and unused hangers. He heard water running in the bathroom. The shower. Light leaked from beneath the door. Federov motioned for Alekseyov to move to the side next to the door handle. Federov stood on the opposite side of the doorframe from Alekseyov.

He nodded and Alekseyov reached for the door handle. Unlocked. He gently pushed on the door. It snapped open and gave a small click. Federov stepped in and swung the barrel of his gun at the shower stall. Water sprayed against the glass and shower pan, with no one to deflect it.

Federov turned to the sink. On the counter was an opened bar of soap and the paper in which it had been wrapped. Someone had used the soap to write on the mirror.

Missed me.

The bus pulled to the curb in Çeşme at just after 6:00 p.m., one of half a dozen buses to arrive. Tourists disembarked, some dragging roller suitcases behind them. The wheels on the cobblestone street rumbled like small jet engines. The sun had nearly set, leaving a reddish-orange winter light and cool temperatures. The Turkish flag, red with a white star and crescent, hung lifeless from a flagpole. Behind it, the bare masts of sailboats protruded above a crowded marina. The street looked to have been recently renovated, with a center divider of stone pavers, immature palm trees—eight to ten feet in height—and decorative streetlights.

Charles Jenkins stepped from the bus wearing a full-length black burka that stopped just above his sandals. The headdress made it difficult to see, but with practice getting on and off buses, he could get by without stumbling.

Jenkins knew Yusuf would have had to tell Federov that Jenkins was on his way by bus to Çeşme. He also knew Federov would make his way to Istanbul, find the bus terminal, and, sooner or later, catch up with him, or with his bus. His detour to Bursa was intended to convince Federov that Jenkins, knowing Yusuf owed him no loyalty and would give up Jenkins's travel plans, had changed how and where he intended to get out of Turkey.

After leaving an easy trail for Federov to follow, Jenkins had walked out the back of the hotel to an alley of restaurants and shops. He made his way to a Muslim clothing store. A woman on the bus had been dressed in a burka, giving him the initial idea. He told the man behind the store counter that he wanted to buy a burka for his daughter, who was almost as tall as Jenkins. The man did not have a garment long enough at the store, but he directed Jenkins to a store close by that did. Jenkins purchased the garment and the sandals, found an empty alley, and slipped them on, along with the headdress. Fully concealed, he made his way to a bus stop, and took a circuitous route to double back to Çeşme. Along the route, Jenkins got off the bus twice, wasted time, then boarded a different bus. He identified two men watching the terminal in Izmir, but nowhere else along the line. He hoped Federov had called off the dogs after he'd arrived in Bursa and read Jenkins's message on the bathroom mirror.

Jenkins crossed to the opposite side of the street, to the stores that apparently did not close until after the arrival of the last tourist buses.

He walked past sparsely populated restaurants emitting mouth-watering smells, and newly constructed two- and three-story apartment buildings wedged in the sloping hillside of red rock, shrubs, and small, spindly trees. He ducked into what looked to be a novelty shop playing loud Turkish music. At the back of the store he found a cheap backpack, bottled water, candy bars, crackers, sunglasses, a red baseball hat with the Turkish flag sewn on the bill, and a black cap with Turkish lettering. He did his best not to speak and not to display his hands any longer than necessary to the woman at the register. This time it was not his intent to draw attention to himself.

Outside, he slid behind temporary fencing for a development under construction and quickly pulled off the headdress and long black dress. The cool air against his perspiring skin felt refreshing. He rolled the clothes into a ball and tucked them into the backpack. Then he tugged the bright-red ball cap low on his head, slid on sunglasses, and made his way out from behind the fence, eventually returning to the marina.

He was immediately discouraged. Most of the vessels were not fishing boats, but pleasure yachts, and clearly owned by people wealthy enough to decline a bribe to take him to Chios, which he could see just across the Aegean Sea. He walked the pier, trying to look like a tourist admiring the impressive boats. He stopped when he saw a man dressed in shorts, despite the brisk temperature, hosing off the deck of a yacht. The man smiled as Jenkins neared, and he held the hose to the side so as not to spray him.

Jenkins asked the man if he spoke English. The man responded with a universal sign, two fingers an inch apart—a little. Jenkins asked if he spoke Russian. The man shook his head and gave an emphatic "No."

"Español?" Jenkins asked.

A shrug. *"Un poco."*

"Es este tu barco?" Is this your boat? Jenkins asked, pointing to the yacht.

The man laughed. *"Ya me gustaría."* *I wish.* In broken Spanish and some English, he told Jenkins he worked at the marina—a good sign—and that the owners came mostly in the spring and summer.

"Espero ir a pescar mañana. ¿Conoces algún barco que me pueda llevar?" I'm looking to go fishing tomorrow. Do you know of any boats that will take me?

"Here? No," the man said in English.

It was as Jenkins suspected.

The man pointed north. *"Por la calle." Down the street.*

"Por la calle?" Jenkins asked.

"*Sí. Por la calle.* Fishing."

Jenkins looked in the direction of the man's outstretched hand. Down the street, perhaps half a mile, he could see boats moored in a much smaller marina.

"Early," the man said in accented English. He pointed at the sky. "*Karanlik* . . . dark."

"Dark," Jenkins repeated, then understood. "*Sí. Mañana.* Early. When it is still dark. *Muchas gracias.*"

41

Jake stepped from his plane into the terminal at Benito Juárez International Airport in Mexico City after a night without sleep. He was running on adrenaline. It had been forty-two degrees when he left Seattle. Early morning in Mexico City, the terminal already felt warm. Still, he didn't dare take off his jacket. Alex had sewn a packet of documents into the lining. She'd also sewn $5,000 into the bottom of his backpack, which Jake would use if he could find the man Charlie referred to as "Uncle Frank."

He followed terminal signs to immigration and customs, had his passport stamped, and located an exchange service. Alex said American dollars were widely accepted in Mexico City, but it would be less conspicuous if Jake used pesos. He then found a duty-free shop and purchased a bottle of Johnny Walker Blue Label Scotch, which Jenkins said had been Uncle Frank's favorite drink. Given the price, it would be anyone's favorite drink.

They had booked David on a fourteen-hour slog from Seattle to Costa Rica with a five-hour layover in Charlotte, North Carolina, hoping to give Jake a several-hour head start. At least that had been the plan.

Jake slung the backpack over his shoulder and, speaking a combination of broken English and even more broken Spanish, he hailed a brown-and-tan taxi outside the terminal. Alex had written down several key phrases and addresses. Having lived in Mexico City, she was familiar with its neighborhoods. Her intent was to send Jake from one side of the city to the other. In each instance, Jake was to walk the neighborhood using the techniques Alex had quickly taught him. She told him to window-shop, focusing on the reflections across the street to determine if he was being followed. She further told him that he should go into and out of stores frequently to determine if anyone paralleled his movements. After ten to fifteen minutes, he'd get into another cab, go to the next destination, and repeat the process.

He did this four times, seeing no one suspicious. At just before 9:00 a.m., he made his way to what the Internet confirmed to still be *Antigüedades y tesoros* in the historic center of Mexico City.

The area reminded Jake a bit of Seattle's Pioneer Square, with low-level brick-and-stone buildings, retail stores, and mature trees in the sidewalks. Jake exited the cab across the street from a stone-and-brick building. With wrought-iron railing across second-floor balconies, it looked like a jail from the Old West. He walked across the street and confirmed the name inscribed on the glass door in antique script: *Antigüedades y tesoros*. Jake breathed his first sigh of relief. Still in business. Hopefully, Uncle Frank was also.

Rather than immediately enter, he strolled the sidewalk. He couldn't window-shop. There were no store windows. The proprietors rolled up metal gates and set out fruits and vegetables in sidewalk stands. They hung T-shirts, hammocks, and other trinkets to attract tourists, then swept their sidewalks with odd-looking brooms while shouting to one another. At the end of the block Jake crossed the street, turned quickly down an alley, and doubled back around the block. No one appeared to be following him or paying him any attention.

He walked back up the far side of the street and entered *Antigüedades y tesoros*. A buzzer announced his entry. Alex had told Jake to be sure no one else came into the store after him—what she had described as an intended coincidence. No one did.

The interior smelled of wood dust and was packed with a menagerie of antiques—everything from furniture to toys, knives, lighters, and jewelry in locked glass cases. Jake walked wood-plank floors as if browsing while considering the man seated behind the counter. He smiled and acknowledged Jake, then went back to polishing a silver pot. He looked a bit like one of Jake's law school professors, dressed in a comfortable brown sweater over a collared shirt, round glasses, and long hair. This was not the man Alex had described. For one, he was far too young. When Jake felt confident, he approached the glass counter.

"Hola," he said. *"Habla inglés?"*

"Sí." The man smiled and put down the silver pot and rag, which held a strong chemical odor. "How can I help you, amigo?"

"I'm looking for someone," Jake said, which drew a smile but no verbal response. "My uncle, Charles Jenkins, told me I could find someone in this store he called Uncle Frank."

Uncle Frank, Charlie had told Alex, was the code name for a man named José. The man behind the counter shook his head and wrinkled his forehead. "I've never heard of anyone by that name," he said. "Are you sure you have the right store?"

"I understand Uncle Frank would be in his seventies, maybe early eighties. Charlie knew him when he worked here in Mexico City. Have you worked in this store long?"

The man nodded. "I have, but I don't know an Uncle Frank. What did you say was your uncle's name?"

"Charlie. Charles Jenkins. He said Uncle Frank was about five feet eight, bald, and wore round wire-rim glasses, like yours. Oh, and he said Uncle Frank liked to drink good Scotch."

The man grinned and leaned against the counter. "You're describing my father," he said. "But his name was José. He owned the store before me. And he liked good Scotch."

Jake felt great relief. He put his backpack on the counter, talking as he unzipped a pouch and pulled out the bottle, setting it on the counter.

"My uncle said to tell Uncle Frank . . . José . . . that I need to talk to him, that it's important."

The man put out a hand. "Slow down, amigo. Slow down. I'm sorry, but my father died seven years ago of lung cancer."

The words felt like a punch in the gut. "He's dead?"

"Sí."

Jake felt paralyzed by the news, not sure what to do.

"Are you all right?" the man asked.

"I'm sorry. I've had a long night and a long morning. He's dead, your father?"

"Sí."

Jake stepped back from the counter, feeling as if he might throw up. "I'm sorry to have bothered you."

"It's no bother, amigo. Was your uncle a friend of my father's?"

"He was," Jake said, still stepping away from the counter.

"Amigo." The man held up the Scotch bottle. "Your Scotch."

"I can't take it on the plane." Jake shrugged. "Enjoy it." He started for the door.

"Did your uncle have a message for my father?"

Jake thought about what Charlie had told Alex when he'd called on the burner phone, but he wasn't about to tell that to the man's son.

"He said that your father was an artist. He said he'd made several purchases from him when he worked here in Mexico City."

"My father an artist?" Again, the man smiled and shook his head like he'd never heard this before. "My father sold antiques all his life. Maybe he sold some artwork to your uncle?"

"Maybe," Jake said.

"What did your uncle do here in Mexico?"

"I'm not sure," Jake said.

The man shook his head and shrugged. Then he picked up the silver pot and returned to polishing it. "I'm sorry you came all this way. Why didn't your uncle call first?"

"I guess he should have," Jake said, and he walked quickly out the door.

The cool air assaulted him. He sucked in several deep breaths. He felt light-headed and nauseated from a lack of food, a lack of sleep, and a lack of options. He needed to eat something to settle his stomach. The area continued to awaken, more cars driving past, and more people walking the sidewalk, some carrying plastic bags. Jake also needed to call Alex and let her know Uncle Frank was a dead end, so she and Charlie could make other arrangements, if they could. He walked down the street, stopping when he came to a lime-green building with a red neon coffee cup illuminated in the window above a display of pastries.

Inside, he ordered a coffee and two cinnamon rolls from a young woman with red hair and freckles, who looked anything but Mexican. She spoke to him in Spanish but Jake shrugged and said he could not understand her.

She made hand gestures. *"Aquí o para ir."*

She was asking if he wanted the coffee and pastries to go or to eat in the store. He saw several small tables pushed up against the store wall, all of them empty.

"Para tomar aquí, por favor," he said. *"Gracias."* He looked about. *"Dónde está el baño?"*

She pointed to the rear of the store.

Jake carried his backpack into the bathroom and shut and latched the door. He considered his face in the mirror above the sink. He looked pale, dark bags developing under his eyes. He turned on the faucet and splashed several handfuls of cold water on his face, chilling his skin, then drying it with coarse brown paper towels.

"Now what?" he said to his reflection.

He checked his watch, which was still set to Seattle time. It was seven thirty in the morning. He'd call Alex and tell her they needed another option. He pulled open the door and walked back into the café. The woman stood behind the counter looking at him with an odd expression. As Jake neared his table he noted only one pastry on his plate and no coffee.

He looked to the woman, using hand gestures. *"¿Dónde está?"* he said. *"Café. Dos."*

The woman pointed to the door. *"El hombre lo tomó."*

"El hombre?"

"Sí. Carlos."

Jake looked to the door and felt an adrenaline rush. Had he been followed after all? *"Carlos? Quién es Carlos?"*

She pointed to the door, smiling. *"Carlos. Antigüedades y tesoros."*

His mind churned. *"Habló . . .* anything? *Carlos habló?"*

"Sí. Dijo que no le gusta el whisky tan temprano en la mañana, pero que le encantaría una taza de café."

Jake didn't understand. He took out his phone and opened a Spanish-to-English translation app he'd downloaded before leaving Seattle. *"Repetir?"* He held his phone out to the woman, and she repeated what she had said into his phone. The app translated to English. "He doesn't like Scotch this early, but he would love coffee and a pastry." Jake looked to the woman and she again pointed to the door. *"Antigüedades y tesoros."*

"Gracias, señorita. Gracias." Jake gathered his backpack.

"Señor." The woman stepped out from behind the counter holding a coffee cup to go and a white bag. *"Dos."*

42

Jenkins rose at four thirty the following morning after another long night with only a couple of hours of fitful sleep. He'd found a hotel room on a hillside above the second marina and headed out the door, hoping people in Çeşme fished as early as people in the United States.

The morning air felt not far above freezing, and he put his hands in his pockets as he walked. Along the coastlines of both Çeşme and Chios, lights sparkled in homes and hotels. Jenkins watched the flashing red lights of an airplane as it approached the Chios airport along the water's edge.

Jenkins found a gap between two buildings terraced above the coast that provided a view of the marina and the parking lot adjacent to it. He searched for signs of someone sitting in a car—the yellow burst of a struck match or a flicked cigarette lighter, the red ember of a cigarette tip, the luminous glow of a cell phone. He also searched the shadows around the marina, looking for anyone standing about and seemingly not having a purpose there. He saw no one.

Headlights approached on the road at the bottom of the hill. The car slowed and turned into the parking lot, stopping in front of garbage bins. A man got out, tossed his cigarette across the ground, and walked to the back of his car. He opened the trunk and unloaded what looked to be a cooler and other items Jenkins could not see from that distance.

He closed the trunk and walked to the marina dock to one of the boat slips.

Jenkins hurried down the hill. As he approached the marina he kept his attention on the parked cars and the shadows, seeing no one. When he reached the marina's dock he slowed his approach, not wanting to frighten the man, who had stepped inside a boat's cabin. An African American man of Jenkins's size could cause fear simply by his presence, at least in the United States. Jenkins waited until the man exited the cabin and made eye contact.

"Affedersiniz. Günaydin," he said. *Excuse me. Good morning.* He had practiced these words during the hours in his hotel room.

"Günaydin," the man responded, sounding cautious.

"Balik tutmak için ariyorum." I am looking to go fishing. Jenkins removed lira from his pocket. "Lira?" he said.

The man was not small and he did not appear intimidated. He also did not look interested. He looked at the money, then again at Jenkins. Jenkins could tell the man was about to turn him down.

"Sakiz gezisi yapmak belki o zaman . . . ," Jenkins said. *Perhaps a ride to Chios then . . .*

This, too, gave the man pause. He looked across the narrow channel. The lights on Chios seemed close enough to touch, no more than a twenty-minute ride. "Chios?"

"Yes," Jenkins said. *"Sadece bir gezinti." Just a ride.*

"Ne kadar?" the man said, rubbing his thumb and fingers together. *How much?*

A good sign, Jenkins thought. *"Beş yüz şimdi,"* he said. *Five hundred lira now.* It should have been more than enough to make the deal, especially if the man was going out anyway. *"Biz indiğimizde beş yüz daha,"* Jenkins said, hoping to seal the deal. *Five hundred more when we land.*

The man looked again to the island, but distrust lingered in his eyes. *"Kimi kaçiyorsun?"*

Jenkins shook his head to indicate he didn't understand what the man was asking. The man pointed to Jenkins, then used two fingers to indicate someone running. *"Kimi kaçiyorsun?"* he said again.

If Jenkins said he was running from Russians, he'd scare the man into rejecting his request.

Jenkins nodded. *"Evet."*

"Kim?" the man said, and Jenkins deduced he was again asking who Jenkins was running from.

Jenkins nodded and smiled. Then he took out his phone and found the translation he was looking for. *"Karim,"* he said. *My wife.*

Initially, the man looked taken aback. Then he grinned and waved Jenkins aboard. *"Belki de seninle gitmeliyim,"* he said. *Maybe I should go with you.*

43

Viktor Federov stood outside the central bus stop in Çeşme, waiting for the next round of buses to arrive. After the debacle in Bursa, Federov had contemplated two possibilities—that the fishermen had lied to him about Jenkins's intention to take a bus to the Turkish coast and attempt to flee to Greece, or, Jenkins, knowing Federov remained in close pursuit, had supplanted those plans with new ones.

Federov dismissed the first possibility as highly unlikely. The fishermen had been paid a price to transport Jenkins across the Black Sea. They owed him nothing more, certainly not their lives or the lives of those they loved. Second, their story made the most sense. The shortest distance out of Turkey was through Greece, where there existed dozens of islands Jenkins could hide on before flying out or taking a ship. That analysis left the latter possibility, that Jenkins, aware that Federov was in pursuit, had changed his plans when he arrived in Bursa, or he wanted Federov to believe he had. In hindsight, Jenkins's cab ride to the hotel had been purposefully easy to trace—Jenkins having spoken English and leaving a large tip to make him memorable. He had clearly intended to lure Federov and his men to that hotel. Jenkins could have then slipped out of Bursa on a bus headed in any of a number of directions. And if that was the case, he could be nearly anywhere by now.

Or . . . that could be precisely what Jenkins wanted Federov to believe, which improved his chances of escaping through Çeşme, as originally planned.

The latter possibility was one of the reasons Federov sat at the bus terminal waiting for the next round of buses to arrive—so he and Alekseyov could ask each driver if he recalled the large American. So far, none had. The other reason was equally as practical. What else was Federov to do? If Jenkins had taken an alternative route out of Turkey, Federov could do little until Jenkins's passport triggered a notice, an asset saw and recognized him, or they learned more about Jenkins's attempts to contact friends in the United States to obtain travel documents.

Alekseyov stepped off the last bus and approached Federov in the courtyard. He'd ditched his suit and dressed as a Turkish tourist in shorts, a colorful shirt, black socks above tennis shoes, and sunglasses. Federov wore slacks, a blue polo shirt, and sandals.

"Nyet," Alekseyov said, shaking his head. "It appears Mr. Jenkins did not come to Çeşme."

"You may be right," Federov said. He had called his contact in the United States, who said it was possible Jenkins was attempting to get travel documents from a source who had boarded a plane to Costa Rica. They were monitoring the man's movements.

Federov turned and peered at the blue-green water of the Aegean Sea and at the boats in the marina's slips, just one of many marinas tucked within the coves and the spits of irregular-shaped land masses of the popular Turkish town. And that did not even account for the many pleasure boats, or the fishermen who could drop anchor in the shallow, calm waters and come into Çeşme for just the day. Jenkins had any number of people he could bribe if he had come to Çeşme for a ride to Greece.

"What should we do?" Alekseyov asked.

Federov took out a roll of Tums and popped two in his mouth, cringing at the chalky taste. "When do the next buses arrive?"

"Not until after five o'clock."

Federov looked at his watch, then at the red tile roofs of the buildings on what had become a gorgeous day of sunshine and pleasant temperatures. There was little more they could do. "We'll eat before the next round of buses. It will give me time to call in and determine if anyone has any further information."

44

Jake pushed open the glass door to *Antigüedades y tesoros* and stepped inside, carrying the white cup of coffee and a bag with two pastries. He crossed the wood-plank floor to the counter where earlier the man had sat cleaning the piece of silver. The pot sat on a tray, along with the red rag and the lingering chemical smell. Behind the counter stood a woman no more than five feet tall with long, straight, black hair. She glanced at the coffee in Jake's hand, and for a moment he thought she would tell him he could not drink or eat inside the store. Then she smiled.

Before Jake could ask about Carlos, the woman walked around the counter and crossed to the front of the store. She turned a sign in the window and locked the door with a click. Then she nodded for Jake to follow her, leading him through a maze of haphazard paths between dressers, tables, bed frames, armoires, and stacks of magazines. She opened a door at the back of the store and stepped to the side. Jake looked down a steep staircase that descended to a dull yellow light.

Jake pointed to the stairs. *"Carlos aquí?"*

The woman smiled and nodded but said nothing.

Jake descended slowly, unsure what to expect. The woman closed the door behind him. He stopped when he heard a click. "Not good," he said. "Not good."

The stairs shook and creaked beneath his weight. As he descended, machines on cobblestones came into view—several copiers, a printing press, and a machine that, he suspected from the clear plastic beside it, laminated cards.

Carlos stood behind an antique partner's desk in an office at the back of the room. The other pastry Jake had ordered sat on a napkin beside a mug of coffee. The yellow lighting emanated from a fixture above Carlos's head.

Carlos smiled as Jake entered. "Please, take a seat."

Jake set down his coffee and bag and sat in a chair on the opposite side of the desk.

Carlos sat and took a bite of his cinnamon roll. He handed a napkin across the desk. "Please. I hate to eat alone, and you look as though you could use some food."

"I could, actually." Jake opened the bag and removed the cinnamon roll, taking a bite.

"Where did you come from?" the man asked.

"Seattle," Jake said.

"And Charles Jenkins is your uncle?"

"He's like an uncle," Jake said.

"I thought so. You don't look alike." After a pause, Carlos smiled. "It was a joke. You look tense. Relax."

"You know him."

"Only from photographs my father has on file." Carlos tore off a piece of pastry, sat back, and dipped the pastry in his coffee. "I had to send you away to be sure you had not been followed and to give me time to review my father's files." He ate the pastry and wiped his fingers on a napkin. "I watched you go into the coffee shop, then hurried down here to determine whether you were telling the truth." He pointed to a laptop on his desk. "I've computerized most of my father's files. There were many. Your uncle's file was in the archives. It appears my father and your uncle did business together, more than once, but many years ago."

"Is your father really dead?"

"Yes. That part is true."

"You took up his profession?"

"I worked with and learned both professions from my father. He made a good living because he was careful in what antiques he purchased and what clients he chose to accept. If he couldn't turn a profit on an antique, he didn't accept it. If he didn't like or believe he could trust the person asking him to make travel documents, he simply feigned ignorance, as I just did. It's the reason my father never conducted business over the telephone. He liked to look a man . . . or woman . . . in the eye. He was highly selective and highly accurate. He was also an artist, as your uncle said, much better than I am, though I don't have to be as good, with the new technology. Much of what my father did for your uncle had to be done by hand. I rely heavily on computers." He set down the coffee. "What is it that you need . . . ?"

"Jake," he said.

"What is it that you need, Jake?"

"May I borrow your knife?"

The man handed Jake the knife. He used the sharp point to cut loose one of the threads Alex had sewn and carefully opened the lining of his jacket. He pulled out the envelope—on an airport X-ray machine it would look as though the envelope was inside his coat pocket. With TSA precheck, Jake never even had to remove his jacket to be scanned. He handed the envelope to Carlos. Carlos opened it and shook out what appeared to be several recent photos of Charlie, along with photocopies of his passport, his birth certificate, and his driver's license. Alex kept these documents, as well as travel documents for her and CJ, in the go bag she brought with her from Camano.

Carlos removed his wire-rimmed glasses, which left red indentations along the bridge of his nose. Without them, he looked younger, his nose and cheekbones more prominent. He read handwritten notes provided by Alex, placing each page facedown as he proceeded. When he had finished reading, he picked up the pages, methodically tapped them on his desk to even the edges, and set them down again.

"Your aunt?" Carlos asked, placing his palm on the written notes.

"Charlie's wife."

"She also was a case officer?"

"Yes. From here, Mexico City."

"I can tell." He pressed the tips of his fingers to his lips and bowed his head as if in solemn prayer. His eyes went back and forth between the materials. After nearly a minute he said, "She said there is urgency. I can get the materials to you by late tomorrow afternoon. That's as fast as I can go."

Jake nodded. "Then I guess that will have to do."

"The price is five thousand dollars."

Jake felt like a large stone dropped in his stomach. It was all the money he had.

"But I can tell that you're worried about your uncle." He tapped the pages again. "So is his wife."

"Very," Jake said.

"I'll do it for twenty-five hundred," he said. "Since your uncle knew my father. Where will you be staying?"

"I don't have a place yet."

"Hang on." Carlos picked up the receiver of an old-fashioned telephone and dialed a single digit. He spoke Spanish, much too quickly for Jake to understand, and replaced the receiver. "I rent out the rooms on the second floor. Veronica tells me we have an opening. You can stay there. I would suggest you stay indoors and largely out of sight. I don't believe you're being followed, but better safe than sorry, as they say. Veronica will bring you food. Leave your jacket and your backpack. Everything your uncle needs will be sewn inside the lining."

45

Upon his early morning arrival in Chios, Charles Jenkins found an isolated hotel with a vacancy up the street from the beach where the fisherman had dropped him—away from the marina and shops, and close to the airport. To the left of the hotel he entered a vacant lot of scrub brush, removed the burka from his backpack, and pulled it on before walking into the hotel to secure a room.

Inside his room, he crashed for the first time in days and did not wake until nearly five in the afternoon. He called Alex, no longer cognizant of the time delay, and awoke her.

"You're safe?" she asked.

"I'm safe."

"Where are you?"

"I'm in a hotel in Chios, not far from the airport. Have you heard from Mexico City?"

"Your papers should be completed late this afternoon. Mexico City has a flight leaving at nine p.m. through Athens. It arrives in Chios at six p.m. the day after tomorrow, Greek time. What's your situation?"

"I've left a trail of misinformation, and at present I'm not picking up any surveillance. I'm hoping they've come to the conclusion that I changed the travel plans I'd been given and that I'm already gone, but the Russian FSB agent is dogged and intuitive. He won't give up easily."

"And you don't exactly blend in."

"Maybe not in America, but I've been wearing a burka when in public. So far it seems to be working."

"For how long, though? How many six-foot-five-inch women dressed in burkas in Greece?"

"Hopefully more than one. Have you heard from David?"

"He landed in Costa Rica a couple of hours ago and picked up a tail at a travel agency. Tomorrow afternoon he's going back to the agency. Hopefully whoever is following will think he's picked up your travel papers and is bringing them to you."

"Where's he flying to?"

"Cyprus."

"Makes sense."

"I thought so. If you had abandoned the fisherman's plans in Bursa you would have taken a bus to the Turkish coast, then across the Mediterranean Sea to Cyprus and from Cyprus into Israel."

"I hope he has frequent flier miles," Jenkins said. He paused. He felt guilt for having lied to Alex and for worrying her. He knew the strain she was under. "How are you holding up?"

"I'm okay as long as I stay busy and keep my mind occupied."

"I'm sorry, Alex. I'm sorry to be putting you through this. I—"

"Don't start apologizing," she said. "Just get home. We'll all be waiting for you here."

He knew she was projecting strength so he would also. Stay on mission. "I'm changing cell phones," he said. "You have the second number?"

"I'm changing on my end as well. I'll give Jake the new numbers when he calls."

"I'm going to go out after dark and see if I can scout out a place where Jake and I can meet."

This time she paused. He heard her voice catch. "Be careful, Charlie. Make sure Jake is careful."

"He makes the drop and heads straight back. Hopefully I'll be right behind him."

"I love you, Charlie. Come home to me."

"I will."

He disconnected and walked to the window. At an angle he had a sliver of a view of the Aegean Sea, and across it to Çeşme. He wondered whether Federov stood there on the other side, perhaps at the marina, looking back across the strait, also wondering.

Federov disconnected the call and went to retrieve Alekseyov, who he had instructed to show Jenkins's photograph around the marina in the unlikely event anyone had seen the American. As he reached the dock, he saw Alekseyov finishing a conversation with a man near a fuel pump.

"Nothing," Alekseyov said when he reached Federov. "No one has seen him."

"Because he's not here in Çeşme."

"What do you mean?"

"I just got off the phone with my contact in America. Mr. Jenkins's likely carrier landed in San José, Costa Rica, and went to a travel agency just before it closed. Surveillance picked him up again when he exited the agency and walked to a nearby hotel."

"Which would make it convenient to walk back in the morning and pick up papers," Alekseyov said.

"Shortly after Mr. Sloane checked into his hotel he made travel arrangements to fly to Cyprus tomorrow afternoon."

"Jenkins took a different bus in Bursa, as you suspected," Alekseyov said.

"That would seem to be the logical conclusion. Alert our assets in Cyprus but tell them to forget the marinas. Mr. Jenkins would have arrived by now. Tell them to get eyes on the airport in Paphos where the carrier is arriving."

"Jenkins could seek to cross to Israel by boat," Alekseyov said.

"Which is why we need to end this in Cyprus."

As they made their way back toward the street, Federov noticed the man at the fuel pump talking to a second man dressed in shorts, flip-flops, and a fleece jacket—a boat owner perhaps. The man at the pump pointed to Federov and Alekseyov, and Federov deduced he was telling the boat owner of his interaction with Alekseyov.

Federov stopped.

"Something wrong?" Alekseyov asked.

Federov realized he had just made a deduction about the two men based upon unconfirmed information, which was exactly what he was doing with respect to Charles Jenkins. He'd deduced, based on Jenkins's excursion to Bursa, and the lack of any sighting of him by any of the bus drivers arriving in Çeşme, that Jenkins had abandoned plans to get to Çeşme and to get across the Aegean Sea to Greece. If Federov was on the run, he, too, would create just as much uncertainty by putting out as much misinformation as he could about his intentions.

"The two men talking down at the dock, did you speak to both men, or just the one?"

"I didn't see the other man."

"They appear to know one another."

"What does it matter?"

"The information regarding the carrier has been made readily available to us, hasn't it?" Federov asked.

"What do you mean?"

"I mean that this carrier"—he pulled out a notepad—"has used his own name to purchase his tickets, and to make a hotel reservation. Much the way Charles Jenkins made his intentions regarding the hotel in Bursa easy for us to follow."

"You think it is to focus our attention on the wrong place again."

"Or the wrong man. If you were seeking to escape, and you knew we would learn of your travel plans from the fishermen, what would you do?"

"I'd change the plans," Alekseyov said.

Federov smiled. "No, you would make us believe you changed the plans. Then when we learned of your supposed new plans, we would think we had outsmarted you, but maybe in so doing, you outsmarted us."

"You think Charles Jenkins could be here in Çeşme? But no one has seen him. He was not on any of the buses. We've asked the drivers here and at stops along the way."

Federov looked again to the two men at the end of the pier. The one Alekseyov had not spoken with was making his way back to a boat. If Jenkins was in Çeşme, and he was seeking passage to Chios, he would come to the marina to hire a boat, or to find out where he could do so.

Federov started walking down the pier toward the man.

"Colonel?" Alekseyov said.

"Do not call anyone . . . yet."

Fifteen minutes later, Federov hurried up the marina's dock. "Jenkins is here," he said to Alekseyov. "Tell our assets to concentrate on Chios. Tell them I want the travel itineraries of any passengers flying from Seattle, Washington, to Athens and . . . No." He stopped. "Tell them I want the identities of any passengers flying to Chios from the United States, or flying under an American passport. Provide every agent with Mr. Jenkins's photograph. I suspect this has been intended to be, what do the American's say . . . a false trail? Whatever. I do not intend to fall for it again."

46

Exhausted, bleary-eyed from a lack of sleep, and sick to his stomach, Jake looked out the window as his flight approached the kidney-shaped island of Chios. The landmass rose from the Aegean Sea's crystal-blue waters to a ridge of lush vegetation. Houses with red tile roofs descended down from that ridge to hotels and shops along the shoreline, where the water was tinted a neon green, and gentle waves lapped against a sandy coastline. The view reminded Jake of the trips he'd taken to Hawaii with David and his mother, back when she'd been alive. It looked like paradise, and under other conditions it might very well have been.

But not for him. Not this trip.

Across the sea, which he assumed Charlie had now crossed, Jake could see Turkey. No one had told Jake any of the specifics of Charlie's efforts to get out of Russia or Turkey, and he knew that had been purposeful. He also knew why. If caught and interrogated, Jake could not tell those questioning him anything of substance. How long it would take such men to reach that conclusion, however, and what they might do to ensure Jake told the truth, was both sobering and frightening.

Jake had spoken to Charlie before getting on the plane in Athens—by way of Frankfurt, Germany. Charlie told Jake to deplane as if he were a college student visiting the island as a tourist. When entering the terminal, Jake was not to look for him. When satisfied Jake was not being followed, Charlie would contact Jake and tell him where to go and what to do.

In keeping with the tourist theme, Jake wore shorts, Teva sandals, and his jacket over a T-shirt, though the January temperature in Chios wasn't exactly balmy. Just before they landed, the pilot announced that daytime temperatures had reached an afternoon high that he calculated to be sixty-one degrees Fahrenheit. When the plane's wheels touched down at just after 6:00 p.m., dusk had descended over the island. Jake grabbed his bag from the overhead compartment along with the wide-brimmed hat he'd bought in Mexico, and he tried to match the other passengers' demeanor and enthusiasm as he walked down the stairs to the tarmac. He hoped it was convincing.

—

Viktor Federov waited inside the terminal building at Chios Island National Airport with three other FSB officers, including Simon Alekseyov. Each was stationed with a view of the airport's two gates. They had stood in the same locations the day before, the same locations at which they would stand tomorrow, if necessary. The men dressed as locals awaiting arriving passengers—shorts or jeans, sandals, and light-weight shirts, with windbreakers to conceal their firearms. The tiny airport accommodated only eighteen to twenty arriving flights per day, all of them from larger airports within Greece.

At just after 6:00 p.m., an overhead voice echoed from the terminal speakers announcing the arrival of flight GQ240 from Athens. According to Federov's FSB sources, three passengers had boarded traveling under US passports. Two were newly married, the trip to Chios an apparent honeymoon. The third passenger, a young man, was traveling alone. Each of the FSB officers had been provided passport photographs.

Federov straightened as the first passengers entered the doors of the terminal building. The young man walked quickly to the line forming at customs and immigration.

Federov touched his ear. "The subject has just entered the building and is standing at the back of the line."

"I have him," Alekseyov said. Alekseyov sat on a bench across the terminal. Since this was the last arriving flight of the evening, Federov sent the other two officers to retrieve their rented car. Federov listened closely to the messages being broadcast over the loudspeakers and watched the young man for any reaction to any message. Federov saw none.

The young man stepped forward in line. Was he looking for someone? Jenkins? A contact perhaps? Federov doubted Jenkins would be so bold as to arrange a drop at the airport, but this young man could also be acting as a go-between, someone to get the documents to a second courier, who would then take them to Jenkins.

The young man stepped to the immigration booth and slid the officer his passport. Federov took another step closer and heard the officer ask the purpose for the young man's visit to Chios.

"Vacation," he said.

The customs officer stamped the passport and slid it back. The young man picked up his bag and walked toward the terminal's front doors. Federov and Alekseyov fell in step behind him.

The young man stopped, pulled out a cell phone, and pressed it to his ear. An incoming call. He continued to talk as he walked outside the terminal doors and crossed the road to a taxi stand. A stiff breeze rustled the leaves of palm trees.

Federov's car pulled to the curb. He and Alekseyov slipped into the back seat. The taxi pulled from the airport onto the two-lane road hugging the coastline, driving north, into Chios.

"Give him room," Federov said.

Minutes later, the taxi stopped at a hotel not far from the marina. The young man stepped out and entered the lobby.

"Pull across the street," Federov said. His driver did so.

The hotel rooms were located off an outdoor balcony, with views of the marina. After several minutes the young man emerged and climbed the outdoor steps to the second floor. He entered the room second from the end.

"How long do we wait?" the driver asked.

Federov rolled down his window and lit a cigarette. "We shall see."

—

Jake descended the stairs to the tarmac, carrying his duffel bag and his backpack. He bypassed the luggage cart and proceeded inside the terminal, standing in line behind the couple he'd met briefly on the plane. Newlyweds from San Francisco, they were honeymooning in the Greek isles and already complaining about the cool temperature.

Jake resisted the urge to look around the terminal and, despite the comfortable temperature, he felt perspiration trickling down his sides. The back of his shirt clung to his skin. He wasn't about to remove his jacket.

The cell phone in his coat pocket vibrated. Jake reached inside to retrieve it, pressing it to his ear so he could hear over the echoing voice thrumming from the airport speakers.

"Do not look around," Jenkins said.

"Okay."

"The terminal is being watched by at least two men. Probably more. Smile like you're happy to be receiving this call."

Jake did.

"Now, look to your right. Do you see the man in the blue windbreaker across the terminal?"

Jake did. "Yes."

"Laugh again."

Jake did. The woman standing in front of him turned and smiled.

"Now, look to your left. Do you see the blond-haired man seated on the bench?"

Jake turned his head to the left. "Yes. What do I do?"

"Nothing. Just proceed forward."

The newlyweds stepped to one of two booths at the front of the line. Jake stepped to the booth on his right when the couple in front of him departed.

"Passport," the customs officer said.

Jake handed the man his passport. The officer opened it and considered the picture, then considered Jake. "Remove your hat, please."

Jake did as the customs officer asked.

The man eyed him for another moment. Then he set down the passport and typed on the computer keyboard. "What is the purpose of your visit?"

"Pleasure," Jake said.

The man pecked at the keyboard, then stamped the passport and handed it back to Jake. "Enjoy your stay in Chios."

Jake picked up his bag and stepped into the terminal. When he did, the man on the bench stood. The man to his right also began to move toward him.

"What do I do?" Jake said into the phone.

"Just walk forward. Do not look around. Smile and look animated for a second. You're happy to be in Chios."

Jake tried, but wasn't certain he was convincing. He departed through the terminal doors. A car pulled to the curb. Jake envisioned the man in the passenger seat stepping out, grabbing him, and shoving Jake into the back seat, but the car drove past him.

Jake let out a held breath.

"You all right?" Jenkins asked.

"Yeah. I'm okay." Jake started for the taxi stand.

"Do not take a taxi. Get a rental car. Take a right out of the parking lot and follow signs for GR-74. Stay on that road for thirty-five minutes. Don't speed. The roads in Greece are dangerous and there are few streetlamps."

"Seriously?" Jake said. "That's what I'm supposed to be worried about? Because at the moment I would say the lack of streetlamps is the least of my problems."

Jake heard Charlie laugh. Then he said, "I'll call you when you get your car and provide you with further instructions. It's good to hear your voice, Jake."

"It's good to hear yours also," Jake said.

Federov considered his watch. They had waited outside the hotel for nearly an hour but no one had come. It might be another hour. It might not be until the morning. Tired and frustrated, he tossed the butt of a cigarette out the window and stepped from the car. The other officers, not expecting the sudden move, scrambled to catch up.

"What about waiting until he makes contact with Jenkins?" Alekseyov asked.

"If he has Mr. Jenkins's travel papers I will convince him to tell us where he intends to meet him."

"He might not be meeting Jenkins. It might just be a drop," Alekseyov said.

"Then I will have someone Mr. Jenkins does not know make that drop."

Federov shuffled up the steps to the second-floor landing and made his way to the second-to-last door on the right. Reaching it, he removed his weapon and knocked. When the young man pulled the door open, Federov did not wait for an invitation to enter. He shoved the man backward. The young man started to protest but Federov quickly covered his mouth with his hand and showed him his weapon. "Not a word. Do you understand?"

The young man nodded, his eyes wide.

"Check the luggage," Federov said to the others.

They rifled through luggage and cut the lining of the young man's suitcase. Federov lifted the man's jacket, flicked open a switchblade, and cut the lining. "Search the room," he said.

"What are you looking for?" the man asked. "Drugs? I don't have any drugs."

"Where are the travel papers?" Federov said.

The young man nodded to the dresser. "They're on the dresser."

Federov considered them. "Where are the travel papers you are delivering?"

"What?"

"Do not play games. I am in no mood."

"I don't know what you're talking about."

Federov stepped closer. "Do not lie to me. I am tired of people lying to me."

"I'm not lying. Please. I don't know what you're looking for."

Federov looked down at the wet spot forming on the front of the man's pants. He swore, then nodded for the others to exit. Before leaving the room, Federov said, "We're going to be watching you very closely. If you tell anyone about this, or attempt to go to the police, we will come back. Do you understand?"

The man nodded.

Federov stepped outside and shut the door. A foreboding feeling enveloped him as he looked out across the blackened waters to the lights of Çeşme. It was possible Mr. Jenkins's courier had not yet arrived in Chios. He could come tomorrow or the next day or the day after that. Or he could have already arrived and Mr. Jenkins was already well on his way home. Federov also knew the courier could be a man or a woman, young or old, and flying under a United States passport or one from anywhere around the world. His contact had underestimated Charles Jenkins's skills. So had Federov. His contact could make all the threats he wanted, but they weren't going to keep Charles Jenkins from getting home.

And then he would no longer be Federov's problem.

He smiled at that thought, at least, and let out a small chuckle.

"Colonel?" Alekseyov said, looking confused.

"Make arrangements for our return to Moscow tomorrow morning," Federov said.

"We're not going to watch the airport tomorrow?" Alekseyov said.

Federov shook his head. "No. Tonight we will go out and have dinner. We will drink vodka and we will toast to Mr. Jenkins. He is no longer our problem."

Jake approached the painted city of Pyrgi, as Charlie had instructed. Though it was night, the city would have been hard to miss. Black-and-white geometric shapes adorned the exterior walls of nearly every building. The narrow streets and alleys would not accommodate a car, and Jake recalled from a history class that many medieval towns were built this way to defend against attacks. He parked outside the city, grabbed his backpack, and headed for the narrow streets. Despite the brisk temperature, a fair number of people walked the streets and alleys beneath stone arches, and men sat at tables playing backgammon while women crocheted, their voices mixing with Greek music spilling from open doorways.

As Jake passed beneath one of the stone archways, the phone in his pocket vibrated.

"Continue walking into the town square," Jenkins said when Jake answered it. "Look across it to the north side. Do you see the restaurant with an unopened red table umbrella near the front door?"

Jake looked across a plaza littered with several dozen unoccupied tables and closed beige umbrellas. He saw the red umbrella. "I see it."

"Ask the waiter for a table on the patio in the back. The temperature is dropping so he'll suggest you sit inside. Tell him it's your first night and you want to experience Greece."

Light spilled from the windows of the shops and restaurants surrounding the plaza. Jake crossed to the restaurant and spoke to the maître d'. As Charlie had predicted, the man suggested Jake would be more comfortable sitting inside, but he relented when Jake said it was his first night in Greece. He lit a candle in a red glass jar, and Jake ordered a Greek beer while he waited.

Minutes after Jake had sat down, he looked up to see Charlie filling the patio doorway and heaved a sigh of relief. He came around the table and gave him a bear hug.

"You shouldn't have done this, Jake," Charlie said, emotion leaking into his voice.

"Yeah, well, there really weren't a lot of choices," Jake said. They took their seats at the table. The waiter reappeared. Charlie ordered a beer.

"Do you know how they ended up at the Chios Airport?" Jake asked. "I was under the impression David led them to Costa Rica, then to Cyprus."

Charlie shook his head, thinking of Federov. He had begrudging respect for the man's counterintelligence skills. "Apparently they figured out that was a ruse. It makes sense. David was too obvious. In counterintelligence you must always have a backup plan. So how did you get through customs without them stopping you? If I were Federov, I would have been looking for anyone entering Chios with a US passport, especially someone traveling alone."

Jake reached into his pocket and handed Charlie a hunter-green booklet with gold lettering.

"A Mexican *pasaporte*," Jenkins said. "Good old Uncle Frank."

Jake shook his head. "Uncle Frank died seven years ago from cancer. His son, Carlos, has taken over the family businesses. And it was Alex who suggested I get a Mexican passport."

He smiled at the mention of his wife. "You have my papers?"

Jake opened his jacket. "Hand me your knife."

Jake picked at the stitching on the inside lining and pulled loose the thread. He removed the envelope and handed it to Charlie, who placed it beneath the napkin in his lap, opened the flap, and considered but did not remove a Greek passport, a Mexican passport, and a Canadian passport, along with corresponding driver's licenses, a couple thousand dollars in US currency, and an airplane ticket leaving Athens tomorrow evening.

"How are you going to get off this island if they're watching the airport?" Jake asked.

"Another principle of good counterintelligence when you're on the run is to keep moving forward—never double back."

"So what are you going to do?"

"There's a ferry leaving Mesta, Greece, early tomorrow morning for Piraeus. You're going to be on it. From Piraeus, it's a cab ride to Athens, and from Athens you fly home."

"What about you?"

"I'll be on a different boat, but not far behind you."

The waiter returned. "I'll bet you're hungry," Charlie said to Jake.

"I'm starving, actually."

Charlie looked to the waiter. "Pyrgi pizza. Extra large. Extra cheese. And two more beers."

PART II

47

After days on the run, Charles Jenkins sat at David Sloane's kitchen table peering out at the blackened waters of Puget Sound, still disbelieving he was actually home. He'd arrived at SeaTac Airport thirty-six hours earlier, groggy from lack of sleep, jet lag, and physical and mental exhaustion—another reminder that he wasn't the twenty-five-year-old man who had chased KGB agents in Mexico City. This ordeal had taken its toll. The mental exhaustion surprised him the most. Escaping Russia had been like a marathon chess match, requiring that he constantly think two moves ahead of Federov, with contingencies for moves Jenkins had not anticipated. He never realized, in the moment, how the constant mental strain could wear on the body. When he had finally arrived home, he'd crashed hard, and he was still trying to recover.

"You hungry?" Alex asked, eyes red from too little sleep and too much worry.

White take-out boxes from a Thai restaurant littered the kitchen table, but the normally intoxicating aroma of chicken pad thai, tom yum soup, and phat khing did little to entice Jenkins's appetite, which remained virtually nonexistent since he'd arrived in the US. Not that he wasn't grateful to be back, grateful to be holding his wife's hand, grateful to read CJ a book before bed, but something gnawed at the recesses of his mind, and he couldn't shake the thought that his ordeal was not yet over.

"Maybe a bit later," he said.

Max, perhaps sensing how close her master had been to never coming home, lay curled at his feet beneath the table. CJ, too, seemed worried for his dad, sensing things had changed though not understanding why. Earlier that evening, when Jenkins put his son to bed, CJ had begged him to continue reading past the usual one chapter. Jenkins realized the request was not an attempt to manipulate, but born from a deeper concern, or fear, of losing his dad. Jenkins had read until CJ drifted to sleep.

He released Alex's hand and cradled a porcelain mug of coffee. The warmth against his palms conjured images of the mug of Turkish coffee he'd held after being plucked from the Black Sea's frigid waters. That feeling evoked memories of Demir Kaplan and his two sons, and of the sacrifices they had made. That thought led to another memory—of Paulina Ponomayova just before she'd departed the beach house to create a diversion.

"Charlie?" David Sloane said.

Jenkins looked at Sloane, uncertain how long he had checked out, but sensing from the concerned looks on the faces seated around the table that it hadn't been for just a moment.

"You okay?" Sloane asked.

"Just tired," he said.

Music emanated from the Echo on Sloane's kitchen counter, a country-western station. Jenkins remained concerned someone could be using directional microphones to listen to their conversations. Since his return, he'd spent four two-hour shifts—the limit of his ability to concentrate—explaining what had led him to Russia, what had transpired there, and why he had ended up running for his life. Now they sought to determine what, if anything, they could do.

"Is there any way to get this information of a leak to the people who might be able to do something about it?" Sloane asked.

"It's not going to be that simple," Jenkins said. "A field officer knows that if an operation is aborted, he is supposed to disappear. He is never to try to contact his case officer."

"Why not?" Sloane asked. He, too, looked tired. Dark bags sagged beneath his eyes, and gray strands now flecked his hair. He no longer had the boyish looks that had so easily charmed juries.

Jenkins started to speak, cleared his throat, and began again. "I was told by Carl Emerson that if the operation went sideways the agency would not publicly acknowledge it, that to do so would be to acknowledge that the seven sisters exist, and possibly put them in greater danger."

"What about going to this guy Emerson?" Sloane said. "Can he be trusted?"

Jenkins blew out a breath. He'd given this question a lot of thought the past few days. "I don't know. Things were certainly not as he represented, but someone could also have been using Emerson." He looked to Alex. "He had a lot of contact with the KGB in Mexico City. We all did."

"You think he could have turned back then?" Alex asked.

"I think anything is possible."

"What do you mean, 'turned'?" Jake said.

"Began to work for the KGB," Jenkins said. "A double agent." He sipped his coffee. He'd also had a lot of time to contemplate this possibility while on the run. "But I think it's more likely that whoever it is—maybe Emerson, maybe someone above him—that person saw an opportunity to sell the names of the seven sisters and took it." He looked at Alex. "I think that's more likely than a Russian mole acting undetected within the CIA for years, maybe decades."

"It's happened before," Alex said.

"It has," Jenkins agreed.

"Why would a well-entrenched mole wait so many years to divulge the names?" Sloane asked.

"Emerson said the names of the seven sisters were known only to a select few at the agency," Jenkins said. "This person might not have known the names until recently, or his circumstances might have changed."

"But if a mole knew the names, why wouldn't he give them all up at once?" Jake asked.

"Again," Jenkins said, "he might not have known them all. Someone could have been feeding him the information one name at a time, which would make this a crime of opportunity—the person is selling the names individually to get the best price for each name. I'm just not certain who that person is—Emerson, someone above him. And I'm not sure how to discreetly find out. If I make the wrong choice I could be alerting the leak, and that could give the person further time to cover their tracks and flee."

"And to come after you," Alex said.

"Possibly," he said, not elaborating on what they both knew—Jenkins was home, but not necessarily safe.

"Did you try calling Emerson?" Sloane asked.

Jenkins nodded. "The number he gave me is no longer in service."

"He gave you the number or something with the number on it?" Sloane asked.

"Just a number on a business card. I'm assuming it's a cell phone."

"Do you still have that card?"

"Not on me."

"Where is it?" Sloane sat up in his chair, clearly interested. "A card is tangible proof of contact, which could be important if Emerson was to deny your operation for some reason."

"It's in my home office," Jenkins said. "But it's just as likely the number will come back registered to some unknown person or unknown company."

"What if we wait and see if Emerson calls?" Jake said. "Seems that if he contacts you, it would be an indication he isn't the leak, wouldn't it?"

"Maybe," Jenkins said. "But it's rare for a handler to call a case officer when a mission has gone sideways, so his keeping quiet isn't indicative of guilt."

"And if he is the leak, a phone call might be to protect himself—to find out how much Charlie knows or to throw him off," Alex said.

"What about going to a reporter," Jake said, "and forcing the CIA to search for the leak internally?"

Jenkins leaned his elbows on the table. "That raises an entirely different set of problems. First, you all had a tough time believing the story when I told it to you, and you know me. A reporter isn't going to believe what I say just because I say it. He'll want confirmation, and I don't have any. An allegation won't get me very far. Not if I can't prove it."

"That's where the card might help," Sloane said.

"Maybe," Jenkins said. "But I'm not comfortable with going public to get to that point. Not yet anyway."

"So maybe you don't say anything. Maybe the leak will know he dodged a bullet, and move on," Sloane said.

"Maybe," Jenkins said. "But I can't do that."

"Can't do what?" Alex asked.

This was the conversation he was dreading. "I can't just let this go."

"Why not?" Alex said. "If the person keeps silent, doesn't do any more damage, why not let it go?"

Jenkins knew Alex was afraid of what could happen to him, and that fear was motivating her questions. "Because someone in the CIA is either a Russian mole capable of continuing to do harm, or an opportunistic leak responsible for the direct deaths of at least three women, and likely others. Beyond that, there are still four more sisters out there. I can't walk away not knowing if that person intends to disclose their names. They have no idea this is going on, which makes them sitting ducks."

"That's not your responsibility," Alex said. "You shouldn't have even been involved in the first place. You were lied to."

"But I am involved, and it is my responsibility. I can't in good conscience leave those remaining four women to die."

"Those women knew what they signed on for," Alex said, becoming more agitated. "They knew the dangers."

"Those women have served this country for decades. I can't abandon them. I won't abandon them. If I do, it means that a very good woman gave her life for nothing. It means that a Turkish family . . . that all of you put your lives at risk for nothing."

"Bullshit," Alex said, pushing back her chair and struggling to stand. "Those people were paid to get you out, and we put our lives at risk to bring home my husband and my children's father. You have a family to think of now."

"I know that."

"Then let this go."

"And every time I open a paper and read of someone dying in Russia, I'll wonder if that was another sister, if I could have saved that person's life."

"Well, that would be a hell of a lot better than me opening the paper and seeing your name. Think about that."

She threw her napkin into her plate, turned, and waddled down the hall to their bedroom as fast as a woman thirty-two weeks pregnant could move.

A silence fell over the room. The Echo played a country song with a sad twang.

Jenkins looked at Sloane. "She'll be okay," he said.

"Let's table this discussion for tonight," Sloane said. "It's late and we're all tired. Let's talk again tomorrow, in my office, just the three of us. She's been through a lot these past few days. We all have." He paused, and then said, "She has a point though. You're home and you're safe. It might be best in this instance to let a sleeping dog lie."

It might be, Jenkins thought, except he had no way to be certain the dog was actually asleep, and not just waiting for another chance to bite.

Jenkins walked past framed photographs of Jake with Sloane and Tina at various points in their lives, before Tina's death. It gave him pause. He looked back to the kitchen. Sloane had turned off the lights and gone up to bed, alone. No one waited in his room for him and hadn't for several years. It made Jenkins think of the decades he had lived alone on his Camano farm, not even realizing the depths of his loneliness. Alex had changed that. CJ too. He had a good life now, a life he never imagined possible during all those years he'd spent alone. He didn't want to lose what he had, but he also couldn't walk away from the people who'd risked so much to keep him alive.

Jenkins pushed open the door to their temporary bedroom with some trepidation. He knew what he'd put Alex through, and he didn't want to be a continual source of worry and concern. He knew the strain that could put on her and on the baby.

A low-watt glow emanated from the bedside lamp. Alex walked in from the adjoining bathroom dressed in her pajamas, her stomach protruding beneath the pale-blue fabric. She eyed him, shook her head, then pulled down the sheets and the comforter and climbed into bed without uttering a word. This was not going to be easy.

"I'm sorry," he said, lingering in the doorway. "I didn't want it to be this way."

"Really? What did you think was going to happen?"

"I thought I could save those women, as was represented to me."

"I suppose paying the company bills had nothing to do with it?"

"Of course it did," he said.

"Of course," she said. "So why didn't you tell me?"

"You know I couldn't, Alex."

"I'm not talking about the operation, Charlie. I'm talking about the extent of CJ Security's financial problems—our company's problems—or did you forget that I am also an owner?"

"I didn't tell you because I didn't want to worry you," he said.

"Oh? And this is better?"

He took another breath, trying to remain calm, not wanting their argument to escalate again and further stress her. "I didn't want to worry you and risk you having complications."

"Well, you failed." She pulled up the covers. Jenkins handed her a glass of water and sat on the edge of the bed.

"I won't push this, if that's what you want," he said. "I'll let it go."

She shook her head, speaking softly, fighting back tears. "I know you can't," she said. "And I know it's the right thing to do, to try and save those women. I just wish it wasn't you who had to do it. Promise me you'll watch your back. I know you didn't want to say it in front of David and Jake, but we both know someone went to great lengths to keep you from coming home, to silence you. If you start talking, that person, whoever he is, will have to respond."

48

The following day, Jenkins drove from Three Tree Point to Sloane's offices in the SoDo district, a term that had originally meant South of the Dome, before demolition of the Kingdome stadium. It now meant South of Downtown. Until the construction of billion-dollar baseball and football stadiums, the area had been primarily industrial. Paul Allen, the Microsoft billionaire, owned one of those stadiums and, sensing an opportunity, spurred redevelopment. Warehouses had been demolished or converted to office buildings, condominiums, nightclubs, restaurants, even distilleries. Sloane's building, a converted warehouse, was one of those.

Jenkins met Sloane in the large conference room behind reception. He knew Sloane sought tangible evidence to support Jenkins's story, to make it credible. Unfortunately, Jenkins did not have a lot to offer.

At noon, Carolyn walked in with a bag of sandwiches. Sloane's secretary and Jenkins had always had a love-hate relationship. "Who gets the pastrami?" she said to Sloane. "You or the Jolly Green Giant?"

"That's mine," Sloane said.

Carolyn looked to Jenkins. "Turkey, plain. You really need to put some spice in your life."

"I've had enough spice to last a lifetime," Jenkins said.

"I got the *Reader's Digest* version." Carolyn paused. "Glad you made it back."

"Was that a civil comment?" Jenkins looked to Sloane. "That was, wasn't it?"

"Don't get used to it," Carolyn said.

After Carolyn left, Sloane said, "I thought a lot about what you said last night, about not being able to go to the CIA, and not being able to go public with what happened. I've got another thought."

"Okay." Jenkins set down his sandwich.

"What if we tell another federal agency about what happened, and let them do the investigation for us?"

"Who'd you have in mind?"

"I have a connection in the FBI's office," Sloane said. "He's not a friend, but he respects me. What if you explain to him, without mentioning a specific operation by name, what happened? You could ask him to follow up with the CIA to confirm you were reactivated and to get further details. It would let the CIA know they either have a mole, or a leak selling classified information to Russia. Even allegations, I would think, would spur some type of investigation."

Jenkins gave the idea some thought. It had merit. The FBI operated within the United States and would have jurisdiction. "Is he dogged?" Jenkins asked. "If I give him bits of information, will he work to verify what I tell him and try to find more?"

"I would think he would—if we give him a reason to. If we tell him the CIA has a mole, or a leak, I would think that would be reason enough," Sloane said.

Jenkins considered his options, limited as they were. "Okay," he said. "Let's do it."

Sloane made the call to Christopher Daugherty, at the FBI's field office on Third Avenue in downtown Seattle. After reacquainting himself, he told Daugherty he had a client who wanted to talk. When Sloane mentioned the CIA, Daugherty said he'd be in Sloane's office within the hour.

For the better part of the afternoon, Jenkins spoke cautiously to Daugherty about CJ Security's relationship to LSR&C, the financial difficulties his company experienced because LSR&C had been late in making payments, and Carl Emerson's timely visit to his Camano farm. He told Daugherty of his two trips to Russia without ever mentioning the seven sisters.

"I can't mention the operation," he said. "It's still in play."

He told Daugherty he'd met with Viktor Federov and, as authorized by Emerson, disclosed the name Alexei Sukurov and the name of the operation, Graystone. He said he later disclosed the name of the Russian nuclear scientist Uliana Artemyeva. Daugherty listened, asked few questions, but took notes—a good sign, Jenkins thought.

When Jenkins had finished, Daugherty rocked back in his chair. "Let me see if I understand this. You received a fifty-thousand-dollar payment to disclose the information?"

"No. The fifty-thousand-dollar payment was part of my fee."

"And you used that money to pay CJ Security's debts and payroll."

"Yes. To keep the business afloat until LSR&C could get caught up."

"Did the Russians ever pay you?"

"No."

"And this man . . ." Daugherty looked at his notes. "Carl Emerson. He was your station chief in Mexico City when you were a field operative?"

"That's right."

"And you hadn't seen him since you left Mexico City."

"Correct. That was decades ago."

"But he came to you and asked you to run this operation in Russia."

"Yes."

Daugherty wrinkled his brow as if trying to solve a complex problem. After another moment he said, "Why would he do that?"

Skepticism crept into his tone, but Jenkins had been expecting it and he had an answer.

"Because I was fluent in Russian and counterintelligence, and it's cheaper and quicker to reactivate an agent than it is to train one."

"And time was of the essence."

"That's what I was told," Jenkins said.

"Okay," Daugherty said. "But you can't tell me the reason Carl Emerson sent you to Russia."

"I can't tell you specifically, no."

"Classified?"

"Yes."

"Operatives' lives potentially in danger?"

"Yes."

"But not Alexei Sukurov or . . ." Daugherty looked down at his notes.

"Uliana Artemyeva," Jenkins said. "Carl Emerson provided me those names. I did not reveal any unauthorized information."

"So, it was authorized."

"It was authorized to me."

Daugherty looked to Sloane, then back to Jenkins. "You understand why I would have a very hard time believing this without more to corroborate what you're telling me."

"I do understand, and I'm telling you there is more to it, more than I can tell you. The CIA has a leak, or a mole, and that person is doing damage to their operations in Russia. If the CIA investigates, they could put an end to it. You'll have to bring in the CIA and have the agency fill in the rest, to whatever extent they're willing."

Daugherty sat back, seemingly studying Jenkins. "Would you be willing to take a polygraph test?"

Jenkins knew polygraph tests were inadmissible in court. He knew that both an examiner and a witness could manipulate the results based upon the phrasing of the questions asked, and the answers given. He also knew that without something more to convince Daugherty that Jenkins was telling the truth, the FBI agent might not be motivated to seek further answers.

"Under certain conditions," Jenkins said.

"Such as?"

"I won't answer questions about the specific operation. I will answer questions about my reactivation, and questions asking if I revealed any unauthorized information." Jenkins wanted to get out as much as he could, but also to protect himself.

Daugherty flipped closed his notebook. "When can you come to the office?"

"I won't," Jenkins said, knowing the environment for the test was important. "We can conduct the polygraph here."

"You want the examiner to come to you?"

"I want a neutral environment, and I want my attorney present to assure the questions are phrased appropriately. I also want the results before you leave the office." Maybe he was being paranoid, but Jenkins didn't want anyone to manipulate the results.

"What time tomorrow?"

"What about this afternoon?" Jenkins said.

"Let me make some phone calls."

Jenkins had only been attached to the machine for twenty minutes, but it would take the examiner time to go through his physiological responses to each question. Night had fallen and Jenkins heard the banging of railroad cars coupling and uncoupling on the tracks behind the building. It sounded like distant thunder.

Sloane's cell phone rang. Daugherty was ready for them in the conference room.

Daugherty stood at the head of the table beside the examiner, a dowdy-looking woman with an officious demeanor. He handed Sloane the report. "No deception indicated."

Jenkins breathed a sigh of relief. Polygraph results could either be NDI—no deception indicated, DI—deception indicated, or INC—inconclusive. All Jenkins cared about was that the test gave Daugherty reason to further investigate.

"So he's telling the truth," Sloane said.

"He didn't lie, not to the questions asked of him," Daugherty said. He looked to Jenkins. "I'll make some calls tomorrow and try to fill in some of the significant blanks in your story. If the CIA confirms you were working for them and some of the other things you told me, we'll go to work and see if we can find the leak. We might have more questions though, depending on what we get. I imagine the CIA might also. You'll be available?"

"I'm not going anywhere."

The men shook hands, and Daugherty and the examiner departed. Shortly thereafter, Sloane shut down the office, and he and Jenkins left for home.

"So far so good," Sloane said.

As Sloane drove, Jenkins checked the side mirror. "We've got a tail."

"What?" Sloane said, eyes darting to the rearview mirror.

"The car behind us. Two men. FBI."

"How do you know it's the FBI?"

"Because the car isn't attempting to conceal itself, which means the two men are not likely CIA operatives or Russians trying to kill me."

"Why would the FBI be following us? Your test proves you're not lying."

"Agent Daugherty wants to keep an eye on me until he can cross all his t's and dot all his i's. I just told him that I disclosed classified information to the FSB."

—

Alex greeted them at the door when they arrived home. Jenkins had called her on the drive and told her of the polygraph test and the results.

"I was just getting CJ ready for bed," she said, sounding more chipper than she had in days. "I have food in the oven if you're hungry."

"Let me put him to bed," Jenkins said. He went upstairs to CJ's room and found his son sitting on the carpet, putting together Legos, one of a dozen different models Jake had pulled out of the attic and given to CJ.

"Hey." Jenkins took a seat on the carpet. "What are you building?"

"It's a Death Star," CJ said. "Dad, when can I go back to school?"

"Pretty soon," he said.

"But when?"

"I can't give you a specific date, son. You miss your friends?"

CJ nodded. "And soccer."

"I know," Jenkins said.

"Are you in some kind of trouble?"

"Why would you ask that?"

"I'm not stupid."

"No, you're definitely not."

"Are you?"

"I'm not in trouble but it's kind of a sticky situation."

"Could you go to jail?"

Jenkins paused, and in that brief moment of hesitation he saw the boy's concern etch on his face. CJ started to cry. "Hey," Jenkins said as CJ fell forward into his arms. "Hey, come on now. Everything is going to be all right." Jenkins had never lied to his son. He considered honesty to be a big part of parenting. "Listen," he said, lowering himself to look CJ in the eye. "Your dad didn't do anything wrong, okay? I want you to know that. I'm telling you the truth. I didn't do anything wrong."

"So you're not going to jail?"

"Why are you worried about me going to jail?"

"Because David's a lawyer and you're always having meetings with him after I go to bed."

It was a logical deduction. "David does a lot of different types of law, CJ. Not just keeping people out of jail."

"So then why are you having meetings with him and why are we living here? Why can't we go home?"

"Those are good questions," Jenkins said, and he thought of where to begin. "Listen, a long time ago I worked for the government, and recently they asked me to work for them again. That's why I was traveling so much. Things have gotten kind of sticky, and I've asked David and Jake to help me. Do you understand?"

"Not really."

"The important thing is I don't want you to be scared. Okay?"

CJ nodded.

"Good man. Let's get you to bed so I don't get in trouble from your mother. Now, she is someone I'm afraid of."

49

Jenkins spent the next three days giving Alex a break from homeschooling CJ and getting him out of Sloane's house so she could get some rest. When not doing schoolwork, they fished from the beach and hunted the shore for polished glass and unbroken sand dollars. They finished putting together the Death Star Lego model as well as two others, and while Jenkins loved the time with his son, he was also stir-crazy and anxious waiting for Daugherty to call. Whenever Jenkins left the house, whether to the library to get books with CJ, or to the local Fred Meyer to buy food and fishing supplies, the two FBI agents accompanied him. Hip-pocket surveillance, they called it.

This morning, Jenkins suggested to CJ that they fish before beginning schoolwork, which would give Alex additional time to sleep. CJ didn't need any more convincing to delay his studies.

They bundled up in winter clothing—a cold spell had dropped the temperature to near freezing—and stood at the water's edge with half a dozen other fishermen, all casting their lures into Puget Sound. Jenkins had just cast his line when his cell phone rang. He recognized the telephone number to the office building in Stanwood that CJ Security shared with several other businesses. He'd forwarded CJ Security's incoming calls to David Sloane's legal office, and Jake had been fielding calls from unpaid vendors and attorneys threatening lawsuits.

"Charlie? It's Claudia Baker."

Baker was the receptionist Jenkins shared with the other businesses in the building. Jenkins apologized for being out of touch.

"I wanted to let you know that, well, you had an FBI agent come into the office yesterday afternoon."

That aroused Jenkins's curiosity. "What did he want?"

"He had a subpoena for documents. I told him you didn't keep documents here in the office, and you didn't have a desktop computer."

"Did the agent leave a card or a name?"

"He wasn't going to, but I asked for a card and for his credentials before I'd answer his questions. His name was Chris Daugherty. I have his card."

Jenkins saw this as a good sign; Daugherty was continuing to dig.

Baker paused and Jenkins could tell she was hesitant to continue.

"What else did he say, Claudia?"

"Well, he just sort of inadvertently said the FBI knew you worked for the CIA, and they needed your files to document it."

Jenkins smiled. Daugherty's digging had confirmed the biggest hurdle, that Jenkins had been acting on behalf of the CIA. His desire to obtain Jenkins's files could only mean he was trying to document what Jenkins had told him.

He thought of Sloane's comment about the business card and need for more tangible proof. "Claudia, I need you to do me a favor."

"Sure," she said, though she sounded tentative.

"I need you to type up what you just told me and attach the business card from the agent to that document. Then I want you to date and sign the document. When you're done, I want you to make a copy. Put the original in an envelope, seal it, and take it to the post office and be certain to get it date stamped today." Jenkins had worked with Sloane long enough to know that a person sending herself certified mail was a way to prove she had written and signed a document on the date stamped on the envelope. He instructed Baker to do this, then said, "When you get the envelope, don't open it. Keep it someplace safe in the office." He gave her David Sloane's name and his law firm mailing address and told her to also send the copy certified mail.

After thanking Baker and disconnecting, Jenkins turned to his son. "Hey, CJ, you about ready for some breakfast?"

"I had a bite," he said. "A few more minutes?"

Jenkins checked his watch. It was just after 8:00 a.m. "Half an hour. Is that fair?"

"Yeah," the boy said, bringing the rod back over his shoulder and flinging the lure out toward Sloane's moored boat. The lure hit the water with a splash and CJ clicked over the bail and started reeling, moving the tip of the rod up and down as Jake had shown him.

"I'll go up and get breakfast ready for your mom," Jenkins said. He wanted to call Sloane, tell him what Claudia had told him, and ask if he had any additional advice.

The tide was out, leaving a thirty-foot stretch of rocky beach from the water's edge to the lawn leading to the covered back porch. When Jenkins reached the porch, he heard the doorbell, quickly crossed through the house, and answered the door. Chris Daugherty stood on the porch dressed in a suit beneath a down jacket and a knit ski cap. A second agent, standing behind him, had also dressed for the cold.

"Mr. Jenkins," Daugherty said. "I hope this isn't too early."

Jenkins was glad he'd left CJ at the beach. "No. It's fine. What can I do for you?"

"I'd like to ask you a few more questions."

"My wife is trying to get some sleep and my son is home."

"We could do it at our offices downtown," Daugherty said.

"Did you speak to the CIA?"

"I did."

"And did they fill in the blanks like I told you?"

"I'm still working on it. Some additional questions were raised. Just a few things I need to clear up."

Jenkins had sent Daugherty on this trail, and the FBI agent appeared, at least, to be digging for answers. He decided it best that he continue to cooperate. "I'll call David and see if he's available."

"We'll see you both in an hour," Daugherty said.

—

An hour later, Jenkins sat beside Jake at a table in a utilitarian conference room at the FBI's field office. Sloane had an arbitration in Port Angeles and told Jenkins to reschedule the meeting with Daugherty, but Jenkins didn't want to do that. He told Sloane of his conversation with Claudia Baker, and said that Daugherty had confirmed that he'd spoken to the CIA and had some follow-up questions.

"I'm anxious to get this behind me. Alex is close to her due date and I want to get home and get things prepared before the baby comes. And CJ wants to go back to school with his friends and play soccer. You and Jake have been more than accommodating, but it's time to get home."

Jake, who had a limited license under Rule 9 that allowed him to practice law, was the compromise. Jake's role primarily would be to take notes, ensure the questions were appropriate, and not allow the FBI to record the conversation.

Chris Daugherty and the second agent walked into the conference room, pulled out chairs, and sat across the table from them. "We made some phone calls, as you suggested," Daugherty said. "Your service record indicates you voluntarily retired from the Central Intelligence Agency in 1978. That was after only a few years of service, correct?"

"Two years and a month."

"Did you leave the CIA on good terms?" Daugherty asked.

"Not particularly, no."

"Why not?" Daugherty asked.

Jake sat forward. "What does this have to do with the current operation in Russia?"

"Just a foundational question . . ." Daugherty looked at the business card Jake had provided him. "Mr. Carter, I want to establish his background, who he worked for at the CIA before he was reactivated. Those kinds of things." He looked to Jenkins. "Why did you not leave on good terms?"

"I still don't see the point of the question," Jake said. "How is it relevant?"

"It's okay," Jenkins said. He knew Jake was just trying to do his job, but he also wanted Daugherty to do his. "I felt that the agency had misled me with regard to a specific operation and as a result people died."

"You were upset with the agency?"

"Back then I was, yes."

"But not any longer?"

"That's a long time to hold a grudge. I'd moved on. I just wanted out. If you checked, then you know that I moved to the farm on Camano Island. I've been there ever since."

"That farm means a lot to you, I take it?"

"It's been home for a long time."

"You're married with a son."

"Correct."

"And another on the way?"

"That's right."

"So how did CJ Security come about?"

"I was approached by the CFO of the investment company LSR&C."

"What's his name?"

"Randy Traeger."

"How did you and Randy Traeger know each other?"

"His son and my son played together, and I must have discussed in passing that I worked as a private investigator and provided security, when asked, for David Sloane and his clients. Traeger said LSR&C was looking to expand overseas into foreign markets and they needed security in those offices for when high-profile investors were brought in."

"And one of those foreign offices was in Moscow?"

"Correct."

"Your wife also works for CJ Security?"

"She did, but she's pregnant and her doctor put her on bed rest."

"Did she also meet with . . ." Daugherty flipped through his notes. "With Carl Emerson?"

"No," Jenkins said.

"Did she ever meet him?"

"No."

"When you started CJ Security, did you take out a business loan?"

Jenkins knew where Daugherty was going. He just didn't know Daugherty's purpose for going there. "Not initially," he said.

"Did those circumstances change?"

"LSR&C began to quickly grow. In order for me to keep up with their security concerns, I needed to hire additional security contractors. I didn't have the capital to do it."

"So you took out loans. What did you use for collateral?"

"The farm."

"Your home."

"Yes."

"And at some point LSR&C stopped paying CJ Security, but you continued to work for them."

"I was told by Randy Traeger that they would get caught up."

"Did that happen?"

"Not initially and not entirely."

"Were you being pressured by your vendors and security contractors?"

"Some."

"Past-due notices, threats to stop providing services?"

"Yes. We went through this before, Agent Daugherty."

"I'm sorry. I'm just trying to be thorough and make sure I understand all of this."

Jenkins was no longer buying that to be the reason for the questions. He now suspected the presence of the second agent was to confirm what Jenkins had to say, since Daugherty had been alone during the first interview. He began to wonder what game Daugherty was playing.

"And in the midst of this shortfall . . . this is when Carl Emerson showed up at your farm, unannounced, and made you an offer to be reactivated?"

"That's right."

"And how much did Mr. Emerson say he would pay you?"

"We agreed on fifty thousand dollars to start."

"And you used that money to pay CJ Security contractors, vendor invoices . . . business expenses, those kinds of things?"

"Again, I told you that I did."

Jake jumped in. "Unless there is something else, Agent Daugherty, we're going to leave. He's answered all of these questions before."

Daugherty sat back but kept his gaze on Jenkins. After a moment he said, "I called the CIA, as you asked. They had no information of an operation in Russia."

"And I told you they won't admit to the specific operation because it would put agents' lives in danger."

"That's not what I meant," Daugherty said. "They had no information of any operation or that you were reactivated."

Jenkins froze.

"If the CIA can't acknowledge you were reactivated, what am I supposed to think?"

Jenkins's mind scrambled for an answer. None came.

"Here's what I don't understand," Daugherty continued. "The CIA said Alexei Sukurov, one of the names you admitted that you divulged to the FSB, was still active."

Jenkins felt another sharp blow. "I was told he had died."

"He did die, but recently and under mysterious circumstances."

Jenkins could not believe what he was hearing. He'd been set up from the start. He felt light-headed and fought against the onset of an anxiety attack. He couldn't breathe and took several quick breaths. It didn't help.

"What the hell have I done?" he said under his breath but loud enough that it caused Jake to turn his head.

"Let's take a break," Jake said.

"Do you want to confess and make a deal, Mr. Jenkins?" Daugherty asked.

"Charlie, let's take a break," Jake said, pushing his chair away from the table.

Jenkins couldn't catch his breath. He felt the walls of the room closing around him. His right hand began to shake. He pulled it from the tabletop. Perspiration rolled down his face. He looked to Daugherty. "This isn't what you think it is. I didn't do it for the reason you think."

"Why did you do it?"

"I took a polygraph," Jenkins said, trying not to sound like a drowning man gasping for a breath of air. "I did not disclose any unauthorized information. The polygraph confirmed that."

"When you were trained as a CIA field officer, did that training including techniques to pass a polygraph test?" Daugherty asked.

"Charlie, let's take a break," Jake said with greater urgency.

"The CIA is also having difficulty reaching another agent in Moscow. Someone they say disappeared from their radar at the same time you said you were over there. Her name is Paulina Ponomayova. Did you have any contact with her?"

"Hang on," Jake said, raising a hand.

But the name anchored Jenkins. He pulled himself together, though not completely. "If I was a spy, Agent Daugherty, a spy guilty of treason . . . as you're intimating, why would the CIA tell you the name of a current operative in Russia and have you ask me to confirm it?"

"I don't know. Why do you think?"

"I don't think they'd be so stupid."

"Are you a spy?"

"I already answered that question," Jenkins said. "And you have a polygraph test confirming I was a spy, and that I didn't disclose any unauthorized information."

The two men stared at one another.

"Am I free to go?" Jenkins asked.

Daugherty motioned to the door as if to say *go ahead*, but Jenkins knew "free" was just an expression. He would have at least one car and two agents following his every move from the moment he left the building.

50

Neither Jenkins nor Jake said much on the drive back to the office. Jenkins now knew the CIA would not come to his defense, would not even acknowledge he had been reactivated. The question was, Why not? Was it because the CIA would do nothing to acknowledge the seven sisters, not even internally? Or was the reason something more nefarious?

In his head, Jenkins heard Alex's warning. *We both know someone went to great lengths to keep you from coming home, to silence you. If you start talking, that person, whoever he is, will have to respond.*

Someone had given Chris Daugherty ammunition to not just discredit Jenkins, but to accuse him of espionage, and possibly put him away, maybe for life. What Jenkins couldn't understand was why Daugherty hadn't arrested him on the spot. Why he had allowed Jenkins to leave the building, even with the escort following them, which had doubled to four agents in two cars, now parked across the street from Sloane's offices.

"I should have cut it off," Jake said. "David would have cut him off."

"You tried," Jenkins said. "I was stupid. I thought the CIA would fill in the blanks for Daugherty, that they would at least acknowledge I had been reactivated."

"It has to be Emerson, doesn't it?"

"Maybe. It could also be that the CIA is protecting an operation that has been ongoing and effective for forty years and will sacrifice both Emerson and me to do so."

"They could try you for espionage," Jake said.

Jenkins looked again at the two Fords parked bumper to bumper at the curb of the undeveloped lot, and he thought again of CJ's question the night he'd gone into the boy's room to put him to bed.

Dad, are you going to jail?

—

Jenkins and Jake looked up from the computer monitor as Sloane returned to his office from Port Angeles. The three had discussed Daugherty's interview on a conference call.

"It looks like we opened a can of worms when we went to the FBI," Jenkins said.

Jake turned his laptop to face Sloane and pulled up the news story that had run earlier that afternoon. "The Securities and Exchange Commission is investigating LSR&C for fraud and corruption," he said. "They're saying the entire company is one big Ponzi scheme." Jake hit the button and the recorded newscast played again.

A female reporter spoke into her microphone outside the Columbia Center, the black monolith in downtown Seattle. The reporter said LSR&C had come under investigation by the IRS two months earlier, but that had gone nowhere.

"That does not appear to be the case with the SEC investigation. The SEC filed its complaint in federal court today alleging fraud against LSR&C's COO, Mitchell Goldstone, and its CFO, Randy Traeger, as well as the company's other officers," the reporter said. "The pleading alleges LSR&C sought wealthy donors through the fraudulent misuse of prominent Seattle names."

Jenkins took out his cell phone and called Traeger, as he had done the first time he saw the newscast, without success. This time Traeger answered.

Jenkins hit the "Speaker" button so Jake and Sloane could hear the conversation.

"Charlie?"

"Randy, what the hell is going on? I'm watching the local news."

"I don't know," Traeger said. "This started several weeks ago with that reporter from the *Seattle Times*. She asked to interview the officers about the company's rapid growth. I had a bad feeling about her then, and I told Mitchell to turn her down. He assured me I was overreacting. A day after the request, we received a letter from the IRS asking for financial information and alleging that the company had failed to pay taxes, but Mitchell again told me not to worry about it. He said it would be taken care of."

"Taken care of how?"

"I don't know how, but the investigation went away."

"Went away? How?" Jenkins asked, knowing that the IRS rarely, if ever, went away.

"I don't know how," Traeger said, clearly on edge. "Mitchell told me he'd handle it, and I never heard anything more about it. I was right about the reporter, though. She wasn't interested in our growth. She was interested in the names of our investors."

"So then what's going on now with the SEC?"

"I don't fully know. All I can tell you is the shit has really hit the fan. They've assigned a bankruptcy trustee and they've seized all of our assets. Have you spoken to Mitchell?"

"No. You haven't either?"

"I have no idea where he is. I haven't seen him since yesterday afternoon. There's money missing, Charlie."

Jenkins looked to Sloane. "How much?"

"I don't know for certain, but it's millions of dollars. I went through my files before they seized our computers."

"Who seized the computers?"

"Federal investigators came in this afternoon and told everyone to get out of the office."

Jenkins paused, thinking, then he said to Traeger, "Where are you now?"

"I'm at home watching the television and waiting for my attorney to call. If this is true . . . I've got a wife and three kids, Charlie. I've got to go. Someone is calling me."

Traeger disconnected. Jenkins looked across the table at Sloane and Jake. "We need to go," he said.

"Go where?" Sloane asked.

"I'll tell you in the car. Jake, pick us up outside the back of the building. I don't want the FBI to follow me."

Fifteen minutes later, Jake pulled into the parking garage beneath the Columbia Center and Jenkins led them up several sets of escalators to the building lobby. They stepped inside an elevator bank that serviced LSR&C's business offices on the fortieth floor. Jenkins swiped his access card and pressed that button, then held his breath that access had not yet been shut off. The light illuminated and the elevator rose.

On the fortieth floor, Jenkins stepped off the elevator and came to an abrupt stop.

The office fixtures, furniture, and other equipment had been completely removed. He didn't see a desk or a cubicle wall anywhere. Every computer had been taken. No prints or paintings adorned the walls. No nameplates identified the persons working in the offices. Jenkins did not see a scrap of paper, a pen, or a discarded paper clip anywhere. Even the carpeting had been removed, the floor now just bare concrete.

51

They returned to Sloane's conference room and continued the conversation they'd started in the car. Jenkins told them the fact that LSR&C's offices had been cleaned out within hours of the SEC news breaking changed things dramatically. This was no longer just about a leak at the CIA. This called into question the very existence of the company Jenkins thought he'd been protecting, and Traeger's statement that money was missing triggered still more red flags.

"Explain to me again what you mean by a CIA proprietary?" Sloane said, clearly still trying to wrap his head around what Jenkins had been telling them.

"Simply put, it's a company owned and operated by the CIA," Jenkins said.

"But not on paper."

"No, never on paper. On paper it looks like a legitimate enterprise. In actuality, it's a means for the CIA to transfer funds to field officers working deep undercover all over the world. The company provides a cover for field officers by providing them with the legitimate employment they need to get into a particular country, and it allows the CIA to funnel them money. It would explain why LSR&C grew so quickly and had offices in Moscow, Dubai, and other foreign locations, and it would explain how an IRS investigation simply disappeared, and how the company's offices could be cleaned out so thoroughly and so quickly. It could also explain why there are millions of dollars missing, as Traeger said. Those could be funds that were either funneled to field operatives or designated for that purpose when the company blew up."

"That's where I'm having difficulty," Sloane said. "If LSR&C was a CIA front, why would the IRS and the Securities and Exchange Commission get involved?"

"Because the CIA doesn't broadcast that these companies are proprietaries, not even to other government agencies," Jenkins said. "To the IRS and the SEC, LSR&C was a legitimate company. I suspect that's the reason why the IRS investigation ended so quickly. Goldstone must have made a phone call to Langley, and Langley called the IRS and told them to back off."

"So why didn't they do the same thing with the SEC investigation?" Sloane said.

"It could be that the SEC's investigation was too far along, or that the story of a Ponzi scheme had already leaked to the media, and investors had become involved. Traeger said the *Seattle Times* reporter knew many of the company details before she set up the interviews."

"So what happens then to Goldstone and Traeger?" Jake asked. "Will the CIA protect them?"

"Not likely. The fact that the offices were cleaned out is an indication the CIA is going to disassociate themselves from LSR&C and anyone who worked for it."

"Could that be what's happening to you—the reason the CIA won't even acknowledge you were reactivated?" Sloane asked.

"I don't know," Jenkins said. "I think what happened to me goes a lot deeper. But from a practical standpoint, the CIA disassociating itself from the officers of the company is a further indication it will not acknowledge me. It means I have no contacts at LSR&C other than the officers being indicted for fraud and corruption."

"It also means that documents that could prove what you're telling us are going to be very difficult to get. There wasn't a scrap of paper in that entire office," Sloane said.

"What I can't yet figure out is why Daugherty didn't just arrest me when I was in his office. Why would he let me walk out?"

"It could be the FBI wanted this news in the public domain to cast doubt on anything you have to say before you have the chance to say it," Sloane said.

"Guilty until proven innocent," Jake said.

"I've seen it done before," Sloane said.

"I'm also concerned about Traeger's comment that there is money missing."

"Why?" Sloane asked.

"Because if someone was selling secrets to the Russians, they'd need a way to wash that money. I saw it happen in Mexico City. Money paid to Russian double agents was washed through businesses, so it couldn't be tied to the CIA."

"Emerson would have known that," Sloane said.

Jenkins nodded. "If LSR&C was a CIA proprietary, Emerson, or someone else, could have been passing money from the Russians through the company. It would be a rational reason why the company imploded now, after we went to the FBI. The implosion could be someone trying to get rid of documents before the FBI could get ahold of them and confirm there are millions of dollars missing."

"That would mean the leak worked for LSR&C?" Jake said. "Could it have been Goldstone? Could that be why he's missing?"

"I don't think so," Jenkins said. "But we need to find him and ask him about it. And I need to talk to Traeger and find out what they both knew about any of this. That isn't going to be easy with the FBI escort watching my every move."

"If they're also getting screwed, they might be looking for a way to save themselves," Sloane said. "And if Goldstone knew LSR&C was a

CIA front, and he has any documents to substantiate it, that gives your story of being recruited greater credibility."

"Which may be why Goldstone is missing," Jenkins said. "And why I'm likely to be arrested for espionage. Someone is trying to discredit us both, and they're well on their way to doing so."

52

The following morning, Jenkins did his best to keep to routine for CJ's sake. They walked down the rocky beach to the water's edge with their fishing poles. Jenkins felt groggy from a lack of sleep. He'd been awake most of the night, filling in Alex on what had transpired, and working with David and Jake on what they could do. Jenkins's further calls to Traeger had gone unanswered. He'd never had a cell number for Goldstone.

Sloane and Jake had both left the office early that morning for Jenkins's Camano Island home. Jenkins had taped the card with Carl Emerson's phone number to the inside cover of a first edition of *Moby Dick*, so the card would not fall out if someone pulled the books from the shelves and fanned the pages. Sloane told Jenkins he also planned to call Daugherty and determine whether the FBI intended to arrest Jenkins. If so, Sloane wanted Jenkins to voluntarily turn himself in. Doing so would avoid the FBI arresting Jenkins in front of CJ and Alex, and it might play better in the news if Jenkins took an early stand that he wanted to vigorously defend himself against any charges.

Puget Sound's waves lapped against the rocks beneath clear blue skies that stretched above Vashon Island to the distant, snowcapped Olympic Mountains.

"You think today's our day?" Jenkins asked his son, as he did each day they'd fished. "Is today the day we catch a big salmon?"

"I think so," CJ said. The boy wasted no time. He clicked the bail open, brought the pole back, and flung his pink Buzz Bomb lure out over the water.

Jenkins brought his pole back over his right shoulder to cast and noticed Chris Daugherty and three men in suits, coats, and sunglasses standing at the railing of the public easement. Daugherty nodded.

"Dad! Dad, I got one," CJ shouted.

The tip of the boy's pole had bent in an accentuated arc, and the fishing line was darting across the water's surface. Jenkins dropped his pole and moved to help his son. "Loosen the drag," he said. "That's a big fish. Let him run a bit but keep him away from the boats. You don't want to get your line tangled around a buoy line."

For fifteen minutes CJ was the picture of concentration, walking three paces to his left and three to his right, reeling when he dropped the tip of the pole, then gently pulling the tip up high. He'd have the fish close to shore, and it would take off running again, his drag whizzing.

"You're tiring him out, CJ."

"Dad, you take him," the boy said, but Jenkins knew the request wasn't motivated by fatigue but by fear that he might lose the fight.

"He's your fish," Jenkins said. "Just keep doing what you're doing. Walk him up the beach." Jenkins picked up the net.

CJ continued to reel as he backed up the beach. Jenkins saw the tail of a big fish slap and pound the water's surface. "You're doing great," he said.

"I think you better take it, Dad. He's too big."

Jenkins bent to a knee and put his hand on his son's back. "This is your fight. You don't need anyone's help."

CJ glanced at him, and when Jenkins smiled, the boy returned it.

Other fishermen along the beach had taken their lines out of the water and cheered CJ on. "Reel him in, CJ. You got this one. Reel him in."

Jenkins looked up at the concrete platform. Daugherty and the other three agents had stepped down onto the beach, waiting. He knew they hadn't come to talk, not that many. The FBI wasn't going to give Jenkins the chance to turn himself in, or to tell the newspapers he was innocent.

Jenkins turned his attention back to the water. "A little more, CJ. Walk back a little more." He waded ankle deep into the water and shoved the net under the fish, lifting the salmon out of the water. The net was almost too small, the tail of the fish hanging over the side.

"It's a king," Jenkins said. He guessed it weighed more than twenty pounds, maybe twenty-five.

On shore, CJ stood over the fish, beaming with pride as the other fishermen congratulated him. Jenkins removed the hook and lure from the fish's mouth and smiled at his son, seeing him through a cloud of tears. He took a small club and hit the fish once over the head, putting it out of any misery.

"Hold it up, CJ," some of the fishermen said. "Let's get a picture for the paper."

CJ dropped his pole and grabbed his prize under one gill. He needed both hands to lift it. The fish stretched from CJ's chin past his knees. This was more than just a fish. This was a trophy.

"Can we show Mom?" CJ asked.

Jenkins looked up to the house. Alex stood on the lawn in front of the Adirondack chairs. Tears streamed down her cheeks. She, too, had seen the four men.

"I think she's seen it," Jenkins said. "And she's so proud of you, she's crying."

CJ turned and waved. Alex waved back.

"Why don't you take it up to her?" Jenkins said. "You and Mom can clean it together. I think she'd like that."

"Don't you want to clean it?"

"You know me," Jenkins said, struggling to hold back his tears. "I'm not too good with fish guts. Go on. Take it up to your mom."

The smile vanished from CJ's face when he saw the four men walking toward them. "I want you to come with me," he said.

"Go ahead, CJ. Everything is going to be fine, just like I told you. You believed me, right?"

CJ nodded, but now tears streaked his cheeks.

"Go on," Jenkins said. "This is my fight now. You understand? And I'm going to win it, just like you won your fight today and landed your fish. Okay?"

Slowly, reluctantly, CJ walked up the beach, occasionally looking back over his shoulder as he went. When he reached Alex, he dropped the fish on the lawn and buried his face in her stomach. Alex waved to Jenkins. He raised his hand and waved back, uncertain when, if ever, he'd have a morning like this one again.

—

Jenkins laid the fishing poles on the lawn next to the tackle box. The other fishermen had returned to fishing, though a few continued to look over their shoulders at the four men in suits and ties.

"I guess you're not going to give me that chance to voluntarily turn myself in?" Jenkins said.

"I'm sorry," Daugherty said. "This wasn't my decision."

"Thanks for not doing it in front of my kid."

"I have three children of my own, Mr. Jenkins. No sense making this harder than it is. We can walk up the easement. I have a car waiting."

"Then let's go," Jenkins said.

Daugherty grimaced. "I'm going to have to put you in handcuffs. I'm just following orders."

"Can we at least wait until we get to the easement?"

"Sure," Daugherty said.

At the easement, Jenkins turned and Daugherty handcuffed his hands behind his back. A news camera filmed Jenkins walking between two marshals, each gripping a bicep. When they reached Daugherty's Ford, one of the marshals put a hand on Jenkins's head, and he lowered into the back seat. Jenkins looked back over his shoulder. Several neighbors stood in their yards, watching the spectacle. Thankfully, Alex and CJ were not among them.

53

Daugherty brought Jenkins to the FBI field office to be booked and processed. He was put in a locked conference room and sat waiting. When the clock in the room neared 5:00 p.m., Jenkins figured he'd be spending the night in the federal jail, but when Daugherty and the three marshals returned, Daugherty said, "Time to be arraigned."

Jenkins looked at the clock on the wall. "It's after five."

"Judge Harden is waiting," Daugherty said, not elaborating.

"What about David Sloane?"

"He'll meet you in court," Daugherty said.

They took Jenkins down the elevator to a car waiting in the garage. At the US District Court on Stewart Street, they pulled to the curb and Jenkins understood the reason for the long delay. A crowd of camera crews and reporters stood in the courtyard leading to the glass-and-copper building entrance. The delay had given the FBI time to alert the media and to get out their side of the story about the arrest.

Guilty until proven innocent.

A marshal opened the back door and helped Jenkins step out. A second marshal moved quickly to his right side. Two others filled in behind them. No one stood in front of Jenkins, which gave the cameras an unobstructed view. When they reached the stairs beside the rectangular wishing pool, Jenkins looked down to navigate the steps and immediately heard the whir and click of cameras. The photographers had waited until he'd lowered his head, looking defeated and guilty.

The marshals escorted him into a cavernous courtroom with ample pews already filling with reporters. Behind the railing, David Sloane waited at the counsel table. On the left stood a team of four lawyers—three men and a woman in dark-blue or gray suits.

When Jenkins reached the counsel table a marshal removed his handcuffs.

"How are you doing?" Sloane asked.

Jenkins shrugged. "I'm hungry. These guys are worse than the Russians. They haven't given me any food all day. You spoke with Alex?"

"She wanted to come. I told her not to."

"Thanks."

"I guess we know now why Daugherty didn't arrest you the other day," Sloane said. "They were getting the media lined up. You've been all over the news and social media. They shipped out press materials before they even arrested you."

"Do we know what I'm going to be charged with?"

Sloane shook his head. "The federal prosecutor hasn't told me. I assume we'll find out in a moment."

"Just get me out on bail so I can go home to my family." Jenkins looked to the government attorneys to his left. "Who among the gaggle is the lead?"

"The woman," Sloane said. "Maria Velasquez. And don't let her diminutive size fool you. We've sparred twice, and both times she put up a hell of a fight. She isn't dishonest, but she isn't forthcoming either. If I don't ask for it in discovery, she won't give it to us. It gets worse," Sloane added.

"Better to pull off that Band-Aid just once," Jenkins said.

"They found Mitchell Goldstone," Sloane said.

"Dead?"

"He's alive, but they found him in a hotel room downtown with his wrists slit and a bottle of prescription painkillers. How well did you know him? Would he try something like this?"

Jenkins shook his head. "I don't know. I didn't know him that well."

"The news is saying Goldstone absconded with money he stole from investors and is facing life in prison."

"We figured that argument out ourselves, didn't we?" Jenkins said. "I don't buy that either. It's too easy. Too convenient."

"And Randy Traeger is cooperating with investigators. I called and spoke to his attorney. Traeger claims he had no knowledge of the Ponzi scheme, and his attorney said he has no knowledge that LSR&C was a CIA proprietary, said he didn't even know the term."

"He's washing his hands of the entire sordid affair."

"Looks that way."

"Any idea why they waited until five o'clock to arraign me?" Jenkins asked. "Other than the media?"

"Judge Harden was finishing up a trial and the government wants him," Sloane said. "He's a former federal prosecutor with a reputation as a hard-ass who does things his way."

The bailiff entered the courtroom from a door to the right of the elevated bench and called out, "All rise, the Honorable Joseph B. Harden presiding."

Jenkins thought Judge Harden looked a bit like Abe Lincoln, a tall, strapping man with jet-black hair, graying at the temples. He entered the courtroom in his black robe, sat at his elevated desk, and picked up several sheets of paper, reading as the clerk called out the case number for the *United States Government v. Charles William Jenkins*.

After a brief pause, Harden said, "State your appearances, please."

The gaggle of attorneys on the left side of the courtroom started, with Velasquez speaking last.

"David Sloane for the defendant," Sloane said.

"Has your client had the opportunity to read the charges against him, Mr. Sloane?" Harden asked.

"No, Your Honor. Nor have I."

"Then I will do so now." Harden read the arraignment word for word. Jenkins was charged with two counts of espionage, two counts of passing classified secrets to the Russians for remuneration, and one count of conspiracy. The government also charged him with disclosing classified information, including the identities of two CIA assets, leading to their deaths. Though Harden did not say it, Jenkins knew he was facing a life sentence.

"How does the defendant plead?"

"Not guilty," Jenkins said.

"Very well. Mr. Jenkins, you will be handed over to the US Marshals Service until such time as you are tried."

"The defense wishes to discuss bail," Sloane said.

"The government opposes," Velasquez stated just as quickly. "We believe the defendant to be a flight risk."

"The defendant is married and the father of a nine-year-old boy," Sloane said. "His wife is pregnant with their second child. She is currently on bed rest from pregnancy complications and is due any day. Mr. Jenkins has no desire to be anywhere but with his family and here in court to defeat these charges."

Velasquez looked to one of the attorneys. He handed her a file. "Your Honor, we have a timeline of the defendant's most recent travels outside the country. We'd like to present it to the court."

Harden nodded and Velasquez hit the buttons on her computer as she handed Sloane a document. A timeline with arrows appeared on the courtroom monitors indicating the dates Charles Jenkins had traveled from Seattle to Heathrow Airport in the United Kingdom, and then to Sheremetyevo International Airport outside Moscow.

"The court will note, Your Honor, that the timeline is incomplete. There is no information pertaining to the defendant's return to this country after his most recent trip to Russia. Yet, here he is. Either Mr. Jenkins is Harry Houdini and he somehow traveled back into this country by magic, or he used a fake passport. The government reiterates that Mr. Jenkins is a former CIA field officer and that he is a flight risk."

Harden looked to Sloane, his eyebrows raised in question. Jenkins knew Sloane faced a dilemma. He couldn't very well tell the court the truth, which would only confirm Velasquez's argument that Jenkins had more than one passport for more than one country.

"Mr. Jenkins can surrender his passport to the US Marshals Service," Sloane said. "And I will assure the court he will remain in the state of Washington to defeat these charges. As I said—"

Harden cut him off with a raised hand. "I'm going to deny bail at this time and find that the defendant is a potential flight risk. Counsel, you are welcome to brief me on this issue. Is there anything else?"

Jenkins felt weak in the knees knowing he would not be going home to his family, and what that would mean for CJ. *Dad, are you going to jail?*

"No," Sloane said.

"Charles William Jenkins, you are hereby remanded to the custody of the US Marshals Service until such further time as the issue of bail is considered or for further proceedings in this matter. Court is adjourned." Harden rapped his gavel once, stood, and quickly departed. The marshals returned to the table, this time with a belly chain they slipped around Jenkins's waist, cuffing his hands to it. The chain extended to the floor and two ankle cuffs. Those two were snapped on.

"Get ahold of Alex, will you?" Jenkins said, worried what the news would do to her and to CJ.

"I'll handle it," Sloane said. "We'll file a motion for bail as soon as we can."

Jenkins knew it would not be soon enough.

54

Jenkins spent the next three days at the Federal Detention Center near the airport in SeaTac. He refused to eat jail food—concerned it could be poisoned. According to Sloane, Mitchell Goldstone had survived, was recovering in a hospital, and was set to be arraigned within the week.

Jenkins tried to sound upbeat when he spoke to Alex and to CJ on the telephone, but he knew the stress his arrest and imprisonment had caused both of them. Sloane had hired a nurse to care for Alex at his home, since he and Jake, who had insisted he be a part of Jenkins's defense team, if only behind the scenes, would be spending long hours at the law firm. Sloane had also hired a retired schoolteacher to home-school CJ. CJ had initially protested, until he learned his teacher had been a professional soccer player who had also agreed to privately coach him if he kept his grades up. The boy nearly flipped.

After thirty hours, Jenkins was transferred to the classification section and issued prison clothing, deloused, given a complete physical examination, and otherwise dehumanized. Sloane filed a motion that Jenkins be placed in administrative segregation, arguing that televisions made it a near certainty Jenkins's arrest, and the charges against him, would be well-known to the other inmates, including military veterans. Harden agreed.

The noise inside the general population—radios blaring rock music and metal banging against metal—was near deafening. The inmates could not see one another and resorted to shouting through the cinder-block walls to keep from going crazy. It didn't always work.

Jenkins didn't speak, concerned everything he said was being recorded, which only further isolated him. He needed to get out so he and Sloane could prepare his defense.

If Jenkins was being paranoid, the fifth day proved it was with good reason. Sloane came to the jail and told him someone had broken into his law office, and that only a tripped security alarm had prevented the person from opening Sloane's safe, which was where he kept Carl Emerson's business card and the sealed envelope with the typed affidavit from Claudia Baker. Those two items were now the only evidence Jenkins had to argue that he'd been reactivated by the CIA. It wasn't much.

Sloane had filed a motion for bail, and Judge Harden had set it to be heard the following morning. "He's pushing us to move this matter quickly."

"Have you gotten anywhere trying to find Emerson?"

"No, and the government isn't helping. They say Emerson is no longer employed by the agency, and they don't know his current whereabouts. It might be why Harden is pushing us. The longer we drag this out, the more time we have to find him."

"What about getting documents that support the government's charges?"

"Jake's working on a motion, but at the moment we're concentrating on getting you out on bail."

"How's Alex?"

"The nurse is taking good care of her. She says the baby's heartbeat is strong and can be delivered by C-section any day now. Alex is waiting until you're home."

"If we lose the motion for bail, tell the nurse to do what has to be done. I don't want anything to happen to Alex or to the baby."

The following morning, Jenkins appeared in court, this time to watch Sloane and Velasquez square off on Sloane's motion for bail. The gallery was full for a relatively mundane motion, indicating again that Jenkins's arrest was big news in Seattle. When the argument finished, Harden took the matter under advisement and said he'd issue an order late that afternoon. Sloane told Jenkins he wasn't sure where Judge Harden would fall in his decision. He said that in a fifty-fifty argument, Jenkins would likely lose.

Harden, however, surprised them. In an afternoon conference call, he granted the motion, setting Jenkins's bail at $1 million, and ordered Jenkins to wear an ankle bracelet that would alert US marshals if he left the Seattle area. Jenkins also had to call into a marshal each morning and each night.

Jenkins didn't care. He was just glad to be out. "Did you hire a security company to sweep your office and home for bugs?" Jenkins asked as he and Sloane drove from the jail to Sloane's home on Three Tree Point.

"Every morning," Sloane said.

Inside the house, Jenkins could tell Alex struggled to hold it together when she saw him. Sloane excused himself and went back to the office.

"How are you doing?" Jenkins asked.

"I'm okay. I'm anxious to get this baby out. The doctor said we can go in any day now that you're home."

Jenkins smiled through tears. "Then let's have a baby," he said. "Where's CJ?"

"Where he is every afternoon; he has a serious bug since catching that thirty-pound salmon."

"Probably a good diversion for him. Does he know anything?"

"He asked me about the men who came to the beach that morning. I told him that he might hear people say unkind things about you, but that those people don't know you the way we do."

Jenkins blew out a breath he felt like he'd been holding for days. He knew from the crowd in the courtroom that there was likely a lot of unfavorable media coverage. It didn't bother him, but he worried about his son. He was glad, at least, that CJ was not in school, where kids could be brutal.

Alex handed Jenkins a small jewelry box. "Open it."

Jenkins opened the box and removed a sterling silver bracelet.

"Read the inside. I had it inscribed."

Jenkins turned the bracelet over, and Alex handed him a pair of reading glasses from the counter. He slipped the glasses onto the bridge of his nose and manipulated the bracelet to catch the light.

THEN YOU WILL KNOW THE TRUTH, AND THE TRUTH SHALL SET YOU FREE. JOHN 8:32

"Whatever happens, we know the truth. No one can take that from us. And that's what we're going to tell CJ."

Jenkins slipped the bracelet over his wrist. "I hope the truth is enough."

55

Sloane and Jake sat across the conference room table from Conrad Levy, a retired CIA operative in his early seventies. In retirement, Levy had become one of the agency's harshest critics for too often leaving field officers hung out to dry. He'd written a book chronicling how good men and women devoted their lives to serve their country, and how the agency had not reciprocated that same loyalty. Sloane sought Levy's opinion on whether Jenkins's story was indicative of the agency's practice of which Levy was so critical.

Levy looked nothing like the James Bond or Jason Bourne characters from the movies. Short, with a slight build, he had receding gray hair and wore glasses, a well-worn suit, and nondescript shirt and tie—the type of person who could eat in the same restaurant each night and not be remembered.

"Obviously I have some questions," Levy said, his voice high-pitched. "But I suspect from what you've told me that your client won't answer those questions."

"You know what we know," Sloane said.

Levy pushed his glasses onto the bridge of his nose. "I'm sorry, Mr. Sloane, but I don't believe Mr. Jenkins's story for a minute."

Sloane had not expected this. "What don't you believe?" he asked.

"All of it . . . For a man who had supposedly played games with the KGB in Mexico City, I don't think it washes. He's either the dumbest intelligence officer who's ever lived, or he's a liar and a traitor." That left little room for doubt.

"Even if his story was true, you won't get anyone at the CIA to back it up."

"Why not?"

"Because if his story is true, it points to the agency's inability to adequately monitor the conduct of a top-level employee, possibly for decades. It makes them look incompetent to intelligence agencies all over the world. Beyond that, the CIA will never publicly acknowledge a company working as a CIA proprietary."

"He told me Carl Emerson was his station chief in Mexico City. Is that not true?" Sloane asked.

"That part is true. But sprinkling a story with verifiable facts is a field officer's technique to get a person to believe that if some of the facts are verifiable, then the others must also be true, such as that Mr. Jenkins was authorized to disclose the names Alexei Sukurov and Uliana Artemyeva to his Russian contact."

"What do you mean?"

"The names Alexei Sukurov and Uliana Artemyeva first originated in the Mexico City field office as potential targets that could be flipped to CIA assets. Mr. Jenkins worked in that office."

"You're saying that because Charlie worked in that office, he would have been familiar with those names?" Sloane said.

"I'm saying it's possible he was familiar with those names, and he used them because he thought, again, that it would add a level of credibility to his story."

"But the government is arguing his disclosure of those names led to the agents' deaths."

"My point is, they were two real CIA assets who could be verified. Think about it. If you're going to say that your former station chief showed up at your farm, unannounced, forty years after you left the agency, doesn't it make sense to use two names your station chief also would have known and used?"

"Are you saying that he made all of this up?" Jake asked.

"I'm telling you what the government will argue. When your client left the CIA he was upset at the agency. The prosecution will beat this point home to the jury like a drum. They'll argue Mr. Jenkins needed money, and by selling secrets to the Russians, he could get even with the CIA for whatever perceived injustice initially made him leave."

Sloane took a sip of water, trying to slow his thoughts.

"I'm sorry, Mr. Sloane. But look at this from the perspective of a person who could be in a position to convict and sentence Mr. Jenkins. Look at it from the perspective of a juror. Mr. Jenkins gets to Russia and makes contact with the FSB. He offers to provide them information for money, which he desperately needs, and it works the first time. He receives fifty thousand dollars—"

"That money came from his CIA contact," Jake said.

"But you can't prove that, and I don't think you're going to want to try."

"Why not?" Jake asked.

"Because I did try to find the source. The funds came from a Swiss bank account, and were deposited directly into CJ Security's business account. There's no way to determine where the money originated, whether from inside Russia or from some account the CIA uses to fund operatives. Regardless, Mr. Jenkins got his money for his actions, which, without some corroborating evidence to prove where the money came from, won't help him. The government will argue that, having succeeded once, Mr. Jenkins determined he had more information to sell, but this time things didn't go as anticipated. After that first payment, the Russians had evidence that he'd accepted fifty thousand dollars, and when Mr. Jenkins returned to Russia, the FSB blackmailed him, which was very typical of the KGB and, I suspect, is of the FSB as well."

"You're saying they threatened to expose him," Sloane said.

"Yes, and Mr. Jenkins, well versed in the game, recognized what was happening, and he took off running. In my opinion, Mr. Jenkins wasn't working for the CIA. He's just a traitor who got caught and is working to get out of it. And that's coming from a guy who'd like nothing better than to expose the CIA, again."

—

After Levy left the office, Jake said, "Charlie would never make this up. I saw men at the airport in Greece who were watching the gate."

Sloane nodded. "Levy's right though. Charlie's story doesn't ring true, and without some concrete evidence to prove it is true, we won't get very far trying to convince twelve jurors."

"So what do we do now?"

"We come up with a better story."

Jake look pained. "I'm not sure that's going to be enough."

"What do you mean?"

"I don't want to be an alarmist," he said. "But I did some research this afternoon, and as far as I can tell, no CIA agent accused of espionage has ever been acquitted by a jury. Not a single one."

56

Jenkins and CJ entered the kitchen after a morning spent fishing, without success. As the days wore on, Jenkins felt less and less sure of his own chances of success.

"We need to go over your math. We don't want you to fall behind."

"I'll get my backpack."

"I'll check on Mom, see if she needs anything."

CJ started up the steps, but stopped. "When did you say she was going to have the baby?"

"Two days," Charlie said. "How are you feeling about becoming a big brother?"

CJ shrugged one shoulder. "Kind of cool, I guess."

Jenkins thought of the impending trial and what it could mean if he were to be convicted. "Being the big brother comes with responsibilities."

"I know, Dad." CJ got quiet. Then he said, "Are you going to be there to help?"

Jenkins nodded. "Sure I will. Why do you ask?"

"I heard some of the fishermen talking. They said you were arrested the morning those men in suits came. They said they were FBI agents and you were a traitor. It isn't true, is it?"

"Come here for a second." CJ came down the stairs. Jenkins sat on the arm of the couch and put his hands on the boy's shoulders. "I was arrested, but the part about me selling secrets and betraying my country isn't true, CJ. I promise you it isn't."

"Then why would they say it?"

Jenkins sighed. "A lot of things that are happening right now are going to be hard for you to understand. But I'm looking you in the eyes and I'm telling you it isn't true. I want to show you something." Jenkins removed the sterling silver bracelet from his wrist and turned it over so CJ could read the engraving. "Mom gave me this. Can you read what she had inscribed?"

CJ moved the bracelet to catch the light, reading slowly. "'Then you will know the truth, and the truth shall set you free. John 8:32.'"

"As long as we know the truth, it doesn't matter what anyone else says. Do you understand?"

CJ nodded. "I think so."

"Things could get ugly around here. There could be more people saying more bad things about your dad."

"I won't believe them," CJ said.

CJ went to his room to get his math book, and Jenkins walked down the hall to their bedroom and pushed open the door. Alex was not in bed. He heard the bathroom fan humming behind the closed door. Alex had to pee just about every ten minutes.

"Alex?" He walked to the bathroom.

She didn't answer.

He knocked three times. "Alex?"

When she didn't answer, he tried the door handle and pushed on the door. Something on the other side obstructed it. He stuck his head between the gap. Alex lay on the floor, her bathrobe bunched about her waist. She looked to have fainted. Beneath her, a pool of blood had smeared the white tiles.

—

Jenkins watched Sloane and Jake enter the hospital waiting room. Jake stepped to a chair where CJ sat, looking scared. "CJ, what do you say we go find the cafeteria and get some food for everybody?"

CJ shook his head and looked up at his father. "I'm not hungry."

Jenkins put a hand on the boy's back. "Mom's in with the doctors," Jenkins said. "And they're taking good care of her. You go with Jake. I promise I'll call if I hear anything from the doctors."

Jake wrapped an arm around the boy's shoulders and led him out of the room and down the hall.

"How's he doing?" Sloane asked.

"He heard the fishermen talking about me being a traitor. Now this. It's a lot to ask of a nine-year-old."

"Yeah, it is," Sloane said. "What are the doctors saying?"

"She lost a lot of blood. I just checked with the nurse. She said I should hear from the doctor any minute."

Sloane pointed to Jenkins's right hand, which had started to shake. "How long have you had that shake?"

Jenkins flexed his hand. "Since I first went to Russia."

"It's not Parkinson's, is it?"

"No. It's anxiety. I'm not as young as I once was . . . And I have a lot more to lose."

The doctor walked into the waiting room dressed in surgical gear. "Mr. Jenkins, you have a healthy baby girl."

"What?" Jenkins said, overwhelmed but also relieved. Sloane gripped his shoulder.

"We delivered the baby," the doctor said. "I'm sorry, but we had to act quickly."

A girl. He had a baby girl. "How's Alex? How's my wife?"

"She's weak and she's tired, but all her vitals are strong and getting better. We're replenishing lost blood. She's anxious to see you."

"I'll call Jake and CJ and let them know," Sloane said.

Jenkins followed the doctor down the corridor and through several swinging doors. Alex was in the third room of the ICU unit with nurses huddled around her bed. She looked pale and tired, but she smiled.

Jenkins kissed her atop the forehead, whispering, "How're you doing?"

"I'm tired but I'm okay," Alex said, her voice weak. "Better now that you're here. Did you see your daughter?"

In the bassinet beside the bed, the top of a pink beanie poked out from a white blanket with pink stripes.

"Not exactly the birth we planned," Alex whispered.

"Not exactly," Jenkins said, mesmerized at the tiny creature in the bassinet. "She's so little. I don't remember CJ being that little."

"He wasn't," Alex said. "But the doctor says she's fine, just a little jaundiced, but that should clear up in a couple of days. Hold your daughter."

Jenkins picked up the bundle. She fit in his hand, from the tips of his long fingers to just past his wrist. He cradled her to his chest. "Hey, little girl." He felt his heart soar as he said it, and he was filled with conflicting emotions. He wanted to hold her close so that no one could ever hurt her, but he also worried that he would not be there to protect her.

"What about a name?" Alex said. They'd decided not to find out the sex, just as with CJ, and early on they'd toyed with several girls' and boys' names, but with everything happening, they hadn't had a chance to come to a consensus. "I thought we could name her after your mother."

Jenkins smiled. "Elizabeth."

"We can call her Lizzie," Alex said.

"What about Paulina?" Jenkins said. "Maybe for a middle name."

"The woman from Russia?" Alex asked.

"She's the reason I'm here, holding our daughter. She never had children. This would be a way for her to live on."

Alex tried out the name. "Elizabeth Paulina Jenkins. It has a nice ring to it."

The curtain pulled back and a nurse stood with CJ. Jenkins moved so CJ could climb onto the bed next to his mother. Alex kissed him, and he became a little boy again, snuggling close to her side. Jenkins bent down so CJ could see his sister. "You want to hold her?"

"Can I?"

"Sure. Hold your arms out like this. You need to support her head."

CJ did and Jenkins placed his daughter in the crook of the boy's arm. CJ smiled up at them. Then, in a serious voice, he whispered, "I'll take care of her, Dad. I promise."

Jenkins smiled back, anything but certain he'd be there, also, to care for them both.

57

A week after Elizabeth's birth, they all returned to Sloane's house on Three Tree Point. As part of his bail requirements, Jenkins had to stay in King County, and they all agreed it was safer for him and his family at Three Tree than on the isolated farm on Camano. Sloane's house was also closer to the courthouse in downtown Seattle, which gave Sloane and Jenkins more opportunities to talk. In between taking care of Alex and the baby, Jenkins made sure CJ kept on top of his homework. The additional responsibilities were a blessing, giving Jenkins something to do, and keeping his mind otherwise occupied, but only to a point.

The trial loomed over him like the glistening blade of a guillotine, even more so now that they had Lizzie.

Thursday afternoon, Sloane asked Jenkins to meet him at the office. Jenkins arrived at four, with dusk settling in. They pulled chilled glasses from the freezer and filled them at a keg in the kitchen, then sat in the main conference room.

"I talked to Maria Velasquez this afternoon," Sloane said, sounding somewhat hesitant. "In exchange for a plea of diminished capacity, she'll recommend two years in a psychiatric ward. Then you're free."

"They want me to plead insanity?"

"Diminished capacity," Sloane said.

"I know what it means," Jenkins said.

"You'd have this behind you. You could all move on."

Jenkins sipped his beer and set it down on the table. He looked to the silver bracelet on his wrist.

"Until one of the kids at CJ's school, or a fisherman, tells him that his father was a nut job in addition to being a traitor. I could move on, David, if it was just me. But my kids would have to live with that admission for the rest of their lives. I don't want to do that to them."

"If you don't take the plea, the government will pursue life in prison."

"We knew that, didn't we?"

Sloane nodded.

"I know you're obligated to present the deal to me, and you have, but I won't agree to any deal that requires me to admit I was crazy."

Again Sloane did not respond, and for the first time, Jenkins sensed uncertainty.

"Do you think I should consider this?" Jenkins asked.

"We haven't been able to come up with any evidence to support our position, Charlie," Sloane said. "And I'm not sure we will. Emerson seems to have vanished. Traeger is cooperating with the government, Goldstone is working on a plea agreement and can't say anything until it's finalized, and we can't get in the polygraph, and we have no documents."

Jenkins said, "Do you think I'm telling the truth?"

"Whether I think you're telling the truth is irrelevant, Charlie," Sloane said.

"Not to me. Do you think I'm telling the truth?"

"Of course, Charlie, but . . ."

"But what?"

"We hired a consultant by the name of Conrad Levy. He's an ex—"

"I know who he is. He's the guy who wrote the book about the CIA and sold out about a dozen former agents."

Sloane told Jenkins the details of his conversation with Levy. Then he said, "Again, Charlie. It's not about the truth. It's about what we can prove. What we heard from Levy is likely what we'll hear from the government. It's a compelling argument."

"But it isn't the truth."

Sloane nodded. "There may be another way," he said. "There's a psychiatrist I've used in the past who could do an evaluation. Depending on the results, it might be the best evidence we have to argue you are telling the truth."

"Then let's do it," Jenkins said.

For the next three days Jenkins submitted to extensive interviews and a battery of psychological tests administered by a psychiatrist named Addison Beckman. A woman in her midfifties, Beckman was held in high esteem by the profession, especially in forensic psychiatry.

Sloane and Jake met with Beckman in the conference room before she'd committed her findings to writing. If she told them Jenkins was crazy as a loon, they'd never mention her and her tests at trial. Beckman declined coffee or tea. She seemed eager to talk. When seated at the conference room table she said, "He's as straight as they come. Too straight. It would be better for him if he'd loosen up a bit."

"What exactly does that mean?" Sloane asked.

"I'm saying, believe your client. I'm saying that in my opinion, he's honest, nondeceptive, and emotionally stable. I gave him a battery of tests, all of which will be summarized in my report. He isn't delusional, and he isn't a sociopath or a pathological liar. It's my opinion that you can believe what he says happened."

They went over every test Beckman had administered. Five hours later, documents littered Sloane's conference room table—charts, graphs, notes, and test results. It was all well and good, but it didn't solve their biggest problem. Sloane still needed evidence to back up Beckman's opinion.

After Beckman had departed, Sloane retreated to his office with Jake to return a phone call he'd received while working with the psychiatrist. Sloane had hired investigator Peter Vanderlay to run a reverse directory search on the telephone number Carl Emerson had given Charlie. Sloane hoped it would provide evidence that the number belonged to Emerson. Vanderlay answered on the third ring. Sloane put him on the speaker so Jake could hear the conversation.

"Mr. Sloane," Vanderlay said. "I was going to call you in the morning. I just arrived at my daughter's basketball game."

"I'm sorry to intrude on family time."

"No worries. They'll be warming up for another ten minutes. I got a hit on that number you provided. You have a pen handy?"

Sloane grabbed a pen and a pad of paper. "Fire away."

"The number belonged to a man named Richard Peterson of TBT Investments."

Sloane had never heard of the person or the company. He looked to Jake, but at the mention of the name, Jake had left his chair and hurried from the office.

"Anything else?" Sloane said.

"That's it. No forwarding number. No address."

Sloane asked Vanderlay a few more questions before disconnecting.

Jake reentered the office and slapped LSR&C's incorporation papers on Sloane's desk. He stabbed at the documents with his finger. "TBT Investments was a subsidiary of LSR&C. It's right there. And the COO of TBT Investments was Richard Peterson."

Sloane read the document carefully to be certain.

"You think Carl Emerson could be Richard Peterson?" Jake asked.

"Sure looks that way," Sloane said. "And if we can prove that he is, it's tangible proof to argue that Charlie met Emerson. The question is, How do we get it into evidence? Even if we can find Emerson, there's no guarantee he'll acknowledge the card or the number." Sloane thought of Beckman's statement that he should put Charlie on the witness stand, but that was always a dicey proposition in a criminal matter. He paced his office, thinking. He stopped at the round table in the front corner and saw the *Seattle Times.* The *Times* had reported that morning that Mitchell Goldstone, the former COO of LSR&C, had accepted a plea agreement that called for substantial prison time. He turned to Jake. "You read that Mitchell Goldstone agreed to a plea deal?"

"Sentencing is within the month," Jake said.

"And until then, Goldstone is at the Federal Detention Center in SeaTac. He might know if Carl Emerson is Richard Peterson."

"He might, but the government will argue Goldstone is a liar," Jake said. "His plea required that he admit he'd lied about LSR&C being a CIA proprietary."

"Yeah, but we now have a number on a business card, and an expert who will testify that the number belonged to Richard Peterson of TBT Investments, *and* we have documents that TBT was a subsidiary of LSR&C. If Goldstone says Peterson is Emerson, it would prove that a CIA officer was acting as the head of an LSR&C subsidiary. It's solid evidence that what Charlie is saying is true." Another thought came to him. "The LSR&C documents—what documents existed anyway—were classified in the Goldstone matter, right?"

"Yeah."

"But with that matter final when Goldstone signed the plea deal—"

"The government will never give up LSR&C's documents," Jake said.

"They're not the government's documents. Those documents belong to a Washington State corporation that is currently in bankruptcy. The firm handling that bankruptcy has control over the documents. With the plea by Goldstone, the criminal case is over and it is now a straight bankruptcy matter. I'm betting the government is no longer even thinking about those documents."

Jake smiled. "You want me to prepare a subpoena to get them?"

"There's no need for a subpoena. The government is arguing that LSR&C has nothing to do with this case, that this is a straight espionage case. We don't have to go through the government to get LSR&C's documents. We can go straight to the law firm handling the LSR&C bankruptcy and get the documents without the government ever knowing it."

58

Sloane left his office and drove to the Federal Detention Center, referred to as the "airport prison" because of its proximity to SeaTac Airport. For the first time, he saw a faint glimmer of hope. Goldstone could fuel that glimmer into a full-blown flame, or extinguish it.

The exterior of the beige building—two cubes with wings and an awning over a glass-door entrance—gave the prison the appearance of a hospital. After the usual red tape, and a lot of forms, Sloane found himself in a beat-up room behind a plexiglass window with several holes that allowed him to speak to the prisoner.

Several minutes after Sloane sat, the door on the other side of the plexiglass opened, and Mitchell Goldstone entered with his hands cuffed to a belly chain at his waist and white bandages wrapping each wrist. Goldstone looked younger than in newspaper photographs and on television. He parted his hair in the middle and it extended over his ears. His complexion was pale and his cheeks flushed. He did not look like a chief operating officer of a multimillion-dollar investment company, and maybe he never had been. According to Jenkins, if LSR&C was a CIA proprietary, then Goldstone was just a figurehead. Decisions came from Langley.

Goldstone gave Sloane a quizzical look.

"I'm David Sloane, the attorney for Charles Jenkins."

"Do you have a card?" Goldstone asked.

Goldstone had every reason to be paranoid. Sloane pushed his card and his driver's license against the plexiglass.

Goldstone leaned forward and considered them closely. Then he said, "I'm sorry about what's happening to him. Tell him I wish him the best."

"He feels the same about what's happened to you."

Goldstone sat back. He looked like he wanted to say something, but he refrained. "What's your question?"

"I wanted to know if the LSR&C documents at the bankruptcy attorney's office make mention of its subsidiaries."

"I'm sure they do. Which subsidiary are you interested in?"

Sloane watched Goldstone closely. "I'm interested in a company called TBT Investments."

Goldstone's eyes flickered and the corner of his mouth inched upward, though he suppressed a grin. "I don't know for certain," he said.

"But TBT was a subsidiary of LSR&C," Sloane said.

Goldstone nodded. "Yeah. It was."

"And were you the chief operating officer of TBT Investments as well as LSR&C?" Sloane knew the answer, but he wanted Goldstone to talk.

Goldstone shook his head. "No."

"The incorporation papers say it was run by someone named Richard Peterson."

Goldstone smiled, as if bemused by the information, but didn't otherwise comment.

"I'm having difficulty locating people to corroborate Charles Jenkins's story," Sloane said. "Do you know how I would find Richard Peterson?"

Goldstone sat back, head tilted, evaluating Sloane.

"Charlie has a wife and two children," Sloane said, knowing Goldstone also had a family. "A new baby girl just a couple weeks old."

Goldstone appeared to be thinking carefully. Sloane thought he was about to leave the window, but he sat forward and said, "Ask Carl Emerson about Richard Peterson."

Sloane did his best to keep a poker face. "He would know?"

Goldstone nodded. "Ask him."

"Have you ever met Carl Emerson?"

"Once. He flew out when we were trying to get money out of the Philippines."

"Can you describe him?"

"He's older. I'd say late seventies, maybe even early eighties. He's tall. Six two or three, and thin. Has a head of white hair and dark eyes. Not brown. Darker. He's also tan."

The description fit the one Jenkins had provided.

"I understand he's retired. Any idea how I might find him?"

Goldstone shook his head.

"You said he flew in to Seattle. Do you know from where?"

"I assume from DC, but I understood from talking to him that he golfs a lot. He talked about the golf courses he'd been playing and it was the middle of winter. So it was someplace warm."

"You don't happen to have any LSR&C documents, do you?"

Goldstone's eyes sparkled, and the corners of his mouth again inched into an impish, boyish grin. Just as quickly, the grin faded. Goldstone rubbed the bandage on his left wrist. "As part of my plea deal with the government I had to relinquish anything I had related to LSR&C."

Sloane realized the facial expression was intended to convey what Mitchell Goldstone could not say. He was savvier than the newspapers had portrayed him. Sloane suspected Goldstone held leverage over the government, documents he had likely secured someplace that would inflict damage if exposed. He suspected that was the reason for the plea deal, and maybe why Goldstone was still alive. He also suspected that Goldstone, not the government, had pushed for that deal. He had no doubt that Goldstone would be sentenced to a long prison term, but Sloane doubted he would spend much time behind bars, and likely at a minimum-security federal penitentiary. The government would wait until all the investor suits against LSR&C concluded and everyone had gotten their pound of flesh and moved on with their lives. When they did, Mitchell Goldstone would come up for parole, and quietly slip back into society.

59

Early the following morning, Jake drove downtown dressed in his best navy-blue suit, white shirt, and red power tie. He'd learned the name of the paralegal in charge of the LSR&C documents and looked up the woman's profile on the law firm's website. She'd been employed for three years, which meant she wasn't fresh out of law school, but she wasn't well seasoned either.

He entered the building and spoke to the receptionist. "Molly Diepenbrock, please. I'm Jake Carter, here to see the LSR&C documents."

Jake tried to appear casual as the receptionist made the call. He listened carefully to her end of the conversation. "That's what he said," the receptionist said twice before hanging up.

Minutes later, a tall, thin woman who looked not much older than Jake stepped off the elevator and introduced herself as Molly Diepenbrock. "What is this about?" she said.

"I need to look through the LSR&C documents," Jake said. "A criminal matter is being finalized this week, so I'm in a bit of a bind and need to see them today. Would you be able to arrange that?"

Diepenbrock said, "I think so. I just have to find them. I'm preparing for trial myself. You'd want copies today, I assume."

Jake pounced on this comment, knowing Diepenbrock was under the gun and she'd be grateful if he took one more thing off her plate.

"Listen, I know what getting prepared for trial can be like. If you just point me in the direction of the documents, I'll arrange for a copy service to come in so you're not put out."

Diepenbrock smiled. "That would be great. I'd appreciate that."

Jake followed her to the bank of elevators. He felt like he'd been given the keys to the Louvre and hoped he was about to walk out with the *Mona Lisa*.

—

Paper plates, used napkins, and empty cans of soda water littered the conference room table. Sloane, Jake, and Jenkins hadn't left the conference room since Jake returned with copies of all the LSR&C documents. As Jenkins suspected, there weren't many—just four bankers boxes. The government had no doubt confiscated the vast majority and, in this day of paperless offices, a large amount likely had only existed on LSR&C's network server. Still, Jenkins was buoyed by what they had found.

"Listen to this." Jake sipped his drink then read out loud from a cable sent in 2015 that outlined the CIA's plan for Goldstone to provide Carl Emerson with a cover. "'Foreign Resources Division requests Mr. Mitchell Goldstone, chairman of the board of LSR&C, to negotiate cover arrangements for Carl Emerson in the alias of Richard Peterson. Foreign Resources Division believes this proposal is operationally sound and should provide solid cover for extended operational use.'"

He set that down and read from a second document. "'The cover should permit Mr. Emerson to portray himself as a representative of, or as the senior officer or owner of a substantial investment company in Seattle, Washington.'" He lowered the document and picked up a third, plowing forward.

"And here's the e-mail to the IRS. 'Headquarters in Langley has contacted IRS and advised to forgo any investigation of tax matters.'"

He set down the document and picked up yet one more. "And here's another document that provides Goldstone with a cover story. 'Tell investigators: Established three companies in question for undisclosed foreign clients who needed US government base for certain unspecified business operations. Goldstone is strictly a nominee in all matters and has no financial interest in the entities.'"

Jenkins suspected that Carl Emerson had formed TBT Investments to distance it from LSR&C and any potential investigation by the IRS. It made sense, especially if Emerson was washing funds he'd received from the Russians.

"Why would Goldstone plead guilty with this kind of evidence?" Jake asked.

"Because he wasn't going to be able to get any of it into evidence," Sloane said. "The judge ruled in a pre-trial motion that Goldstone's alleged ties to the CIA were irrelevant to the charges brought against him—that he ran a Ponzi scheme and bilked investors out of their life savings."

"So how are *we* going to get it in?" Jenkins asked.

"Your case is different. They've alleged espionage, and your entire defense is that you acted at the behest of a senior officer within the CIA. The documents are clearly relevant."

"Doesn't mean we'll get them in, especially if someone in the government gets to the judge," Jenkins said.

"I've thought about that also. We need to turn around Harden's opinion of you and of the government's case," Sloane said. "Harden's only human. He'll be upset if he's convinced you sold secrets to the Russians. We need to find a way to let him know you're telling the truth and the government's lying. In my experience, if there's one thing judges hate, it's attorneys and witnesses who lie."

"So how do we do that?" Jenkins asked. "How do we get the government to lie?"

Sloane smiled. "We just get them to move their lips."

60

The following day, Sloane and Jake filed the defense's motion to compel production pursuant to federal Rule 16, the evidentiary discovery rule. They'd tailored their request to specifically ask for the documents they already possessed. The rule required the government to produce any within the government's possession, custody, or control, which would include many of the documents within the four bankers boxes. They further requested the government produce Carl Emerson's last-known address.

The government's responsive pleading, filed six days later, predictably denied the existence of any such documents and added, "The government has no intention of participating in, or furthering, Mr. Jenkins's fantasy." Despite this response, the government sought to have the motion and the response sealed, and they asked that the hearing be held in the judge's chambers, or that the courtroom be emptied of spectators, because of what it called the sensitive nature of the requested materials.

Jenkins smiled when he read that sentence calling his request a fantasy and the government's further response that it had no knowledge of Carl Emerson's last-known address.

"Maybe they know we have the documents," Sloane said, with respect to the request to seal the matter. "Or maybe they're just being cautious."

The next day Sloane filed a motion to compel, and he requested oral argument. He also opposed the government's request to close the proceedings. "I want to draw another crowd," he told Jenkins, "which we can use to hopefully alter the public's perception of you."

—

The following week, Sloane, Jenkins, and Jake appeared in court before Judge Harden, who had granted the government's request to seal the pleadings and close the hearing to the public. Sloane told Jenkins not to worry, that their foremost intent had been to change Judge Harden's opinion. As before, the government brought a gaggle of attorneys to stand beside Velasquez.

After Harden took the bench and opened the proceedings, Sloane explained that Jenkins intended to argue that he had been authorized by Carl Emerson—acting for the CIA—to disclose certain information to the Russians as part of a CIA operation. "The documents are therefore critical to my client's defense, as is Mr. Emerson."

Jenkins could almost hear the crackle of intensity in the courtroom.

After Sloane's argument, Velasquez responded in a dismissive tone intended to convey incredulity. "Your Honor, the government is unaware of the existence of any such documents, because the defendant's supposed defense is a fantasy. The government cannot produce what does not exist. There are no documents relevant to the make-believe theory that Mr. Jenkins was working for the CIA when he traded agency secrets for money. As for Mr. Emerson, he worked with Mr. Jenkins in 1978 in Mexico City."

Harden looked to Sloane. "Mr. Sloane, the government cannot produce what it doesn't have."

"Certainly not," Sloane said. "But I would ask the court to ask Ms. Velasquez if the government actually searched for the requested documents."

Harden looked to Velasquez. "Counsel?"

Jenkins watched closely. Velasquez sighed. "Your Honor, the defense can't look for something that doesn't exist. The defense is pulling rabbits out of its hat and creating a total fabrication to confuse the very simple issue before this court: Did the defendant trade government secrets for money?"

Jenkins suppressed a smile.

Harden again looked to Sloane. "Mr. Sloane?"

Jenkins knew Sloane would push the matter further so Velasquez could not later vacillate.

Sloane did just that. "Your Honor, with all due respect, we can't tell from the government's written response, or from the statements made by counsel in court this morning, if the government did not search for the documents, in which case Ms. Velasquez's response is based on ignorance, or if the government looked, but Ms. Velasquez is deliberately attempting to mislead this court because such documents would reveal damning information that Mr. Jenkins's 'fantasy,' as the government put it, is in fact a reality."

Velasquez bristled at the accusation, which Jenkins knew Sloane had intended. "Your Honor, I resent the insinuation made by counsel, and I reiterate that the defendant's argument is a total fabrication. To look for nonexistent documents would be a waste of time and resources, and Mr. Sloane knows this."

And there it was, Jenkins thought, anticipating what was to come.

Sloane turned to Jake, who provided him with a stack of documents, all date stamped with letters and numbers to show that Sloane possessed the "nonexistent" documents. Jake also provided a memorandum summarizing each request to which the documents specifically related. "Your Honor, if I may approach," Sloane said.

Harden waved Sloane forward, curiosity creasing his otherwise impassive face. Sloane handed the stack of documents to the clerk, who handed them to the judge. Once they were securely in Harden's hands,

Sloane returned to the counsel table and handed a duplicate set to Velasquez. Jenkins watched her reaction as Sloane continued his attack.

"What the defense has just presented are copies of LSR&C documents that state, very clearly, that LSR&C was a CIA proprietary, that Mitchell Goldstone was working under CIA authority, and that Carl Emerson—whom the government has already acknowledged worked for the CIA, but who has apparently vanished into thin air—was utilizing the alias Richard Peterson to serve as the COO of an LSR&C subsidiary, TBT Investments. We'd simply like to know what additional documents exist."

Velasquez looked about to explode, but Sloane pressed on before she could interrupt him. "Mr. Jenkins's security company, CJ Security, provided security for the employees and the clients of LSR&C in offices all over the world, and it was to be paid to provide those services by LSR&C—aka the CIA."

"Objection, Your Honor," Velasquez said. Red in the face, she clearly struggled to control the volume of her voice. "Those documents are classified."

"Your Honor, would those documents that the government now claims to be classified be the same 'fantasy' documents the government contends don't exist?" Sloane asked. "Because I don't believe the government can move to classify documents that don't exist. That would be a 'total fabrication,' wouldn't it?"

"Enough," Harden said in a soft but bemused tone. He went through the documents for several minutes before setting them down. He took another minute. When he spoke his voice was calm, but stern, like a father talking to a child who had broken curfew. "Ms. Velasquez, earlier I asked you a direct question, whether you had looked for the documents requested by the defense."

"Your Honor—"

"It's a simple question, Counselor," Harden said, raising his voice to speak over her. "Did the government look for these documents?"

"No. The government did not. Might I add, Your Honor, that the government has no control over LSR&C's documents and therefore—"

Harden smiled, clearly having anticipated the argument. He shook his head as he interrupted her. "No. No. No. Ms. Velasquez. I'm looking at documents that originated from the CIA and from other government offices. Mr. Sloane, are there additional responsive documents?"

"There are, Your Honor."

"Please present them to the court."

Sloane directed Jake to present the four bankers boxes.

Harden clenched his jaw. "I will review the documents in camera and make three determinations. First, whether the documents are responsive and relevant to the requests. Second, whether the government has willfully withheld relevant documents and lied to this court, and, third, whether these documents are admissible in the defendant's upcoming trial. Anything else, Mr. Sloane?"

With a clear change in Harden's attitude, Sloane remained on the attack. "Yes, Your Honor. The defense requests the government be compelled to provide Carl Emerson's last-known address, as well as the date he retired from the Central Intelligence Agency, along with relevant documents."

Velasquez said, "Your Honor, the government can't produce what it doesn't have."

Harden scoffed. "Look a little harder, Counselor. Maybe you'll find that information in the same location you would have found these documents. When you do, I'm ordering you to provide the last-known address to defense counsel. Counsel will have my written ruling this afternoon." He rapped his gavel once. "We're adjourned."

—

Jenkins returned to Sloane's office buoyed by their victory, despite Sloane cautioning him and Jake not to get too excited. "This is going to be a marathon, not a sprint," Sloane said. "We can celebrate when we cross the finish line."

As the day came to a close, Carolyn walked into the conference room holding copies of a document. "Hot off the judicial presses," she said, handing them the document and then departing.

Harden had considered all of the LSR&C documents thoroughly and ruled that Jenkins's stated defense—that he had a reasonable belief that a CIA agent had authorized him to reveal information—mandated that the documents be produced as relevant.

Jake said, "It's a whole new ball game."

"Yeah, well, don't get picked off first base just yet," Sloane said. "The government isn't going to let this go without a fight."

No sooner had Sloane spoken than Carolyn walked in carrying another document. "Don't they sleep over there?" She looked at Jenkins. "Whatever you did, you've accomplished the impossible. You've actually motivated government workers to work."

Sloane and Jake quickly flipped through the pages of the pleading as Jenkins stood looking over their shoulders. "They're arguing that under the Classified Information Procedures Act, or CIPA, the government has the right to classify the documents as a danger to national security and prevent them from coming into evidence, even if those documents would substantiate our defense," Jake said.

"There's no way they prepared this motion this quickly," Sloane said. "There's a lot of boilerplate codes and case law they could have pulled from motions filed in the Goldstone matter, but there are also specifics related to this case and to the particular documents the government seeks to have classified. They had to have had this motion ready to go, which means they anticipated this ruling. Harden will know that, and hopefully it will piss him off even more."

"But can they do this?" Jenkins asked, feeling suddenly deflated. "Can they exclude the documents?"

"Harden doesn't think so. You can tell from his decision. It's clear he wrote it anticipating the government would appeal and likely argue CIPA. Look on the third page. He says a criminal defendant has a constitutional right to insist that the government prove his guilt beyond a reasonable doubt. Harden says excluding documents as classified would, in effect, deny you the right to a trial because it would prevent you from putting on a defense."

"He's given us a road map to prepare an opposition to the court of appeals," Jake said.

Sloane looked to Jenkins. "The important thing is he knows what's in those documents, and Judge Harden now knows you're telling the truth."

Jenkins wasn't so confident.

"The trial date is going to have to be vacated until after the appeal," Jake said.

"Do you think they'll make another plea offer?" Jenkins asked. He wanted to be found innocent, but he wasn't adverse to a quick resolution—for Alex and his children's sake, so long as he didn't have to admit guilt.

"They might," Sloane said. "Especially if they lose the appeal."

Near six o'clock, after further discussion, Jenkins said, "I better get home and give Alex a break. Call me if you need anything."

Jenkins grabbed his jacket and walked to the door. The phone in the center of the conference room table rang. Since the receptionist had left for the evening, Sloane had forwarded his calls to the conference room. The lights on the telephone console indicated the call was from outside the firm, but when Sloane answered, the telephone number did not register on the small screen.

He hit the "Speaker" button. "Law offices of David Sloane."

"David Sloane?" The caller's accent stopped Jenkins's retreat. He turned to the phone as if hearing a ghost.

"Yes," Sloane said.

"Good. Mr. Sloane, my name is Viktor Federov. Your client Charles Jenkins is well familiar with me."

Sloane looked to Jenkins. He nodded, returned to the table, and sat down.

"You have placed me on the speakerphone," Federov said. "May I presume that Mr. Jenkins is there with you now?"

"I'm here, Viktor," Jenkins said.

"Mr. Jenkins. How are you?" Federov asked the question as if they were two old friends getting reacquainted.

"I've been better, Viktor."

"Yes, I have been reading with great interest of your arrest and pending trial. In Russia, we are not so fortunate. My failure was viewed as an embarrassment to the government and I was summarily dismissed."

"I can't say I'm sorry to hear that," Jenkins said.

Federov laughed. "No. I did not think you would be. I never had the chance to congratulate you on your escape. You are a formidable foe, one I think I might like to know under other circumstances. Maybe someday I will come to United States and we will have a toast."

Jenkins gave Sloane a puzzled look. "Did you call just to congratulate me, Viktor?"

"No. I did not. I called to tell you that in Russia the government is direct. In your country, not so much. I would let bygones be bygones, but what I think does not matter. There are those in your country who do not want to see you go to trial. It would be . . . embarrassment to them. I thought you should know."

"Are you referring to Carl Emerson?" Jenkins said.

"Me, I am not referring to anyone. To do so would not be so good for *my* health."

"Why are you telling me this, Viktor?"

Federov sighed. "I say again, we are not so different, Mr. Jenkins. We work for bureaucracies that do not always appreciate what we do, but that are swift to punish us when we fail."

Jenkins gave that comment a moment of thought. Then he said, "Thanks for the heads-up."

"Is no problem."

"What will you do?" Jenkins asked.

"Me? My brother runs a concrete business and does much work for the government. I will make more money working for him, though not nearly as much as others have made at our expense, Mr. Jenkins."

Jenkins again looked to Sloane. He interpreted the comment to confirm what he had suspected, that someone, possibly Carl Emerson, had made millions of dollars. "I understand."

"Then it is good that I called. Until we meet again, Mr. Jenkins. *Za zdaróvye!*"

Federov disconnected the call. Jake pressed a button on his phone. He had recorded the conversation. "I have it," Jake said. "We can take this to Harden and play it for him."

Sloane shook his head. "It would never come into evidence. You taped it without Federov's knowledge, and the government will argue they had no ability to cross-examine Federov on what he said."

"That's not the biggest problem," Jenkins said. "It also confirms my relationship with a Russian FSB agent, and it makes us sound like we're friends. The government could spin it and use it to convict me."

No one spoke for a moment. Then Jake said, "Do you think he was trying to set you up somehow?"

"No," Jenkins said. "He has no stake in this game anymore. I think his warning was from one agent to another. I think he also wanted me to know that someone made millions of dollars at both our expense. He's pissed. It's why he called. He wants me to win."

"Why? What's in it for him?" Jake asked.

Jenkins smiled, thinking of Federov, and of the respect he had developed for the man's counterespionage skills. It appeared Federov had developed a similar respect for Jenkins.

"Absolutely nothing," Jenkins said, "which is why I believe him. He and I are the same in one respect—his government screwed him and mine is trying to screw me. This is his way of helping."

"But if you believe there are people who could try to kill you, why are you so calm?" Jake said.

"Because no contract killer will honor that contract, if one exists. It's a small fraternity, and I'm sure they sense what has happened. They'll want to find out the result. Because they know that if this can happen to me, it can happen to them."

The appeal resulted in a four-month delay of the trial. Jenkins spent that time with Alex and the kids. School was out for the summer, which caused CJ to scale back his request to go back to his school. Alex was working part-time at a supermarket. Jenkins, however, was unemployable because of the publicity surrounding his arrest and the pre-trial activities. He was dipping into what retirement they had to make ends meet. Sloane would not take any money, either for rent or for food. "What good is my money if I can't use it to take care of my family?" he'd said one night.

Midweek on a warm July afternoon, Sloane called Jenkins to tell him that three Ninth Circuit judges had unanimously agreed with Judge Harden's decision and rejected the government's appeal to classify the documents under CIPA. Jenkins hung up the phone and let out a contented yell. He was more confident than ever the government would either let the case go or offer another plea agreement, one that did not require Jenkins to plead insanity.

Jenkins's euphoria, however, was short-lived. Sloane called back at the end of the day to tell him the government had again appealed, this time seeking an expedited decision from the full panel of twelve Ninth Circuit judges. Sloane explained that it was highly unlikely the full panel would overturn a unanimous decision of three of their colleagues, but when it came to the power of the CIA and the FBI, Jenkins was not so naïve.

On the eve of the new trial date, the Ninth Circuit ruled seven to five to reverse Judge Harden's decision, as well as the affirmation by the three-judge panel. All of the LSR&C documents Jake had gathered were deemed classified under CIPA, and therefore inadmissible. Sloane tried to console Jenkins by pointing out that Judge Harden, at least, knew the contents of those documents.

The jury, however, would not.

Not surprisingly, the government did not offer another plea deal.

That evening Jenkins walked down to the water's edge. He now knew that those in power would never let the truth come out, never allow him to have a fair chance, never allow him to be free. He stared across Puget Sound. The sun had started its descent, coloring the sky in ominous hues of red and orange, and it reminded him of the sky over Moscow on his first trip to Russia.

He faced three life sentences, and he could offer virtually nothing to substantiate his defense.

Late in the evening before the start of trial, Jenkins sat on Sloane's covered porch listening to the waves from a passing cargo ship pound the shore, like bursts of thunder. He understood now why the government had never lost an espionage case. It was like playing blackjack in Las Vegas. The odds of winning were not favorable, especially when the house controlled the cards.

Sloane stepped onto the porch, letting the screen door slap shut behind him. He carried two bottles of beer and handed one to Jenkins. They sat in rocking chairs, looking out at Puget Sound's darkened waters. Jenkins knew Sloane had bought the two chairs before Tina's death, and that he had anticipated sitting on this porch with her, admiring this view, well into his old age. How quickly and dramatically life can change.

Jenkins sipped his beer. "You get everything done?"

Sloane had spent all day in court, arguing pre-trial motions. If Judge Harden was pissed off at the government for lying about the LSR&C documents, or for being reversed by the court of appeals, he didn't show it. He'd been efficient and professional. The defense won and lost the pre-trial motions pretty much as Sloane had predicted.

"Did the government produce Emerson's last-known address?" Jenkins asked.

"Nope," Sloane said. "And I'm not holding my breath they will. If they do, they'll likely produce an address to a PO box in some town in the middle of nowhere. And if he's out of state, he won't come willingly, and I doubt we could get an order to force him. If we could even find him."

Jenkins considered that for a moment. Then he said, "Might be for the best, especially if he knows you now have no documents to impeach him. We have to assume he won't have anything positive to say about me, and if he's the leak, or a mole, he's had plenty of time to cover his tracks. Emerson has always been smart. He's played this game for forty years. He could burn me if we put him on the stand."

Sloane sipped his beer, then said, "I want it on the record that we tried to get him, and we asked the government to provide his address. It could be grounds for an appeal."

Jenkins knew an appeal would only be necessary if he lost. "Did they produce a witness list?"

Sloane smirked. "Not a minute before five this afternoon. Twenty-seven names, and no information what any of the twenty-seven will say."

Flying blind, Jenkins thought, not for the first time. The runners of Jenkins's chair caused the planks of the old porch to creak and moan.

It sounded like the sound of a man hung from the gallows in an old Western, his body twisting in a breeze.

"I won't ask you to look after Alex and my kids," he said, keeping his view on the darkened landscape. "Just to be there for them, if they need help."

"I'll take care of them as if they were my own," Sloane said. "You know that. But we're not giving up just yet."

"I'll never give up, David, but some things are not in our control."

Inside the house, Lizzie cried. Jenkins looked at his watch. "She's nothing if not punctual." He handed Sloane his beer. "I told Alex I'd feed her so she could get some rest. Didn't figure I'd sleep much anyway, and I'm not sure how many more of these opportunities I'll have to hold her."

61

The following morning, the government brought a motion asking Judge Harden to recuse himself because he had been made privy to the documents protected by CIPA. Harden rejected the motion, asserting that the documents would not prejudice his handling of the trial.

Sloane told Jenkins the motion was a good move, that he suspected the government filed it intending the motion to hang over Harden's head to ensure his rulings followed the law.

After Harden denied the motion, the selection of jurors was as efficient as the pre-trial motions. In federal court, the judge asked most of the questions of prospective jurors. Sloane and the government were each limited to three questions. Sloane told Jenkins that most jurors entered a courtroom assuming that if a case had made it to trial, the allegations were likely true. Therefore, his first question had to cause jurors to rethink, or at least reconsider, their preconceived opinions about Charles Jenkins, the spy.

At the lectern, Sloane said, "By a show of hands, how many of you believe the United States has in its employ spies who work behind the scenes and in the shadows to protect our country's national interests and national security?"

In an era of daily terrorist threats, almost everyone on the panel raised his or her hand. Jenkins noted on a legal pad those who did not.

"And how many of you believe, by a show of hands, that in order to protect our country's national interests, the government doesn't always provide the public with information about where their spies are working and what they are doing?"

Again, nearly every prospective juror raised his or her hand.

"How many of you would agree that sometimes the government makes mistakes?"

This time everyone in the jury pool raised a hand. Sloane sat, and Jenkins felt that the tide had, at least, turned slightly before the government had the chance to brand him a traitor.

Velasquez did just that.

"How many of you, by a show of hands," she said, "believe that persons who sell classified information to a foreign government should be punished?"

The show of hands was unanimous. Velasquez's two follow-up questions were equally stinging and equally persuasive.

In the end, Sloane utilized eighteen of his twenty preemptory challenges to dismiss certain jurors. Velasquez used seventeen. Just two hours after starting the voir dire process, they had a jury of nine women and three men. Most were well educated and held positions of responsibility. Sloane told Jenkins he was pleased with the group.

Harden wasted no time moving the case forward. "Is the government prepared to give its opening statement?"

It wasn't a question. Velasquez slid back her chair and stood. If she wasn't prepared, she didn't show it. Confident and poised in a navy-blue, single-breasted jacket and skirt, she placed a laptop on the lectern but abandoned it to face the jury.

Emphasizing the theme that she had first raised in voir dire, Velasquez said, "The Justice Department doesn't move forward on a case of this nature unless there is full consultation and evidence to support it."

Jenkins saw Sloane move as if to stand, but he remained seated. The statement was argumentative, but he deduced from the jurors' expressions that they didn't believe it, at least not all of them.

"During the course of this trial you will hear evidence that the defendant, Charles Jenkins, was facing both personal and professional setbacks. His security company, CJ Security, was teetering on the edge of bankruptcy, and so was he. Mr. Jenkins's company was in debt to its security contractors and to various vendors. He was also on the verge of personal financial collapse. He had used his family farm on Camano Island as collateral for business loans to get his company off the ground. In simple terms, he needed money or he'd lose his home."

Velasquez took small paces to her left and told the jury of Alex's complicated pregnancy and her preeclampsia. She paced to her right. "So, what could Mr. Jenkins do? How could he save his family?" Velasquez paused as if expecting a juror to answer. "He could rely on a skill he'd once possessed, against a foe he had once combatted, a foe he knew would be very anxious to receive the type of unique information Mr. Jenkins could deliver. You see, Mr. Jenkins was once a spy for the Central Intelligence Agency. In the late 1970s, he worked out of the CIA's Mexico City field office for a man named Carl Emerson. Mr. Jenkins ran operations against the Soviet Union and its KGB officers stationed in Mexico City. Mr. Jenkins therefore had access to confidential information on American agents working in Russia, and on double agents—Russians spying for America."

Velasquez discussed Jenkins's abrupt departure from the CIA and his admitted dissatisfaction with the agency. She then turned toward Jenkins and raised a finger. "And so, facing both a personal and a professional catastrophe, what did Mr. Jenkins do? He had a perfect cover to travel to Russia. LSR&C had opened an office in Moscow and it was CJ Security's job to provide security to the workers and investors there."

Velasquez went through the trips Jenkins had made to Moscow, the information he had allegedly disclosed, and how that information had first originated in Mexico City. "Those two agents who Mr. Jenkins disclosed to the FSB," she said, "paid for Mr. Jenkins's betrayal with their lives."

Jenkins could feel the eyes of the jurors boring into him and fought not to react.

Velasquez explained how, upon Jenkins's first return from Moscow, his company received a $50,000 wire transfer from somewhere in Switzerland. "It was a straight trade—money for information. He was debt ridden and he was desperate."

Fluctuating between being outraged and being pragmatic, Velasquez explained to the jurors Jenkins's mysterious return to the United States after a second trip to Russia, seemingly without the use of his passport. She told them about his interactions with FBI agent Chris Daugherty, insinuating the meetings had been motivated by a fear of being caught. Then she said, "And he made up a story."

Velasquez explained what she called "Mr. Jenkins's fantasy." Then she asked, "Would this great nation—the United States of America—leave one of its own agents out in the cold if he were truly in the service of his country?"

She scowled. "Ask yourself, where is the evidence, any evidence, to support his story? Ask yourself, is it likely that during his personal and professional hardship a CIA agent would materialize on his farm carrying a pot of gold? That's the sort of story one reads in poorly written mysteries, what any discerning reader would laugh at and toss aside as pure, unadulterated fantasy."

After just twenty minutes, Velasquez had left a strong impression on the jury. As she turned for the government's table, the only sound in the room was the rocking of jurors' chairs as they swiveled toward the defense table.

—

Sloane was already walking to the lectern when Harden said, "Mr. Sloane, do you wish to give an opening statement at this time or defer?"

"The defense very much wishes to be heard," he said.

Sloane had explained to Jenkins that he had about thirty words, maximum, to change the impression Velasquez would create before the jurors tuned him out, and that he had to involve the jurors in Jenkins's case.

He didn't even bother to greet the jurors. Instead, he pointed his finger at Jenkins. "Is this man a spy?" He looked each juror in the eyes. Then he said, "You bet he is. He's a spy for the United States of America. He was a spy in the 1970s, and he was reactivated November 2017. Is it coincidence, as the government contends, that we are here? Absolutely not. We are here because Mr. Jenkins is the victim of a rogue CIA agent who was bilking an investment firm."

Sloane paced as he spoke. He told the jurors what Velasquez had not, that Carl Emerson had worked as Richard Peterson for TBT Investments, a subsidiary of LSR&C, which served as a CIA front for agents all over the country. It was a risk. Opening statements were not facts. Facts came in through evidence. Without the documents to support the opening statement, it could be a risk that would backfire, but it was a risk he and Jenkins agreed they had to take.

"Was it coincidence that Mr. Jenkins's company was going bankrupt? Of course not. Mr. Jenkins couldn't pay CJ Security's bills because LSR&C had stopped paying CJ Security. Was it coincidence that Carl Emerson showed up on Charles Jenkins's farm at this critical financial moment? Of course not. Carl Emerson showed up at this critical moment because Carl Emerson had been Mr. Jenkins's superior officer in the CIA, knew why Mr. Jenkins had quit, and knew he would not agree to be reactivated unless something mandated it—something catastrophic, as counsel said—something like his business going bankrupt and his family losing their home."

Sloane paused to let his outrage and the significant amount of information sink in. Did he care whether each juror absorbed each nuance? Not at this moment—especially if he couldn't get in information to support it. What he wanted to convey was the government's disloyalty and dirty dealing. Things, he hoped, each juror could understand.

"Carl Emerson also knew Mr. Jenkins was a skilled agent who spoke Russian, and Carl Emerson knew Mr. Jenkins had the perfect cover for getting into and out of Russia—he had a company providing security services to a business in Moscow. Was it a coincidence that Mr. Jenkins would disclose the identities of two American assets working in Russia who had first started working for the CIA in Mexico City? Of course not. That information was authorized for disclosure by Carl Emerson, who, as the former Mexico City station chief, knew of both operations."

Sloane paused, watching each juror. He'd told Jenkins that his hope was to make the jurors uncomfortable and hopefully cause them to change their perspective, or at least realize there was another story and withhold judgment. "Counsel asks whether you would believe that an agency of this great government would leave an agent hung out to dry. When you hear the evidence, I'm confident your answer will be: yes, they did."

Sloane brought his hands to his lips as if in prayer. "Ladies and gentlemen, under American law, the burden of proof that Charles Jenkins is guilty lies with the government. In any criminal case, the defendant is innocent until guilt is proven beyond a reasonable doubt. He doesn't have to testify." He lowered his hands, as if what he was about to say was spontaneous. Nothing was spontaneous. He and Jenkins had talked about the risk of this part of the opening for several hours the prior evening. "But in this particular trial we're going to do it differently. Yes, we are." He looked to Jenkins and nodded. Then he pointed to the government attorneys. "We're going to relieve the prosecution of their burden. We are going to assume that burden and we are going to prove to you, beyond doubt, that the defendant did not break the law and that he was a loyal American who believed at all times that he was serving his country."

Sloane thanked the jurors and returned to the counsel table. When he did, Jenkins noted that the jurors' expressions had changed, from disdain to curiosity, and he knew that was all he could have hoped for.

62

After lunch, Harden again wasted no time. He spoke as he arranged papers on his desk. "Is the government prepared to move forward?"

Again, it was not a question. Again, Velasquez, already on her feet, didn't hesitate. "We are, Your Honor."

"Call your first witness."

Velasquez called Nathaniel Ikeda, a records clerk at the CIA's offices in Langley, Virginia. Ikeda was a good-looking Japanese man with graying black hair. After establishing Ikeda's credentials and his job responsibilities, Velasquez asked, "Did your records check turn up any information that a Charles William Jenkins was employed by the Central Intelligence Agency?"

"It did," Ikeda said in a confident tone.

"Will you explain to the jury what the records revealed?"

Ikeda faced the jurors, no doubt as instructed, or from years of experience testifying in a courtroom. He held documents in his lap, which the prosecution had turned over to Sloane only the night before, and he explained that Jenkins had been employed from roughly June 1976 to approximately July 1978.

"Do they indicate how his employment ended?"

"Assumed voluntary retirement after unsuccessful attempts to contact Mr. Jenkins."

"Did your records reveal that Mr. Jenkins was reactivated as a field operative in November or December 2017?"

"No, they do not."

"Did you search for any records pertaining to a Carl Emerson?"

Ikeda again turned to the jury and said that he had. After Velasquez had the documents marked and admitted, Ikeda explained what those records revealed. Then he said, "Mr. Emerson was deactivated from his position as station chief in Mexico City and was working in Langley, Virginia."

"Do the records reveal whether Carl Emerson was running an operation in Russia in December 2017?"

"They do not."

Ikeda explained what records he would have expected to find if such an operation had been initiated, then said he had found no such documents.

"Is there a record of a fifty-thousand-dollar payment being made to Mr. Jenkins or to Mr. Emerson in December 2017?"

"There is not."

Velasquez then asked Ikeda about the two assets Jenkins had revealed to the FSB—Alexei Sukurov and Uliana Artemyeva. "Do your records indicate whether either of those individuals or their operations were active files?"

"Active in the sense that the files remained open, yes."

"When were those operations first activated?"

"They were first activated in 1972 and 1973."

"Out of which field office?"

"Mexico City."

"Who opened those files?"

"Carl Emerson."

Velasquez thanked Ikeda and sat.

Jenkins and Sloane had only had the morning to pore through the records, and Jenkins knew that to some extent, Sloane would have to wing his cross-examination. He'd told Jenkins his goal was to establish that Carl Emerson existed, that he wasn't some phantom figure. He wanted to establish that Emerson ran the Alexei Sukurov and Uliana Artemyeva operations, and that there were no records tying Jenkins to either. He also wanted to establish that Emerson had been fired from the CIA at about the same time LSR&C blew up and Jenkins was charged with espionage. "I hope," Sloane told Jenkins, "that where the jury sees smoke, they'll assume there is a fire."

"Who was the station chief in Mexico City in 1972 and 1973?" he asked Ikeda.

"Carl Emerson," Ikeda said.

"Do your records indicate whether Mr. Jenkins worked on either of the two operations previously mentioned?"

"I'm not sure," Ikeda said. "He could have."

"Please, feel free to consult your records and tell me if Mr. Jenkins's name appears on any document in either of those files."

For the next couple minutes Ikeda looked through his documents. Jenkins watched him, and he watched the jurors' reactions. "I don't find his name in either file," Ikeda finally said.

"You have no information in your records that Mr. Jenkins even knew of those operations, do you?"

"Not in my records, no."

"Do you have records with you today documenting that Carl Emerson worked for TBT Investments in Seattle, Washington?"

"Objection," Velasquez said, "the question violates the CIPA ruling."

"Sustained," Harden said.

"Do you have records with you today that Richard Peterson worked for TBT Investments in Seattle, Washington?"

"Same objection," Velasquez said.

"Sustained."

"Were you asked to look for such records?"

"Same objection."

"Sustained." Harden shot Sloane a look not to try that again.

"Do you have records—plane reservations, hotel receipts, dinner receipts—from Mr. Emerson seeking expense reimbursement for travel from Langley, Virginia, to Seattle, Washington, between November 2017 and January 2018?"

"I don't know. I wasn't asked to look for those records."

"But Mr. Emerson did work for the CIA in November and December 2017 and January 2018, didn't he?"

"According to the records, he did."

"Your records don't reveal that Mr. Emerson traveled to Seattle in his capacity as the chief operating officer of TBT Investments?"

"Same objection," Velasquez said.

"Sustained," Harden replied.

"How about records for reimbursable expenses sought by Carl Emerson or a Richard Peterson for that same time period? Did you find any of those records?"

"I wasn't asked to look for any such records."

"Wasn't asked to look for those either," Sloane said, as if perplexed. He turned as if to retake his seat at the counsel table, though Jenkins knew he wasn't finished. Sloane wheeled and walked back to the lectern, looking perplexed. "I'm sorry, Mr. Ikeda, but just a few additional questions. Do your files provide a termination date for Carl Emerson's employment with the CIA?"

"Yes. January 25, 2018."

"He was fired?"

Ikeda looked to Velasquez, who shot out of her seat. "Objection, Your Honor. It misstates testimony."

Harden shook his head. "Not this witness's testimony. He hasn't answered the question. Do you need the question repeated, Mr. Ikeda?"

Ikeda looked uncomfortable. "No," he said. He looked to Sloane. "He was terminated."

"Fired," Sloane said.

"He was terminated," Ikeda persisted.

"The records don't say Carl Emerson retired, do they?"

"No."

"Quit?"

"No."

"Leave of absence? Sabbatical?"

"No."

"It says he was terminated, correct? Canned, fired, dismissed."

"It says 'terminated.'"

"Do your records say why Carl Emerson, who worked for the CIA since at least the 1970s, was fired?"

"No."

Sloane paused, as if to give that information some thought. Jenkins knew the jurors would do so as well.

Velasquez took about five minutes on redirect, then excused Ikeda. The remainder of the afternoon was a parade of witnesses from the twenty-seven on the government's witness list. None were particularly damaging, but by the end of the day Jenkins had started to feel like a piñata.

Early the following morning, after a late night, Sloane returned to his office with Jenkins and Jake and found an unmarked envelope on the floor just inside the glass-door entrance. The exterior of the envelope did not have a stamp or a postmark, which meant it had been hand delivered.

Sloane opened the envelope and pulled out a single sheet of paper. He shook his head and held it up. "Carl Emerson's last-known address."

"They've had it all along," Jake said. "Where is he?"

"Santa Barbara," Sloane said. "See if the address is still good. If it is, get him served with a trial subpoena."

"It's outside of a hundred miles. We can't compel him to appear," Jake said.

"I understand," Sloane said. "But if Emerson isn't at least called, after I've brought up his name so often, the jury is going to want to know why not. I want to put that turd in the government's pocket when I give my closing. I want to be able to say we subpoenaed Emerson, but he wouldn't come, and the government could have called him as a witness but chose not to. Maybe the insinuation will be enough to cast reasonable doubt."

63

To start the second day of trial, Maria Velasquez called FBI agent Chris Daugherty to the stand. Daugherty looked the part in a dark-blue suit, button-down white shirt, and solid-red tie. He couldn't have come across as more American if Velasquez had hung a flag around his shoulders.

Velasquez took Daugherty through the circumstances that led to him interviewing Charles Jenkins and, with prompting, Daugherty explained in detail the nature of each conversation.

Then she asked, "Did Mr. Jenkins ever ask that a CIA representative be present before talking to you?"

"No, he did not."

"In your experience, would that have been customary for a man telling you of a sensitive CIA operation?"

"In my experience it is customary."

"Do you have an understanding why that is customary?"

"The FBI is responsible for what happens within the United States. The CIA is responsible for what happens outside the United States. The two agencies can't and don't know what the other is working on at all times, so a CIA agent questioned by the FBI will seek a CIA representative to make certain that confidential information is not disclosed."

"When Mr. Jenkins finished telling you his story, what was your response?"

"I told him that I didn't believe him. I told him the story was ridiculous."

"What was his response?"

Daugherty shrugged. "He said, 'Trust me. I wouldn't lie to you. I can't tell you everything. You need to fill in the blanks from the CIA.' I said, 'Why can't you tell me?' And he said, 'Because I was told that anything I said could endanger an ongoing, critical operation.'"

"Did you call the CIA and attempt to verify what Mr. Jenkins told you?"

"I couldn't verify anything he'd told me. The CIA told me they had no record of Mr. Jenkins being reactivated, and they had no record of any operation involving him inside Russia or anywhere else. They also advised that they had looked into the two operations that Mr. Jenkins told me to ask about. They said both operations had been deactivated years before, but that the two assets had recently died in Russia under suspicious circumstances."

Velasquez paused, as if flipping through her notes. She wanted that information to stick with the jurors. It did. Several looked at the defense table. Then she asked, "What did you do next?"

Daugherty said, "The FBI opened an investigation into Mr. Jenkins's actions and learned that CJ Security had received a payment of fifty thousand dollars into its checking account shortly after Mr. Jenkins's return from his first trip to Russia."

"Did you attempt to determine the source for those funds?" Velasquez asked.

"We asked a forensic accountant to trace the source of those funds."

Jenkins and Sloane had a copy of the report and had agreed to its admissibility.

"What does the report conclude?"

"The accountant determined that the funds had originated from a Swiss bank account. He was not able to further trace the source of those funds."

Velasquez led Daugherty through what Jenkins had told him during their second conversation at the FBI's field office in downtown Seattle.

"Did you tell Mr. Jenkins what you had learned with respect to the two operations he disclosed to the Russians?"

"I did."

"What was his response, if any?"

"He shook his head and he said, 'What the hell have I done?'"

Again, Velasquez let that response linger a moment before she asked, "Did you respond?"

"I asked him if he wanted to confess and make a deal."

"What was his response?"

"He said, 'This isn't what you think it is. I didn't do it for the reason you think I did.'"

With that seemingly damning statement, Velasquez thanked Daugherty and sat.

Sloane rose and slowly walked to the lectern. "Agent Daugherty, you mentioned that you asked Mr. Jenkins if he wanted to confess to having committed a crime, is that right?"

"Yes."

"Would you please produce to the court the confession that Mr. Jenkins signed in your offices that day."

Daugherty cleared his throat. "I don't have a signed confession."

"How about an unsigned confession then?"

"No."

"Wouldn't it be standard procedure, when interrogating a witness who confesses, for you to get the witness to sign and date a confession before the witness leaves your office?"

"There are a lot of different procedures—"

"And wouldn't one of those procedures be that the FBI agent—you—would get a signed confession before the witness leaves the meeting?"

"It would."

"You never even pursued a confession, did you?"

"No."

Jenkins watched the jurors. Two of the men smirked, amused.

"You said Mr. Jenkins told you, 'This isn't what you think it is. I didn't do it for the reason you think I did.' Is that right?"

"That's what he said."

"Didn't he say he revealed those two names because Carl Emerson authorized him to do so?"

"He said he didn't reveal any unauthorized information, but I couldn't find any corroborating evidence to support that it was authorized."

Sloane flipped the pages of the typed document. "You did write in notes that Mr. Jenkins said, 'That isn't the whole story. For the whole story you need to go to the CIA.'"

"Yes."

"And you claim that you called the CIA, and you were told they had no record of any operation in which Mr. Jenkins had been reactivated, as you put it. Is that correct?"

"They said they had no record of it."

"So, you assumed no such operation existed, right?"

"I suppose that is correct."

"But you also told this court that the FBI handles what happens inside the country and the CIA handles what happens outside the country, didn't you?"

"Something like that."

"You would agree, wouldn't you, that one agency doesn't always know what the other agency is doing, and the two agencies don't always tell one another what they're doing?"

"Yes, I would agree with that."

"Wouldn't it also be true that while the FBI and the CIA's ultimate objectives might be the same, how those two agencies achieve their objectives are not the same?"

"I don't understand."

"Let me see if I can make it clearer for you." Sloane had handled an FBI case before. "Isn't your motto at the FBI, one of them anyway, 'AIJ—put the asshole in jail'? You've heard that among FBI agents, haven't you?"

"I've heard that, yes."

"Black-and-white, isn't it? Just put the asshole in jail."

"I'll agree to that."

"What's the CIA's creed among its case operatives, do you know?"

"I don't."

"'And you shall know the truth, and the truth shall piss you off.' Have you heard that?"

Daugherty smiled. So did several jurors. "No, I haven't."

"Any idea what that means?"

"No."

"It's not so black-and-white then, is it?"

Velasquez stood. "Objection, Your Honor, this is speculation. He said he doesn't know the creed."

"Overruled," Harden said.

"It's not so black-and-white, is it, Agent Daugherty?"

"Not to me it isn't," Daugherty said.

64

Following Daugherty, Velasquez called Randy Traeger, the former CFO of LSR&C. She established Traeger's background, then proceeded to establish that LSR&C had been unable to make payments to CJ Security for approximately three months leading up to the end of 2017. She also established that Jenkins had told Traeger he'd exhausted his line of credit with the bank.

Sloane stood when Velasquez sat down. "You were the chief financial officer of LSR&C, in charge of all the money coming into and out of the company, weren't you?"

"In a sense."

Sloane was in no mood for half answers. "That was your job, wasn't it?"

"Yes, in part."

"So why wasn't LSR&C paying CJ Security?"

"I asked Mitchell Goldstone that same question and—"

"All due respect," Sloane said, cutting him off. "But I want to know from the *chief financial officer* why LSR&C could not make payment to CJ Security."

"We just didn't have the cash flow during those months."

"And why was that?"

"I don't know."

"It was your job to know, wasn't it?"

"Well, yes, but . . ."

"But you didn't take steps to figure it out?"

"I tried."

"You asked the chief operating officer. What else did you do?"

"I tried to determine what was happening to our profits."

"And what was happening to LSR&C's profits?"

"I couldn't make a determination."

"You didn't know."

"No."

Sloane took Traeger through his educational and professional background, which was extensive, then asked, "And with all this education, even you couldn't figure out where millions of dollars were going?"

"No."

"Are you aware that your chief operating officer, Mitchell Goldstone, contends that LSR&C was a CIA-backed company through which the CIA funneled money to operatives all over the world?"

Velasquez stood. "Objection, Your Honor, violates the CIPA ruling."

Harden considered this, then said, "Overruled."

Sloane was not asking about the documents, but rather what Mitchell Goldstone had alleged, and hopefully would testify to. Harden, for one, seemed curious. So did several jurors. It remained a risk. Sloane could state the accusation and Goldstone would confirm it, but the government would paint Goldstone as a liar, and without the LSR&C documents, Sloane had nothing to back up the testimony.

"I didn't know about that accusation until I read it in the paper."

Sloane returned to the table and picked up the government's complaint against LSR&C. "Charges were brought against you in the same case as Mr. Goldstone, weren't they?"

"Yes."

"You agreed to provide testimony against Mr. Goldstone in exchange for immunity, didn't you?"

"That was the agreement my attorneys reached."

"Don't go blaming us attorneys," Sloane said, which drew a smattering of laughter from the jury box. "You signed that agreement yourself, didn't you?"

"Yes."

Sloane introduced the signed agreement. "You sold out Mitchell Goldstone to keep your own hide out of jail, didn't you?"

Velasquez stood. "Objection, Your Honor. Counsel is badgering the witness."

"Cross-examination," Harden said. "I'll allow it."

"I agreed to provide testimony about what I knew and didn't know," Traeger said.

"And you found out you didn't know a lot, didn't you?"

"I don't think that . . ." Traeger paused and looked to Jenkins. Then he said, "I guess that's true. I didn't."

Sloane followed up with a question to draw the jurors' attention to the CIA, the implication being that even the CFO of the company didn't know what was going on. "Mr. Traeger, did you ever meet Carl Emerson?"

"No."

"Did you at least know who he was?"

"No."

"Did you know a Richard Peterson?"

"He was the CEO of TBT Investments."

Bingo. The defense now had confirmation, without relying on the documents or on Goldstone's testimony. "And TBT Investments was a subsidiary of what company?"

"LSR&C."

"Your company," Sloane said. "The company for which you were the CFO, correct?"

"Yes."

"Did anyone ever tell you that Richard Peterson was actually Carl Emerson?"

"No."

"Now, when the indictment was issued against LSR&C, Mr. Goldstone, you, and the other officers, did you try to reach Mr. Goldstone?"

"I tried, but I wasn't able to reach him."

"Did you drive into the office looking for him?"

"Yes."

"When was that?"

"The next day."

"And by that you mean the day after the indictment came down?"

"Correct."

"And did you find him in the office?"

Traeger started to look uncomfortable. "No."

"What did you find when you drove to LSR&C's offices in the Columbia Center the day after the indictment came down?"

"Nothing. Everything was gone."

"Everything? The cubicles and the computers?"

"Yes."

"Gone. How about the carpeting? Also gone?"

"It was just concrete floors."

"The entire office was completely dismantled in what, less than twelve hours since you had been there?"

"Yes."

"And all the company files? Did you find those?"

"The physical files were also gone, and the network server was gone."

"Who took all of this?"

"I don't know."

"And what about all the investment money? Was it also gone?"

"I couldn't access the company's server, so . . ."

"Millions of dollars just vanished, along with the entire office. Everything just went *poof*, like a magic act, correct?"

"I suppose, yes."

Sloane sat, and after a brief redirect of Traeger, Velasquez dismissed him.

Near five o'clock, Harden dismissed the jury. For once, the government had no motions to argue.

"Who will the government call in the morning?" Harden asked.

"We haven't made that determination yet, Judge," Velasquez said.

"Whoever it is, let the defense know tonight." Harden rapped his gavel. "We're adjourned for the day."

65

The following morning, as Jenkins settled into his seat, Maria Velasquez had a surprise for the defense, and this one was problematic. Sloane and Jenkins expected the prosecution to continue its case, though Velasquez had not called the prior evening to advise which witnesses she would call that day. When Harden took the bench and instructed the government to call its next witness, Velasquez stood and said, "Your Honor, the government rests."

Sloane did not physically react, but Jenkins knew that, inside, his attorney was scrambling. Judges liked nothing less than an unprepared attorney, especially one of Sloane's caliber. Any complaint by Sloane that the government had again sandbagged the defense would be met with disinterest. Velasquez could have told Sloane, and the court, of the government's decision the night before, but she would no doubt have a readymade response why she had not.

The real question was: Why had the government rested its case with at least twelve more names on its witness list? It was possible the prosecution believed it had proven its case. It was also possible the government was dumping the case back in the defense's lap and intended to impugn Sloane on his opening promise to take the prosecution's burden and prove Jenkins's innocence.

If Harden was surprised by the government's position, he also didn't show it. He turned to Sloane. "Call your first witness, Mr. Sloane."

That was all well and good, except Jenkins knew Sloane's witnesses were not yet in court. Sloane stood and said, "Your Honor, may I have a minute?"

"A minute," Harden said.

Sloane looked to the gallery and motioned Jake forward. At the railing, Sloane whispered, "Go out and call Carolyn. Tell her to get the Columbia Center leasing agent here ASAP, as well as Addy Beckman."

"Tell her to also call Claudia Baker," Jenkins said. "Have Carolyn tell Claudia that I need a favor. She'll come. It will take an hour or more to drive down, but she'll come."

"What are you going to do in the interim?" Jake asked.

"Stall."

"Mr. Sloane," Judge Harden said. "Call your first witness."

Sloane straightened as Jake hurried from the courtroom, punching in numbers on his cell phone. Across the courtroom, Velasquez and her entourage of lawyers sat as if waiting for Sloane to complain. He didn't. "Certainly, Your Honor. The defense calls Alex Jenkins."

Alex had been in the court the first day, and then every chance she could. Sloane arranged for a babysitter to watch CJ and Lizzie and for the next hour, Sloane led Alex on a slow and methodical journey of her marriage to Charlie and their children. She outlined the formation of CJ Security, their relationship with CFO Randy Traeger, and CJ Security's relationship with LSR&C. She testified that she had never heard of TBT Investments until the trial.

She continued until Jake returned to the courtroom and nodded to Sloane, who approached the railing. Jake handed him a sheet of paper.

Leasing agent and Baker in the hallway waiting to be called. Beckman on way.

Sloane thanked Alex and excused her. Velasquez had no questions.

Sloane then called the Columbia Center leasing agent, who confirmed Randy Traeger's testimony that LSR&C's offices had been cleaned out the day after the story broke of an SEC investigation.

"The entire company was gone," the agent said. "I mean everything was gone, even the carpet. I took pictures because I'd never seen anything like it."

The jurors loved the man's incredulity, as well as the photos Sloane broadcast on the court's computer monitors.

Again, Velasquez declined to cross-examine.

After the leasing agent, Sloane called Claudia Baker and established her job as the receptionist at the building where CJ Security maintained an office. Then he said, "At any time during your employment did the FBI come to CJ Security's offices?"

"Yes," she said. "An agent by the name of Chris Daugherty came to the office."

Upon prompting, Baker provided the date of Daugherty's visit.

"Did Agent Daugherty say why he was there?"

"He said he knew Charles Jenkins worked for the CIA. He said he wanted the files of CJ Security so he could confirm the relationship."

Sloane thanked Baker and sat.

Velasquez quickly stood. It was possible, Jenkins thought, as he watched Velasquez charge the lectern, that they had underestimated her preparation. Then again, he knew Sloane had laid a trap and was hoping Velasquez stepped in it. "Ms. Baker, you fielded calls for CJ Security, including calls for Mr. Jenkins?"

"Yes."

"At any time in your employment did you field a call from a man named Carl Emerson?"

"I don't recall. It's possible but . . ."

"You don't recall that name. How about Richard Peterson?"

"I don't recall that name either."

"Did Mr. Jenkins ever tell you he was traveling to Russia?"

"No."

"Did he ever tell you that he worked for the CIA?"

"No."

"Did he ever tell you that he had once worked for the CIA?"

"No. I didn't know about it until I read it in the newspaper."

"You said FBI agent Daugherty came to CJ Security's offices and said 'we know Mr. Jenkins worked for the CIA,' is that correct?"

"Yes."

"You didn't write down any notes detailing such a conversation, did you?"

Velasquez had just stepped in Sloane's trap and made her first mistake of the trial. She'd asked a question to which she did not know the answer.

"I did, actually."

Velasquez froze, and in that instance, Baker pushed on. "I called Mr. Jenkins and told him what the FBI agent said to me, and Mr. Jenkins asked me to transcribe what the FBI agent said, date, and sign it. He said I should mail the document to myself and to his attorney."

Velasquez knew she'd backed herself into a corner. She had no choice but to ask the next question. If she didn't, Sloane would. "And you did that?"

"I have the envelope right here." She pulled it from her bag. "It's still sealed."

Sloane stood when Velasquez sat. After establishing the date of the postmark, he had Baker open the envelope and read her statement. Then he said, "Did you field calls made to Mr. Jenkins's cell phone?"

"No. Not unless he forwarded his cell phone to the office."

Sloane thanked and dismissed her.

After the lunch recess—a much-needed reprieve that allowed Sloane to catch his breath and go over Addison Beckman's testimony with her—he called the forensic psychiatrist. He established her background and went through each test and its purpose. "What conclusions did you reach as a result of putting Mr. Jenkins through all of these tests?"

"I concluded Mr. Jenkins was telling the truth, and I told you to believe him. I also concluded that Mr. Jenkins was fiercely loyal to his country."

Sloane sat and Velasquez took the lectern.

"Ms. Beckman, did you question Mr. Jenkins as to the reasons why he left the CIA in 1978?"

"I did not."

"He didn't tell you that he walked away from the agency without even telling his station chief that he was quitting?"

"No. My focus was on the present."

"He didn't tell you he left the agency because he was disgruntled?"

"We didn't discuss it."

"He didn't tell you he was disillusioned?"

"We didn't discuss his reason for leaving in 1978."

"But you did conclude he was fiercely loyal to his country, right?"

"Yes."

Velasquez's tone became increasingly more incredulous. "But in reaching that conclusion you didn't consider that he left his job at the CIA and walked away without telling anyone why he was leaving or where he was going?"

"He walked away. He didn't betray his country."

"Not then he didn't," Velasquez said.

Sloane shot to his feet. "Objection."

"Sustained," Harden said, not waiting for anything more to be said, and shooting Velasquez a reproachful look.

"You also administered tests and concluded that Mr. Jenkins was telling the truth—is that right?"

"That's right."

"Did Mr. Jenkins tell you that his training to become a CIA operative included how to pass an interrogation?"

"No."

"You didn't know that he'd been trained to get an interrogator to believe he was telling the truth when he was, in fact, lying?"

"I don't know whether he had that training or not, but I'm not an interrogator. I'm a forensic psychiatrist. I would have known if he was lying."

Velasquez gave that answer a smile, and let the jurors see it. "If we were to believe his current story, we'd have to believe he was skilled at lying, wouldn't we?"

"I don't follow."

"Wouldn't we have to believe that he successfully lied to Russian FSB officers and got those officers to believe he was telling them the truth? Wouldn't we have to believe that?"

"I suppose we would," Beckman said.

"So, we can assume Mr. Jenkins is a pretty good liar, can't we?"

"Objection, Your Honor, argumentative," Sloane said.

"Sustained."

Velasquez, having made her point, sat.

After a brief redirect, with the end of the day approaching, Harden adjourned the proceedings. Velasquez waited until the jurors had left the courtroom, then said, "Your Honor, we have a motion concerning the defense's subpoenaing of Carl Emerson to appear and testify and would request that the courtroom be cleared."

"So, you found him," Harden said.

"We did," Velasquez said.

"A blank envelope was slipped under my law firm's door with the address inside. I found the envelope yesterday morning," Sloane said.

Harden cleared the courtroom, then looked to Velasquez. "Proceed with your motion, Ms. Velasquez."

"Your Honor, based on the Ninth Circuit's decision that the LSR&C documents are classified under CIPA, the government objects to the defense's subpoenaing Mr. Emerson. Mr. Emerson cannot testify as to subjects set forth in documents designated by the court of appeals as classified and potentially damaging to national security. Nor can those documents be used to impeach him. Therefore, the government moves to quash the subpoena to Mr. Emerson."

"Mr. Sloane?"

"Mr. Emerson's testimony is not the same as asking him about classified documents. We certainly don't intend to introduce the documents, but that does not preclude us from asking Mr. Emerson questions about his relationship with TBT Investments and TBT's relationship to LSR&C. This is a critical portion of our defense, and it is the defendant's constitutional right to defend himself."

Harden continued flipping through the government's motion, then flipped it back to its original page and set it down. "I agree, Mr. Sloane. CIPA protects the documents. It doesn't prohibit you from asking Mr. Emerson questions about his relationship to the two companies. The defendant has a constitutional right to defend himself, and while I will not allow you to go so far as to injure national security, I do believe you have the right to ask Mr. Emerson questions, and I believe this jury has a right to hear him testify. I'm hereby ordering the government to produce Mr. Emerson in this courtroom, tomorrow morning at nine a.m. at the defense's expense."

"Your Honor," Velasquez started.

Harden cut her off. "Do not, Ms. Velasquez, give me the same song and dance about the government having no authority over Mr. Emerson. I'm willing to accept that the envelope that appeared under Mr. Sloane's office door did so by magic, as opposed to the other possibilities, such as the government deliberately misleading this court from the outset, but my suspension of disbelief will only go so far. Have Mr. Emerson here tomorrow morning, or I will hold the government in contempt."

"I'm not sure he did us any favors," Jenkins said to Sloane as they walked from the courtroom. "Emerson could admit he was working for the CIA, even go so far as to say that LSR&C was set up to provide funds to operatives and operations, but deny that he met with me, which will bolster the government's argument that my defense is nothing more than a convenient excuse I fabricated, after Mitchell Goldstone and LSR&C were indicted, to keep my ass out of jail."

"If Emerson is going to be here, the jury is going to expect me to put him on," Sloane said. "My thought is we keep his testimony short, establish that he worked for TBT Investments, and that he came to Seattle at roughly the same time you claim to have met with him. If he lies, I can argue to the judge that I should be able to use the documents to impeach him, that he can clear the courtroom of all but the jurors, but I'm not sure he'll allow it."

They worked late into the night, until everyone started to fade. Jenkins followed Sloane into his office to wait while Sloane checked his e-mail.

Sloane did so and groaned. Then he swore under his breath and said, "Maybe we won't have to worry about questioning Emerson after all."

66

The following morning, Judge Harden's clerk entered the courtroom and advised that Harden wished to see counsel in his chambers. Sloane looked to Jenkins and nodded. Both knew the reason.

Jenkins and Sloane followed Velasquez and the other government attorneys down a narrow hall to the judge's chamber. The court reporter was tucked into a corner of the room with her machine. Judge Harden stood behind his desk. His judicial robe hung from his coatrack, along with his suit jacket. At the side of his desk he'd placed the four boxes containing the LSR&C documents.

Harden held a document, reading as the attorneys entered. He brought the proceeding to order, asked counsel to state their presence in his chambers for the court reporter, then said, "Mr. Sloane, I assume you have not seen Judge Pence's order, which I received early this morning?"

Pence was the Ninth Circuit Court judge who had written the order reversing Harden's decision to allow the use of the LSR&C documents. Sloane had not seen an order, though he had read the government's interlocutory appeal to keep Sloane from calling Carl Emerson.

"I saw the appeal. I have not seen the judge's order."

Harden handed Sloane the order across his desk. "Judge Pence apparently works late nights." He looked to Velasquez when he said this, but she remained stone-faced and impassive. "In any event, Judge Pence's order prevents the defense from asking questions of

Mr. Emerson that pertain to subjects covered in the documents the Ninth Circuit has already held to be classified under CIPA. He also has issued a number of other restrictions with respect to questions the defense may ask of Mr. Emerson. I don't expect you to make a decision at this time regarding what you intend to do, whether you still intend to call Mr. Emerson. But if you do, these restrictions would apply."

Sloane and Jenkins quickly flipped through the two-page order, reading the restrictions. They would prevent Sloane from asking Emerson much of anything. Emerson would have a green light to lie, knowing Sloane could not impeach him. On the other hand, if Emerson was present in court and the defense did not call him, the jurors would wonder why not. It could be fatal to Jenkins's defense.

"We will let you know, Judge," Sloane said in as confident a voice as he could muster.

Velasquez, now imbued with confidence bordering on arrogance, said, "The government requests a decision now. We need to let Mr. Emerson know whether he is free to go, so as not to inconvenience him, or we need to prepare him for questioning."

Harden rubbed his chin as if he'd just taken a right cross and the impact had surprised him. "Counsel," he said to Velasquez. "You can tell Mr. Emerson that if the defense decides to call him today, tomorrow, or the next day, or the day after that, I expect him to be in that hallway. Do I make myself clear?"

"You do, Your Honor," Velasquez said.

"Your Honor," Sloane said, thinking on the fly. "If the defense opts not to call Mr. Emerson, I would request an order preventing the government from commenting on Mr. Emerson's presence here, or on the defense's decision not to call him. It would be highly prejudicial, especially because the defense could not comment that it had been forbidden to use LSR&C documents to impeach Mr. Emerson, were he to lie."

"That motion, I will grant," Harden said, and quickly added, "We're finished in here, counsel."

After Harden went through preliminary matters, the jurors returned and took their seats. Sloane called Mitchell Goldstone, LSR&C's chief operating officer. Goldstone had been driven to the courthouse that morning from the Federal Detention Center at SeaTac, and his wife had provided him a suit, a tie, and appropriate shoes to wear in court.

Jenkins thought Goldstone looked at ease on the stand, perhaps because the trial subpoena had both compelled and freed him to testify. He told the court that LSR&C had been run as a CIA proprietary from the start of its existence, and that LSR&C had been paid by the CIA to provide cover stories for its field operatives, including providing them with "legitimate" employment. He testified that Carl Emerson had initially been employed as an officer of LSR&C, but that it was subsequently decided at CIA headquarters in Langley, Virginia, that it would be more prudent if he was an officer of a subsidiary, TBT Investments, to keep the money separated from investor funds. Goldstone said CIA money was funneled through TBT Investments to fund agents and their operations. He also testified that he'd met Emerson when Emerson came to the offices in November 2017. That piece of information would allow Sloane to argue in closing argument that Emerson was in Seattle at the same time Jenkins said he met Emerson on Camano Island.

Goldstone answered Sloane's questions without hesitation and appeared calm and confident. But Jenkins and Sloane both knew that, because of the plea agreement he'd signed, Goldstone was easy pickings for Velasquez, and she wasted little time shoving that agreement down Goldstone's throat.

"Mr. Goldstone," Velasquez said. "It's true, isn't it, that you pled guilty to ninety-four counts of perjury, fraud, and tax evasion?"

"Yes," he said. "I did."

"You pled guilty to lying under oath nearly one hundred times, correct?"

"That is correct."

"And your lies pertained to statements you had made that your company was a CIA proprietary, correct?"

"Yes," Goldstone said.

"You also pled guilty to defrauding investors in LSR&C, didn't you?"

"Yes," Goldstone said.

"You pled guilty to running a Ponzi scheme, didn't you?"

"I did."

"After your arrest, for fraud, you didn't call the CIA and ask someone to bail you out, did you?"

"I guess I just thought they would."

"You didn't call the CIA and ask someone to bail you out, did you?" Velasquez asked again, this time a little more forceful.

"No, I didn't."

"And nowhere in the plea agreement you signed does it say you were working for the CIA or that LSR&C was a CIA proprietary, does it?"

"No," Goldstone conceded.

Velasquez was more than happy to sit down. Sloane looked to Jenkins. They both knew that any attempt to rehabilitate Goldstone would just make the defense look desperate. They dismissed him.

During the lunch recess, the defense sat at a restaurant table staring at their food. "That went a lot worse than I anticipated," Sloane said.

"Not your fault," Jenkins said. "Without the ability to introduce documents, Goldstone does look like a liar. But we had to put him on. What do we do about Emerson?"

They talked in detail about Judge Pence's ruling, and decided it was too risky to call Emerson as a witness. "He'd carve you into little chunks," Sloane said. "And the documents to prove he's lying will be sitting in boxes in Judge Harden's chambers. They might as well be somewhere on the moon, given the restrictions Judge Pence has placed on us."

"Put me on the stand," Jenkins said. He knew the risks, but he'd talked it over with Alex. If he was going down, it would be with a fight. He didn't want to be convicted without ever getting the chance to look the jury in the eyes before they called him a liar.

Sloane turned to him. "Without the documents—" Sloane started.

"I know the ramifications and the risks, David. This isn't on you. It's on me. Put me on the stand. Let me talk directly to the jury. If the government is going to call me a liar, let them do it to my face."

"It could backfire," Sloane said. "The jury could see it as a desperate act—"

"Of a condemned man," Jenkins said. "I know. And maybe I am, but I prefer to go down swinging."

67

In the courtroom, as Jenkins had requested, Sloane stood and called him to the stand. Jenkins saw Velasquez look at Sloane as if he was crazy, but she also flipped through her binder. She had prepared for this possibility.

Jenkins felt his anxiety rise as he walked to the witness chair, but he managed to keep his right hand from quivering when he took the oath to tell the truth.

Sloane and Jenkins had agreed that it was important, as it had been in voir dire and in Sloane's opening statement, to immediately alter the negative connotation of the word "spy" and to get the jury to acknowledge that America uses spies to protect national security.

"Are you a spy?" he asked.

Jenkins spoke to the jury. "Yes."

"What country did you spy for?"

"The United States of America."

"What agency were you working for?"

"The Central Intelligence Agency of the United States of America."

"Did you at any time provide to a Russian FSB officer, or to anyone else, any information that you were not authorized to provide?"

"No. All of the information I gave was authorized."

"Did you do anything other than follow CIA orders?"

"No."

"Who was your case officer in the CIA?"

"Carl Emerson."

"And you followed Mr. Emerson's orders and instructions?"

"Yes."

Sloane then asked, and Jenkins answered, questions concerning Vietnam, his initial recruitment by the CIA, and his time in Mexico City. Jenkins answered each question in about twenty-five words or less, to prevent the government from asking questions about subjects outside the scope of his answers. "Can you tell the court why you left the employ of the CIA?"

"Again, I can't provide specifics. I left because I felt that the government had not been truthful with me about the intentions of a certain operation, and that operation had resulted in unnecessary deaths. I decided to leave."

"Did you kill anyone?"

"No. But I provided intelligence."

"Were you upset when you left the CIA?"

"No. I was saddened."

"Why?"

"I thought I had found a career, something I was good at and loved. But I didn't want to be a part of anything like what had happened."

"When you left your employ with the CIA, did you tell anyone you were leaving?"

"No."

"Why not?"

"In hindsight I wish I had. I wish I'd done a lot of things differently when I was in my early twenties. Now that I'm older and have a better perspective I would do things differently, but I can't change the past. I just wanted to get out and get as far away as I could."

"Did you go back to your childhood home in New Jersey?"

"No. I wanted a fresh start, so I went to Camano Island in Washington State."

"Were you hiding from the government?"

"Pretty hard to hide when your name is on a deed to a ten-acre parcel of land and you pay income tax every year."

Sloane asked why Jenkins had started CJ Security.

"I was looking for something that would give my son opportunities in life to be whatever he wanted to be. He's smart. He takes after his mother."

Several of the jurors smiled.

Jenkins told the jury of Randy Traeger's proposal.

"Did you consider it an odd coincidence that Traeger would have a job seemingly right up your alley?"

"Not at the time, no."

"What about now?"

"Now I wonder."

"Did you have any suspicion that LSR&C was a CIA front for agents and their operations overseas, as Mitchell Goldstone testified?"

"No."

"Did you know Carl Emerson was running TBT Investments as Mitchell Goldstone testified?"

"No. I hadn't seen Carl Emerson or heard his name since I'd left Mexico City. He just showed up on my farm one day in November, after Alex had taken CJ to school."

Jenkins told the details of his meetings with Emerson and what Emerson asked him to do.

"Did you think it an odd coincidence for Mr. Emerson to show up on your farm?"

"Not then, but I do now."

Jenkins answered Sloane's questions about the financial difficulties CJ Security endured, about the personal guaranties, and about the business loans the company owed.

"Is that why you accepted the job?"

"It's one of the reasons, certainly," he said. "But there was another reason."

"And what was that?"

"Carl Emerson said agents' lives were in danger. He said they would likely die if the operation wasn't successful."

"What was your cover supposed to be?"

"The best cover is one closest to the truth. I was a former CIA field officer, disillusioned and upset at the agency, and I had classified information to sell. I was told by Carl Emerson that I would go in, set the hook, and get certain things to occur. Then other agents would take over the operation."

"How were you to contact Mr. Emerson, if needed?"

"He gave me a business card with a number on it."

Sloane projected that card on the court's computer monitors and Jenkins confirmed it to be the one Carl Emerson gave him.

"Did Emerson say anything to you about what would happen if the operation fell apart?"

"I was told that if anything went wrong, the agency would not acknowledge the operation."

"Did you think they would acknowledge that you had been reactivated?"

"Not publicly, but yes, in private."

"Is that why you voluntarily went to the FBI and spoke to Agent Daugherty?"

"Yes. I asked him to look into the matter. I thought the CIA would acknowledge my reactivation and would investigate what I was telling Daugherty."

Sloane and Jenkins got out the basic story. It was time to finish up.

"Did you at any time, give to the FSB, or to anyone else, any information that was not authorized?"

"No. I hadn't been a field officer for decades. I didn't have any information that wasn't authorized." They had discussed this the night before and considered it a strong argument.

"Did you do anything other than follow CIA orders?"

"No."

The final two questions were designed to impress to the jury that Jenkins was one of the good guys.

"Are you loyal to the United States of America?"

"I always have been. I love my country."

Sloane let that answer linger, turned, and sat down.

Velasquez stood and approached the lectern. "That's quite a story, Mr. Jenkins. It dovetails nicely with Mr. Goldstone's story, doesn't it?"

"It's the truth."

"You knew, didn't you, Mr. Goldstone's allegation that he, too, had been working for the Central Intelligence Agency?"

"I learned of it. I'm not sure when, but I learned of it."

"Mr. Sloane asked you about coincidences. I'd like to ask you about that as well. It's quite a coincidence, isn't it, that Carl Emerson, whom you hadn't seen in some forty years, just happened to show up on your farm at the same time your business was on the verge of financial collapse, isn't it?"

Jenkins had to be careful here. If he said no, he would have to testify, without the documents to support him, that Emerson, or someone else, had orchestrated withholding payment to CJ Security to put Jenkins under duress. It might be too much for a jury to believe. Instead, he piggybacked on Goldstone's testimony that he had met Emerson at LSR&C in November. "I didn't think so at the time because I didn't think the two were related. Now that I know Mr. Emerson was working at LSR&C, no, I don't think it was a coincidence."

"You were a trained CIA field officer and you didn't question your former station chief showing up, unannounced, decades after you left, offering you a job when you just happened to need money?"

"I didn't question his motives at that time. But I did question why he was there. You bet I did."

"Isn't it true, Mr. Jenkins, that when you met with FBI agents, you didn't ask for a CIA representative to be present at those interrogations?"

"That is true."

"You told Agent Daugherty that you had disclosed information to a Russian FSB agent."

"I told Agent Daugherty that I had not disclosed any unauthorized information."

"The two agents whose names you disclosed originally became CIA assets in Mexico City, where you also worked, correct?"

"I didn't know that at the time."

"But when Agent Daugherty told you both agents had died, you said, quote, 'What have I done?' didn't you?"

"I might have said that, yes. I couldn't believe it. Carl Emerson told me that both of those agents were safe and the operations had been over for years."

"Agent Daugherty also told you that the CIA had no record of you being reactivated. Didn't he tell you that?"

"That's what he said."

Velasquez kept up her attack for another forty-five minutes. Jenkins did his best to weather the storm. Beneath the confident exterior, however, Jenkins felt his T-shirt sticking to his back.

"Isn't it true, Mr. Jenkins, that you didn't tell Agent Daugherty the whole story because you didn't know the whole story when you met with him; that you were still making it up as you went along?"

"No, that's not true."

"You knew, Mr. Jenkins, did you not, that if the CIA didn't confirm your story, you could be tried for espionage, didn't you?"

"Yes, I knew that."

"And yet, you are asking this jury to believe that, with a wife suffering from pregnancy complications, and a nine-year-old son, you didn't tell Agent Daugherty the whole story out of loyalty to an agency that, you knew, would not support you and that would try you for espionage? Is that what you're asking this jury to believe?"

"I didn't tell him the whole story because I was concerned that if I did, I would expose agents and their operations, and those agents could die."

"So even now . . . you would have us believe that you still haven't told us the whole story—is that your testimony?"

"I can't tell you the whole story," he said. "I'm sorry, but I can't."

Velasquez looked to the jurors. "And neither can the CIA, can they?"

"I don't know whether they can or can't," Jenkins said. "All I know is they won't."

Velasquez finished her cross-examination at just after three in the afternoon, and Sloane finished a brief redirect. Jenkins was excused and returned to the counsel table, physically and emotionally drained.

When Jenkins sat, Harden said, "Mr. Sloane, you may call your next witness."

Sloane stood. During a break he and Jenkins had decided that if Sloane felt Jenkins's testimony was strong, they would rest their case.

"Your Honor," Sloane said. "The defense rests."

Harden looked mildly surprised. He directed his attention to Velasquez, who spoke in hushed whispers with her co-counsel before standing. "The government also rests."

Sloane would be giving his closing argument in the morning. They all waited for Harden to thank, admonish, and excuse the jurors, as he had done at the end of each day. Instead, Harden sat forward.

"Ladies and gentlemen of the jury, the defense has rested its case. So, too, has the government, but I believe there is another witness the jury should hear from and I am therefore calling Carl Emerson as a witness. I am calling him because I want the evidence of his testimony in the record," Harden continued. "And I don't want either party to feel in any way obligated to call him, and they are not obligated to call him, but I think the jury needs Mr. Emerson to answer some questions."

"I'll be damned," Sloane said under his breath.

68

Velasquez quickly stood. "Your Honor, the government objects."

"Overruled."

"Your Honor, the government intended to call Mr. Emerson as a rebuttal witness."

"No, Ms. Velasquez, the government very clearly rested its case, and I believe the jurors should hear from this witness."

"Your Honor, we request that the government's objection be noted in the record, and that the court adjourn for the day to allow us to take this matter up to the Ninth Circuit on an interlocutory appeal."

Judge Harden sat forward. "So noted," he said. "The government's motion is denied. Anything else?"

"No, Your Honor," Velasquez said.

Harden looked to his bailiff. "Please go into the hallway and ask Mr. Emerson to enter."

And just like that, the reason for Harden's decision to call Emerson at the end of the day became apparent. He did not want to give Velasquez time to again run to the Ninth Circuit for an order.

Jenkins looked to Sloane, who leaned close and kept his voice low. "Haven't seen this happen in all my years practicing," Sloane said. "But so far, I'm enjoying it."

Emerson entered the court in a blue power suit. The fact that every juror considered him from the moment he entered was proof of their curiosity about this man whose name they kept hearing. Though Emerson was in his late seventies, he looked younger, with a full head of silver hair, and the glow of a man who spent time in the sun. His bearing and his gaze emitted the feeling that he considered the whole judicial process to be beneath him and was eager to get it behind him.

After he'd taken the stand and was administered the oath to tell the truth, Emerson unbuttoned his coat, sat, and crossed his legs. He looked to the lectern, then to Jenkins's side of the courtroom, and seemed genuinely perplexed when the first question came from Harden.

"Please state your name for the record," Harden said.

Emerson looked to Velasquez, then to the judge. "Excuse me?"

"State your name for the record," Harden said.

"Carl Edward Emerson."

"Are you presently employed?"

Emerson uncrossed his legs and sat up. "No, I'm retired."

"What are you retired from?"

"The Central Intelligence Agency."

"Did you retire from the CIA or were you terminated?"

"I decided that forty-five years of government service was sufficient and I retired."

"Mr. Emerson," Harden said, pulling out the documents that the CIA records clerk had introduced. "I have employment documents here indicating your employment was terminated. Are you telling me these documents are inaccurate?"

Emerson gave a smug smile. "I suppose it is how one looks at it. I didn't consider myself terminated. If I was, it was after I had already decided to retire."

"The documents also indicate you were reprimanded for exercising poor judgment in dealings with the companies TBT Investments and LSR&C. Are you saying you weren't aware of that?"

"No, I'm aware of it."

"So you were terminated?"

"I suppose I was," Emerson said, that slight smile still on his lips.

"And why were you reprimanded?"

Emerson again looked to Velasquez before answering. "For investing personal money in those companies."

"You invested your own money?"

Jenkins leaned into Sloane. "I was right," he whispered. "Emerson's the leak. He was using TBT to wash the money he received from the FSB."

"I did," Emerson said. "It was a mistake, given how everything turned out."

"There has been testimony that you previously served as the Mexico City CIA station chief. Is that true?"

"That is correct."

"And you were the defendant's, Charles Jenkins's, boss."

"For a brief time when I was his special agent in charge. Charles was an excellent agent, but he abruptly left the CIA. He was upset and angry. I cannot discuss the operation that caused Charles to quit, but he was angry at the CIA and the United States government, and I guess at me."

"He told you this?"

Emerson stumbled, then sought to recover. "No. I never heard from him. He just left."

Judge Harden paused, and Jenkins looked to the jurors, several of whom appeared to have caught the inconsistency. If Jenkins had abruptly left and had not spoken to Emerson, then how did Emerson know the reason for Jenkins's departure?

"There has been testimony that you served as an officer of the company TBT Investments. Is that true?"

"Nice," Sloane said under his breath to Jenkins. "He's relying on testimony, not on the documents."

"That is true."

Jenkins had expected Emerson to lie, but maybe Harden's decision to call him so quickly prevented the government from telling Emerson that the LSR&C documents had been classified.

"Did you have a TBT business card with your phone number on it?"

"I had a business card with a number on it, yes."

"And there has been testimony that TBT was a subsidiary of a company called LSR&C. Is that correct?"

"That is correct."

"There has been testimony that TBT Investments was a company used to funnel money to CIA field officers and their operations in other countries. Is that true?"

"Yes, that is true."

Jenkins leaned close to Sloane. "We have confirmation that Goldstone isn't a liar."

"There has also been testimony that in your capacity as an officer of TBT Investments, you used the alias Richard Peterson. Is that true?"

"I did."

Jenkins watched the jurors' reactions. They looked intrigued.

"During November 2017, did you have occasion to travel to Camano Island and meet with the defendant, Charles William Jenkins?"

Jenkins knew that was the key question. If Emerson was going to lie, now would be the moment.

"No," Emerson said. "That is not true."

It was as Jenkins had speculated. Emerson would admit that LSR&C was a CIA front but deny that Jenkins had been reactivated. That would allow Velasquez to argue that Jenkins had made up the story after Mitchell Goldstone raised it as his defense. The difference now, however, was Emerson had confirmed that Goldstone had told the truth.

"When was the last time you saw Mr. Jenkins?"

"The last time?" Emerson looked to Jenkins, the smug smile still on his face. "That would have been decades ago, in Mexico City."

"You haven't seen him since?"

"No."

"You're excused," Harden said.

Emerson never lost the smug smile. He stood, buttoned his suit jacket, and stepped down.

Harden turned to the jury. "That is the court's evidence. Ladies and gentlemen, let me give you another status report. The defendant has concluded the evidence that he is going to put on, and I have plugged in the evidence that the court felt you ought to have. And now the government, if it is inclined to do so, may put on rebuttal evidence. Counsel, are you so inclined?"

Jenkins knew the government had been painted into a corner. The judge's questions clearly showed Carl Emerson had a connection to the CIA and to LSR&C through TBT Investments, as Jenkins and Mitchell Goldstone had both testified. Jenkins suspected the government attorneys would not leave well enough alone and would question Emerson.

Velasquez stood. "Yes, Your Honor. The government recalls Carl Emerson."

Emerson wheeled as if it were a great inconvenience and retook the stand.

"Mr. Emerson," Velasquez said, "I want to draw your attention to an FBI agent named Chris Daugherty. Did you have occasion to speak to Agent Daugherty on or about January 2018?"

"I don't recall the specific date, but yes, I spoke to Agent Daugherty on the telephone."

"And would you tell the jury the substance of that conversation."

"Agent Daugherty called and said Charles Jenkins had spoken to him. I said, 'Who?' I was surprised to hear that name. Agent Daugherty then said Mr. Jenkins said he worked for me and that I would have details regarding work Mr. Jenkins was doing on behalf of the CIA in Russia."

"And what did you tell Agent Daugherty?"

"I asked him if this was some sort of joke. I told him I hadn't seen Charles Jenkins in more than forty years."

"I take it you didn't tell Agent Daugherty about any operations Mr. Jenkins was running for you in Russia?"

"There were no operations."

"You didn't authorize Mr. Jenkins to give information about CIA assets inside Russia?"

"I didn't authorize it, no."

Velasquez thanked Emerson and sat.

Sloane stood. "Isn't it a fact, Mr. Emerson, that TBT Investments was a company arranged for you so you could distance yourself from LSR&C?"

"Objection," Velasquez said.

"Overruled."

"Yes, that is true."

"What was the phone number on the business card for TBT Investments?"

"I don't recall."

Sloane provided the number. "Would that be the number?"

"I don't recall."

"Isn't it true that you were terminated from the CIA within days of the collapse of LSR&C?" Sloane asked.

"My leaving had nothing to do with the collapse of LSR&C."

"Well, correct me if I'm wrong, but didn't the collapse of LSR&C also result in the collapse of TBT Investments?"

"I assume TBT Investments ceased to exist."

"As did Richard Peterson?"

"I don't understand your question."

"Was there any money in bank accounts controlled by TBT Investments—that is, by you—that was unaccounted for at the time you were terminated?"

"I wouldn't know."

"You were the chief operating officer of that company, weren't you?"

"Only on paper."

"Isn't it true that when you were terminated, you and your superiors at the CIA reached an agreement that no legal proceedings would be brought against you?"

"No, that is not true."

"Didn't TBT Investments receive millions of dollars from LSR&C, ostensibly to funnel money to agents all over the world?"

"Objection."

"Sustained."

"Wouldn't you, Mr. Emerson, as the COO of TBT Investments, using the alias Richard Peterson, have been responsible for funneling money to agents?"

"Objection. Violates the CIPA order."

"Sustained."

Jenkins knew Sloane didn't care, and that Judge Harden didn't either. Sloane just wanted to get the questions before the jury. He'd accomplished what he wanted, a link between the CIA, LSR&C, and Carl Emerson. Whether that would be enough remained to be determined. Sloane surprised Jenkins when he continued.

"You testified that you haven't laid eyes on Charles Jenkins since the day he left Mexico City forty years ago. Is that right?"

"That is correct."

"Perhaps you can explain to me how it is that Mr. Jenkins had in his possession a business card with the number for TBT Investments?"

Sloane produced the document and handed it to the clerk, who handed it to Emerson. The business card with just the phone number was put up on the courtroom computer screens. Jenkins didn't know where Sloane was headed, but he was curious. The jurors also looked interested.

"I wouldn't know," Emerson said. "Perhaps he came into the office and took it to facilitate the story he intended to tell here in court."

"Perhaps," Sloane said. "Except . . . According to the government's theory, Mr. Jenkins's story wasn't concocted until sometime after LSR&C had been shut down, and there is testimony that the offices had been stripped to the concrete floor within hours of that event."

Jenkins smiled. "Son of a bitch," he said under his breath. Three jurors sat back in their chairs, nodding.

"Objection. Move to strike," Velasquez said. "That is Mr. Sloane's argument, not a question."

"Sustained."

"My question, Mr. Emerson, is how could Mr. Jenkins have gone into the office and taken a card, if the office, and every scrap of paper in that office, had vanished just hours after the news broke on the television?"

"I wouldn't know," Emerson said.

They left the courtroom that afternoon in better spirits than any other day of the trial. Sloane and Jake returned to Sloane's office so Sloane could prepare his closing argument. Jenkins went to Three Tree Point with Alex. They had a family dinner with CJ and the baby. They were both dog tired, but they thought it important. They left unsaid that it could be the last dinner they would share as a family.

After reading CJ several chapters of Harry Potter, Jenkins found Alex on the porch, sitting in one of the rocking chairs, feeding Lizzie.

"How many chapters tonight?" she asked.

"Three." Jenkins sat in the adjacent chair.

"You'll spoil him."

"The first two were for him. The last one was for me."

They sat in silence, the chairs creaking as they rocked forward and back. Jenkins said, "Do you think I should have taken the plea? A year or two wouldn't have been terrible, would it?"

"It wasn't just a year or two, Charlie. It would have been a lifetime of people believing you were guilty."

"I'm not worried about what people think of me anymore. I'm worried about you and the kids. I'm worried about them growing up not knowing their father. I could miss it all."

"We're not there yet. Don't go there," Alex said.

"I want you to promise me that if I'm found guilty, you won't wait around for me."

"Charlie, stop."

"You're too young, and the kids need a father."

"They have a father." She reached over with her free hand and grabbed his. Her touch calmed him, if only a little.

"We'll get through this, whatever the outcome," she said. "We could have taken the plea, but we chose to fight, Charlie, and not just for you, but for CJ and Lizzie, and for all those other agents out there who might someday find themselves left out in the cold."

"No agent has ever won."

"Then you'll be the first."

"Emerson is going to get away with it, isn't he? He's betrayed agents and he's betrayed his country. He's responsible for those women's deaths, maybe more, and he's going to get away with it and live like a king."

"Nobody gets away with anything, Charlie. Eventually we all have to answer for our actions."

"I wish he had to answer here."

"Maybe he will."

"No," Jenkins said, shaking his head. "He knows where the bodies are buried, and likely has the documents to prove it. The CIA doesn't want to have those secrets come out and embarrass them. It's easier for them to sacrifice Goldstone and me."

69

Maria Velasquez's closing stuck closely to her opening statement. Jenkins was a man in a desperate financial situation who sold out his country to the Russians to pay his bills.

"He sold what he had—his honor, his oath, and classified information," she said.

Sloane told Jenkins the most important thing was to keep his closing argument integrally related to the opening, and to keep his promises. Sloane had promised to prove Jenkins's innocence. Without any documentary evidence, that had been a difficult promise to keep, but they'd caught a break when Judge Harden called Carl Emerson to the stand. Emerson had admitted a connection between the CIA and TBT Investments and between TBT and LSR&C. He'd lied when he said he hadn't seen or spoken with Jenkins since Mexico City, but Sloane did his best to refute that testimony with the card bearing the phone number. If nothing else, it gave Sloane something to argue.

Sloane brought a schoolhouse blackboard and chalk from home and placed the chalkboard in front of the jury. Tina had once used the blackboard to teach Jake. Several jurors sat forward, curious about what he had in store. Judge Harden also looked interested.

"On the first day of trial, I told you the defense would accept the burden of proving that Charles Jenkins is not guilty of the charges brought against him. I told you there would be no signed confession, though the prosecution contends Mr. Jenkins confessed. There is no signed confession. I told you we would prove the CIA was involved with LSR&C. We proved that. I told you Charles Jenkins had a phone number we traced to the company TBT Investments. We've proven that also. We've also proven that Carl Emerson was in Seattle in November 2017, and that Mr. Emerson continued his employment with the CIA until terminated at a later date. How would Charles Jenkins have known that Carl Emerson was in Seattle in November 2017 unless he'd met with him? How would Charles Jenkins have received a card with TBT Investments' number on it unless Carl Emerson gave it to him before LSR&C's offices were closed down and cleaned of every scrap of paper?"

Jenkins thought both were legitimate questions, and he noted several jurors furiously scribbling in their notebooks.

"Now, here's the reality," Sloane said. "Here's what this case is really all about. In the winter of 2018, the CIA pulled the plug on two companies in Seattle that it was using as CIA proprietaries, and Charles Jenkins got left out in the cold. The government has charged him with two counts of espionage, one count of conspiracy, and two counts of selling US secrets to the Russians. The law says the burden of proof is on the government. But they haven't proven a thing.

"I am going to list the issues the government has failed to prove. Write these down with me in your notebooks so you don't forget them."

Sloane took the fat piece of chalk and wrote on the blackboard as he ticked off each item. Sure enough, the jurors wrote right along in their notebooks.

1. *They have not denied that the CIA had ties to LSR&C.*
2. *They have not denied that Carl Emerson was working for TBT Investments, an LSR&C subsidiary.*
3. *They have not denied that Carl Emerson had a Seattle phone number that rang at TBT Investments or that Charles Jenkins had a copy of that number in his possession.*

4. *They have not denied that Chris Daugherty, a Seattle FBI agent, told CJ Security's receptionist that he knew Charles Jenkins worked for the CIA.*
5. *They have not produced a single piece of paper to substantiate their assertion that Charles Jenkins confessed to his crimes.*

The list went on. When Sloane finished writing, he said, "These are the facts, and the government hasn't denied them. Unless they explain these facts, they must be true. And if these facts are true, then we have proven that Charles Jenkins is innocent."

Sloane pointed to Velasquez. "I challenge the government to answer any of these. Now, the government has one more chance to make their case. But we don't have another chance. You have to accept what we're telling you right now, because this is it for us. This is the last chance we get to speak to you. The government gets one more chance, and I've given them a list of questions they need to answer. If they can't answer even a single one of these questions, then your duty is to find this man not guilty."

Sloane set down the chalk and wiped his hands of the dust. "Sometimes, with all the gadgetry that is now used in a courtroom, with all the testimony from experts, computer graphics, and expensive photographs, we lose sight of one fundamental principle. Your ultimate responsibility is to find the truth, and sometimes, the truth is not complicated. It doesn't require fancy graphs and diagrams or computer technology." Sloane looked to the blackboard. "Sometimes, the truth is simple and straightforward. Sometimes, it is staring us all in the face. Sometimes, the truth is in black and white."

Velasquez did not take Sloane's bait. Her second closing was a forty-minute tirade intended to incite juror emotions. She pounded on the lectern and raised her voice, but she never addressed a single point Sloane had written on the blackboard.

"I do agree with Mr. Sloane on one thing," she said. "The truth in this case is very simple. I stated it in my opening and I am reiterating it now. This man sold his honor and his integrity and his knowledge. It was a straight trade—information for money. He had the information. He traveled to Russia. And fifty thousand dollars materialized in his account shortly after he returned. The defense attorney and I agree, at least on this one fundamental principle. The truth sometimes is easy to see. And the truth in this instance is that Charles Jenkins is guilty."

It was a powerful response.

The only thing left to do now was to wait.

70

Sloane told Jenkins he expected the jury to be out deliberating for four to five days, and the longer the better. In a criminal trial, the longer a jury debated a matter, the more likely it meant one or more of the jurors could not reach a verdict without reasonable doubt. Harden told both sides he wanted them to remain in the building, in the event the jurors had questions during their deliberations. He offered the defense a jury room in one of the vacant courtrooms to wait.

Near five o'clock, Alex and Jake cleared half-eaten sandwiches and wrappers from the table and tossed the uneaten food into the garbage.

"I imagine the bailiff will come to let us go for the night," Sloane said. "That's a good thing."

Minutes later, Jenkins heard footsteps outside their door, followed by a quiet knock.

Sloane looked at his watch. "Time to go home." He slipped on his jacket as Jake answered the door.

The bailiff stood in the hallway. "We have a verdict."

Jenkins's heart sank. David Sloane looked equally stunned. The jury had been out less than five hours. They all gathered their belongings. No one said a word.

As they stepped into the hallway, people streamed toward Judge Harden's courtroom, and as the defense team approached the courtroom doors, an overflow crowd, including reporters and television crews, stood in the hall. The reporters shouted questions. Jenkins ignored them. He felt numb, uncertain even how his legs were functioning. He felt his right hand shake.

Then he felt Alex take hold of his hand.

As they neared the courtroom doors, officers created a wedge so the defense team could enter.

"David?" someone called. A familiar voice. Jenkins turned and saw Carolyn.

"She's an expert witness," Sloane said to one of the marshals, who allowed Carolyn through. She stepped beside Alex and they locked arms.

Velasquez and her team already sat at the counsel table. They looked ready to celebrate.

With everyone assembled, Judge Harden quickly retook the bench and asked the bailiff to escort the jury into the courtroom.

The nine women and three men entered without looking at Jenkins, also not a good sign.

When the jurors were seated, Harden addressed them. "Have you reached a verdict on all five counts of the indictment?"

Juror number four, a mother of two who ran her own business, stood. "We have, Your Honor."

Jenkins's chest gripped.

"Will the bailiff please hand the verdict to the clerk of the court?" Harden said.

The bailiff did. The clerk handed Harden the verdict. Harden read through the pages without giving any hint of the jury's findings. Jenkins could hear his breath rattling in his chest. The rest of the courtroom was deathly quiet. He thought of what he would miss—the birthdays and the holidays, reading to CJ, feeding Lizzie, holding his wife in bed.

Harden returned the document to the court clerk. "The defendant will please rise and face the jury."

Jenkins needed Sloane's assistance to get to his feet. He put his hands on the table to steady himself. His heart pounded and his ears rang. He turned his head and looked over his shoulder to the first row in the gallery. Alex gave him a small smile, but he could see she was fighting back tears. So, too, was Carolyn.

The jury foreman took the verdict.

"The jury foreman will now read the verdict," Harden said.

"On the first count," the woman began, "we the jury find the defendant, Charles William Jenkins, not guilty."

Jenkins felt Sloane's hand on his back. He took a breath to keep from hyperventilating, then a second and a third. He looked to Sloane for confirmation. Sloane nodded, smiling. Behind him, it sounded as if the entire courtroom had exhaled.

"On the second count," the foreman said, her voice growing stronger, "we the jury find the defendant, Charles William Jenkins, not guilty." This time the foreman allowed herself to glance over at Jenkins. Other jurors also looked at him. Some smiled. Several women had tears in their eyes.

Jenkins felt Sloane reach around and hug his shoulders. On the remaining three counts, the foreman's verdict was the same. "Not guilty."

The courtroom gallery erupted. Harden banged his gavel to restore order, thanked the jury, and excused them. Velasquez and her team looked stunned by the verdict.

"Mr. Jenkins," Judge Harden said.

Jenkins turned to face the bench. Harden didn't smile, but there was a glint in his eyes. "We're adjourned," he said. "And you, sir, are free to go."

Epilogue

In the days, weeks, and months following the verdict, Jenkins's life slowly returned to normal. For a period of time he was asked to give interviews and to appear on television programs. He didn't want to do any of it, but Alex had persuaded him that it was important he do so. She said that being the first agent found not guilty of espionage by a jury was a story other agents needed to hear, first and foremost as a precautionary tale about how quickly things could go wrong, and how an agent could be left out in the cold.

They also needed the money.

In interviews, Jenkins told reporters he continued to love his country and always would, that it wasn't perfect, but he still considered it the best place in the world to live.

Several jurors also did interviews. Their statements were more pointed. The majority indicated they didn't have the same confidence in the government that other generations once had. They'd become much more skeptical of politicians and government agencies. One had said, "Where there is smoke, there is usually a fire, and this trial had a lot of smoke."

David Sloane couldn't have scripted it any better.

When the euphoria of his not-guilty verdict finally evaporated, and Jenkins no longer warranted coverage, he returned his family to Camano Island, to his farm. His reception in the small town of

Stanwood was cordial. At school and on the sidelines of CJ's soccer games—CJ had improved dramatically from his one-on-one training with his tutor—one of the other parents would occasionally stop to congratulate Jenkins, and to tell him they had been pulling for him. He thanked them. He also didn't believe them. He knew, human nature being what it is, that they had condemned him the moment he had been arrested, and they had absolved him only after the verdict. Some anyway. Others would always consider him a traitor who had managed to dodge a bullet.

Jenkins didn't care. He knew the truth, and the truth had set him free.

He entertained a six-figure book deal and spent most of his days taking care of his baby daughter while Alex worked in Jake's classroom. He'd have to eventually look for a full-time job, or write that book, but for the time being he was happy doing part-time work for Sloane again, and being a househusband.

When Elizabeth turned six months, they drove down to Three Tree Point to celebrate news that Jake had passed the Washington State bar exam. No one would say it, but the gathering had another purpose. They'd never celebrated the verdict.

Alex worked in the kitchen making tacos while Lizzie slept. Jenkins, seeing an opportunity to spend time with CJ, slipped out the back door with his son, and they walked to the water's edge with fishing poles and the tackle box.

CJ had become a patient and skilled fisherman, having already caught three kings and multiple silvers. The other fishermen had come to know him by name. If they knew him as the son of a man acquitted of espionage, they didn't say it. When it came to fishermen, they had a single purpose with each cast.

Jenkins handed CJ a fishing pole, and the young boy cast. Jenkins prepared his pole, noting that his right hand no longer shook, and hadn't since the verdict. He cast and began to reel.

Fifteen minutes into their task, Jenkins's cell phone rang. Caller ID did not identify the caller or the number. Jenkins almost ignored the call, thinking it was another person seeking an interview, or a writer calling to ask whether Jenkins was interested in telling his story. He wasn't, not yet.

"Hello?" he said.

"Mr. Jenkins."

Jenkins recognized the accent. "Viktor," he said.

"You are a hard man to track down."

"I've had to screen my calls." Jenkins stepped away so CJ would not hear his conversation. The young boy glanced at him, still not completely trusting that his dad would not be taken away again. Jenkins smiled and gave CJ a thumbs-up, and the boy returned his attention to reeling in his lure.

"I followed with great interest the news of your trial. It seemed as though I was reading about a trial here, in Russia, where the truth would never be allowed to come out. I am happy you were found not guilty."

"Thank you," Jenkins said.

"So you see, again I say that your country and mine are not so different."

Jenkins smiled. "How do you like working for your brother?"

"I decided is not for me. There is too much red tape, and that is coming from someone who worked for the government." Viktor laughed.

"What will you do?"

"I'm private detective," Federov said. "So far I have one client. I thought you might like to know about my first case."

"Why is that?" Jenkins asked.

"Because I believe you know the man I tracked down."

"Who would that be?"

"He served as your station chief in Mexico City, and more recently he worked in Washington, DC. Your trial helped me to find him."

Jenkins felt a lump in his throat.

"You see, Mr. Jenkins, though I joke, Russia is not United States. In Russia, we have long memories, and justice is always served, if not one way then another."

"What do you mean, Viktor?"

"Follow your news. I assume they will cover it soon."

Jenkins thought of his statement to Alex, that he wanted Carl Emerson to pay for his crimes here and now, rather than in the afterlife.

"Do you have pen or pencil and paper?" Federov asked.

"Why?" Jenkins asked.

"I want to give you some numbers."

"Hang on," Jenkins said. He went to the tackle box, found the back of a lure package and the stub of a pencil.

"Okay, go ahead."

He expected ten digits—a phone number—but he got more than that.

"What is it?" Jenkins asked. "Not a phone number."

"It is the number to a Swiss bank account. I opened it in your name."

"In my name? Why would you open an account in my name?"

"Because you were my client."

"Me?"

"Okay, so I have two clients—you and me, and I thought you deserved the money almost as much as me. I decided on sixty-forty, because I did all the work." Viktor again laughed.

"Viktor, if this is the money Carl Emerson stole, I can't keep it."

"No, Mr. Jenkins, I didn't think you would. I believe you are a man of much integrity. But the money was not stolen. It is money paid by Russia."

"Emerson was the leak."

"Leak? I know nothing of leak unless it is below my sink."

"How much money are we talking about?" Jenkins said, curiosity getting the better of him.

"Enough," Viktor said. "Enough for everything our two governments have put us through. No?"

"I can't take that money," Jenkins said. It was blood money. It was money given to Emerson that had cost three of the seven sisters their lives.

"It is there, Mr. Jenkins. What you choose to do with it is your business. And now I must be going. I fear our meeting again will not happen."

"Don't be so sure," Jenkins said. "We both know lives can change in an instant, and in ways neither of us ever could have imagined."

Viktor laughed long and loud. "Then until we meet, I will be drinking to your good health. *Boo-deem zdarovov.*"

CJ yelled, "Dad! Dad! I think I have a fish."

Jenkins disconnected and slipped his phone in his jacket pocket. CJ's line was in one spot, not moving. "Let me see." He took the fishing pole, still thinking of what Federov had told him. "I think it's just a snag, CJ."

"Really?" the boy said, disappointed.

Jenkins pointed the tip of the pole at the snag and yanked the lure free. He handed the pole back to his son. "Reel it in and cast again."

"Let's just go in," CJ said. "We're not going to catch anything."

Jenkins put a hand on top of the boy's head. "You're going to get a lot of snags in life, CJ, but you can't let the snags keep you from trying. You keep trying and eventually you'll catch something big again."

"You really think so?"

"Charlie? Charlie!"

Alex called out to him from the porch. Everyone else had gone inside. "You're going to want to come up and watch the news. You're never going to believe it. David is taping it."

Through the large windows, Jenkins could see the guests gathered in the family room. They had their backs to him, facing the glow of the flat-screen television.

Jenkins nearly put down his pole. He was tempted to go up and find out what exactly had happened, but he decided he knew enough. He thought of Viktor Federov and of Carl Emerson, and of justice, often meted out in ways unexpected, for all of them. He wanted nothing more than to watch his son cast his lure far out over the water, and reel in his line with a fisherman's faith that, despite exceedingly long odds, this cast would be different.

"Flip back the bail and cast again," he said to CJ.

ACKNOWLEDGMENTS

A few years ago, I read the novel *The Nightingale* by Kristin Hannah. I was so impressed with the novel, the documentation, and the details that I wrote the author. We share the same literary agency. I asked her, "Where did you find this story?" Kristin responded, "Sometimes good stories fall into our laps, and we just need to get out of the way."

I agree. *The Eighth Sister* is not a true story. It is complete fiction. But I did receive a call from a gentleman who had a story to tell. I took him up on the invitation, and that meeting spurred me to write this novel. I'm grateful to have had coffee with him, and for the help he lent me.

In the midst of writing this novel, I met another man at an event in Seattle. He told me that he worked in the Soviet Union at the Metropol Hotel during the 1970s. It was not a hotel at that time. We got to chatting, and he, too, had another career. He, too, helped with the writing of this novel.

In addition, I want to thank John Black, whom I met while teaching a writing class. John is a former international oil and gas lawyer who worked for oil companies in Moscow and Yuzhno-Sakhalinsk, Russia, from 1991 to 2008. He was trained in the Russian language by the US military during the Vietnam conflict. John read the manuscript and helped me with its accuracy. Thanks also to Rodger Davis, who lived and worked in the Soviet Union and contacted individuals to further help me write the novel. Rodger gave me great tips on Russia and Russian culture. He introduced me to several books as well: *Peter the Great,* by Robert K. Massie; *Black Wind, White Snow*, by Charles Clover; and *Wheel of Fortune*, by Thane Gustafson. Rodger is a talented writer and generous colleague. Thank you also to Tim Tigner, a novelist and a friend. Tim worked in the Soviet Union for a number of years and has written about the country in his novels, which include *Coercion* and *The Lies of Spies*. Tim also recommended Bill Browder's book, *Red Notice*, which I devoured.

I also want to thank Jon Coon, who was trained as a hard-hat diver and explosives specialist and served as a dive safety officer and project leader on commercial salvage, archaeology, and scientific projects internationally. He's written three novels and numerous articles. His photographs have illustrated textbooks and magazines for more than thirty years. He is a PADI course director, former PADI regional manager, cave diver, and trains emergency first response instructors.

I am indebted to all of these people for their help. If there are mistakes, they are mine and mine alone.

In addition to the above, I read a number of other books, fiction and nonfiction, including *A Gentleman in Moscow*, by Amor Towles; *The Main Enemy: The Inside Story of the CIA's Final Showdown with the KGB*, by Milton Bearden and James Risen; *Moscow City*, by A. R. Zander; *The Honest Spy*, by Andreas Kollender; *The Defector*, by Daniel Silva; *The Spy Who Came in from the Cold*, by John Le Carré; *Gorky Park*, by Martin Cruz Smith; and *Istanbul Passage*, by Joseph Kanon.

I also spent three weeks in Russia. In 1998, a Russian opera singer, who had defected years earlier from the Soviet Union, and who had sung at my wedding in Seattle, was going home. She offered to help facilitate a trip to Russia. My wife and I, and our then eighteen-month-old son, my brother-in-law and sister-in-law, my parents, and my wife's parents, took her up on the offer. Prior to departing, my brother-in-law and I decided to get flattop haircuts. We were told that conditions in Russia could be primitive and washing our hair would be a pain. (That proved inaccurate.) I got a flattop. My brother-in-law chickened out. We also decided to wear navy-blue berets to keep our heads warm. Are you starting to get the picture?

When we arrived at Sheremetyevo International Airport in Moscow, the officer checking my passport sternly uttered, *"Nyet."* I was taken out of the passport line to a room where all of my belongings were thoroughly searched. When we finally arrived at the Hotel Rossiya in Moscow, each couple received a room assignment. Interestingly, we were assigned every other room on the same floor, and in each of our rooms hung a large mirror on the wall of the adjacent, and presumably empty, room. We joked that we were being watched, and each morning I'd parade in front of the mirror naked. That first afternoon, we all agreed to take a short nap and to meet for dinner at 6:00 p.m.

None of us made it.

Each of us, all eight adults, said we tried to get up from the bed and couldn't, that we felt drugged when we tried to sit up. We didn't meet until the following morning.

We ventured out to Red Square and the Kremlin. As we walked the grounds from St. Basil's to the Lenin Mausoleum and other attractions, my brother-in-law approached and said, "We're being followed." He then pointed out a woman in white boots. He said, "She's been with us everywhere we've gone." And she continued to follow us through the GUM department store and other locations. We went to Detsky Mir, the huge children's toy store, and we walked around Lubyanka Square and marveled at what had been the famed KGB headquarters. The woman came with us, until we returned to the Hotel Rossiya.

I also recall that when we went to the Church of the Twelve Apostles, we encountered a group of schoolchildren. They looked at us and smiled knowingly. One young boy, finding the courage, walked up to me and said, "You military." I assured him I wasn't. My assurances were not believed. His friends, now emboldened, came forward and soon many were repeating, "You military."

So, if we hadn't attracted enough attention, two nights later, my brother-in-law, in search of a stone from Red Square, convinced me to go out at midnight to smoke a Cuban cigar. We stood near the platform where Ivan the Terrible was said to have executed many. There was a small, loose stone in the bricks. My brother-in-law said, "How do I get it?"

I said, "Drop your cigar and when you pick it up, pick up the stone."

My brother-in-law dropped his cigar. When he did, a car across the square turned on its headlights and shot straight for us, stopping about ten feet in front of us. My brother-in-law, concerned, said, "What should I do?"

I said, "Shut up." Then I said, "Step on your cigar."

He did, and we walked back to the hotel on our best behavior.

I later learned, through research, that the Hotel Rossiya was the hotel where all international visitors were placed. I also learned that when the hotel was purchased to be remodeled, they found listening devices, cameras, and pipes, apparently to dispense gas, embedded in the walls. The hotel had to be torn down. A park was created. Vladimir Putin took credit. I also learned that Red Square had directional microphones everywhere, and they were said to be so sensitive they could pick up a whisper. I don't doubt it.

So, were the Russians interested in me and my family? Probably not. We were a pretty boring lot in terms of careers and espionage. But all of the above sure made for great intrigue, didn't it? And that was the beginning of my fascination with Russia. We all agree that the trip to Moscow, St. Petersburg, and Zagorsk was the most interesting and fascinating we have experienced. Russia is a country of incredible beauty and wealth and just as incredible poverty. The people generally walked with their heads down, as if hoping not to be noticed, but when approached, they would go out of their way to assist us and take us wherever we were trying to go. We were not on a tour, which meant interaction in newly formed food stores and restaurants was imperative. Few spoke English. In St. Petersburg, we stayed in an apartment the family had lived in for five generations. They gave it to us because the rent we paid for the week was more than the owner made in a year. I watched ice float up the Neva River and thought of Napoleon.

A friend said I had to go back to write this novel. That was just not in the cards. So I pulled out my photo albums, and read many books, and I went back over the restaurants we went to and the places we explored.

Russia was the last big trip I took with my father. He died of melanoma on Father's Day in 2008. I want to remember him in the square in St. Petersburg, kissing my mother, who bent one leg backward, like a movie star in some iconic film. I keep that picture on my wall.

I could never write a Charles Jenkins novel without acknowledging and thanking my law school roommate and dear friend, Charles Jenkins. Chaz, as we called him, is a living legend. At six foot five and 230 pounds of sculpted muscle, we were in awe of him in the weight room, but more so outside of it. Chaz is a gentle soul, quiet and funny with a unique perspective of the happenings in life. A good man and a wonderful father, he's also one of my dearest friends. I told Chaz long ago that he was larger than life, and that someday I'd write a book and use his name and likeness. Now I have. I also hope I captured his essence.

Thanks to Meg Ruley, Rebecca Scherer, and the team at the Jane Rotrosen Agency, my incredible agents. I am so blessed to have them. They are tireless advocates, knowledgeable advisors, and truly wonderful people who make travel to New York always a blast.

Thanks to Thomas & Mercer. This is the tenth book I've written for them, and they have made each one better with their edits and suggestions. They have sold and promoted me and my novels all over the world, and I have had the pleasure of meeting the Amazon Publishing teams from the UK, Ireland, France, Germany, Italy, and Spain. Wonderful people in every sense of the word. I am so very grateful for all they have done and continue to do for me and for my novels.

Thanks to Sarah Shaw, author relations, who never seems to have a bad day. She is always smiling. Again, thank you for always brightening my day.

Thanks to Sean Baker, head of production; Laura Barrett, production manager; and Oisin O'Malley, art director. I love the covers and the titles of each of my novels, and I have them to thank. Thanks to Dennelle Catlett, Amazon Publishing PR, for all the work promoting me and my novels. Dennelle takes care of me whenever I'm traveling and it always feels like first-class. Thanks to the marketing team, Gabrielle Guarnero, Laura Costantino, and Kyla Pigoni, for all of their dedicated work helping me to create an author platform both interesting and accessible to you, the reader. Thanks to publisher Mikyla Bruder, associate publisher Galen Maynard, and Jeff Belle, vice president of Amazon Publishing, all truly good people.

Special thanks to Thomas & Mercer's editorial director, Gracie Doyle. She is with me from the concept to the final written novel, always with ideas on how to make it better. She pushes me to write the best novels I can, and I'm so very lucky to have her on my team. She's also become a close friend whom I enjoy traveling with.

Thank you to Charlotte Herscher, developmental editor. This is book ten together, and she has the unenviable task of telling me when things in the book don't work. I pout for an hour, realize she's right, and get back to work making the novel better. Thanks to Scott Calamar, copyeditor. When you recognize a weakness, it is a wonderful thing—because then you can ask for help. He makes me look a lot smarter than I am, and I'm grateful he does so.

Thanks to Tami Taylor, who runs my website, creates my newsletters, and creates some of my foreign-language book covers. Thanks to Pam Binder and the Pacific Northwest Writers Association for their support of my work. Thanks to Seattle7Writers, a nonprofit collective of Pacific Northwest authors who foster and support the written word.

Thanks to all of you tireless readers, for finding my novels and for your incredible support of my work all over the world. Thanks for posting your reviews and for e-mailing me to let me know you've enjoyed my novels. It sounds trite, but you push me to put out a book worthy of your time.

Thank you to my wife, Cristina, and my two children, Joe and Catherine. Joe went off to college four years ago and I thought that was a tough day. This year Catherine followed. Catherine is our baby girl. She is my Bubster, as everyone on Facebook has come to know. She makes me laugh and smile. Just seeing her makes me happy. Taking her to college was going to be one of the hardest things I've ever done as a dad. And then one day, she got word that she'd been accepted to her first choice, a school close by. Her first words to me were, "Dad, now I don't have to go." She did have to go, for herself, and she's having a ball and doing wonderfully. I get to see her at sporting events, and for dinners, and I see how happy she is and I imagine all the wonderful years God has in store for her and for all of us. I love the classic movies, like *Peter Pan*. Time to crow, Catherine. Time to fly. Love you.

Truly blessed. I give him all my thanks for all the special people God has placed in my life.

ABOUT THE AUTHOR

Photo © 2018 Douglas Sonders

Robert Dugoni is the critically acclaimed *New York Times*, *Wall Street Journal*, and Amazon bestselling author of the Tracy Crosswhite Series, which has sold more than 4 million books worldwide. He is also the author of the bestselling David Sloane Series; the stand-alone novels *The 7th Canon*, *Damage Control*, and *The Extraordinary Life of Sam Hell*, for which he won an AudioFile Earphones Award for the narration; and the nonfiction exposé *The Cyanide Canary*, a *Washington Post* Best Book of the Year. He is the recipient of the Nancy Pearl Award for Fiction and the Friends of Mystery Spotted Owl Award for best novel set in the Pacific Northwest. He is a two-time finalist for the International Thriller Award, the Harper Lee Prize for Legal Fiction, the Silver Falchion Award for mystery, and the Mystery Writers of America Edgar Award. His books are sold in more than twenty-five countries and have been translated into more than two dozen languages. Visit his website at www.robertdugoni.com.